Pixie Noir

Cedar Sanderson

Dedicated to Cedar's Grampa Bob, who told her the Tanana River story, and her Great-Uncle Dave, herein referred to as Raven. May you both live forever in story and song.

This story would not have been possible without the man who inspired the first scene, I wrote it to make him laugh. My First Reader, Sanford Begley, who patiently let me bounce almost every scene off him until it felt right. If the men are manly in this tale, it's due to him!

Contents

Chapter 1

Sawdust Pie

The woman who answered the door was wearing the most amazing shirt. Knitted silk, I think, it clung to her like a second skin, and even though it was dark blue, managed to be transparent. I could see the shadowed curves of a truly magnificent rack, terminating in the slightly darker shadows of her aureoles. I swallowed hard, my mouth suddenly dry. She was looking over my head, and I had seen all this in the time it took her to utter a grumpy "what the hell?" and look down at me.

It was heroic, but I managed to meet her eyes. They widened as she took in all four foot five of me. "You're a pixie," she blurted.

I must have been thrown off balance by the boobs, that's all I can figure. We're not supposed to admit anything of the sort, dammit. I croaked out a witty response.

"Um, yah."

She slammed the door in my face. Through it, I could make out a shouted, "wait there."

I waited. I didn't have much choice, really. I'd come here to get her, and even though she wasn't supposed to know who or what she was, I'd

1

already figured out in the brief time I'd known her that Belladonna Traycroft knew more than she was supposed to. Besides, I really wanted to look at her again.

It's not that I have a thing for tall women, it's that all human women are taller than me. There aren't a lot of pixie women around any longer, we're a dying breed, and the ones I had met were all airy fairy and sparkles. Not my kind of girl. Belladonna, however, had made an impression on me, even before I had seen her. I'd been struck while reading her dossier that she was a very competent female.

She opened the door again, and now she was fully dressed, to my disappointment. The shirt was gone - or at least hidden, as I caught a glimpse of the cuff of it under the thick wool plaid shirt she had thrown on. The ratty pyjama bottoms were replaced by jeans, and the wool socks had disappeared into heavy winter boots. Like I said, my kind of girl. We kept staring at one another for a minute longer in silence.

She broke the tension with a reluctant sigh. "You'd better come in."

I knew why she was reluctant. Pixies in your house could lead to trouble. I didn't intend her harm, but depending on what stories she'd heard, she was right to be wary. I stomped the snow off my boots and followed her into the tiny cabin. It was warm, at least.

Why the girl had to be in Alaska, I didn't know. And why they had sent me to get her... well, that was easier. I'm tall, for a pixie. LeBron tall in human terms, as it happens, and that mean I didn't get the hassles when traveling in the open most of my kind do. I don't like it, being taken for a midget and getting pitying glances, but it could be worse. My cousin had to glamour himself as a puppy and travel in a crate last time he needed to fly. I was spared that kind of humiliation.

Inside, I set down the attaché case I was carrying and held out my hands toward the stove in appreciation. She eyed me for a moment. I knew what she was seeing. I'm proportioned like a human, I don't have pointy ears or wings, but I still look like a bloody leprechaun. I hadn't put on gloves when I got out of the car, I didn't expect to be kept standing on the porch in who knows who many below freezing degrees. My cheeks were probably rosy above the stubble, even. I scowled at the stove, not looking at her.

"Coffee?"

She melted my bad mood with a single word. Well, that, and she had... nevermind. The hot nectar of the gods would be enough.

"Thanks." I looked at her as she pulled cups out of a cupboard. The pot was still sputtering. She must have started it just as I knocked before. No wonder she's pissed, I thought, girl hasn't had her coffee yet. I realized something else. She was wearing glasses now. She hadn't had them on before, which must be why she hadn't seen me right away.

Dammit. I might not have a thing for tall girls, but glasses... I put my coat on the back of the other kitchen chair, lifted the attaché case onto the table, and sat down uninvited. I needed to focus. This was a simple courier job, I was going to deliver the paper, get a signature, and go home.

She pushed a thick pottery mug to me and I took it gratefully. She sat down in the other chair.

"Grandma told me a lot of stories. So I know what you are. But I can't figure out why you are here. I mean, your home tor is about half around the world from here. And I can see that you know who I am. Care to introduce yourself and explain?"

I smiled at her. Beautiful and smart, a wicked combination. I was going to have to play this very carefully.

"You can call me Lom. I'm a courier, and all I came to do is deliver some family documents to you, Ms. Traycroft."

She raised an eyebrow slightly. "That's all? You flew into Alaska and drove what, 200 miles, to deliver papers?"

"How do you know I drove that far?" Yes, I was ducking the question, but I was curious as to what had given it away.

"Your rental car is from Fairbanks. I'm hoping you didn't drive overnight, that would make me even more uncomfortable with this." She had her entire attention focused on me, and I could feel the heat of her gaze. Literally. She had power, whether she knew it or not. I looked away and ran a finger under my collar.

"FedEx does come out this far." she went on. "So there is more to this than you are telling me."

"I stayed at the Tok Lodge last night." I offered, finally meeting her eyes again. "And the papers are, hm, how do I say this. Sensitive."

Now both eyebrows were up. I sighed and popped open the latch on the case. "It's going to be better to just show you."

I slid the thick packet of leather and vellum out and put it on the table. It looked decidedly odd on the battered wood. She stared at it while I placed the case back on the floor. The gilded knotwork on the case fit into her kitchen decor about as well as a Louis XIV chair would have.

"What," she asked in a distant tone, "is this about?"

I could tell she wasn't happy. Well, I had guessed from her background she might not be, whatever my employers had thought. It wasn't my choice to be sitting here in a Bush cabin, although I found it a much more welcoming environment than when the packet had been handed to me just three days ago.

She slid the case closer to her and looked at it. "Lovely." She commented on the design without looking up at me, then she opened it and slid the stack of papers out. Some were ordinary modern white paper, computer-printed. But under them were darker sheets of real vellum, weathered and yellow with age. She started to read. I leaned back and sipped my coffee. She brewed a pretty good cup. Strong, but not too bitter. This might take a while.

I was working on my second cup when she looked up from the last sheet. Her blue eyes were bleak. She hadn't looked at me for quite a while, I had gotten the refill on my own, adding cream from the pot she had left on the counter next to the coffeepot. It was cute, a little ceramic rabbit. I'd wandered around a bit, too, stretching my legs. She hadn't stopped me, although I was aware of her attention when I stood at the bookshelves reading titles. I was never out of her sight, nor she out of mine. One of the other instructions from my employers, the papers were not to leave my sight.

"Do you know what these are?" she asked quietly.

"Not entirely," I admitted.

"How did a pixie come to be playing messenger for Fae?" She changed her tack a little.

"I had a debt to pay. This seemed like an easy way to get out of it. Take a trip to exotic Alaska, the Final Frontier."

She blinked, then laughed. "Well, you must be a very different pixie. My grandmother told me that they hated to travel."

"Oh, I do," I assured her with a heartfelt tone. "But sometimes it's necessary. And my family uses me as courier more often than I would like."

I don't know why I'd just admitted that to her. I frowned as I realized that was the second time she had provoked me into admittances.

She tucked the papers back into their case. "Well, I'm glad your debt has been paid with this, Mr. Lom. It was nice to meet you, but," She checked her watch. "I'm late for work."

She slid the case across the table with a little more force than strictly necessary. I could tell that they had upset her.

"It's not Mr. Lom, it's just Lom. And, um, my debt isn't paid until you have signed some of those."

Now the anger was unleashed at me, and her Power lashed out. "I will not sign any of those."

"I can't leave until you do," I told her firmly, trying to keep the nervousness out of my voice. She had a potent force I was fairly sure she was unaware of.

"Then prepare for a long stay. I recommend the Sawdust Pie at the Lodge, it's quite good." She got up and walked over to the door and held it open.

I sighed. This was not going to be easy. I don't know why I had thought it was going to. Pushing the case back into my attaché hastily, I plunged back out into the cold. "I will be back, Ms. Traycroft."

"You'll be lucky if I don't meet you at the door with a shotgun, Mr. Lom." She spat the honorific. "Get off my property."

The door slammed behind me.

I went back into the speck of a town and found someplace to sit and think about this development. There were only a couple of restaurants, and one was closed. The other had a bar, but it wasn't open before lunch. Shame, that, I could have used a stiff drink or two.

Instead I wound up at the local truck stop and diner, waiting for my eggs to arrive and contemplating whether she really would shoot me. She had that ring of authenticity in her voice, and I was certain she owned the weapon to back it up. I had pulled out my phone and was checking to see if had service in town when I became aware that the two guys who had just walked in were stopping by my table. I looked up.

And up, and up. The older man was something over six feet tall, and sitting in the booth bench, my feet didn't hit the floor. I was immediately unhappy, even before I got to the expression on his face. He wasn't happy. Also, I suspected I knew why.

The other man stood slightly behind him, his face almost obscured behind a bushy black beard that looked as though it might jump off his face and start chasing its tail. Or bite my dangling ankles. I cleared my throat.

"Would you two, er, gentleman, care to sit down?" There was no point in delaying the inevitable. They wanted to talk to me. I preferred they do so in public. Here was as good a place as any.

"Are you the one tha' went to see Bella this morning?" the older man asked in a low, menacing rumble. Yep, definitely her family.

"I am." I admitted. The waitress showed up, juggling my plate of eggs and bacon, three cups of coffee, a saucer full of creamers, and a full carafe of steaming coffee. I eyed her in awe as she glared at the men.

"Sit, already, Bob." She expertly delivered her load to the table without a drop of coffee going astray. The big man deflated slightly and meekly allowed her to shepherd him onto the bench, followed by his shadow. She sniffed, poured, and vanished back into the kitchen.

"Now there," I commented, "is a woman I hope never to cross."

I surprised Bob into a guffaw. "May is something, for sure," he admitted before remembering that he wasn't here to chat about women. At least, not that one. "What were you doing at Bella's?"

"I had some paperwork for her." I picked up the cup and took a sip, although more coffee wasn't really what I needed just then. This was going to be ticklish, I had enough adrenaline to keep me alert already.

"About?" He prompted when he could see I wasn't going to go on.

"About none of your business. I don't know who you are, sir, and my business was with Belladonna Traycroft, and her alone." I put a touch of ice, and a hint of Power, into my voice, hoping he would get the hint.

He leaned across the table, his eyes narrowing. "Well, well... you're one of them, aren't you?"

I was beginning to wonder just what was going on. First, Bella, now this Bob. "One of whom?"

He settled back and folded his arms. "Dan, why don't you go ask May about some pancakes for us."

The younger man shadowing him simply nodded slightly at this obvious dismissal and got up. As soon as he was on the other side of the room, Bob nodded at me. "I'm Lavendar's widower, lad. That makes me Belladonna's grandfather, and I know why you are here, even if she doesn't."

"She does. I showed her the papers this morning. Did she tell you I was here?" I found it difficult to believe, for some reason, that she had gone crying to anyone, even this formidable old man.

"Nope. I heard one of your kind was in town, and I'd hoped to catch you before you went out there, I could have saved you some trouble."

I sighed. "My kind?"

He raised one bushy eyebrow and I knew where Bella had gotten that expression. "You're a pixie."

So much for the humans not knowing about the Olde Folke. "Yes, I am."

"There's bad blood between you and her people."

I had an intuition suddenly that this was not only about Belladonna. He was referring to his late wife. And late? How had Lavendar come to be dead? That wasn't in the dossier, and was fairly unlikely, as fairy live for a very long time indeed. Not quite immortal, but close, from a human perspective.

"Not any longer, sir. There was a pact created about 300 years ago." I rubbed my eyes. Lavendar had not been covered in the dossier I was given, except as a name in the genealogy, and I was convinced that had been a mistake on someone's part. Or, more likely, a deliberate omission. There were a lot of folk who would like me to fail in this mission.

I went on. "I just need to have Ms. Traycroft sign some papers. She has... come into an inheritance."

His blue eyes, much like hers, narrowed again. "Are you a lawyer, lad?"

I shook my head, smiling. I liked this man already. "No, sir. I'm just a messenger boy."

Dan returned and slid into the booth, still silent. I regarded him for a moment. Steely gray eyes met mine, and I was surprised to see the laugh lines around them deepen slightly. The beard hid any trace of a smile.

Bob sighed. "Bella doesn't need any troubles, son."

I realized he was talking to me, not Dan. Something in the bearded man's approval had completed Bob's assessment of me and he'd decided I was not going to die today, at least. I relaxed minutely.

"What troubles has she been having?" I asked him and he ran a hand through his silvering hair, leaving it standing askew.

"Well, now. it started about a year ago, when she came back to town."

I nodded. I knew she had been hired to do a census of local wildlife by the National Park Service. Given the sheer scale of the state, that had to be a work of a lifetime.

"At first, we thought it was just local idiots who hadn't thought it through. She wasn't going to limit hunting, she was going to find data that would in all likelihood loosen the regulations that have been strangling us." His speech pattern changed as he started to talk about his granddaughter's work, and I wondered if he realized how thin his 'good ol' boy' facade was getting.

"We had a talk with some guys." He indicated Dan with a motion. "And they denied it was them, entirely, although we did clear up a couple of incidents. Dan and the boys can be a mite formidable when they try." He stopped to chuckle in reminiscence. "Her cousins are fond of Bella. And they know how important her work is to what they do."

"What do they do?" My curiosity is going to be the death of me, I swear. I shut my mouth, but it had already slipped out. For all I knew, they were the equivalent of the Alaskan Mafia. Bob certainly had that godfather aura.

"Big game hunters and guides." He smiled at me. "Best in the Bush. We need the tourists for our economy, and hunting gets big money into town."

I nodded. This made sense. He went on.

"But that didn't stop it. She had her brake lines cut, and only a patch of muskeg and some canny steering on her part saved her. That was the last time, before snow flew. She's stayed pretty close to home since the freeze, compiling her observations. We're keeping an eye on strangers, since the locals don't seem to be the problem..." He shrugged, his giant shoulders still showing their power under his worn plaid shirt. He might be old, but this man was a powerhouse. Bella was a lucky girl.

"I see." And I did see, a lot more than he did, because the threats against her had likely originated a lot closer to where I had just come from. Well, shit. My job had just moved from difficult to "deck stacked against me."

The enemies moving against her wouldn't be seen by Bob and her cousins, unless some of them had the Sight. I did, but the prospect of going up against them for a girl I barely knew was not appetizing. Duty be damned, I didn't relish dying. For one thing, that meant the family honor debt would pass onto someone who was not equipped to fulfill it. The family has been getting thinner with every generation, and little cousin Devon was barely fifteen. He wouldn't even be as noticeable as a speed bump to the fairies who wanted Bella and my whole family dead.

I switched my attention back to Bob. "So what do you want from me? I can assure you, I mean her no harm. As a matter of fact, the inheritance would give her more power."

He raised that eyebrow again. "Really, Power, is it?"

I nodded. I was not at liberty to tell him what was in those papers that rested under my hand in my attaché case. I wasn't so melodramatic as to cuff it to myself, but anyone trying to take it away would get a nasty surprise. I could, however, give him a clue, if he was astute as I thought he was, and Lavandar had told him enough.

"Well, then..." he mused out loud. The he nodded abruptly. "What did she say?"

"She told me to get out or she would shoot me." I told him drily.

He burst into laughter. Dan even laughed quietly. I waited until he was done and had wiped the tears out of his eyes. "Don't know why I expected any less from my girl," he grinned. "Don't give up, son, she'll come around."

He nudged Dan. "Time to be getting home."

Before they walked away, he tossed a couple of bills on the table. May had invisibly delivered their order a while back. I was certain she had been listening as hard as she could, too. He delivered his parting shot.

"I'll talk t' Bella, and tell her she should sign those papers."

I watched them walk out. I didn't think he really understood what was in those papers, or he would be taking me someplace they would never find the body, about now. I was still going to have a hard time with this, and I wasn't entirely sure I wanted to succeed in it.

I added to the money on the table. He'd left enough, but I figured having May on my good side was worth it.

I went straight back to the hotel. Time to think this through, and make a decision. I hadn't been straight with Bella or Bob, but that wasn't about them, it was about the depth of my involvement. Unless you were born to a destiny that you really didn't want, and had to be dragged kicking and screaming into, you won't understand my dilemma. I was supposed to get her to sign the papers, but I wanted her to not sign them, ever.

Back in the room I shed my outer layers onto the chair. I was grateful for them... Damn, it was cold outside... but they made me feel like a fat little man. Little was bad enough without being round. Then I flopped on the bed and closed my eyes. It had been a very long three days.

Chapter 2

Raven Wings

I had started out in Underhill, of course, safe at home, my feet propped on the hearth, a good pipe going, and book in my hand. All was right with my world. Then the summons had come, and dragged me all the way out to the end of the world. I knew, lying on that musty bed in a cold hotel room, alone and with danger closing in, that I'd never get back there. It had the force of a Sight, and I sat up with a growl.

"No, dammit. Not going to just lie down and let Fate walk all over me with her stiletto heels, the bitch!" I spoke a little louder than I'd planned, and someone banged on the wall.

I stared at the wall. It was a vanilla hotel room wall, something I knew better than I wanted to. I hadn't been entirely truthful with them. I wasn't just a messenger boy, although that was how it had started. Just not with me, but with my great-great grandfather.

The Pixie clans and the Fae who ruled Underhill had been at war since before humans started scratching down records on birch bark. We were peoples of a cold, wet land, scattered over islands, back then, even on the mainland of what would become France. There just weren't enough resources for both of us, it was proclaimed, and the feud carried on cold and hot from generation to generation.

The rise of humans gave us something. The Fae preferred to use humans as tools, the pixies used them as well, but more as refuges. The legends of the brownies, knockers, and coblyns (which gave rise to the word goblin) all came from my ancestors. For the Pixie clans had fragmented by then, into several discrete groups which had their own codes of honor. Fae had remained united, but two-faced, as High Court and Low, the light and dark of Fae. Only the Dark Hunt lay outside the Court's rule, and they were a horror. I shuddered in the overly warm room as a touch of the cold hound's breath lingered in my mind.

They had almost had me, that once. I'd been young and foolish, trying to do something heroic, of course. I wouldn't do that again anytime soon. Now, I worked for duty, but nothing more than was necessary to fulfill the family debt.

My clan, a sept of the Brownies, had fallen on hard times somewhere around the reign of the human Queen Elizabeth. The Fae were in ascendance, and the feud had quietened. But my great-great had done the math, and had seen the population of his people plunging. Pixies are shorter-lived than the near-immortal fairies, and neither group reproduces like humans. He had done the unthinkable, trying to keep his family going.

I wondered what he'd been like, he had been long dead by the time I was born. The Family hated his guts, of course. With all our reverence for family and tradition, I had never seen the portrait of him that ought to be hanging in the tor along with the others. Rumor had that it existed, though. I had no sympathy for him, his bargain had cost me my life.

There are things worse than being dead. Some days, I wondered what would have been wrong with letting that Direhound close his jaws over me. That would have ended it. Well, except that then wee Devon would have been on the hook for the Debt. I grunted, a soft sound in the heavy silence of the room. Time to get over myself and get the job done.

It was lunchtime, but I wasn't hungry after the hearty breakfast at the Northstar. I wondered if I dared venture back to her, if Bob had had the time to soften her up a little. Frankly, I was bored, sitting in an empty room. The television was a blank eye looking at me, but I didn't feel up to that level of vapidity any more than sitting in silence.

I had looked it up, it would be dark in a couple of hours. Maybe it was time to look around town a little, see what was here, and who was from out of town. Bob and Dan couple probably do that far better than I, of course, but I might recognize one of the Folke. And it beat sitting here twiddling my thumbs.

I was mostly bundled back up when there was a loud knock at the door. I unzipped the parka to give me more flexibility of motion and cursed the modern air travel security as I went to the door. There were no peepholes on the wood door, and I had no illusions about the chain keeping someone from entering, even though I had engaged it. Without a weapon, there wasn't much I could do about it.

I popped the door open and peered out and up into Bella's eyes. You could have knocked me over with a feather. She was smiling.

"Er..." I really needed to regain some semblance of suave around this woman. "Hang on a sec."

I shut the door in her face and popped the chain, then swung it back open. "Sorry."

She chuckled. "I knew what you were doing. May I come in?"

I stepped back and she slid by me into the little room. I hesitated to shut the door, then shrugged. This wasn't Court, where being alone with her would spawn whispers for a hundred years.

She plopped into the only chair. I opted to stand, which put me eye to eye with her.

We looked at each other for a long moment in silence. I was seeing her in better light, here. Her skin was a pale cream that looked shockingly pale contrasted with her black hair, and dark violet eyes. In appearance she was not a typical fairy, at all. I wondered what her father had looked like. The dossier had been more concerned with Lavendar and her mother Daisy. Fae bloodlines were matrilineal.

She looked very relaxed. This concerned me. She had gotten pretty big news today, and it didn't seem to have affected her. Perhaps she wasn't aware of the import of it.

"So, you came all this way to tell me that I am a fairy princess?"

Well, she knew. So why was she so at ease?

"Yes, sort of. I have a job to do, which was to bring you those papers, and get a signature." I wanted to see how much she understood.

She nodded. "And when I sign, I bind myself to a life at Court. I must never again leave Underhill. My family here, my house, my work, I abandon it all."

I nodded. She understood, all right.

"Come with me for a drive?" She invited abruptly, standing. I looked up at her, trying to follow what she was thinking. I shrugged, there was no reason not to, and I wanted some more time with her. Wear her down, maybe.

I followed her out to her little truck. She climbed in in silence and I got in the passenger side. At least it wasn't so tall I needed a stepstool to get in. I noted the rifle case tucked behind the seat as I climbed in, and wondered what she was carrying. It didn't surprise me to see the gun. Alaska has a certain reputation.

"Where are we going?" I didn't figure she was going to take me out and make me disappear, Alaska is not that lawless. But at twenty-five below zero, I would be in trouble fast should she decide I was walking back to town.

"I thought I would show you my world, before I send you back with the bad news." She turned her head briefly and grinned at me. My heart sank. She wasn't going to make this easy.

We hadn't gone far when she pulled into a gravel parking lot. I looked around. A small store and a hotel even smaller than the one I was staying in. Everything was painted brown and what might have once been white, a decade or so ago. Bella hopped out. I decided that I'd follow her.

A short woman with curly brown hair looked up from a book that she had laid flat on the counter and was bent over, reading. "Bella!"

"Hi, Kathy." My fairy princess met the older woman at the counter gate and hugged her briefly.

"Could you watch...?" Kathy popped the gate open. Bella laughed.

"Go, go. No kids today?"

The brunette trotted toward the back of the store, tossing her reply over her shoulder. "No, they're off on the trapline today."

Bella stepped behind the counter while I tried to figure out what had just happened. She looked at the book and chuckled. "Kathy must be bored if she's reading this."

"Ah, do you..." I tried to phrase it properly. "Work here?"

"What?" She looked across the counter at me, propping her elbows on it and nesting her chin in her hands. "Oh, no. It's just that she can't leave the front, there's no one else here. When her kids come in they can help, so she can, ah..." Bella gestured toward the back and it dawned on me why Kathy had been so urgent. "Or stock shelves and such."

"Oh." I looked around. There was a little of everything on those shelves. I stepped closer and saw the prices with shock. Two to three times what it would cost elsewhere in the First World.

"Why don't you find what we came in here for?" Bella suggested.

I looked over my shoulder at her and she grinned. "We have to bribe someone to talk to you."

I looked back at the cluttered shelves. "Am I that bad?"

"Nah, he's just suspicious of anyone new. Grab some chocolate bars, beef stew, and jerky."

I explored the little store for the items, half-listening as Kathy came back and joined Bella behind the counter.

"So how are the kids?" Bella asked her friend.

"Good, can't wait for spring."

I could hear the exasperation in the mother's voice. I wondered what it would be like to have to stay mostly indoors for six months at a time. Poor lady, no wonder she read all the time. There were four brands of beef stew on the shelf. A popular item, it looked like. I picked out one of each. I'd have to be bribed to talk to me, too, some days.

Back at the counter with the requested items, I waved off Bella's offer to pay. "I'll pay for information, more often than not it's worth any amount."

She nodded and stepped back. I could feel her scrutiny. The plastic card Kathy swiped in the old-fashioned machine didn't tell either woman what I had in the bank, unlike the old days of Fairy gold. A bag of gold coins would draw unwanted attention, then and now. But I didn't think that was what she was thinking about.

The bag of goodies rode by my feet as we headed south out of town. I wondered where we were headed; the next major landmark in this direction was the Canadian border, and I wasn't carrying my passport. Bella didn't seem to feel a need to chat, so I looked out the window.

The world outside was a study in black and white today, with a heavy overcast sky. I wondered if it would snow. The trees that lined the highway were tiny, sticks of conifers that looked black in the low light, with their feet in the snow and clumps of it scattered over their branches. We'd driven out of town after just a couple of minutes, and now there was no sign of human habitation, except the snowmobile tracks next to the highway. I fully expected to see a sled dog team at any moment.

"Quite a change from the merry Olde, isn't it? You're used to a lot more green, and wet, I'd think." Her voice broke my reverie.

I looked over at her profile. She was completely focused on the road, and I thought I understood why. Her parents' death had been covered in the dossier, with an article reporting that Daisy and Ben Traycroft had been traveling up the Alaska Highway when they'd struck a moose. They were both killed on impact. The article had gone on to speculate that Ben, a known alcoholic, had been drunk, and possibly driving at speeds of up to one hundred miles an hour at the time of impact.

Small wonder that she had become a very self-sufficient young lady. I answered her slowly.

"It's beautiful, but frightening."

She nodded. "Yes, it's deadly out there if you don't know how to prepare for it."

"The same could be said of almost any situation, I suppose."

She flicked me an amused glance with those violet eyes that made me melt a little. "The people who have lived here for generations respect the land highly. They have to, because if you let down your guard it will kill you. Add to that immense tracts of land with very few people, and you could die out there with no chance of anyone finding your body, ever."

I grinned. This was my kind of woman. "Is that a threat?"

"Nah." She grinned as well. "See that bridge coming up?"

I did, it was an impressive old steel span.

"That's the Tanana River. Right now it's frozen almost solid, and in the old days it was the highway." She slowed as we crossed the bridge and I looked down at the rumpled ice surface with interest. It would not have been easy to travel on that, with sleds or on foot, and add the cold to it... travel in the modern era was so much more convenient. Bella went on. "In summer it's full of silt, small rocks, the water looks more like soup. I am told - mind you, I've never put this to the proof, but I'd heard stories - that if you drop a body in the Tanana all that suspension will grind it up within a few miles."

She sped back up as we climbed out of the river valley. I pondered what she had been telling me between the lines of her stories. No overt threat to me, perhaps, but she had a lot of power here in her own right. With a large family that was very fond of her, and only two state troopers covering an area the size of my island kingdom home, I was vulnerable. If she felt threatened by me I was in trouble, not her. I was fine with that.

She put on her turn signal and I looked around. A narrow break in the trees with a roughly plowed driveway that vanished into the depths of the forest was the only place we could possibly turn off.

"He likes company, but prefers not to have people around all the time." Bella grunted softly as the truck bounced over the berm and left the paved road.

I was becoming very curious about this mystery man. Not only who he was to Bella, but why she wanted me to talk to him. I knew it had to do with my being a Pixie. I also knew there were no Folke living in the area beside Lavendar's family, at least that were recorded. The Court kept very close track of the Folke. That was mostly self-protection. A rogue fairy, goblin, or pixie even, could do a lot of damage. And that was what my job really had been for a long time now. Tracking down strays.

We jolted to a stop in front of a tiny cabin, even smaller than Bella's place. It looked like something from a postcard of Alaska, with the cache on stilts just behind the cabin, and a truly magnificent rack of moose antlers suspended over the front door. There was no other vehicle there, but tracks to the porch led me to think someone with a snowmobile had been to visit recently.

Bella took the bag of groceries so I could get my attaché. Even out in the boonies I didn't want to leave it unguarded. I had carried it into the little store earlier, to Bella's unspoken amusement. At least now she knew what was in it, and yet she showed no real emotion toward it. We crunched through dry snow and the quickly falling darkness to the porch.

Bella rapped on the door, which struck me as redundant. The inhabitant of this remote dwelling almost certainly knew we were coming as soon as we had turned off the highway. There was no immediate answer.

"How do you know he's home?"

Another of her quick, amused glances. "Uncle is always home."

The door swung open with a creak, startling me. The wizened old man who stood there cackled slightly at my reaction.

"Come in, come in, you're letting the cold in." He hopped back with an agility I would not have expected from his appearance.

Bella handed him the bag as she went by him, headed for the battered couch that formed the living room quadrant of the one-room cabin. He peered into it. "Oh, goodies. What brought on this generosity?"

"I need you to talk to this Pixie for me." She gestured to me, and I could see her frustration for the first time since she had chased me out of her house.

He looked at me, sharp black eyes framed by a million feathery wrinkles. His thick black hair was cut short and seemed almost out of place above that tanned leather face. He didn't speak, and I couldn't look away from those eyes.

I felt myself falling, and the darkness of his eyes expanded until I was soaring in a night sky on rustling wings... I swore out loud as I realized that she'd tricked me. He was an old spirit. Older than any I had ever soul-gazed with before, although I tried to avoid that with anyone, much less a spirit-being. I flapped my wings to gain altitude and heard his distant laugh.

I've never put too much stock in the spirit walks you read about. Yeah, I'm a pixie. Magic is part of my life. That doesn't mean that I'm all happy in the metaphysical, looking for some deep spiritual meaning in everything. I'm Folke, not a hippie, dammit. That, and Raven's chortling was getting on my nerves.

"I don't mean her any harm." I snapped. I grabbed a little more air, then went into a slow bank, looking at the frozen Alaska scenery below me.

"Then why is she afraid of you?" He asked. His voice in my head was warmly amused. This was not a being who feared others. Or at least not me.

"Hell if I know. I brought her good news."

The forests stretched out endlessly under my raven-host. The spruces were so close to one another it was almost an unbroken carpet. I wondered if he was showing me *Now*, or *Then*.

"She does not come to me lightly, my niece. So why would good news have set her feathers on edge?"

"Your niece? Whatthehell?"

I'd finally seen the landmark I was looking for, the snake of white that was the river she'd driven us over. I stooped toward it, my feathers rustling in the wind.

"She is my blood. Answer me."

The tone of that last rang with command and I winced. So far three people had manipulated me since my arrival. I didn't like it, but the words came out almost on their own. "She's also of the Fae. Her grandmother's blood in her makes her the heir to the throne, Underhill. I came to bring her news of her heritage, and to bring her back to Underhill, to Court."

"You want to take her from her home?" He sounded deeply surprised. I was following the river, now, hoping for the bridge.

"No, I want to bring her home." I hoped my terse reply would satisfy him, before I revealed more than was good for me.

"This is her home. She is bound here by blood and love. You call only on a forgotten part of her heritage, one that Lavendar set aside long before you were born, Boy."

"I have my duty," and I had found the bridge. I swooped low over it, and then followed the highway. I was close, now.

"You have told her. She chooses." His voice had lost the amusement.

"She is coming back with me." I gritted through a closed beak, a very odd sensation. I could spot the clearing, now.

"She gets the choice, boy. You are not in your people's territory, now, and the tales make me a fool, but they also make me free with other's body parts." His laugh now was positively chilling.

"Mine are too small to be worthwhile." I flapped for airbrake effect and touched down on her truck. The door to the cabin was closed, of course.

Now the chuckle was indulgent. "Want in? And don't put yourself down, Boy, you have great potential. Mind, you hurt her, and I'll be in line to hurt you. Got that?"

"Yeah, in spades. Let me in, it's cold enough to freeze my…" I stopped there, suddenly unable to think of a lewd enough metaphor.

Chapter 3

Troll on the Bridge

A cackling Raven in man form swung the door open and I fluttered into the warmth. My body was leaning on a kitchen chair, eyes closed and slack-jawed. I looked quickly away. That was not a comforting sight. The lights were out and no-one was home.

Bella was sprawled on the couch with a book. She didn't look up, and I figured that was on purpose. She didn't want to make eye contact with me, who she'd betrayed into this. I hopped up onto her chest. As a bird, I figured I could get away with it. Cats do it all the time. She grabbed me and held me up in the air, finally looking me in the eye. I squawked.

Raven came and grabbed both her hands and me. I started to feel a bit squashed, and pissed as hell. Well, that wasn't just starting. I'd felt that way since the bird had pulled me into his trap. He opened his mouth and I was looking forward to home, sweet body, when something made a sharp tone.

Bella let go, leaving me in the old man's hands, and while the tone ululated, pulled a pager out of her pocket and dialed the volume even higher than the ear-piercing initial sound had been.

A scratchy radio transmission burst forth. "Respond to a motor vehicle accident on the Tanana Bridge. Injuries reported."

Bella jumped up. "I have to go. I'm probably closest," she blurted to Raven and I, and bolted for the door.

I shouted, but only the old man heard me, as I was still in the bird. "Wait!"

She was gone, the door banging behind her. "Shit."

"What is wrong?" He reached out for my body with one hand, and I leaned on the link as well, leaping back into my own consciousness.

I staggered toward the door. "There - there was no one on the bridge when I flew over it."

I felt woozy. The jump from bird back to human form had been too quick. The old man slid an arm around me with surprising strength. "I mean, there could have been an accident, but for there to have been a response that fast..." We made it out the door, the Raven, his bird, and I, but she was gone already.

"Argh." Not eloquent, but that summed up how I felt about this. Something bad was happening.

Raven steered me down the steps. I was still tripping over my own feet, so I obediently followed him. It wasn't like I could go charging down the driveway after the woman in the pickup.

"I'm going to let go, now, can you stand alone?" He peered at me from a distance of mere inches away.

"Personal space..." I leaned back a bit. "Yeah, I'm fine."

He grunted and stepped away from me. Feathers were starting to sprout from his skin, and his nose was lengthening into an impressive beak. I stared, fascinated, as he transformed into a glossy black raven, taller than I was. He turned a vivid grey eye on me and stretched his wings.

"Ah..." He croaked, and I took a step back. "That feels good. Been a while for me."

Hearing human speech come from him, even as raspy as it was, I relaxed. Then I shivered. It was damn cold out here, and even with my coat still on, I was chilled through. I looked around. There was no garage hiding a vehicle, so how was I going to follow her?

The giant Raven laughed at me. "Climb aboard, Boy."

I looked up at the smooth expanse of wing he was presenting me. "Oh, hell no."

"You would prefer to stay here?"

I backed up a step, and again that piercing gray eye fixed me. I could tell he expected me to turn tail and run. Instead, I grinned at him and ran full speed ahead, up the leading edge of his offered wing and onto his back. He wasn't the first oversized avian to give me a ride.

Silently, he launched himself skyward. I held on for dear life, pressing my face into his feathers. I dug my hands in deep, holding on near the skin and feeling the heat of his body. I kept my face down as we rocketed up. I didn't need to see where we were going, and the wind chill would have me solid in no time. I could tell from his wingbeats that we were still climbing.

As I pressed my face into soft, cool feathers I could smell the old bird. Smoked leather, salmon, the beef jerky we had brought him: who knows what else, but this was a spirit being at least as old as any of the Fae at my home Court. He was different, powerful, and he was giving me hope for the first time since I had been bidden to this, the final task of my life as a freelancer.

He hit the peak of his arc and I could feel the tension in his shoulders as he pitched his wings for a long dive. His pinion feathers fairly crackled as we picked up speed. I risked a peek.

I caught a blurred glimpse of the bridge looming below us, before my eyes streamed with tears in the cold wind. I put my face back down, trying to blot my tears on his feathers. I didn't dare let go with even one hand while we were in this dive. I was beginning to wonder how I was going to get off at the end of it. Flung out like a stone from a slingshot, it felt like.

Raven spoke for the first time. "I see trouble, all right. I'm going to drop you by her truck to provide distraction."

"Where's Bella?" I didn't dare take another peek, I needed clear eyes for this when I finally got back on the ground.

"He has her." I felt a jolt as he angled his pinions against the air flowing over them, and we dropped like a stone. "Get ready."

I was going into a fight blind, no idea what the enemy looked like, what weapon I would find, even if there was one in the rifle case I'd gotten a glimpse of. My ally was a trickster spirit not known for loyalty, and a fairy princess was in trouble. My fairy princess. It was my job to save her cute little ass. I really hate my job.

"Go!" Raven rasped, and I rolled off his wing in the direction he'd banked, and hit the ground running.

Straight into the side of the truck. "Oof..." I could hear all the wind leave my lungs, and I reeled backward for a second, windmilling. Smooth, Lom, real smooth.

The door handle popped open easily, she hadn't locked it. Why would she, out in this godforsaken wilderness? Well, all right, not so god forsaken. One god, with feathers optional. I looked over my shoulder down the length of the bridge to see where he had gone, and got my first look at the hairball I was walking into.

I pulled the rifle case out by feel while I sized it up. There was indeed a wrecked car midway down, although it looked to me like a fake-up. I had used such a set-up a time or two myself. Bang into the rail just enough to break a light or two, scattering glass and the ridiculous brittle plastic cars are made of these days, then play possum until your target stops to check on you. I wasn't proud of it, because that was how you caught someone who still had some soul left.

Bella was in the air, clutched by a Norwegian Troll, unless I missed my guess, and I never do. It's my livelihood to know all the weird creatures out there, and what they are capable of. This one had looked like an ordinary man, possibly with a creative blood smear on his forehead and a dazed look in his eyes, right up until she had leaned in to take his vitals...

Then he had changed, into his real appearance, brutish, huge, but the dazed look would still have been there. Trolls are not smart.

Now, he towered twice my height, and seemed to be using Bella as a shield against the angry Raven-god who was trying to pick his eyes out. The way he was holding her, with both hands so he pinned her arms against her body, made me think she had done something to protect herself and had injured him. I had the rifle out of the case, now, mostly by feel, and I tore my gaze from the bizarre fight to look at what I was going to be using.

A nice little 30-30, lever action. Scope, and a rubber recoil suppressor on the butt, which I would appreciate tomorrow. I jacked the chamber open and pulled the cartridges rapidly, finding three, then reloaded as fast as I had pulled them. You aren't supposed to carry a loaded weapon in a vehicle. Naughty girl. I was liking her more and more.

There was no time to look for more ammo. This was just going to have to be enough. I departed the truck at a jog, headed for the action. The rifle was heavy for me, but not too much.

I knew that the Troll was not an easy being to kill or incapacitate. I was going to have to get it either in the eye, or the nose. Anyplace else, and the heavy plates of its skull bone would deflect the bullet. Also, he was so distracted by Raven that he hadn't yet noticed me.

"Hey, butt-ugly!" I stopped, braced the rifle to my shoulder, and bellowed at him all in one smooth move. I was in my element, finally. He swung around from trying to bat the annoying bird out of the air and stared at me, mouth hanging open. He held Bella awkwardly in front of him.

She looked at me and stopped trying to kick him, instead curling her head toward her chest, and her legs up. The best attempt at a fetal position while being pinioned by troll mitts. Not bad. I appreciated her consideration for letting me take a shot, as well as keeping her own pretty skin out of the way, and then breathed out as I gently squeezed the trigger.

The first shot knocked his head back, and he dropped Bella. She landed in an ungainly heap, but I couldn't watch her sort herself out, I was still watching him to see if I had hit the right place. He staggered back and then clutched his head with both hands. Shit... I'd hit him right between the eyes. Blackish blood bubbled out, but I knew it wasn't a fatal wound. He shook his head, spraying blood in all directions, and then opened his mouth in a roar as he charged toward me.

I had gained his full and undivided attention. I had two bullets, and less than fifty feet between us, and a rifle that wasn't sighted in properly. I fired again, sighting below the scope, along the barrel sights this time. The troll staggered, and I heard 'boom, boom, boom' from behind him. He fell to his knees, one eye destroyed, the other still with a dazed look tinged now with confusion. Slowly, he fell forward onto his face.

I looked over his body at Bella, who was still in her shooter's stance.

"Why the hell didn't you shoot him before?" I was pissed, and it may have come out in my voice.

Hers was very tart as she holstered the hand cannon she'd been carrying in a shoulder holster. "I don't usually shoot my patients out of hand."

I put the rifle over my arm and walked up to the troll. It was a short walk. I looked down at the back of his head, with the grayish, wrinkled scalp visible through the wispy hairs. "And when he turned into the big ugly?"

"I didn't have time before he grabbed me. You saw how he was holding me. All I could do was give him a fat lip and a sore crotch."

Despite myself, that made me chuckle. All right, more like a short bark of bitter laughter. I looked at her. She was beautiful, standing there with her cheeks all rosy and fire in her eyes. The laughter vanished.

"We need to talk. Now, before another monster pops out of the woodwork."

She looked down at the troll. "What's going on? What did you do?"

"He wasn't coming for me, lady. They are after you."

"What?" Her eyes snapped back to me. She had been contemplating the troll like she was trying to figure out his genus and phyla. Understandable, given her job. She wasn't going to get it, though, this was way out of the experiences of all but an unlucky few. I was one of those, sadly.

I turned away from her and walked back to the truck. I felt tired. I always did, at those moments, when the adrenaline drained away and left wobbly legs and nausea in its wake. The case was hanging half out of the door, and I fumbled at it with numb fingers. I had not noticed the cold until now, and I was fast losing the ability to use my hands. Bella came up behind me and helped, wordlessly.

A rare woman, this one. She knew when not to talk, and she could handle a gun.

"Your scope is off."

"I don't doubt it. It's sensitive to bumps."

"I was in a hurry." I sighed then. "Good thing you had it. Where's your ammo?"

She pulled a plastic case halfway out and I nodded. If I needed it again, I knew where it was. In that single gesture she'd shown me she was going to trust me. I trudged over to the passenger door and climbed in, my legs leaden. She started the truck's heater blasting as soon as I got in.

"What are we going to do about the troll's body?" I asked her.

"Raven will take care of it." She pointed and I saw that he was still in giant bird, form, and pecking at the troll. There were a bunch of other ravens there, and clouds of them flying in. I looked away. I really didn't need this image in my dreams.

Bella looked a little pale, too. "I'll take you back to Raven's cabin. We can't get past him to Tok right now."

"What about other traffic?" I didn't really care, but I was curious if she had ever dealt with this before.

She peered skyward through the windshield. "I don't think this will take long."

I followed her gaze to the cloud of birds. "I think you're right. Let's go."

31

She made a nice tight turn and got us headed away from the growing flock of carrion birds. Neither of us talked again on the way back to the cabin. I was nodding in the drowsy heat by the time she turned back onto the driveway and jolted me awake. But at least I was warm again.

Inside, she looked rather helplessly at me, and I could tell she was unhappy and out of her element. The first time I had seen her like that, now that I thought of it. I filed that away as useful information. It took a lot to shake this one, she was steady under fire, but afterward, the reaction.

"Coffee? Or would you rather tea? Raven's version of tea is... execrable, but..."

I stopped her before she could go on. "Coffee is good. I'm not that English."

I sat on the couch and watched her get it brewing with quick, economical motions. She knew her way around this kitchen.

I went on. It was time to make her aware of who I was, at least to some of me. "Actually, I have spent as little time there as I could since I was old enough to leave."

"I thought pixies were bound to their home tor?"

I wriggled out of my coat. The wood stove was keeping the cabin nicely warm. "Not bound, no. Just it's a trait of our kind to be homebodies. I'm a very odd Pixie, by my family's opinion."

"That explains why you have no accent."

"Well, that, and I tried to get rid of it."

"Oh." She brought me a chipped mug full of coffee. It smelled heavenly.

"So, um, Lom, what do you really do? What was that thing?" She sat down on the couch next to me. There really wasn't anywhere else to sit in the tiny dwelling. I took a gulp of too hot coffee to try and delay my answers to those loaded questions.

"Well, I am not doing any longer what I've spent most of my adult life at. I got called into service a few days ago."

She lifted that eyebrow at me. I regarded the line of her jaw as it tightened with a slight head tilt, and thought for about the dozenth time since I had first seen her that I was going to have to either learn control or become an eunuch.

"The service of the Court?"

I felt apologetic as I explained. "Not exactly. Your service, specifically."

I might as well have struck her in the face. She flinched back. "What? I don't want that."

I sighed. I wanted to rub my face, but a half cup of still steaming coffee in my hand kept me from it.

"I told you we needed to talk. Let me begin at the beginning?"

She leaned back and nodded. Her face was tight and unhappy. I took a deep breath, and then decided I needed to stand and pace a little.

"How much do you know about your heritage?"

She closed her eyes and sighed. "My grandmother used to tell stories. About fairies, and then when I was older I realized that they were about real people. After my mother died, when I moved in with them, she told me more. And she taught me how to use my Sight."

"That's why you knew I was a pixie."

She nodded. "I should have used it on the troll."

She looked so dejected I took pity on her. "Why would you? You weren't expecting trouble. I'm guessing you do not scan for the Folke everytime you meet a stranger." Which meant she had been looking for me? Now, that was an interesting thought.

"No, well, sometimes when I meet someone I've never seen before."

"Have you ever met any?" I walked into the kitchen and put the empty coffee cup on the counter.

"Other than you? Yes, a couple others."

"So you know that there are other things than fairies out there, you knew I was a pixie. What did Lavendar tell you about your magic, and that of other species?"

"I don't have any magic!" She looked as startled as she sounded. "I'm only a little bit of fairy. I just don't understand why they want me to come back to them. Lavendar left, and she wouldn't talk about why, but I do know she never wanted to go back, or for me to go back. She told me..." Bella stopped talking and looked away from me, toward the door, pressing her lips together.

I sighed and ran my fingers through my hair. She didn't trust me, even now. "Let me guess, she told you to never trust a fairy or a pixie. To run if you saw a goblin coming."

She shook her head. "Nothing bad about pixies. She told me that fairies never meant what they said, and goblins are defilers of all that is good."

I was surprised to hear that Lavendar had borne no ill-will toward pixies. That would have been an interesting story, but it was too late to hear it.

"I don't have time to give you all the details. That will have to be filled in later. You really are an heir to the High Court."

"An heir?" She interrupted me. "How many are there? And how can I possibly be an heir, I'm not..." She waved her hand. "All fairy."

"The fairy line hasn't been pure since the human race came along." I chuckled. "Fairies and humans don't cross breed easily, but that doesn't keep them from trying."

She looked taken aback at that. Evidently she had never thought through her grandparents having sex before.

I went on. "And that has been part of the problem, too. Fairy is... not a fertile species. Children borne to fairy and human parents are usually sterile, like a mule."

Now she raised both her eyebrows, but I had her full attention.

"The succession for the Queen of High Court is matrilineal and it's partly a meritocracy. Out of the females of each generation to the royal family, one is chosen to be Queen. In order to choose one, they are required to serve at Court for a time. That is what you are going to have to do."

She sat up straight. "I do not want to. How do I say no?"

I shook my head. "You don't have a choice. It's a duty that you are required to fulfill."

"No one can make me."

"Ordinarily, I would say that was something you could get away with." I sat down next to her, facing her. She was very tense, and on the verge of jumping up, I could see. "But there is something else going on here. That's why the troll was after you."

"After me? It was an accident." She had forgotten what I told her at the scene. No surprise, she was under a lot of stress.

"No, it was an ambush." I was speaking softly and as matter-of-factly as I could. She was practically vibrating with unhappiness. "He, or whoever he was working with," I couldn't get the dumb look in his eyes out of my head, "used magic to send a fake radio message they knew you would respond to. He's a troll, he had an affinity for bridges, that's likely why they used that."

I took her hand, and she didn't resist. Her hand was warm and calloused. "He was going to kill you and it is my job to stop that from happening."

"I..." she stopped. She looked like she had lost all the breath in her body.

"It's going to happen again. This is why I was sent, instead of overnight mail. Because the heirs have been dying. Your mother's generation is almost gone. Two of your generation are dead. There were only seven of you to begin with." I was doing my best to sound reasonable, rather than 'listen to me you silly twit.'

She sank back into the cushions, her face pale. She didn't let go of my hand.

"I'm not important enough to bother with." She told me quietly. "Can't I renounce it, or something? Abdicate?"

In this position I was very close to her. She smelled of soap and water and girl, and I swallowed. I would have given anything to assure her it would be all right, she could just say no and everything would leave her alone.

"That is not an option. They are going to come after you, after anyone who they can use as a lever, until they get to you."

"Who are 'they,' and are you saying my family might be in danger?"

The door rattled, and we both jumped.

Chapter 4

Flight from Alaska

Raven walked in, back in his guise of wrinkled old codger. I no longer bought into this; having seen him in action I knew he was ageless. I found that I was standing between her and the door, I had moved into defensive position without even being aware of it. I sighed, and sat back down.

Bella sat up straight. "Uncle." She reached her hands out to him and he dropped his coat on a chair with mine and took them.

"You have to go, I know." The way he said that, sadly but with certainty, surprised me. I had expected an argument from both of them.

"I don't have to go anywhere." She insisted. She looked at me.

"Child," he told her gently, "I can protect you, if you stayed here, in my house."

"Then that is what I will do." She set her chin in what I was beginning to associate with her more stubborn moments.

"But for how long, and what about your family?"

I had to wonder how long he had been listening at the door. I didn't buy into his knowing everything. Powerful, certainly. A god, certainly not.

"You love too well, child."

I looked at her and saw her face crumple. There were no tears, yet, although I had a sense that she was fighting it.

"Then I must go."

He nodded. "I can make sure you are safe until you leave my territory. After you are gone, I can make certain your family is safe." He looked at me with those grey eyes. "Are her enemies likely to come after the family?"

I shook my head at him. Bella was the only person they wanted here.

"Then you must go."

She buried her face in her hands. I almost didn't hear her muffled question. "Can I ever come home again?"

I looked at the old man, and we stared at one another for a long moment. He had decided to trust me, I saw. His eyes were relaxed and he nodded slightly.

"I don't know." I answered her honestly, after deciding that I had better start telling her the truth as much as I was able to. "There are five remaining heirs. If one of the others is chosen for Queen, then you will be released from Court."

"Like Lavendar was." She looked up and I could see the tears had started. "So how long will it take?"

"Service in the court is timeless." I told her formally, hoping she would catch from my tone that I was quoting.

"Lavendar told me that fairies live long, Underhill. That they only age while they are in the human realm, and humans are affected oddly by the passing of time between the two planes. That is where the stories of men who live a hundred years Underhill, yet age and die in days when they return home, come from."

I nodded. She had the idea. It could be a very long time before she came back here. "You can't say goodbye. But you ought to be able to get in touch with them as we travel, and during your time at Court. These aren't the days of paper mail, any longer."

"We need to leave..." she faltered a little. "Right now?"

Raven answered for me. "Yes, and not go to the airport." He cocked his head to one side, a far-off look in his eyes, as though he were listening to something outside our perceptions. "There are enemies between you and your return ticket, I am afraid." He looked at me and grinned. "Lom."

He knew my real name. During that foray into spirit journey he must have seen into my mind. I frowned back at him, trying to convey my deep displeasure at his discovery. He cackled like the bird he was.

"In town?" I asked him, hoping he'd keep the secret to himself. He had a reputation for enjoying a good joke. Of course, some of the stories about his jokes also involved a woman wearing bird droppings and thinking they were high fashion.

He shook his head. "They have found the car on the bridge. You will have to return to town by another route. Also, I believe they know where you are staying, Lom. There are two strange men who are hanging out in the Tok Lodge bar. They arrived about the time the Troll passed through town."

I shook my head in disgust. "Figures. Well, not the first time I have had to cut and run. The rental car is easily taken care of, and this," I patted the case that was standing near the couch. "Is all that really matters."

Bella eyed it. "Destroying or losing it will not help you, princess." I warned her. She gave me a dirty look indeed.

Raven held up his hand, palm outward. Even that was wrinkled, and had what appeared to be centuries-old dirt embedded in wrinkles and scars. A hand with a lot of character. We both stopped talking obediently and looked at him. He beamed at us.

"Before you leave, children, I will give you a meal."

Bella groaned. My stomach grumbled. It had been a long time, and a fight, between breakfast and now, whenever now was. I looked at my watch. Well past lunchtime, verging on dinner.

"We don't have much daylight, Uncle," she protested.

"You need your strength."

Silently, I agreed with him. Now that food had been mentioned, I was starving.

"Bella girl, set the table. Lom, put some wood on the fire." He shot his orders at us and turned his back, reaching into the crude cupboards that made up his pantry. I shrugged at her helpless look and grabbed my jacket and gloves. I had seen the woodpile, so I could handle this little chore.

I stepped out the door and noticed two things instantly. One, it was a lot colder than it had been when we'd come in. Two, the reason for that was, it was dark now. I had not realized just how short the days were here. It was almost spring, and still it was dark. Dammit. I hated not being able to see them coming.

The snow reflected the starlight well, so I found the woodpile and gathered an armload with no incidents. I stood there in silence for a long moment, listening. The old spirit might have his spies out, but I preferred to rely on my own senses.

It was quieter than any place I had ever been before. Only a slight, muffled clatter from the house broke the stillness. I closed my eyes and used my inner sight to look for Power. It was like seeing stars in the sky, Underhill. Sparks bright and dim would spangle the world around me. Here, the old man glowed like a beacon. Bella's warm yellow flame drew me, then I looked upward and saw the dull lights of the ravens under his control.

I opened my eyes and relinquished the power, blinking to get my eyes back in focus. The clearing around the house remained empty, and I walked across the squeaking snow back to the door. I stamped my feet to get snow off and Bella opened the door. I smiled my thanks as I pushed by into the house.

She showed me the wood box behind the stove and I dumped the stack into it.

"Cold out there."

She nodded and took my coat as I peeled it off. "Probably about twenty below. Not bad at all."

I felt my eyebrows lift. "Not bad?"

She grinned suddenly. "How much did you research the area?"

"Obviously, not enough." I sniffed. "What is that?"

"Moose burgers." Raven announced. "You took long enough. Almost ready."

I sat at the little table. A pair of folding chairs had been produced to join the single upholstered one that appeared to be almost as old as Raven. Spattered enamel plates and mismatched cutlery finished the set-up. It felt... homey. I relaxed a little. It wasn't often I could stop worrying about the next threat, but Raven had the watch.

Bella sat in the other folding chair with a suppressed moan.

"Bruised?"

"A bit. I went down right on my..." She rubbed at the affected area. "When that monster dropped me. What was that, anyway?"

"Norwegian Troll." Raven put two slabs of homemade bread on my plate and walked back to the stove where a skillet was sizzling and sending off mouth-watering odors of cooking meat. "Big and dumb. They have an affinity for bridges, and while they're hard enough to kill at any time, on a bridge it's damn near impossible."

"I put three .44 hollow points in his back," she asserted as she leaned back from Raven, who was now wielding a hot pan. He slid a moose patty onto her bread. She flipped the other piece on top and gave it a little squish.

"Yeah, that got his attention until I put a bullet in his eye. It wouldn't have stopped him, though."

"Oh." She took a big bite and chewed thoughtfully. I imitated her. "Mmmm..." She purred. "Raven, you make the best burgers."

He grinned, showing a set of improbably white and perfect teeth. "Flattery will get you everywhere, niece."

I had to agree with her. I didn't know what he had put in to flavor the meat, but now I understood why there were no condiments on the table. Garlic, onion, spices... and juicy. I swallowed and sighed.

"Thank you." I inclined my head to him in a formal Japanese style, and he returned that gravely.

"There are three things one should never do on an empty stomach. Fleeing, fighting and..."

"Uncle!" Bella interrupted him with a laugh.

"I get it." I was chuckling at their byplay. "And I appreciate you feeding us. But how are we supposed to get back to town?"

"Snowgo," he answered promptly. "You can take it in to town, and call your cousin Tex to fly you out from there." This part he addressed to Bella, who nodded. I was still trying to figure out what a snowgo was.

He stood up, reached behind the ratty couch, and hauled out a snow-shoe. I stared at it in horror. It was damned cold outside, and more than twenty miles back to town, and he expected us to walk?

Raven offered the snowshoe to Bella. "Dessert?"

She burst into laughter as I wondered if they had both gone mad.

When she got her giggles mostly under control she turned to me, "Aunt Mya made Raven a birthday cake a few years back. She's a really good cake decorator, so she decided she would make a snowshoe-shaped cake for him. He took one look at it and refused to eat it."

Raven broke in. "It looked real. And you don't know that woman's sense of humor! I wouldn't put it past her."

His exaggerated look of grievance made me chuckle again. I understood what he was doing, clowning about to keep Bella's mind off the events of the day. She was looking better, more color in her cheeks with food and the laugh. Time to get moving, while we could still evade our enemies.

She put her plate on the counter next to a dishpan and I imitated her.

"You're not washing up, girl." he scolded her. "Get some more layers for this boy." He pointed at me. I was amused at his command.

She looked at me, and smiled. Suddenly I wasn't so amused. That look held a lot of mischief, and she had reasons not to be happy with me.

Ten minutes later I waddled out the door. I was wearing about three more layers than I had been, and most of them had obviously been made for children. Even my shoes had been stuffed into a backpack, while my feet (in an extra layer of socks) were stuffed into a pair of moon boots I would have bet good money were made sometime in the 1980s. They were warmer than my shoes had been, I would admit.

The crowning insult was the hat, an erratically knitted affair made from variegated rainbow yarn. It was lined with rabbit fur, had a bobble on top, and earflaps. Bella had handed it to me with a funny little smile. I had looked at the thing in my hand in horror.

"I made that." She told me.

I looked up at her and wondered whether to tell her the truth.

"Horrible, isn't it?" she went on cheerfully. "I was eight, and just learning how to knit. I gave it up after a few tries, I think this might be the only thing left. It is warm, though, really."

I sighed, and put it on. She hid her mouth behind her hand, but I could see the smile in her eyes.

Now, standing on the porch, I had to admit that at least I couldn't see it, and it was keeping my ears warm. Bella went around the corner, having asked me to stay put. A moment later I hear the roar of a small engine, and she reappeared on a snowmachine.

I trudged down the steps as she dismounted and held out a hand for the attache case. Silently, she tied it down to the rear of the seat, then remounted. With a deep sigh I gathered my temper and climbed on behind her. I had never ridden on one of these before. Motorcycle, yes, horses, many wheeled vehicles, but this was completely different.

Bella shouted over her shoulder, "hang on!"

This was getting to be a pattern. I held on tightly to her waist and couldn't see much of anything as she accelerated around the cabin and toward the woods at an insane speed. Peeking over her shoulder, I could see the narrow trail she was heading for.

The forest in this area was made up of conifers, black and thickly crowded in the dim light of the moon and stars. Only the reflection of that light off the snow kept it from being pitch black. If we had a headlight on this thing, she hadn't switched it on yet. The light level dropped the instant we slid into the trees, and Bella lit up the scene with a brilliant headlight. I really wished she hadn't.

The feel of the snow under my butt was different, here, and as she took us around a curve it felt disconcertingly like water as we sank into it. I held on tighter, frustrated at being out of control. I couldn't even see any further than the trail, now the light was on and disrupting my night vision. I closed my eyes, and opened up my Sight. If it was all I could do, at least we wouldn't zip into an ambush.

For the second time that day I found myself with my face in someone's shoulder. This day was just getting worse and worse. I didn't dare think about the ways it could be worse, actually. These things had a way of coming to be.

It's not that I am superstitious. I'm a magical being, but I don't believe in greater forces manipulating our lives. We're too small and the world too big. Well, Bella was important enough to mobilize the forces of the world I knew best, the one hidden in the shadows of the human world. We peek out around the edges, but daren't come out too far, lest we all be cut off.

Humanity has never dealt well with outliers. We may have magic, in its various forms, and at one time, before the rise of technology, we had enough power to worry them. Now, they could and likely would wipe us out. Those of us they didn't keep as pets.

Bella hit a curve at a wild speed and I clutched tighter at her middle. With all the layers in the way, I couldn't tell if I had waist, or something further up. Not that it mattered... I couldn't appreciate it anyway. Damn my life. Up until this morning it had been all beer and skittles, or at least monster hunting with the occasional threat of death by dismemberment, and the rare evening by the fire with my pipe. Now I had a fairy princess to protect, and no way to do it. Until I got her safely back Underhill, into the thick of the conspiracies and politics of Fairy, shifting like quicksand. Dammit.

She shouted something over her shoulder I didn't catch. I opened my eyes, releasing the Sight and re-engaging with the visible. My eyes teared up and I blinked rapidly to clear them. She was slowing down, and the reduced wind chill helped me get my eyes clear.

We were on the bank of the Tanana. She slowed almost to a stop and pointed. I understood that she was warning me it was about to get rough.

"Ok!" I shouted into her ear, and we tipped over the bank.

I leaned in the same direction she did. Same principle as balancing a motorcycle. The ice on the river was rougher than I had expected, and she slowed down as we crossed. I had a chance to look around.

The moon had fully risen, and it was almost bright as day now that we were out of the thick forest. It was a world of black and white, with shadings of grey. The river ice that had looked smooth from high up on the bridge earlier today was revealed to be as cracked and ridged as a crocodile's skin. She slowed even further.

"What's wrong?"

"I'm listening. When the water flows under the ice, sometimes it leaves hollow places that just have a thin skin over them. If I hear cracking, we change course."

"Wouldn't going faster be better?" I wondered if she could hear the concern in my voice. I felt like someone had just dumped a bucket of that ice down my back.

She'd heard it. I could hear the laughter in her voice. "You mean like the idiots that try skimming over open water? We wouldn't know how big the hole was, and on this surface we couldn't go fast enough to make it, more than likely."

We were almost all the way across. I could see the trail opening in the trees above us, and the bank was shallower on this side. I breathed out... and then gulped for air as the ice gave out under us.

We were in freefall for a fraction of a second, just long enough for her to squeak in terror and me to tighten my grip on her. Then the machine hit bottom with a crunch. We had dropped perhaps three feet. I let go of her and stood up. Yep, I could see out of the top, we weren't down far. She had let go of the throttle and the engine was idling.

Bella looked up at me. "We're stuck?"

The way the pocket was shaped, it looked like it. Sheer ice, layered and banded with sediment, it curved ahead of us. I looked around. It was very beautiful. Where the headlight was shining into the ice I could see faint blues and cloudy whites. It wasn't a perfect circle, rather a sort of pointed oval shape. And there was no way to drive out of it.

"We're still about five miles from town?"

She nodded at me. Wrapped in her warm layers, only her eyes showed, but I could see her worry. It was night, it was very cold, and we had no chance if we had to walk into town. I looked up toward the distant bridge. It was only a half mile at a guess, but our enemies were expecting us there, and no guarantee of a neutral passer-by.

"Shut it down."

"What?"

"Turn it off. And get off, and stand over there." I pointed at a spot well away from the machine.

She didn't hesitate now, hopping off as she shut the engine down. I walked around the front of the snowmobile, kicking at the ice. It was really solid. The top edge curved in a little at neck height, where it hadn't broken when we fell in.

"Ok, let's get you up there." I turned to her and waved her to come over.

"What are you doing?" she asked nervously, but obediently came to my side.

"I'm getting us out of here. Do you need a boost?"

"We cannot walk to town," she told me flatly. Then Bella accepted my cupped hands and I gave her a gentle hoist. She scrambled up and stood looking down at me. I decided I had better start explaining. This was a good time to start teaching her, before the bad guys really caught up with us.

"You know why the Folke are different from humans, right?"

She peered down at me. I grabbed the front of the snowmobile and pulled upward. Heavy, but more awkward than anything, especially with a hot engine. I really didn't want to burn myself, that smarts.

"We have special powers?" She sounded hesitant, like she didn't quite believe it.

"We do. Magic, Bella," her name tasted strange, rolling off my tongue. I would think about that later. "Magic that is linked to who and what we are."

I heaved upward and got the machine up over my head, the skis on the edge of the hole. I ducked out from under it. She had backed off from the edge a little.

"Are you using magic now?" she sounded a little nervous now.

"A little. Pixies are also quite strong. I don't have full access to my magic, I'm an earth being. All this ice is..." I tried to decide how best to describe how it felt. "Muffling my magic."

I looked up. She was near the edge again. "Back way up, the machine's coming up."

She retreated to safety, and I got to the rear of the machine and breathed deeply. I reached out with my senses and could feel the resonance of the thin layers of sediment trapped in the ice. That was all I could access, the ice under my boots kept me from tapping into the earth fully. It was enough. I heaved upward, and the machine caught a little on the ice, breaking more of it as it left the hole and landed above me with a crunch.

"Heh." I panted. "Not bad for an old man." Bella hadn't heard that, I realized, she was still way back from the edge. I grinned and looked at the ice layers. Using the sediment as toeholds, I got up and out faster than I'd hoisted her up.

Her eyes were very wide. I couldn't see their color in the moonlight.

"Ready to get going again?"

She nodded and approached the machine slowly. "Lom..."

"Yeah?" I waited for her to mount before I climbed on behind her.

"What else can you do?"

"Lots. And yes, you have magic. I will teach you how to access it once we get somewhere and settled." I answered her unspoken question and evaded having to explain too much about my abilities.

"And is mine... earth magic?"

"No, Fairies have air magic. Some of them also have an affinity for fire."

She nodded, which I felt more than saw, and gunned the engine. We were off again. I hoped for a smooth ride into town. Now, I had other things to worry about. We couldn't just swing by her place and pick up her travel documents. I didn't even know if she had a passport. I wasn't going to ask her about it now, though. We were back up to her favorite speed level: insane, and that was going to make talking impossible over the whine of the engine.

The trail broadened a bit here, and we were now riding on a trail that was beaten down by other snowmobiles, it no longer felt like water under us. She did something I didn't think was possible and opened the throttle even further. I went back to my safe position behind her shoulder and pondered her reactions while I opened my sight again. This close to town, enemies were more likely.

Bella hadn't said anything about being afraid, but her need for speed was telling me loud and clear she was worried, and feeling unsafe out here in the woods. I didn't really blame her. This had to all be a shock: the Troll, my revelations, and now a pell-mell flight through a frigid winter night. I may have impressed her with my snowmobile toss, she was impressing me with her fortitude. All this would come at a cost, though. I was worn to the bone from my magic use earlier, and she was going to hit the end of her endurance eventually.

Properly grounded - literally, that is, bare feet to the earth - I could go on almost forever. I had come close to my limits once, and it had kept me alive through a Hunt that would have killed anyone, anything, else. But on the ice, with only a little sediment to draw from, I had drained my own reserves. I hadn't told Bella that because she didn't need to know. Not where my weaknesses were, only that I was a lot stronger than she would have been.

What it meant was that I was going to need to rest, soon, and refuel. Hopefully there would be food at the airport. We zipped past a house, making the sled dogs tied in their yard start barking uproariously. She didn't even turn her head. I could see the dim glows of their life, seven of them, then we were turning. I kept my eyes closed. She knew where we going, and I needed to See more than watch the road. So far, only ordinary lives were visible.

She turned again, and I guessed that we were following a road now, from the feel, and the corners rather than curves. We must be getting close, there were more people around, although we were moving fast enough I was just registering and letting the glows pass, like the lights of oncoming traffic. When the really bright one showed up directly in front of us, like a lighthouse beacon, I opened my eyes quickly.

Breaking out of the Sight can be a little disorienting. For all the times I have had to do it in a hurry, it has never gotten any better. I opened my mouth to shout a warning at her, and then realized she was slowing. We were at the airport.

"Bella, wait," I spoke into her ear, sure she would hear me now. She came to a stop, just outside a small building with the grandiose sign "Tok International Airport" over it.

""What is it?" She turned to look at me as I let go and slid off.

"There is..." I wasn't sure how to explain it. The door opened and two men walked out. One was wearing brown coveralls, the other was in a parka and jeans. Both were heavily bearded, something I had come to expect of Alaskan males.

"Bella. You ok?" The shorter one, still taller than she was by six inches, which meant he towered over me, hugged her. "Uncle sent me to wait for you, I was beginning to worry."

She hugged him back and I thought I heard a small sigh, before she gestured at me as he let her down.

"I'm fine. A bit bruised. This is Lom, he's been helping me."

She looked at me, then. "Lom, this is my cousin Mark, and Tex, who isn't a cousin, but might as well be."

Mark surveyed me with dark hazel eyes as he took my hand briefly. Then I looked up at Tex, who had to stoop a little to shake my hand. He was taller than her grandfather, a skinny rake of a man in greasy coveralls.

"You're our ride out of here?" I surmised, and he grinned.

"Yup, sure am. Come into the warm, though, like to freeze my..."

"Tex!" Bella interrupted. An old-fashioned girl, that one. But inside sounded good. Maybe there would be food, too.

I followed the girl in, content to let the men wait chivalrously for us to go in. They may also have been assessing me for threat, not that I gave a damn at the moment. I'd seen that Mark was of Lavendar's blood when he'd hugged Bella and their lifeglows were identical. I was safe, for values of safe. In the building was a large waiting area, a universal design and decor, and on the counter where tickets were no doubt sold from, were two large pizza boxes.

I headed for them. Mark grabbed a stack of paper plates and handed Bella and I each a slice of pizza.

"Fast Eddie's Mad Trapper Pie." He announced cheerfully. I didn't care what it was called, I needed it. I was already taking a bite.

It was good. Spicy - my mouth was already burning, but hot and greasy and perfect. Mark watched me eat, and slid another piece on my plate before I could even ask. I was most of the way through that piece before I remembered what I needed to ask.

"Bella, have you a passport?"

She looked startled. I guessed it hadn't crossed her mind, just like it hadn't really sunk in that she was leaving home.

"Yes, but..." she turned to Mark. "It is in my cabin, and I don't know how we will get it. Some clothes and things would be nice." She looked back at me, a pleading expression. "And the cat. Who will feed him?

Mark snorted. "Rasputin will feed himself. Nothing short of a wolverine would take that mangy excuse on. As for the rest of it, let me make a call."

I interrupted. "Whoever goes needs to use caution. And I need to get my case off the snow machine, dammit." I had completely forgotten it in my need to get food in my system. That wasn't good. I could not let my guard down like this.

I got up; when had I sat down? I couldn't remember. Tex materialized. "Hey, settle back. Here's your briefcase." He set it down next to me. "You're looking a little peaky. Guess you needed to eat."

I knew he hadn't tried to open it. If he had, there would be some melted snow outside. The elaborate tooling on the case was for more than decoration. I patted it and went back to eating.

Mark handed me another slice on a fresh plate. I sighed and intoned. "Bless you, my son."

He snorted. "I'll call Dan to get her things. I think you met him this morning."

"Is it still today?"

Bella laughed. "I need to talk to him, Mark. He'll need my combination." She made a face. "And I will change it when I get back, just so you all know!"

Mark adopted an expression of abused innocence while I watched the byplay with amusement. They were more like siblings than most cousins. I went back to eating while they talked to Dan on the counter phone.

Bella came and perched on the arm of the dilapidated couch I was sitting on when she was done. "This won't take long. Raven told Tex to take us to Haines, when we do leave."

"Where?" I was surprised at how many feathers the old spirit was sticking into the pot. Bella must be something special to him.

She nodded. "Exactly. It's unlikely your, um, cohorts, will know where it is, either."

"Not my cohorts." I felt utterly tired, now, but the warm glow in my stomach was soothing my unsettled humor.

"What are they then?"

"Yes," Mark joined the conversation, sitting across from me. "I'd like to know, too."

"I told Bella earlier, she has an inheritance from her grandmother. I know, she'd like to be able to decline it, but that's not an option. These people are going to come after her, no matter what. And they will use you - her family - as leverage to get to her."

"Yes," Bella broke in, "I've accepted that. But who are 'they'?"

I rubbed my face. This was not going to be easy. I wasn't supposed to tell Mark, an outsider, anything. Oh, hell, he is Lavendar's blood.

"Look, Fairy, the world Underhill, is broken into two courts. Just like in the stories."

She wrinkled her nose, an expression I was finding rather endearing. "Summer and Winter? Low and High? Grandmother's stories were always changing."

Mark nodded at this. "She didn't tell me the same stories as Bella, but I learned very young the value of sitting still and being quiet."

"Always a useful skill," I told him, still trying to marshal my thoughts. "Summer, Winter, light, dark, good, evil... No one quite knows how it happened, but over the centuries each court has become a magnet for certain personalities. It isn't always linked to bloodlines, of course, although there are certain families who are always Summer, or always Winter. Lavendar was Summer court, and thus you are, Bella."

Mark got up and brought the pizza over and put it in front of me. I nodded my gratitude as I took another piece, and went on.

"For some time now, Summer has been on the wane. Nothing overt was ever done, but Winter would prefer that Summer stay out of the way, so it was assumed that certain accidents... weren't."

I stopped to finish eating. I needed the fuel badly, still. I took another piece.

She went on, "so I am being targeted by Winter fairies? And they have Troll allies?"

Mark gave her a startled look. Raven must not have told him about that fight.

I swallowed. The pizza was very good, but I was eating too fast to appreciate much. Tex materialized and handed me a bottle of soda.

"Dan's on his way," he informed us laconically. "I am going to go tighten the rubber bands."

When he'd gone outside, I looked at the others. "Tighten the rubber bands?"

It gave me the chance to finish - was this my fourth, or fifth piece? - while Mark answered. "When Tex came here he was used to flying larger planes. The running joke is that he loves the little bush planes, but he never misses an opportunity to down-talk them. Says the J-5 he will be flying today runs on two rubber bands... ever play with a toy airplane?"

I nodded, my mouth full. I got the joke, now. Bella reminded me gently, "what about the Winter court?"

"I am not convinced it's the Winter court alone. I know they have allies, and some of them may be Summer Court, I'm sorry to tell you." What I wasn't going to tell her was that I trusted no-one. Not even her sweet, innocent little face. It might look to them like I was only talking, and stuffing my face. I was also watching their every reaction to what I was saying. Mark was looking slightly concerned, with protective glances at his cousin from time to time. She might think of herself as competent and independent, but she had a pack of family who looked after her.

Bella was solemnly focused on me. I went on, "among other allies, the worst will be the goblins. They are known as the defilers for a good reason. Do not," I emphasized grimly, holding her eyes with mine, "let them take you captive. The women and children are worse than the warriors, and that is no exaggeration."

She nodded, looking a little pale. I picked up the last piece.

"Do you always eat like that?" She followed the arc as I lifted it to my mouth and took a big bite.

I shook my head and swallowed. "No, but I burned a lot of energy back there. Remember that. Magic use comes with a cost, always. Try to do too much, and it will kill you."

She sighed, "I have so much to learn, and so little time."

I nodded. Not much more I could say, to that. The door swung open and I was on my feet and between her and the newcomer before Mark could even look around. I relaxed, recognizing the man stamping snow off his boots. While I was up, I grabbed the other box, the one with half a pizza left in it.

Dan brought a thick envelope and a backpack to Bella. She stood up and hugged her cousin, and he glared at me over her shoulder while he rubbed her back. I nodded at him, acknowledging his anger and frustration. The burly, bearded man rather intimidated me, and he didn't have a bit of magic.

Bella kept her face turned away from me when she let go of him, but I could tell from her hand movements that she was wiping her tears away. Dan came to me.

"Anything else we can do?" He asked me in a deep, quiet voice. I shook my head. The food had me alert again, and now I had to think through how we were going to get safely away from here, without any collateral damage. We needed to leave, soon. My power signature was damped, I knew, but she had no such training, nor did Mark. I mentally debated taking him with us. No - they would leave him alone, he was male and posed no danger to them.

"No. We need to leave, before trouble finds us."

Bella swung the backpack over her shoulder. "I'm ready as I'll ever be."

She looked down at the box in front of me, then looked me in the eyes, raising an eyebrow. "It's amazing you aren't round, the way you eat."

She had a right to snark at me, I had eaten a pizza and a half, it looked like.

"Remember to have food on hand when you learn to do that. Then you will understand." And I was looking forward to training her, and getting a chance to prove it to her as she tossed back the calories afterward.

"I'm going to be able to toss a snowmobile?" She grinned.

To my surprise, I grinned back, demurring, "I didn't exactly toss it."

Chapter 5

Encounter with a Roc

Tex meandered in, something I was learning was his speed. "You two ready?"

We turned and answered "yes" in unison. He grinned, and gestured toward the rear. "Ladies first."

"No." They both looked at me in surprise, that must have come out pretty firmly. "I go first, always, Bella. Part of my job."

I was walking as I talked to her, and went into the back hall with a glance around, then motioned her to follow me. Tex trailed behind, a very amused look on his face. I was guessing the Alaskan princess was used to ruling this part of the world with velvet gloves. None of the men in her life let her pretend to be a delicate flower, but they all treated her like a jewel. I approved. The more I got to know this family, the more I hoped they weren't part of this nasty business. But I couldn't trust just yet.

Once we were onboard, I relaxed. Tex had the engine going and the plane preflighted. I was going to trust that part. I have no idea how to fly a plane of any size.

Bella buckled up, then looked over her shoulder at me. "Need help?"

I shook my head. I might not be able to fly one, but I had flown in one many times. She handed me a pair of headphones and I put them on, just as the engine whine rose to a higher level.

"On our way," Tex announced and we began to roll across the tarmac, bouncing gently.

"So, where is Haines?" I asked. I hadn't wanted to talk about it before we were in the air. You never knew when ears were perked in your direction. But the clatter of the plane ought to keep them from prying too much.

Bella answered. Tex seemed to be ignoring us. "Southeast Alaska. I have a great-aunt there. I'm not sure why Raven is sending us to Aunt Min, but I am sure we will find out soon."

"How soon is soon?"

"Well, if we drove, it would take about eight hours. Up here, we can go the path the, er, Raven flies. We'll be there in about four hours."

"At least we don't have to walk." I find that my short stature sometimes has advantages, as I curled up in the seat. "I'm going to take a nap. If you can, Bella, you might want to sleep. Tex, please don't."

The tall man chuckled in response to that sally. I closed my eyes and let my mind drift, sleeping might not be an option, but I could probably achieve a drowse. My mind was going a mile a minute, like it always did, and sleep was difficult on a good day, which this was not.

I was awakened by a jolt. "Huh, wha?" I asked, sitting up. I had fallen asleep, remarkably.

"I don't know what it was." Bella answered me, even though she couldn't have understood the words. I looked out the window. It was clear and bright, we had flown into the dawn.

"Not turbulence." Tex was looking down at the instrument panel. "Should be smooth sailing. Bella, can you see if we still have a tail?"

Now I was really awake. "What?"

Tex laughed. "It's a joke, greenhorn."

I bared my teeth at his back in an angry grin. He couldn't see me, I knew, he was looking out the window. Bella was looking out her side.

"What, did we run into something, up here?" I asked, looking out the window myself. The same direction as Bella, which meant neither of us were looking in the direction of the attack. One minute we were more or less straight and level, the next I was looking straight down at the frozen Alaskan landscape below us. Bella shrieked, and I let out a strangled grunt as I hit the end of the tether that was my seat harness.

Tex was silent, but once I had myself righted, I could see the look on his face as he wrestled the little plane back under control. Scared half out of his mind. I closed my eyes and opened the Sight. It was big, and close.

"Put us in a dive!" I shouted without opening my eyes. Tex didn't hesitate. Good man.

"Bank left." Bella gasped as he did that maneuver, and I guessed she had finally seen what was attacking us. I was more concerned with anticipating the big bird's moves, and keeping us out of its reach. Without opening my eyes to look I couldn't identify it, but I knew it had to be a bird, we were too high, and it was too big, for it to be anything else.

It overshot us badly. "Take us back up. Tex, get as much altitude as you can."

I was still studying it with my eyes closed. I had seen this before in a lifeglow. Tendrils of black penetrated the light from the outside edges, clouding it completely in places. This was a creature with a parasite. Hag-ridden, they used to call it. Nothing I could do about it, that was irrelevant... But it might slow the natural reflexes of the creature.

"Dive!" I yelled as it looped back around and above us. I opened my eyes and grabbed the back of Bella's seat. My gorge rose and I swallowed, hard, trying not to let the pizza come back out. In retrospect, stuffing myself was a bad idea. Tex added his own little fillip to the maneuver, twisting us around to the right tightly, almost throwing us into a spin before he straightened back out.

Bella gasped and pointed. I looked, and identified our enemy.

"Tex, do you have a gun? That's a Roc. He's bigger than this damn plane, and right now he's toying with us. When he wants us down, we will go down."

Bella twisted around and pointed. "There's a box under your seat, Tex's pistol is in it, and it's loaded for bear."

The Roc, looking like an overgrown Golden Eagle, glided alongside us. I could see him watching us. Birds aren't equipped to smile, and still I could see his smirk. I fumbled under the seat for the box with one hand and unlatched my harness with another.

"Why isn't it attacking?" Bella's voice was shaking. I didn't blame her. We were flying over lovely, snowcapped mountains right now, and there was a limit to how high we could go. Which meant the ground was coming up to meet us, and there was not a lot of room for error, much less a dogfight with a big bird.

"He's toying with us. Roc's tend to be sadistic SOB's. How far out are we, Tex?"

"About thirty minutes." The man's knuckles were white on the yoke. I sympathized, and admired his fortitude in flying straight despite the bird keeping pace with us.

"So we don't have long, and neither does he." I looked back out at the bird. "How do I open the window?"

"You don't open that one. Only the door windows open, and not very far." Bella's voice was more in control already.

"Ah. I'm coming up there, then." I didn't give them time to object before I abandoned my position, ripping the headphones off.

I scrambled over the seat, trying not to kick Tex, who grunted and leaned out of my way. This left me in Bella's lap, as she squeaked a little in surprise. She flipped one latch and I got the other, and then realized this was going to be a challenge. The little plane was not designed for offensive purposes, the window opened at the bottom and swung out a few inches, then stopped. I could get the gun through it, but any visions I'd had of hanging out like a helicopter gunner were dashed.

"Tex, want me to shoot forward, or aft?" I could get the pistol out, but couldn't bend my arm and hold it steady to shoot the bird, who was looking even more amused. The looks he was giving me were pissing me off.

"Aft," he replied after a long second of thought. "Less chance of prop damage. Let's do this quick, you're throwing my trim off."

"You have an idea?" I asked him.

"Yup. Brace yourself."

I glanced at Bella. I was straddling her lap so I could aim out the window, my knees on either side of hers. She nodded, and grabbed me around the waist, holding on for dear life and essentially burying her face in my midsection. Damn, life was unfair. I didn't have time for a reaction before Tex put us into a steep climb.

I held on tight to the gun, hoping this didn't break my wrists. The bird peeled away and looped below us. I lost sight of it, then watched it rising rapidly up at us. I held my fire. The big revolver only gave me six shots. "What's the plan?" I yelled to Tex, hoping he would hear me. The headphones were on my seat in the back, and the noise and cold with the window open were becoming overwhelming. I needed to get a shot, fast.

"Put it into a spin, and hope the wings don't fall off." He grunted and twisted the yoke, throwing us up and around. Only Bella's arms kept me in place as the plane went over. The bird missed us, and I fired twice into the massive breast as he brushed our wing. The third shot went through the wingtip of the plane.

"Oops." I muttered, eyeing the neat hole in the aluminum. The bird was spiraling towards the ground, a few feathers drifting in his wake.

Tex couldn't hear me, he was focused on pulling us out of the danger of slamming into a mountainside. I pulled the gun back in. My hands were so numb I was afraid I would drop it.

"Bella, close the window." I managed, my teeth chattering.

She didn't hear me. I shuddered and dropped the gun in between us as she looked up. "Sorry..." My hands just weren't working properly. She grabbed the window latch and pulled it closed. Tex cranked the heat up. I was shaking now. I hadn't thought about not having my coat on, I had taken it off to use as a pillow. Bella hugged me close, now that I wasn't kneeling, we were face to face, and I could see the concern in her eyes. I was sitting fully on her lap at this point, and her body heat was delicious.

"Is it gone?" I could feel the warmth of her breath and hear the concern in her voice, even without headphones. I nodded, trying to control the chattering of my teeth.

"I don't see it." Tex was looking out his window, below us. "Not in the air, or down there, either."

"I don' think I killed it." I managed through stiff lips.

"Well, as long as we scared it off." He looked over at us. "You two gonna canoodle, or let me get back in trim?"

"I could go for canoodling." I said before I could stop myself. Bella laughed out loud. She let go of me and carefully picked the gun up from between us. I blurted out, "Dear lord, that was a joke, you don't need to shoot me."

Now Tex started laughing along with Bella. I climbed over the seat much more carefully, finding it far more awkward to manage than it had been going the other way. Adrenaline rushes made a lot of things possible that you wouldn't even consider under other circumstances. I found that although I was warming up, I had the shakes. This was going to be a long trip.

We would be in Haines shortly, and I didn't know where we would be going from there. Until I had her safely Underhill, we were subject to attack from any side. This midair encounter had shaken me, although I didn't plan to let her know that. Something was changing. The accidents that had been happening had been subtle, up until now. This was not subtle at all. I didn't know what I was going to tell Tex to keep him quiet once the plane ride was over.

All my training, my life's work, had been to keep humans at large from knowing about Folke, and the magical world that had once been strong on

Earth, but was now fading away into the shadows. Would it come back, like the Winter Court believed, if magic were allowed to reign again?

I doubted that. My thoughts were that it would lead to war, and death and destruction on both sides. Far better to stay in the shadows and play it conservative. But it was unlikely I would be consulted, by either side. I could just do my job. The more I found out about Bella and her family, the better I liked that job.

When we landed, I was warm again, and had my eyes tightly closed and Sight stretched to its fullest extent. Meeting the Roc had shaken me. I suspected the Tok Airport had been under surveillance, and they could not have known we were headed to Haines rather than one of the cities, but I wasn't taking chances. I had also made a decision.

Chapter 6

Ferry Boring

"Are we flying out of here, or what?" I asked Bella as we stopped in front of another tiny airport terminal. She shook her head as she climbed out.

"I don't know. Aunt Min is supposed to meet us here."

I led the way toward the building, letting Tex precede me into the warmth. His complexion was a little greenish, still, and I was guessing the gravity of our midair encounter was finally sinking in for him. A man with shoulder length grey hair and a face most charitably described as craggy met us just inside the door.

"Tex." They clasped hands. "Min's waiting for ya."

He nodded at us, but didn't seek an invitation.

"Thanks, Drake." Tex waved us further into the building, and we passed through the mechanic's shop, it looked like, before another doorway took us into the waiting room.

Min was the only person in the room, standing and looking out the window. Her dark brown braid surprised me, I had been thinking old lady when Bella said great-aunt. She turned to meet us, a broad smile on her face, and outstretched arms for Bella. I could see the small signs of age now, the shot silver in the hair at the temples, the laugh lines framing her eyes. Bella simply leaned into the older woman with a little hiccup that might have had tears behind it. I was struck by their beauty, and realized I was seeing what my girl would look like in forty years.

When had she become my girl? Dammit. I was being dangerously sentimental. She was my charge, sure, but not mine.

I walked around them and checked the rest of the room and the outside as seen from the windows. Then I closed my eyes and looked again. Min and Tex had no magic. Bella glowed a pretty periwinkle blue. A pair of normals in the hangar area. We were all clear, for the moment. I opened my eyes again. Bella and Min were looking at me with matching serenity.

"Aunt Min, this is Lom." Bella introduced me formally. I held out my hand and Min took it gently in her warm one.

"Pleased to meet you, I think." Min's voice was a husky soprano.

"It could have been under better circumstances," I admitted. She let go of my hand and I ran a hand through my hair, which was already on end. She smiled. I must look pretty funny, at that.

"What is the plan?" I looked at Tex, who'd sat in a chair and was quietly contemplating us. I was going to have to talk to him, but I didn't need to make this op any messier than it already was. Min had no need to know we had been attacked by a Troll and a Roc in the last 24 hours.

"Uncle said that you two need to get to the Lower 48, and flying wasn't an option. I have tickets for you to board the ferry in two hours, and I'm going to take you to breakfast before I put you on the ship to Seattle." She finished by turning toward the door, and I understood there was no arguing with this woman.

"I'll be right behind you two." Sometimes you just can't clear all of the Alaskan wilderness for your charge, and Min looked like she could hold her own, too. I needed to talk to Tex before we left.

He was looking a bit shocky. I stood in front of him, and he focused on me.

"You going to be all right?"

He nodded. I frowned at him. "You can't talk about this, you know."

"No one would believe me." He buried his face in his hands. "I'm not sure I believe me."

I sighed. An emotional Texan was not something I needed right now. I pulled out my wallet and fished a card out of it.

"Look, we will be out of communication for a while. There's no cell towers where we are going. But I can check my voicemail from time to time. If you need me, give me a call. And when you get back to Tok," I added on a whim, as it occurred to me. "Get in touch with Bella's Uncle."

He looked at me. We were eye to eye, him seated, me standing. "Her Uncle Ray?"

So that was what Raven went by in this modern world. I nodded. He reached out and took the card. "Thanks."

He stood up, like a scarecrow unfolding, and offered me a massive hand. It swallowed mine when I shook it.

"Better hurry, Min's a force of nature." He smiled, a return to his normal self beginning already. The human mind is a resilient thing.

I took his advice and hurried. I could believe that about Bella's aunt. I left the airport building wondering what Tex would do. I was trusting a man I barely knew with a lot of sensitive information, and that trust was largely based on her unblinking trust in him. Min's truck was idling at the door, and I climbed into the back jumpseat before Bella took the passenger side.

"We'll have a hearty meal at the Fireweed Restaurant, then I'll get you on the boat." Min reminded me cheerfully while we pulled onto the road. I was looking out the window. There was a lot more snow here, close to the ocean, than there had been in the interior. As we got into town, I could see the ocean, the small chop sparkling in the morning sun like a field full of moving jewels. The beauty was lost on me, I was wondering how I was going to keep us safe on a ferry.

"How long will it take us to get to Seattle?" I asked.

Min answered without taking her eyes off the road. "About three days, and it's Bellingham, just north of Seattle."

"Slow boat ride." I frowned at the pretty scenery outside.

"Well, if you can't fly..." She responded tartly.

Bella spoke up. "Aunt Min, enough. It's not his fault. We can't talk about it, so can you just trust me? We can't risk going out of, or flying into, any big airports right now."

I could see Min's frown as she looked at Bella. Bella went on, "Lom will take good care of me. He's stronger than he looks."

I was fighting to keep my face straight, but neither of them looked back at me.

Min sighed. "All right. I know you'd tell me if you could. Just know, all you have to do is call." I couldn't see what she did, but I think she reached her hand out to Bella and Bella took it, as she answered.

"I know."

We were all silent until we walked into the kitschy restaurant. My stomach growled at the smell. Min chuckled, "Never send a man off to face the unknown on an empty stomach."

A man came out of the kitchen, wiping his hands on a cloth. His clean white apron strained over his belly.

"Min! Who'd you drag in with you?" He seized her in a bear hug that had her inches off the floor.

"Oof! Gary, put me down!"

When he did, she shrugged out of her jacket, and we followed her lead. "Gary, this is my niece Bella, and her friend Lom. They need breakfast before they catch the ferry."

"Ah! We haven't much time, then." He gave us a mock bow and vanished back into the kitchen.

"Booth, or table?" Min asked, indicating the dining room.

"Bathroom?" Bella responded and Min laughed, pointed the way, and both Bella and I made haste for the necessary room.

When we came out, Min was seated at a table reading a newspaper.

"I ordered for you, I'm afraid." She didn't sound sorry, but I found myself smiling at her. She was impossible to hold a grudge against.

"What are we having, then?" I sat facing the entrance.

"Crab omelettes. Fresh king crab, and Gary does a fabulous omelette. I'd put him up against the best chefs in the Lower 48."

A waitress, young, pretty, and obviously Aleut, brought us coffee with a broad smile. She wasn't much taller than I.

"Leave the pot, please?" I asked her.

She wrinkled her nose in thought, and I guessed she was about sixteen. I beseeched her, playfully.

"I need the black ichor of the gods to sustain me before I brave the Old Ones of the Deep." I pressed one hand to my heart.

She responded to my sally with a laugh. "Cthulhu'd freeze in the Gulf."

She took me by surprise, and Min must have caught that, because as the girl disappeared back into the kitchen, the pot safely in my possession, she told me, "It's a long winter. Everyone reads a lot."

I nodded, "I approve of that." We smiled at one another, and I went on, "Lovecraft doesn't do it for me, but some of the modern re-interpretations, like Correia, are fun to read." She could have no idea of why I enjoyed reading about monster hunters, of course. She shook her head.

"Never heard of him. I prefer mystery, myself."

Bella rolled her eyes at us, but I ignored her, and talked authors with Min until Gary appeared with two plates, his pert waitress on his heels with the third. He served us with a flourish, and stood back with a beaming smile.

"Gary, it smells wonderful." Bella told him.

I took a bite. "Tastes as good as it smells. Asparagus?"

"Works well with the crab." Satisfied at the praise, he left us to it. None of us talked much until we had finished.

"Ah..." I leaned back with a sigh. "Min, you can order for me anytime."

"I'll remember that," she laughed. "Ready?"

"Not really, but we had better go, I suppose." Bella answered her quietly.

Gary came back out for a hug from Min, and handshakes from Bella and I, along with promises to return. As we walked to the ferry terminal, the ocean breeze nipping at my cheeks, I wondered about that. Bella was special. Once Underhill, that certain something might lead to her stay becoming permanent. She didn't understand that, and I was coming to understand that she had a family who would come looking for her.

Of course, before that danger, I had to keep her alive and whole until the coronation. Something that did not look like an easy task.

The ferry was a very big boat. Cruise ship sized. I sighed, remembering a certain Brownie family and a cruise ship. All had been well until the first mate had put a stop to the housekeepers leaving little plates of food out for them...

Min stopped. "Either of you need Dramamine?" She pointed to a little shop that obviously catered to ferry passengers. I shook my head and looked at Bella.

"I'm fine. I spent some time in Japan counting seals during college, remember?"

"That's right." Her aunt frowned, "I guess this is goodbye, then."

Bella hugged her. "Goodbye, I love you."

Min sounded choked up as she told the younger woman, "love you too, Bell."

Min turned to me, her eyes very bright. "You take care of her."

"I promise. Dan scares me." I was serious.

That made her laugh, and we shook hands. Bella waved me onward, impatient, and I understood that she hated goodbyes. Once aboard, I was surprised to learn we were sharing a small stateroom.

"Sorry," Bella looked at me out of the corner of her eye. "I guess Aunt Min misinterpreted 'friend.'"

"I suspect Raven had a wingfeather in this, actually."

"Really? Why?"

"Because I can best protect you if we are always together." And I was rather flattered that he saw me as capable of that, and not harming her.

"What if I don't want you around all the time?" she protested. "I need my privacy."

"Tough, princess." I told her bluntly.

She looked disgusted at that.

I soothed her a little by offering her a treat. "Besides, this means I can begin teaching you."

She brightened. "Magic?"

"Among other things."

"When can we start?"

"Let's go up on deck." I stepped out into the hall and looked both ways, then held up my hand to stop her while I closed my eyes and opened my Sight as wide as I could. The ferry was too large for me to scan entirely, but if there were Folke aboard, they weren't radiating. Which did not mean they were not there. I opened my eyes slowly.

"All clear. You'll have to get used to that."

"I will try to remember. Do you really expect to find... something... onboard?"

"No, but I didn't expect the Roc, either," I told her ruefully. "And it's good practice."

She shivered, and I didn't think it was from the cold Arctic wind as we left the enclosed cabin area.

"When will I be safe again, Lom?"

She stopped very close to me and looked down into my eyes. I could read the concern, even fear, in hers.

"After coronation." I admitted.

"And when is that?"

I sighed, and admitted, "there is no set date. Once the King chooses his Consort."

"His... consort?" She faltered and looked utterly horrified.

"Not what you're thinking. The King and the Queen aren't necessarily married, although many of them have been. It's a political alliance, not one for love or sex."

She sighed deeply. "Whew. I am glad I don't have to jump overboard and try to swim ashore."

I was pleased to hear her humor come back, at least a little. I hoped she was joking about that. I couldn't have let her jump, of course, and it might have been awkward to keep her in the cabin the rest of the trip; humans frown on kidnapping. The wind bit my cheeks, reminding me why I had brought her out here, and putting me back on track to finish this quickly.

"Want to learn some magic?"

"Will it take long?" She looked around at the empty deck and huddled into her jacket. I didn't blame her.

"It shouldn't, but I needed the wind, that's why I brought you up here."

I led her near the bow. "Spread out your arms. Catch the wind." I told her. She did so, looking at me and waiting for the next command. I let her stand there for a moment. Then I asked, "feel the pressure?"

"Yes, I feel... warm." She dropped her arms and looked amazed. "What was that?"

"That's your air magic kicking in. Spells will take a while to learn, but your body already uses just a little to protect you; in this case, keeping you warm. Now, let's go in. I don't have that magic to use right now."

She nodded and followed me to the door. Back inside the hall, I rubbed my cheeks to try and get feeling back in them. "Whew. Next lesson I think waits until warmer weather."

"That was magic? I still have trouble believing it actually exists, much less that I have it. How?"

"Let's get back to the cabin."

She fell silent and followed me. As we reached our door, she spoke again. "I thought bodyguards followed their principal."

I unlocked the cabin and looked in - it wasn't large enough to need more than that to see no-one had entered in our absence. "Go ahead, Princess. Now I'll follow you."

She gave me a dirty look as she slipped past me. I closed the door and locked it behind me. "There will be times I'll lurk. But unless I'm expecting a stern chase, I want to walk into trouble first. So get used to it."

"You keep telling me that."

I shrugged, acknowledging her wounded pride. "It's that or get used to being dead."

She flopped into the sole chair, leaving me the bed. "I'm still getting used to that, too."

"I know this is hard on you." I sat cross-legged on the bed facing her, even though she had her eyes closed and was no doubt trying to will herself back to a time when I didn't exist and her life was normal. "But this is the new reality, and unless you learn how to act and react, you won't live long."

She sat up straight and looked at me. "What's in it for you? Why are you not only protecting me, but teaching me?"

"Teaching you is protecting you. When we are Underhill, there will be times I won't be able to be right there. You need to be able to tap into your magic for both defense and some offense."

"Well, we have a couple days stuck on a boat. I suppose I'd better cram, then, Teacher." She cocked her head a little to one side. "You didn't answer the 'why' part of my question."

"You won't like the answer."

"I'm a big girl, if you hadn't noticed."

Yes, I had, and sharing a room with her for two nights was going to be a challenge. I fed that frustration into a little snarl as I answered her as unpleasantly as I could. "It's my job. To get you there in one piece, Princess."

"Stop calling me that," she shot back.

"It's your title, get used to it."

She closed her eyes again. I guessed that because she couldn't leave the room, that was her equivalent of walking out and slamming the door behind her. I stood up, and she kept them closed.

"Stay here. I'm going to go get us some lunch, and when I get back, lessons."

"What if I don't stay here?"

"Then I will have to find you."

"How do I know I can trust you?" She had opened her eyes again and was looking intently at me.

"You don't."

I left the room, locking the door behind me. It wouldn't keep her in, she had a key, but it might slow a monster down. And she needed a little space to digest what I had just said to her. Sure, I had saved her life back on the bridge with the Troll. But that didn't automatically make me the man with the white hat. In my experience, there was no such guy, and she needed to learn that, fast. This was lesson one. Trust no-one.

Lunch was sodas and pre-packaged sandwiches. Nothing like the crab omelette we'd enjoyed early that morning. But it would keep body and soul together, which was all we needed for now. She was sitting cross-legged on the chair with her laptop when I came back in the room. Her eyes were closed.

"You didn't challenge me?" I asked her curiously.

"Well, you have a key, and I was watching you."

"You figured out how to use your Sight." I grinned, suddenly seeing how a smart student could be a real asset.

"I think so. I'd seen you this way that first morning at the cabin, so I figured I'd recognize you again."

She opened her eyes, then winced and blinked rapidly. "Ow. Now I'm seeing double."

I put the food on the tiny table and came to stand in front of her. "Switching back and forth between Sight and real vision isn't a fast process. That's why you have to be cautious about relying on it."

74

She tried to focus on me, tears in her eyes. "Does it get better with practice?"

"Yes," I held out my hands toward her. "May I?"

"Ok." She closed her eyes again and I gently touched her temples, rubbing the taut muscles.

Her skin was soft, and the scent of it, as she bowed her head almost into my chest, was overwhelming. I stepped back quickly. "Better?"

"Yes, thank you." she opened her eyes, and I could tell she was seeing clearer. "Lom?"

"Yes?" I didn't like this. This was a messy situation rapidly becoming more difficult, and I was afraid what she was going to ask me.

"Can we not fight? I know I shouldn't trust you, but I have to trust someone, and I have a feeling you are..." She trailed off.

"I'm no good guy." She was echoing my thoughts from earlier, in a way.

She grinned suddenly. "Fine, a rogue, a scoundrel, but MY bad guy, then."

I stepped back slightly and swept into a low bow, trying not to hit either the bed behind me, or her, in the limited space. "Your very own ethically-challenged henchman, Princess."

That made her laugh. "I suppose if I must be a princess, I at least have a henchman. Is that food?"

Now I laughed. Magical use made her hungry, too. I'd expected it, and had brought her two sandwiches. She made appreciative noises as she tore into the first one.

"I'm glad you aren't a picky eater, at least."

"Not a fairy-tale princess," she insisted. "I'll eat almost anything, once, and I know enough to not ask 'what is it?' in a foreign country."

"You said you spent some time in Japan?" I prompted.

She didn't need more encouragement to talk about that, around bites of her sandwich. She might not be a fairy-tale princess, but she was a tidy eater, I was pleased to see. There would be no need to teach her deportment before presenting her in Court. Now, some of the Court might shock and repulse her, but that was not my concern.

My princess had manners, and style. And she was tough. The girl might have a fighting chance. I refused to think about what would happen were she crowned Queen. The evil of the day was sufficient to worry about. We had a long path to walk before I even presented her at Court - and wasn't that a peculiar thing, to be her guard and sponsor. Her family had almost no connections left Underhill. Lavendar had been the last of her line, and although she had been unusually prolific for an elf in the mortal world, there still were few of her bloodline remaining.

Bella cocked her head at me, and I realized I'd missed something, and apologized. "Sorry. I'm wool-gathering."

"I was asking if you needed a nap. You look tired."

I yawned hugely at the word nap. "I suppose you are right. Going to sit watch over me?" My attempt at teasing fell a bit flat when she nodded seriously.

"Wake me in an hour."

"Will do." She pulled a slim case out of her bag and flipped it open to reveal a tablet.

I fell back on the bed and closed my eyes, slipping into sleep far too easily.

Chapter 7

Dream Diversion

"Your drains are clogged." The old man was sitting on the edge of a trench, his feet in the muddy water.

"What the hell?" Lom looked around at the eerie landscape. A ditch stretched out seemingly forever. Trees blocked out the horizon to either side, and if he looked at them too long, their limbs began to writhe. The sky was lowering overcast, swirling with unhealthy greens and purples. "Where am I?"

The graybeard waved his pipe at Lom, the smoke falling listlessly toward the ground. "A particularly nasty bit of Underhill. Very useful for setting young lads at tasks that keep their nose to the grindstone."

Lom looked again. He remembered the mud, but the trees were new. It had been brown grass on dry fields before, and he had thought he was digging an irrigation ditch. "Dammit, Alger, I'm too old for your games. Why are you in my head? And how the hell did you get in, I thought I'd had you blocked."

Alger shrugged eloquently. He'd had centuries of practice, and Lom really thought he'd spent a few of those years in front of a mirror perfecting his Aged Wizard routine. "There's a back door in that spell."

"I didn't get it from you," Lom pointed out through gritted teeth.

"No, but I developed it. Look, we need to actually talk, not bicker." Alger waved his hand, using the fingers of both the moving and stationary hand to build a spell, then they were sitting in a cozy room with a fire flickering in the grate. "Ah..." Alger stretched his feet out to the warmth, easing back in Lom's own chair. "This is better. But I wanted to illustrate that your drains are blocked, dear boy."

Lom felt himself wince. Alger's metaphors were usually heavy-handed, this one was worse than normal. Settling into the chair felt good, though, it had been a while - too long - since he had been home. Even in a dream, it was reassuring. "And what do you mean by that?"

"I mean, of course, that every time you use magic, it's a toxin building up inside you," Alger leaned forward and stabbed his pipe stem in the direction of Lom's chest. "And if you channel her, it's that much faster."

"I'm teaching her magic so she doesn't need me to channel her."

"And how much is she going to learn in a few days? I had a few years with you and look at you now..." Alger sighed, leaning back. "This new generation, always in such a hurry."

"I know how hard change is for the elderly, Alger," Lom snarked at him. "We have less time than you have, and more to do."

Alger spluttered. "Elderly?"

Getting Alger's goat had always been Lom's favorite pastime, but he had work to do, Lom couldn't spend all afternoon in a dream with his great-great-it was forgotten how many times uncle. Besides, Alger was dangerous. He had great power, but his prices tended to be rough on those he helped.

"I know only too well what is happening to me. I was there when the spell was set. I've spent years refining my tolerance levels, and I know where my limits are."

"She's Lavendar's kin. She'll push your limits, boy." Alger eyed Lom for a second, then stared into the fire. "Her grandmother," Alger's voice was softer than Lom had ever heard from him, "was a remarkable woman."

"Please don't tell me…" Lom stumbled on his words, and couldn't even finish that thought.

"Eh?" Alger laughed after a moment when he understood what Lom had said. "No, no, not like that. She was her own girl, and far too young for me. But a powerhouse. Simply brought out the best and worst in all around her. I wonder if this girl of yours is the same way."

"She may be," Lom reflected on her family and friends he had met so far. "But I have a job to do, and I intend to complete it, then go back to what I was doing before."

"You'll be killed, you know."

Lom throttled back his irritation. Alger had this way of cocking a bushy brow at him and delivering the most annoying statements deadpan. "In escorting her to Underhill? I expect opposition, but not that heavy."

Alger fluttered his good hand at Lom in irritation. The other one sat in his lap, leaden, as always. "No, no… Well, yes, you could get killed doing that. It would be a glorious death! Reflect well on the Family, and all that."

Lom bit his tongue. "Hell with the Family. This was absolutely the last chore I was doing for them."

Alger chided him, "you keep saying that, too."

He went on, "No, the whole tracking down rogue magic users. Going to get you killed, m'boy. Bound to. You keep moving up the food chain, and you will find something with bigger teeth than you have."

"Maybe I am at the top of the food chain." Lom knew better. There were creatures bound to Underhill he had always been glad were so bound.

"Mphm…" Alger subsided again, having sat erect with his outburst about family. "You're the head of the Family, you have a duty."

"The Family can go to hell." Lom repeated himself. "And since when did you start taking my mother's lines?"

"Other than young Devon, who else is there?"

"Not much of a family, ours. Besides, you're the oldest, not I. That makes you the Head."

"I abdicated *that* role before your grandfather was out of training pants," Alger returned calmly. "I'm just the advisor."

"Oh, some advice you give. What do you want, Uncle Alger? Stop beating around the bush, I don't have time to rehash ancient family business."

Alger attempted a hurt look. Lom suppressed a snarky comment on it needing more practice. "I only want to make sure your mission is success-ful, boy."

"I neither need nor want your help. And I can't afford the price."

"Tut, tut..."

Now Lom did interrupt him. "Really? You just said tut, tut?"

Alger laughed, he couldn't help it. "You don't respect my gravitas at all."

"I would if you had it. Can you go on without the flourishes?"

"This time, boy, you can owe me. You're going to need help with her." Alger leaned forward, the jovial mask gone, and his eyes glittered in the firelight. "There are those even in High Court who will do anything to keep her from being presented. Should it appear she will become Consort... well, the gloves will come off. And Low Court is restless. Word is that the Hunt is preparing."

"It's been a while since they rode out. They were pretty well dispersed the last time." Lom spoke more calmly than he felt. He remembered the last time all too well. The breath of the hounds...

"Yes, and they have had a few years to lick their wounds, boy." Alger's voice had softened again, and Lom knew he was remembering, too. Lom would have been dead if it weren't for him. He owed Alger for that, if nothing else.

"And just how do you propose to help me?" Lom was still wary of him.

"You are teaching her magic?"

"Just barely started." Lom admitted, running my hands through my hair and making him smile. Lom knew he must look silly with it all on end, but it was a habit.

"I can help."

"I am not letting you run around in her mind." Lom pointed at him. "Just because you make yourself at home in mind, does not mean you are allowed to do it with her. You don't have permission from her, and I will tell her not to grant it if you asked."

Alger looked hurt, and this time it was much more genuine. "I am not given to trespassing. You are... unique."

"You mean I'm the only mind you've violated? Pull the other one, it has bells on."

Alger sighed. "I will give you a spell for her. Teach it to her, and it will give her access to a library, of sorts. My only fear is that she won't understand it."

Lom thought back to his recent conversation with her about her college years and the affection for research that had led her into the line of work she was doing. "No, I rather think she is a library kind of girl. That might work." He eyed Alger dubiously, "what's the price?"

"I don't know yet."

Lom blinked at him. "What do you mean, you don't know?"

"I mean it's a favor you will owe me, and I'll collect in time. Or maybe never. Right now, just take it and get your duty fulfilled."

"I don't think I can afford this."

"She can help with repayment, then."

"The hell she can," Lom stood up and pointed at Alger. "You leave her alone, old man." He smiled, which just made Lom madder. "This is my job, and I'll do it. Give me the spell, and let me get out of this dream."

Alger reached into a pocket in his coat and brought out a ratty book. Lom held out his hand, and he placed it gently on Lom's palm. Spells in reality were sometimes visible as energy, but here in the dream it had a physical weight, and a faint smell of old book.

Lom sniffed, "I'll admit I'm rather fond of that odor." He tucked it under his arm, lacking a pocket large enough to hold it. Alger stood up.

"Best of luck, boy. You don't know how much hangs on your success. I shall be in the wings, watching, but I cannot interfere too much once you are Underhill."

Lom shook his head. "Get caught interfering at all and you will be banished, and I know it. You've done too much, over the years, and the fairies have long memories."

"Teach your grandmother to suck eggs." Alger chuckled. "I shall be *discreet*."

"Can you do that?" Lom mocked at him gently. The old man wasn't someone Lom could spend too much time with, but Alger was family, and had been his teacher from when Lom could remember. "Be safe. I can manage delivering the girl, and she isn't a helpless thing."

Alger reached out and they shook hands, awkwardly, Lom remembering that he wasn't really there, and Alger with a look that meant he'd rather hug Lom. Lom had made his feelings about that clear long ago. Alger let go of his hand and Lom felt the dream dissolving, and closed his eyes.

Chapter 8

The Magical Library

When I opened them again, I was staring at the ceiling of the stateroom on the ferry. I turned my head. Bella was sitting and reading, still.

"How long was I out?"

She jumped. I smiled, and made a mental note to take her books away if she ever had to stand watch.

"Oh, about an hour..." She looked down at the tablet. "Or two."

"Good book?" I sat up and stretched. The spell was no longer visible, but I could feel the pull of it, attached to me.

"Yes. Do you... do that often?"

"That wasn't a nap," I assured her dryly. "That was someone's heavy-handed attempt at communicating with me in a dream."

"Oh. You can do that?"

"I'm not going to teach it to you. The problem with being able to do it is, it's too hard to make sure the person you've given permission to enter your mind can't get in whenever they like. I didn't think this person could any longer, for instance."

"Oh!" She repeated, her eyes wide. "So this was an enemy?"

I shook my head. "He's my old teacher, and a relative. But he always extracts a price for his help, and sometimes that price can be... well, let's just say that the stories of Puck having ass's ears have a basis in reality. And for Alger, that wasn't much of a price. More a prank."

I remembered the years of servitude to him that my mother had paid for what she wanted. Only it had been me, serving, not her. I suppressed the familiar flare of resentment and rage, and the fear at what he was going to ask for, this time, and went on.

"He wanted to help me teach you magic."

"And how much will it cost?" She looked a little nervous, and I didn't blame her.

"Nothing to you. This is something he and I will work out, later. Evidently it's important to him that you make it to Court, and he gave me a spell for you to learn. It will give you access to a library of spells, and it will be a whole lot faster than me teaching you babysteps."

She looked me in the eyes. "Do you trust him?"

I sighed. There was the heart of the matter. No matter what else, he'd been good to me in the long run. I'd become his student, not just a servant, and although I'd chafed at being tied to him, the reality was that I'd be dead many times over if it weren't for the skills I'd learned from Alger.

"Yeah. I do, and furthermore, he has motivation to keep you safe and sane."

She nodded. "What do I do, then?"

"Spells, to boil it down to the simplest level, are a form of energy. We compel them, and release them, with hand gestures. Most use both hands, some simple ones only use one, or just finger movements. I'm going to lay this," I pulled the spell free of my aura and it appeared as a golden flicker of energy, vaguely book-shaped. I smiled. Alger was a master craftsman at the things he really cared about.

I held it out to Bella, who was staring at it in awe. I went on, "in your hands, and when you close your fingers around it and squeeze, it will activate. It will probably take a while for you to assimilate, I remember some of his teaching spells from when I was a lad."

She nodded, eyes wide and apprehensive.

"It won't hurt." I promised her, and put the book in her hands. She held it tightly, and there was a brief flare of the golden light, then it disappeared.

Bella shuddered and leaned back, closing her eyes. I let her be. Alger's spells were compact and efficient, and that had been a large one. This would take some time. I looked at my watch and decided that food would be a good idea for her when she came out of it. I couldn't leave her like this, though, she would be helpless.

I sat on the bed and closed my eyes, opening the Sight as wide as I could without boosting it with my magic. Alger was right, I really needed to be careful how much magic I used. I'd been careless in Tok, but special circumstances. These days, I got by on cunning and speed as much as magic. I'd pushed my limits a few times right after the battle that had won me this particular scar, and I knew that it would leave me sick and helpless if I let it build up too far. At least it seeped out slowly when I wasn't using magic at all, or I would be dead by now.

The Sight showed no other magical activity on the boat, besides Bella. She was... I took a moment to watch her with the inner Sight. Her usual signature, a pale blue flare, was intricately overlaid with spinning golden letters, runes, numbers... I looked away. That spell was hypnotic with the dance of light on light she presented at the moment. I couldn't afford the time or magic to get sucked into it with her.

I opened my eyes slowly, and practiced just breathing while they readjusted. It wasn't meditation, per se, which I'd long ago decided was froufrou trappings for what my brain really needed. Peace, and oxygen. Not necessarily in that order. Getting my brain to stop a whirl of thoughts was all but impossible. I could slow it down, at least.

I stood up. Bella still half-laid in the chair. Her eyes flickered rapidly under her thin eyelids, and I suppressed a sudden and irrational urge to bend over her and kiss those closed eyes... I found that I'd take a step closer to her, and forced myself to walk past her, to the door.

Out in the hall I practiced my breathing again. The racing thoughts and feeling of the last few minutes had been overwhelming. I'd have to be more careful. I kept saying that about her, and I was beginning to feel like a moth, drawn to the flame. Falling for the princess was fatal, outside fairy tales.

When I returned to the room with a bag of the same sandwiches we'd had earlier, she was still where I had left her. I put the sandwiches on the night stand, locked the door, and lay down to get some real sleep. Dream talking was not at all restful. If she moved, it would wake me.

As it turned out, she didn't wake me, nor did anything else. I woke up groggy, slightly disoriented, and six hours later. It was still dark outside the tiny porthole window. I rolled over and looked at her. She was sitting just as I'd left her, eyes closed, breathing, I could see her chest move slightly.

Now I was alarmed. It should not be taking this long for the spell to work. I got up and stood in front of her. If she opened her eyes we would be eye to eye, but she didn't.

"Bella?" I asked in a low voice. Still no response. I reached out and took her hand.

Her eyes flew open, and after a second she focused on me. Her face animated again from the soft relaxation she had been showing before, and she frowned. "Leave me alone. I'm trying to figure out this damned archaic card catalogue system. Who uses these things anymore, anyway?"

I let go of her hand, and her head fell back, eyes already closed. She was in a trance, mentally in the library Alger had given her. With the era he'd learned to use a library, it was no surprise the indexing system was complicated and obscure. I'd leave her to it until she was ready to come out. My stomach growled, reminding me that I still needed to feed her, too.

I wound up giving Bella bites of the sandwich, which she took without ever really opening her eyes, chewing and swallowing almost mechanically. Then she got up, disappeared into the bathroom, and returned, all without fully opening her eyes. I tried not to be freaked out. There wasn't much I could do about it, short of calling Alger, and I didn't think he'd respond, or even think anything was wrong with this behaviour. I did start to wonder just how large the library he had given her was, though.

Speaking of a library, now I was bored. With her out of it, I had nothing to keep my mind occupied except for the endless circle of worries. Who was after us, what minions were moving in the shadows against us, just why were they targeting Bella so hard... I couldn't get answers without more data. My turn to login to the wifi on the ship.

My little laptop could run on the regular internet, of course, but what I needed was somewhere Google couldn't go. Spells locked into the case let me reach across the border into Underhill, and send a message to my nephew Devon. I hated to bring the boy into this, but he was one of the very few I could trust right now. I couldn't walk into Court blind, not now that I knew an ambush was waiting.

He responded in seconds, making me wonder how closely he had been watching for my message. The little text box blinked, and his words scrolled up.

:Uncle Lom, where are you? Mother and Grandmother are worried.:

I smiled. He was refreshingly mannered compared to the human youth I encountered. I typed back, :All is well, on my way to Court. I need your help with something.:

:Anything, you know that.:

:I need to be sure you will be discreet. It is getting dangerous in Court.:

I remembered that age, charging headlong into heroic efforts. It was amazing I had survived, and I definitely was no longer 'intact' from my idealistic youth. I didn't want him following in my footsteps.

:Yes, Uncle. It is my duty to the Family to be around to produce the next generation.:

I could almost hear the sarcasm in the writing. He had gotten something from me, after all.

:I need to know who is at Court, and who plans to arrive in the next week. Listen to your mother's conversations. She always has all the gossip.:

:Ugh. I will, but really, isn't there an easier task to do? The Augean stables, perhaps?:

I suppressed a chuckle with a glance at Bella. She was unmoving. The kid had a sense of humor, also from me.

:Sorry, kid. I'd rather shovel shit, too. I'll check in before we cross the border. Thanks, Devon.:

:YW, Lom:

He typed back, and I signed off with a sigh. He was good about text speak with me, but at the moment I felt a little like Alger. What was the younger generation coming to? I knew, having spent most of my adult life in the human realm, after a childhood all but imprisoned Underhill, that humans were far different than Folke. Most of the Folke, though, had no idea, choosing to spend all their lives in their own realm. Not a bad thing. Too much magic up above and bad things happened. Which is why I had job security.

Humanity might be obsessed with cute fairy tales, supernatural creatures, and the ilk, if you watched enough popular entertainment. But if they met the real thing, there was going to be trouble. A banshee alone could wreak more havoc than an average human could imagine. And now what was I doing? Why, teaching a half-fairy half-human magic, and how to cross the border to Underhill.

There were times it just didn't pay to get up in the morning. To top it all off, I was going to need to venture out and collect some essential supplies. With Bella in a trance, which I hadn't anticipated, I was in dire need of reading material. I spoke to her, softly, telling her that I would be back in a few minutes. She didn't acknowledge me, but I knew from experience that she would have processed it unconsciously.

Following my usual procedures, I left the room secure, and made my way to the lounge. It was abandoned, but I had noted something in passing, and now I made my way directly to the small bookshelf. Stuffed full of ratty magazines and paperbacks left by passing travellers, it looked wonderful to me. I doubted there would be a title on it that I wanted to read, but I was willing to settle for the back of a cereal box, at the moment. As long as action was happening, I didn't mind, but when life was slow, I needed to read.

The battered copy of a blackpowder magazine was a pleasant surprise, the closest thing on the shelf to what I considered professional reading. The copies of Soldier of Fortune I left well enough alone. It had devolved from useful entertainment to conspiracy mall ninja theories that were worse than useless. A few slim paperback novels by my favorite Western author I pounced on. To a Faerie world kid those had been pure fantasy for me, growing up.

I finished off my stack with a couple more whose covers looked attractive, and looked around. No one seemed to have noticed or cared about the short guy pilfering the ship's library. I made my escape. Back in the room, Bella remained still, and I dropped my loot on the bed to decide where to start.

Reading allowed me to stay quietly in the room for the rest of the day, only venturing out for food. I skipped the sandwiches, which I was mightily tired of, and ventured into the restaurant for a take-out meal, which I shared with the compliant Bella. We had no refrigerator for leftovers, which would have been convenient so I didn't have to keep leaving her.

I slept fitfully that night, having decided that if Bella was still out of it in the morning, I was going to have to contact Alger. We docked in early afternoon, and I couldn't explain a woman in a trance state to the authorities. Sure, I could use a wheelchair and take her off that way, but people had seen her board normal and under her own power. There would be raised eyebrows about what I had done to her if she left in this state.

Breakfast was cinnamon rolls, messy to feed her, but tasty. She ate like a little bird from my hand, soft-faced and off in her own little world. I hoped she would remember much of this when she snapped out of it, because I was pretty sure she would not be happy to have been catered to like this. I got her into the bathroom, and was contemplating how to bathe her if necessary. Not the way I wanted to see her body, but again, she wasn't going to be able to do it on her own.

I sat on the bed, facing her. Her eyes were half-open, but no-one was home. I had seen this before, but it was always unsettling.

"Bella. I know you're in there. I need you to be with me, for a while, so we can leave the ferry."

"Going to see Fairy," she mumbled.

I sighed and rubbed my face with both hands. Well, at least I'd gotten a response. She was close enough to the surface to be aware of me. I'd try again later. I picked a book out of the stack on the floor and lounged on the bed.

A short while later, that book hit the wall with a satisfying thud. The scuzzy writer had attempted to take a classic H. Beam Piper series and redo it, and had wound up creating a cynical, depressive, PC pile of crap. My copies of the Fuzzy books were too far away to wash my brain out, and I was feeling rather sick.

"Lom?" Bella's voice surprised me, and I rolled over to sit up and look at her. She looked back with clear eyes and a little smile. "I always thought the book against the wall was a metaphorical thing. I was raised to treat books with respect."

"That one didn't deserve anything other than to be put out of it's misery."

She stood up and luxuriously stretched, and I swallowed and looked away. At least now I wasn't thinking about stories that were merely thinly veiled propaganda. This might be worse, though. I could hear her little moans as she found stiff muscles and worked them out, and tried frantically to distract myself. The sounds she was making were involuntary, and not loud, but my mind was wondering if she made them during other activities, too.

She wound up on her knees in front of me, and I couldn't help looking into her eyes, slightly below mine, for a change. She was smiling again. "Thank you for the wonderful gift, Lom." She reached out and took my face between her palms and kissed me softly.

I froze. The world went away for a long moment. I'd had no idea that she saw me as anything other than an unwanted intruder, and barely tolerated escort. The kiss lasted an instant of her thanks, and then she leaned into me with a little murmur of surprise and the contact deepened. I lost my mind and kissed her back, thoroughly. If you've ever kissed someone well enough to lose the outside world and create a pocket universe with only the two of you in it, time and cares locked out, then you know what it was like. If not, I'm sorry. Keep trying.

Chapter 9

Moire LeFay

I don't know how long that lasted. It can't have been as long or as short as it seemed. She leaned back, slowly, with a sigh, her eyes half closed. I snapped back to reality, where kissing my charge might well be a crime punishable by death and disgrace to my family, and rolled off the bed and away from her.

"Let's get off this boat." I announced over my shoulder, shoving things into our bags willy-nilly.

She didn't speak to me again, just took a spot to my left and a half-stride behind me. I thought it was a good compromise to my need for her to let me take the lead without making her look like a beaten woman. My head was spinning from the aftereffects of that kiss. If I explained to her why it wasn't going to happen again - ever - I risked both giving her a lot of leverage over not only me, but my family. Almost equally as bad, I could hurt Bella by rejecting her. I knew what I was expected to do. I didn't know if I was going to do it.

We could run. Who would come after us? I was, no immodesty, just fact, the best in the business. I could keep us safe for a human's lifetime. My family, though, would bear the brunt of my disloyalty.

I stumbled through the debarking procedure and somehow found myself standing in the building we debarked into, not having our own vehicle like most of those riding the ferry. I shook my head to try and clear it and focus on the job at hand. I needed to rent a car, and get us out of here, fast. There were bad guys, and distraction could get us both killed. I really wished she hadn't kissed me... no, I didn't wish that. It couldn't happen again, but that didn't mean I wasn't going to remember it for a long time.

I fished my cell phone out of my bag, noting that it finally had bars again. it hadn't for a good part of the last day. We had had intermittent wifi on the ferry, and cell service only a little better. I didn't have contacts in town, so a straight rental car would be my only option until we reached Oregon.

Bella sat down on a nearby bench and closed her eyes again. I conducted my business with half my mind on her, concerned about this development now, on top of the kiss. Once I had scheduled a car delivered to the terminal in a half-hour, I hung up and bent close to her.

"Bella?"

"Yes?" She answered without opening her eyes.

"Are you all right?"

"I'm..." She sounded faint and far off. "Still processing."

"Oh, sh..." I broke it off. Time to make a plan B.

I made a few more calls, and by the time the car arrived and I signed over my life to get the keys, I knew what I was going to do. Bella was compliant but visibly not-right as I helped her into the car and buckled her up. She closed her eyes and leaned back, so I lowered the seat back a little for her.

The hotel I'd called around to find was on the outskirts of town, right off Highway 5 headed toward Seattle. I left her in the car and nervously checked in. The clerk gave me a suspicious glare. Evidently requesting a ground floor room on the corner was a red flag. I hoped she didn't see me helping Bella in, or she'd label me a serial killer for sure.

I know I looked odd, helping a woman who was a head taller and had a few pounds on me, into the room. I got her laid down on the bed, and then looked around the room and swore out loud. There was only one bed. In getting the room strategically placed, I'd neglected to make sure it was a double bed room. Bella curled up on her side, murmured something unintelligible, and was out again.

I walked outside and called Alger. This was decidedly not normal, and he had some explaining to do. The whole Family was liable for this girl's safety and well-being, and he had endangered that.

His voice crackled oddly on the phone. "Hello? Lom, is that you?"

"Yes, Alger. Who else would it be? Everyone else can use magic to contact you."

"True, true. And how is our Princess?"

"Don't ever let her hear you call her that. She'll have your balls on a plate."

I could almost hear his wince. "So vulgar, my boy. I'm rather attached to them."

"She's still in a trance. She came out of it, I thought, and I got her off the ferry, and then she told me she is still processing, whatever that means. Oh, and she absolutely hates your indexing system."

"She understands the card catalog?" His voice was a mixture of taken aback and elated.

"Um, I guess so, but she sounded annoyed about it."

"Excellent news, m'boy!" he boomed over the phone. The crackling got worse, and I pulled the phone away from my ear. That hurt.

He went on, "I never thought she would be able to access the library on that level. Why, this means we will have an Archivist again!"

"Alger!" I raised my voice, then looked around to make sure no one had heard me. I went on in a more normal tone. "We have a girl to deliver safe and sane, remember? She's not a member of the Family, and Whatthehells did you do to her?"

"I gave her the library."

"The whole library? I thought you said it was something to help her learn magic."

"Well, yes, that was the surface layer. But you know, you can never know too much."

"Alger..." I gritted out through clenched teeth. "How long will she be in trance state? We have very bad things after us, and I need to get her Underhill. I cannot do that while she's like this."

"Oh, I know. I have no idea when she will finish sorting through it. Everyone's brains are different, you know."

At his smug tone I looked around for a wall to beat my head on. Not being near a handy one, I settled for hanging up on my uncle. Then I went looking for food. We had a small refrigerator in the room, and obviously I needed to stock it, because she was going to be ravenous when she was done digesting this spell.

I had been blinking in and out of the Sight all day, watching for magical use, and I was exhausted. It was still daylight outside when I sat down in the chair to watch over her, and nodded off. I twitched in and out of sleep a couple of times, and then drifted into a nightmare I'd hoped to never have again.

The banshee was my friend. I'd met her when I was a wee child, on the day everyone was crying. The tor rang with wailing, and I crept silently in the hall on wobbly legs, trying to find someone who would explain to me the grief that had washed through our halls. The woman in grey who languished in Father's chair, her long, thin white fingers caressing the wolfhounds carved into the arms was perhaps not a logical choice of person to approach and ask, but even as a toddler my relationship with my mother had been uncertain.

"Why are you cryin'?" I asked her in my high baby voice. She stopped, abruptly, and looked down at me. It was only later with the eyes of adulthood in the dreams that haunted me I could see the terrifying eyes of the banshee, rimmed with red, and the thin face that clung to the bones of her skull.

"You..." her hoarse voice grated at my ears, but it was better than the thin wailing. I held my ground on stumpy legs. "Are not afraid?" she finished, wonderingly.

I waited for her to answer. Adults, I had already learned, did not behave in predictable fashions. I would ask again if she didn't answer, but not too soon, for that would earn a smack of punishment.

She crooked a finger at me, one of those impossibly slender fingers, tipped in a shiny green polish. I obeyed the unspoken wish, and ventured to her knees, resting one starfish splayed hand on hers when I got there. In the dream lucidity, I looked down at those little fingers which were mine and wondered just how young I had been when this happened.

Her tone now was different, "you are not afraid." This was calm, even warm, as she held out her arms to me in the universal gesture of a woman to a small child. I climbed into her lap, and she cuddled me close to a bony chest as she sang a short, sad song. I didn't mind that as much as the wailing, but I was still waiting for my answer.

I ventured to ask again. "Why is everyone crying?"

"Ach, now. Your Father has gone to the great sleep, and shall return no more."

"Does that mean he is dead?"

"It does child, it does." She sighed over me, and gave me a little squeeze. "You maun run along now, darlint, and let me do my wailin'."

"But why must you? It hurts my ears, and I would rather have a story from you." I ended on a hopeful note, with an attempt at a winsome smile, for I did love stories.

"It is my duty, childling. I promise you a story another time. Do not forget." She admonished, which I thought was unnecessary. I never forgot anything, my mother often told me so.

She put me down, and I clung to her dress for a moment while she petted my head and cooed over me. "Go put cotton in your ears, baybee, and rest a little." She sent me out of the room, and I fled for my own bed to do as I was told, her wailing already beginning behind me.

My dream jerked a little, and suddenly I was taller, stronger, and running down the corridor of dark trees rather than my ancestral hall. I stumbled, but kept on, for I remembered this part of the dream all too well. There was a monster chasing me. If I fell, I would feel the hot breath and crack of my skull, then all would go black. The dream usually ended that way, and I would awaken with a strangled cry, my bedclothing wrapped tightly around me, and bathed in cold sweat.

I ran anyway, even knowing how it would end. Maybe someday I would outrun the monster... The banshee stood in front of me, her arms outstretched and surrounded by an eldritch green light. She screamed at what was behind me.

"It is not his time! You shall not touch mine!"

I fell at her feet. This was not part of the dream. I was still a youth, I could feel the difference in myself, the vitality with no pulls of old scars and the lagging sense of achiness that kept me company since the poison had entered my body. I rolled over and looked up at my rescuer, her face still contorted into a snarl, and realized this was no dream.

I was remembering. For all the horror of the nightmare, it had ended mercifully soon for all these years. I scrabbled at the muddy ground and got to my feet, slightly to one side and behind her, and faced my nightmarish pursuer for the first time since that night. In the lucid dream, I was both aware of me, the young man facing a horror, and my self trying to wake up in a Washington hotel room. I couldn't wake up and escape the dream, or the memory that I had suppressed for so long, whichever this damn well was.

The darkness obscured much of what I was facing. The Wild Hunt, not a single monster, stopped in its tracks. The leader astride his massive stag had one hand raised, presumably in the motion that had checked the onslaught of the others. One of the steeds near him stamped and champed, but I heard no sound. All wore enveloping black armor, muddy with the chase. No gleams of silver or gold broke the sombre ensembles, and the steeds were bizarre creatures. Some, like the great stag with his gaping jaws that revealed sharpened teeth covered in bloody slobber, I could identify, even if I didn't want to. Others appeared to be several creatures knit together in some unholy fashion.

"Why do you chase the child?" She challenged them.

The huntsman appeared to contemplate her for a long moment. I say appeared, for his eyes were completely concealed behind the ebon helm. His voice emanated from it in a deep boom. "We are bidden."

She sneered at him verbally. A banshee's voice is a spell unto itself, and she was exerting terrible effort in her scorn of him. I shrank into her shadow, away from the worst of the effect. "Who dares bid the Wild Hunt? We go where we will, when we will. And this innocent child is not our prey."

"Stand aside, Moire LeFay," he boomed. The stag reared, and one of the flanking riders threw something at us.

Moire screamed and threw herself *at* them, her outstretched arms becoming great grey wings, and her fingers talons, dripping venom. I threw myself to the ground, but not fast enough. The spell... stuck to me. It burned into my skin, and I found myself trying to scratch it off frantically, but it stuck to every part it touched. Now I was screaming, and I'd lost track of the Wild Hunt. The screaming stopped, sort of, when I started vomiting. I think I lost everything I had ever eaten.

When I had lost last week's dinner, I no longer cared if the Wild Hunt ran over me. In fact, I wanted to die, so the pain would stop. The two arms that cradled me especially hurt, and the whimper that I couldn't stop hurt the throat I had screamed raw. I was being carried, and I wanted down, to let the stag finish what the beast-borne fairy had started.

I'm fairly sure that was why I was whispering "Kill me, kill me..." anyway. The lucid dreaming part of me took note of that, the younger self was somewhere out of my head. Only when my rescuer dumped me unceremoniously on Alger's floor did I have a flicker of rational thought.

"Elfshot." The voice was improbably deep, and I wondered why the Huntsman was there, then I slid away into a blissful tunnel of black velvety darkness. In the hotel room, I jerked awake, leaping to my feet and looking around. It was full dark. Bella was still asleep on the bed. I could hear my own breaths coming in harsh pants.

Chapter 10

Ghoulish Procurer

I stumbled to the bathroom and closed the door behind me before I put on the light. Looking in the mirror was both a scary and comforting experience. My eyes were bloodshot and hair standing on end, but it was the Lom who had been through hell, not the one who was just starting that journey. I preferred to live in the present. I ran cold water in the sink and splashed it on my face, washing away some of the cold sweat and awakening myself fully.

It couldn't possibly have been the huntsman who had taken me to Alger's hall. I had misheard the voice, or was blending dreams with memories. I had never seen Moire after that day, and could only assume she had sacrificed herself for me, but why? Only Alger's skills had kept me alive, and I was handicapped by the toxins that accumulated every time I aroused the malice of the elfshot by using magic. She had to have thought I was dead when she flew at the hunt, elfshot never left survivors. I was unique.

I'd rather not be. Normal would have been nice. A fat, balding pixie warming his toes by the fire with a pipe in one hand and a book in another... I sighed and rubbed my dripping face with a towel. Time to see if

Bella was ready and move out before our hunters found us. We had been flying under the radar by doing the unexpected, but we would be found. I didn't doubt that.

For one thing, I had to present her at court, and that was as good as walking into the kettle with the water boiling. I opened the bathroom door without turning off the light. The splash of illumination outlined her, lying there with the gentle curve of her hip and shoulder turned toward me. I crossed the room and gently shook her shoulder.

"Bella."

She opened her eyes and looked up at me, rolling partly onto her back. The shirt stretched across her breasts and I tried to ignore them.

"Lom?" She rubbed her eyes with her hands like a little child.

"Can you stay awake for a while? We really need to move and get Underhill."

She nodded. "Yeah. I think the majority of the spell is... absorbed."

She focused behind me, "is it still dark?"

"Best time to travel. No traffic," I pointed out, collecting the few things I had out of my bag. She sat up and stretched.

"Do I have time to shower?" She asked plaintively, wrinkling her nose.

"Please do." I waved at the bathroom and turned on a lamp. She headed into the bathroom while I policed the room for any forgotten items. By the time she came out I was lounging on the bed, reading. I'd snagged the novels by my favorite author from the ferry. A small pilferage, but a worthy one.

"Sorry I took so long." She was still toweling her hair as she spoke. She had taken her bag in, and was in fresh clothes.

"Not a problem. You never know when you'll get another chance at a time like this."

"Time like this?" She dropped the towel on the bed. I stood up and grabbed my bag.

"Yeah, when you're on the run from the Big Bad." I opened the door, looked out, and clicked the unlock button on the car's keyfob. I stepped back in, "after you, my lady." I swept her a mocking bow, and she laughed as she swept by me.

I made a call once we were back on the road. We would stop in Seattle, then keep south down the coast. But we needed supplies, and not reading material, this time.

She stayed alert on the ride, looking out the window at the scenery. I was glad, I didn't feel much like chatting, and between the kiss and the dream, just wanted to crawl in a hole and pull it shut behind me.

The only good thing was, she seemed to have forgotten there ever was such a thing as a kiss. Maybe she thought it had been a dream, or just didn't recall from her brain being occupied with the spell as it was. I'd take either way. Remembering Moire had been a splash of cold water on my half-wondering thoughts of following through on that contact with Bella. She was a job. Get her in, and get out myself.

Getting involved at Court was a sure way to have Moire's sisters come wail for me. Bella wasn't Family, and I had a duty, that was all. So why was I still arguing with myself? The GPS spoke to me, and I stopped thinking so much and followed the voice to an old friend's haunt. At one point, I'd known my way in and out of here like the back of my hand. But time passed, and a city grew.

Georgio's was literally a haunt, too. The tall man was a ghoul, and I don't mean that in a metaphorical morbid guy sort of way. He lived by eating dead bodies, and there were enough forgotten ones in the back alleys to keep him alive, in a manner of speaking. He refused to go Underhill, and we had a deal. I left him alone, he left the living alone, and he provided me with supplies when I was in town.

It was foggy, no big surprise in Seattle. The world was a smear of colors from neon and headlights, and then we pulled into the back alley behind Georgio's, and when I had it in park, I closed my eyes. Bella nudged me.

"I can do that."

I opened my eyes and looked at her. She was pale in the dim light, but even so, I could see the determination written on her face. I nodded. It would speed my reaction times up if she could do the watching with the Sight and I could stay in the real world the whole time.

"Thanks."

She closed her eyes. "I see a flare of magic in there," she pointed without opening her eyes. "Sort of greenish."

"That's Georgio. Anything else?"

She concentrated for a moment longer and then shook her head. "No, no more magic."

"Want to stay here?"

She opened her eyes and winced slightly. "No, I'd like to stay with you."

I got out of the car and she followed on my heels as I rapped at the heavy steel door. It swung open almost immediately. He'd been expecting me. He was almost seven feet tall of bad road, with a side order of roadkill that you smelled right away. When my eyes started watering, I choked out, "Georgio, remember we talked about soap?"

"You threatened me with a pressure washer, last time." He grinned, and I could feel Bella's flinch at the sight of ghoul teeth. Closely related to sharks, I sometimes thought, rows of sharp, serrated things. They shed them like sharks, too, he'd given me one, once. I'd bleached the hell out of it when I got home, and it still smelled faintly of death and rottenness.

He looked at her. "Welcome, Lady. Come into my humble abode, please." He made a little bow stiffly, and we followed him up a short, dim hallway into a large, dim room. Ghouls are not overly fond of bright light.

He spoke to her again, rather than me. I was mildly amused. Women were a rare commodity to him, and he was enjoying this, although I doubted Bella was; she seemed to have a normal sense of smell.

"Can I offer you some refreshment?"

"Oh, that..." I could tell she was torn between graciousness and horror at the idea of ingesting anything from his pantry. I intervened.

"No time, Georgio. I need to get back on the road."

I saw a flash of disappointment, and then he shrugged. "Sure thing, Lom. I have it for you."

He reached behind a dusty sofa and hoisted out a leather satchel that had seen the last century - maybe two. "Everything you asked for, boss."

I handed him the cash I'd agreed on with him. "We were never here, see?"

He nodded. "Bad things coming, Lom. Real bad." He turned to Bella. "You ok with him, pretty lady?"

She smiled up at him, craning her neck almost as much as I had to. "He's good to me, yeah. Thank you, Georgio. Maybe we will meet again."

He smiled real big, and she didn't flinch this time. Good self-control, that girl. "I'd like that."

I hefted the bag with one hand, which took considerable effort. "Hang loose, Georgio. Might be time to go underground for a while." Again, with a ghoul this was literal. He considered being buried alive restful.

He nodded. We left. Back into the fog and dark alley. As we stepped out of the back door, I felt a cold touch of doubt and looked back into the hall. I couldn't see anything, but... I closed my eyes. Only Georgio's olive green glow was visible. Bella took my elbow, and I let her half-guide me back to the car. Once the bag was on the back seat I was functional enough to drive again.

Chapter 11

Ogre, Ogre!

Bella let me get back into traffic before speaking. "You didn't ask him any questions?"

I grunted and avoided an idiot turning without his directionals. "We have a deal. He's no snitch, so I don't even ask. He did offer some information, though."

"What?" she sounded confused.

"Ghouls are incredibly strong, and really damn hard to kill. They're also unpredictable in a fight. I've had one just slump down, I thought I'd got her, and when I went in for the finish, she grabbed my throat with her foot." I shook my head at the memory of the cold, slimy grip and the choking smell. The foot hadn't let go even after I'd blown her head off, and it took me breathless moments to pry it loose. I'd gone after ghouls from a greater distance after that encounter.

"When Georgio says very bad things are coming, I listen." I went on, getting us back on the highway finally and out of city traffic. "There aren't many beings ghouls respect."

"You," she pointed out. "Which is reassuring, I suppose."

"Thanks, Princess." I responded dryly, continuing, "also, ogres and dragons."

"Dragons are real?" The intrigue in her voice made me smile. There's something powerful about the mystique of the ancient lizards.

"There have been rumors about sightings in the last century, in unlikely places like Colorado, but no one has seen a living dragon in recent memory." I didn't tell her how far back my personal memory went, let alone Alger's. "So ogres are much more likely, I deduce."

"So he was telling you what to expect. And how are ogres different from trolls?"

I knew she had to be thinking back to that ambush on the bridge, which seemed so far behind us, but the bruises were still faintly visible on her throat.

"Can you use the library?" I didn't mind answering her, but I was curious how much she could manipulate the data she had been given.

"Oh! I didn't even think of that. Let me try..." She trailed off, and I glanced over to see a very distracted expression on her face. I looked back at the road. Now that we were out of the Seattle area the fog had lifted, and it wasn't sunny, but a bright morning for the Northwest.

"Ew!" I heard, and sneaked another look. Her nose was scrunched up in disgust, so I guessed she had found the information about ogres.

"They really aren't cannibals. They don't eat one another. They will, however, eat any other species they can get their teeth into, and it's a point of pride to them to eat talking species." I shrugged. "Dietary habits are just that. The fact that their hide is damn near tough as dragonscale is a lot harder to deal with."

"Like the troll, you have to hit them in a certain spot?"

"Only ogres are smarter than trolls. Not geniuses, good thing, or we'd be overrun. But they did figure out that goggles made from lexan protect the eyes."

"The, um, book I found didn't say how to kill them."

"No, most of the tales and legends just tell you how to avoid them. In this case, we can't, they are waiting for us, and I'm pretty sure I know where."

I had been hearing rumors out of this area for a while now, and when I'd read that the trails to the top of Mt. St. Helens had been closed down after the mysterious death of a hiker, I'd known I would be sent into the area for clean-up. It just hadn't happened yet, and now I had to run the gauntlet with Bella.

"Surely in a car we can outrun them?"

"Probably. Then we will have ogres in Hummers on our tail. They favor big, ugly gas hogs. Suits them. So what we are going to do is unwrap the goodies I had Georgio pack up for us. Have you ever used a grenade launcher?"

She squeaked, "are you serious?" as she unbuckled and twisted around so she could open the bag and look in it. A moment later I rolled the windows down some, because when she opened the bag it emitted eau de ghoul residence, and I could hear her gagging as she leaned over the seat.

"What the hell is this thing?" She asked when she had recovered.

"If it looks like an abomination of a shotgun mated to a Thompson machine gun and blown up in scale, it's a M32 MGL," I focused on driving. The exit I wanted would be coming up soon. We were going into battle with little time to prepare and ever fewer resources.

"MGL?" She asked, leaning further back. I had thigh pressed against my shoulder.

"Multiple grenade launcher. Range is something shy of 400 yards. So it gives you the ability to stand off and make an impression."

"Okay..." she drew that out slowly, like she was humoring me. "It looks like it fires with a trigger pull, and that's the safety." I could hear her turning it over. "I can do this. Bet it kicks like a mule on steroids, though."

"Yeah, it does. Can you handle that?"

"I'll want an icepack after. But yes. What else is in here?"

"Backup supplies. Sit your butt back down in the seat, Princess, I need to make a turn."

She wiggled back into position, leaving me with delightful impressions of warm womanflesh on my cheek and shoulder. My exit had come up, and she clicked the seat belt as I took it into the rest area. I disobeyed the signs and entered the truck area, scanning for what I wanted. It wasn't hard to find, but finding just the right one... ah... there.

I pulled in between two of the big trucks, effectively hiding the rental sedan, and shut it down. I turned to look at Bella. Her face was serious, and I knew she was reading my mood. Playtime was over. "Here's the plan. You're going to drive the car, and I'm going to lure them out with that truck." I pointed upward at the big logging truck I had parked us next to.

"Wha... Ok." She squared her shoulders. "I need a little more detail."

I grinned at her. "You got it, Princess."

"And stop calling me that," she protested weakly.

When I was done explaining we got the car ready, then she made a trip to the bathroom. I covered the MGL on the front seat with my jacket. It was warm enough down in the lower 48 to get away without it, and I was sure the logging truck would have heat. When I left it, on the other hand... I'd live. I hoped. Pretty sure I wouldn't die of cold, anyway.

Once I was done fussing over her preparation, I started my own. Using a tiny bit of don't-see-me glamour, I climbed up the side of the truck and stuck the gray, putty-like explosive pellets I'd made with a spell in the heart of each one onto chain links in strategic places. Then I unlocked the door of the truck with my feet on the dirty asphalt and my hand on the lower edge of the door. I could hear the lock click. Getting up into the truck was quite a scramble for me, and I was grateful I didn't have to haul the trucker out, as he was nowhere in sight. Getting a meal, I guessed, or some shut-eye. This wasn't a sleeper.

Bella appeared at the open door. "Lom?" She questioned, her eyes focused on a point about two feet from me. I still had the glamour on.

"Try the Sight," I told her. She closed her eyes briefly.

"Oh. Now I see what you did." She looked directly at me now. "Are we ready?"

"Can you pass me that bag? I need to sit on something so I can see out the window."

She eyed me uncertainly. "Will you be able to reach the pedals?"

"Yeah, close but I can. It will do for a few miles, anyway. Now you, scoot. Find out how to shut down your magical signature?"

She nodded, looking pale and serious. I grinned down at her, having shoved the bag under me. "Don't worry, Princess, it's a drive in the Park."

She glared at me. "Are you ever serious?"

"Nope. Close that door, will you?"

She slammed it and got into the car without a backward glance. I watched her pull away and thought about her unspoken question. Yes, I was scared. Maybe not as much as she was, but I didn't know if this was going to work, I was improvising as fast as I could pull it out of my... well, it wasn't the first time I'd faced Ogres. One Pixie was worth a half dozen of the big monsters.

As it turned out, there were seven of them. I could see the faint glows of their magical signatures as I squinted at the upcoming bridge over the Toutle River. Off to my right the ashy delta of the Toutle merged with the cleaner Cowlitz, carrying the debris of the still-active volcano down toward the sea. I was radiating as hard as I could, had been pretty much for the last five miles to make sure they would see me coming, and the magical use was making me sick to my stomach. Driving with one eye closed to use the Sight was also disorienting and sick making. I opened it and blinked rapidly. I'd be able to see them in real vision soon enough, not that I wanted to look at Ogres.

They were lurking under the bridge, all right. They swarmed up and onto the road as I barreled towards them, spreading out to form a road-block of formidable proportions. I don't know what they expected me to do, but it probably wasn't what I did. I accelerated, passing seventy on that flat stretch in the big truck, and waited until I could see the reds of their eyes. They were just standing there watching me come, and I could almost see the wheels in their brains turning, and the smoke rising from their ugly, greasy green skulls.

They started to scatter, having realized that I wasn't going to stop, and I threw the wheel hard to the right and set off the explosives as I felt the truck start to go over. I've always thought the movies had it wrong, trucks sliding sideways down the road at top speed. I wasn't counting on the truck, I was counting on the twenty foot long logs of Western Red Cedar on that truck. There wasn't a one on board that was less than eighteen inches in diameter, and at least two were almost as wide as I was tall.

I wasn't wearing a seatbelt, and had my window down, planning for this contingency. As the truck started to roll onto its side, I went out the skyward window. I could feel my wings tear through my shirt, and I darted for the sky, pulling as much altitude as I could get. My head started to throb, not from altitude - I wasn't that high - but from the use of magic. I didn't have long, and I needed to find Bella. I banked to the South, and only then looked down at the chaos I'd created.

The roads had been empty, it still being just about dawn, since we had left the hotel in the middle of the night. I could see the logs and truck breaking through the barrier on the bridge and falling into the river, taking some of the beasts with them. One seemed to be sitting in the middle of the bridge with a smaller log jutting out of his torso. I had at the very least taken them out of the game for the time being.

I looked for the sedan and found it, pulled over to the side about a mile from the bridge. I could feel the effects of my flight acutely, and vomited in midair as I started to fly toward her. I wasn't going to make it all the way there. I was about to lose my wings, I could feel the toxin levels climbing to intolerable, and I needed to be on the ground. I started dumping altitude, and saw her get out of the car, holding the MGL.

I was a few hundred feet short when I finally hit the ground, rolling on the cold, wet asphalt like a broken doll. That was going to hurt later. I added it to the list, and climbed to my feet, staggering toward her. She was looking past me, at something coming from the bridge. It couldn't be traffic, I had effectively blocked the road with logs and debris. I tried to shamble faster.

I could feel it, now, the heavy thumps of running footsteps. It had to be a big one to make that much noise, but I didn't dare look over my shoulder, I was having enough trouble staying upright as it was. I just kept going forward. She lifted the big weapon to her shoulder and her face smoothed out. I recognized that look of utter focus and veered slightly more out of her way as she fired. The first round missed, I could tell from the look on her face, but she didn't pause, just angled the barrel a little upward and fired again.

Smart girl. She had figured out that it might look like a shotgun, but it fired like a bow. I heard a meaty thunk. She shouted as she fired the third time.

"Dammit! That just blew a hole in him, but he's not stopping!"

I could imagine what it looked like, the ogre coming on like a freight train, bloody gobbets of his flesh in his wake. I pushed my last bit of strength for a burst of speed that wasn't going to take me far... She fired the fourth time, and I knew there would be no time for a fifth round.

The projectile passed over my left shoulder, it felt like. I did feel the warmth on my cheek, and then processed that sensation. There were not supposed to have been incendiary rounds, he'd said he couldn't get them... The explosion behind me lifted me off my feet. Not much, just enough to send me stumbling into the tail of the car. I did turn and look, then, holding onto the trunk for support.

There were two feet standing in the middle of the road, one slightly in front of the other like he had been in mid-step when she blew him apart. The rest of the ogre was scattered in flaming chunks across both lanes, and some of him was still floating downward, sparkling slightly.

"Holy Mother Titania, how did you do that?" I breathed.

"I used the library." She slung the weapon and smiled sweetly at me. "There was a handy fire spell that stuck nicely to the grenade."

I felt myself sliding off the car. She caught me before I hit the ground. I whispered "Well done. Very well done," before I passed out.

Chapter 12

Bella Takes the Wheel

She drove through or around Vancouver and Portland, I wasn't sure which. I was in and out of it, trying not to vomit any more, and answering her questions of "are you all right?" with grunts.

She stopped in a small town I didn't recognize around noon, having traveled below Portland, and got us lunch. I turned food down and sipped gratefully at the bottle of water.

"Lom, where are we going?"

I looked at her. She had leaned my seat back, so I was looking up at her. Well, further up than normal.

"Underhill." I didn't mean to be snappy, I was just tired and hurting.

"I expected us to hit the airport in Seattle. Or Portland, at least. Instead we've been driving for about four hours, and you don't seem to have a destination."

"What do you mean?" I was confused, trying to remember when I had said anything about taking a plane.

"Going to England? To get Underhill? You made sure I had my passport."

"Oh. Um, there are ways to get Underhill that are close. We don't need to fly anywhere, and the passport was for Canada, and because I don't know where you will come out of Underhill."

"So, how much further? I fueled up a while back, so we're good to go another couple hundred miles. But I think you need rest." She eyed me. I must look pretty green.

"I appreciate you driving." I told her. She waved it off. "We're headed for Florence, Oregon, and then a few miles out of town, it's a pretty little town."

"OK, I can put that in the GPS, and you can sleep. How long?"

"I know it's three hours from Portland."

"A while then, yet. Have you been there before?"

"So many questions." I smiled at her as I teased her. "Yes, I have. It's kind of a back door to Underhill. As you can see, I'm a bit under the weather, so I don't want to make a splashy entrance."

"I'm fine with that. What is wrong with you?" She had a firm tone in her voice, and I knew I couldn't evade this question.

I sighed and rubbed my face, buying a moment. She needed to know, it was going to make me less effective in protecting her, but she was showing me she was quite capable of taking care of herself. And me, if need be.

"I have to be careful how much magic I use. It's... toxic to me. When I use it, the toxins build up to critical levels, and it needs time to bleed off again. If I push it too much, it will kill me."

"So, this is from you using magic?" She tuned out on me for a moment.

I wanted patiently, having learned to recognize the signs of her accessing the library. I didn't think she would find anything. I was fairly sure I was the only Folke to have anything like this. I didn't mind the delay, though, I was tired...

I woke up to find we were back on the road again. The gentle rumble of road noise was reassuring. Bella was driving with purpose, focussed on the highway. "Hey. Sorry I faded out on you." I told her. She glanced over at me with a little smile.

"I was worried. Glad to see your eyes again."

I yawned and rubbed my chin, feeling the stubble there. "How much longer?"

"About 30 minutes, according to the GPS. Pretty stretch of road, but tricky driving."

"We on Hwy 1?" I sat up. The ocean was to my immediate right, and about a hundred feet below us. "Damn. I guess so."

She didn't look at me, and I didn't blame her. "Can we stop for dinner when we get to Florence? I'm starving again already."

"I think we should stop for the night, honestly. I want to cross just after daylight, not risk it getting dark while we find the door."

"Find the door?" She echoed skeptically. "I thought you knew this place."

"Well, two things. One, it's been a while. Two, the borders and thin places we call doors move. Not a lot, but there's some drift."

"I see," she told me in a tone that told me she didn't fully understand. "I could use some sleep, too."

"Hey, you've earned it. You blew up an ogre with magic today."

She perked up at that. "Yes, I did, didn't I? I had no idea I could do that, but I tapped into the library and it just came to me."

"I can't wait to see what else you can pull out of there."

She sighed. "I'm hoping for not having to do that again. That was just too exciting."

"I wish I could tell you that Underhill is safe. But it's not. You're unlikely to face Ogres there, though."

"That's a comfort." She responded dryly.

I looked out the window at the vast Pacific. It crossed my mind again that if we ran, I could... No, look at me, I'm a wreck. I couldn't take care of a kitten, let alone the two of us.

She must have heard my sigh, and although she couldn't possibly have known what it was for, she reached over without looking and patted my shoulder. I accepted the comfort. Keep going forward. She pulled into a mom-and-pop diner and we both got out. I was wobbly and stiff. She got a booth, and I hit the bathroom.

Washing my face helped a little. I got back to the booth and slid in. She eyed my damp hair. "Feel better?"

"Yeah."

"I ordered already. I was starting to worry about you."

"You take after your Aunt Min, don't you?"

She chuckled. "I hope so." The laugh trailed off into a little misty eyed moment. "I miss them already."

"It won't be long."

"Really? Because I've been researching the selection process. And I'm having a little trouble with the time differences between Underhill and um, the human world. Does it have another name?"

"Not really. And everyone has trouble with the time differences. There's no logical algorithm for determining the passage of time in the two planes."

"So I could go in, and come out 300 years later?"

"Oh. That story."

"Yes, that story."

The waitress arrived with our plates. She slid them onto the table and Bella smiled at her. I looked at what she'd ordered for me. A hamburger, big and juicy, with all the fixings on the side.

"I didn't know how you liked it." She made a wry, apologetic face.

I was struck by something, looking at her. This girl - no, woman - was something else. She was considerate, endlessly patient, brave... I looked quickly back down at my plate, aware I was staring at her. She was also beautiful. She was going to make a splash in Court, where a real woman was a rare commodity.

"This is perfect." I told her and assembled my burger.

"There's a chance," I told her when I had put the last bite in my stomach, "that you might experience severe time slip. But it does not happen often. Most of the time I transit between worlds, I don't experience any time dilation."

She nodded. "I suppose I don't have much choice."

I shook my head. "I'm afraid not. We have to keep moving toward Court."

"Why do I feel like we are being herded?"

"Because they know where we are going. They are trying to stop us from getting there."

"Will they stop once I am presented at Court?"

"I think it will just get more subtle. Hey..."

She was drooping a little. I reached out to her, and she took my hand. The warmth reassured me. "I have your back. And you have mine. You showed me that today, and it impressed me. We're a team, ok?"

She nodded, the corners of her lips quirking. "I like that idea. I need someone I can trust."

I took a breath, knowing she wouldn't understand this. "My hands are yours, my blade is at your service."

Her eyes widened. I'd forgotten the library knowledge she could tap into. "Lom..."

"Yes, I'm serious. Now shush, finish your dinner, and lets get some rest." I got up and went out into the cool evening air to calm myself. I'd just sworn fealty to her, dammit. Yes, my family duty was to her and should she be crowned Queen of Fairy I would be life-bound to her, but this wasn't part of the plan. I also didn't think she would hold me to a life-bond, if she got back to her family. So this was... temporary.

She came out and looked at me. "I did trust you before, you know."

"I know. But this... has some magical power, too. Now I need sleep."

She nodded, accepting that I didn't want to talk about it more. We spent the night in a cheap hotel with decent beds, and I slept like a rock. In the morning we drove out to the Siuslaw River, and I called in a favor to return the rental car. We left it sitting on the side of the road where a sprite would pick it up and return it to the terminal. Bags on our shoulders, I led her up the hillside.

It had been clearcut last time I'd been through this way, about twenty mortal years before, and the undergrowth was wild. Rhododendrons, vine maple, and huckleberries tangled together with the regrowing cedars and firs. We walked in silence most of the way, and then broke out into a tiny glade with the sun shining into it. The golden shaft of light fell onto the tiny waterfall, no taller than I was high, where it splashed into a little pool. The gnarled old vine maple still hung over it, of no value to the loggers when they had passed though, so unmolested. It still pinned one corner of the door, just as I had left it.

I knelt and splashed water onto my face. The spring sunshine, rare for the Oregon coast, was warm. She had insisted we bring the MGL, and the damned thing was heavy. I wouldn't let her carry it, though. I was still not up to strength, but she wasn't going to lug things. She joined me in kneeling by the pool.

"It's so beautiful."

I looked up at the sunbeam hitting the water. "It always is. One of my favorite places."

"What are the yellow flowers growing from the rock?"

"Monkey flowers. If you squint a bit, you can see the face in the center of the flower."

"They are pretty, in spite of the silly name."

I smiled and let her absorb the place for a few moments, the birdsong filtering through the trees and adding to the splashing water. Then I smiled and told her, "Close your eyes and look with your Sight."

She did so obediently, and gasped out loud. She reached out for me, and I took her hand. "Lom! Is that?"

"That's the border to Underhill," I confirmed.

"Oh, that's amazing. It's like the northern lights, only... more."

"Yes. I'm glad you like it."

Her eyes opened again, slowly. "I wish we could just stay here."

"Nervous?"

"Yes," she nodded. "I'm not sure what to do."

"Just be yourself."

We got up, and I held out my hand again. I was rather liking all this handholding, even if I couldn't get used to it. "Ready?"

"No. But let's go." She squared her shoulders, and we walked through the door together.

Chapter 13

Fairy Wings

Passing through the door to Underhill and the realm of the Folke was a chancy proposition. For one thing, there was always that chance of temporal slip that could put you back out into the human plane a hundred years later after a day in fairy land. For another, it felt strange, in a different way for any being who passed through that door. For me, that meant an intense itching between my shoulderblades, where my wings would erupt when I wanted to fly somewhere. Pixies get a choice. Fairies don't.

Bella looked up at me. "That tasted like raspberries and cream." Then her forehead wrinkled as she realized something. She was looking up at *me*. "Lom? Did you... grow?"

I shook my head, sadly. Her eyes widened. "What happened to me?" she blurted out, looking down at herself.

In her excitement, her iridescent wings fluttered into a blur, lifting her feet off the ground. She clutched at my arm, but didn't scream. Instead she hissed in pure fury. "What. The. Hell. Did you do?"

"Easy, Bella." I put my hand over hers where it was clamped onto my arm. "This wasn't me. When you come Underhill, your fairy blood comes to the forefront, and you take fairy form."

"Who is in charge of that idiotic idea?" She demanded indignantly and I suppressed a smile, she wasn't entirely being rational.

"I'm fairly sure that's a law of Underhill that can't be changed, it's like a law of physics in the plane above."

She quivered with frustration, rising another few inches above the ground. "Bella. Look around."

She wasn't going to be distracted. "You knew. You knew this was going to happen, and you didn't warn me. You... you..." She sputtered to a halt in sheer fury at my neglect to tell her about her upcoming transformation.

"Was afraid you wouldn't agree to cross over, yeah."

She slapped me. I didn't see it coming, but I had to agree I had it coming. She didn't know her own strength yet, so I could feel that she had split my lip as she let go of me and flew across the field we were standing in. She shouted over her shoulder.

"Don't you dare follow me!"

I started to go after her, and then swiped blood from my chin. She'd really gotten me. And I was tired from the toxic magic. She would come back when she had gotten over her mad, and had a chance to look around her. I knew Bella. She wouldn't be able to resist the beauty of this wild, forgotten corner of Underhill.

I, however, was in no mood for it. I needed more sleep, and time to purge the poison out of me, so I'd be able to use magic at Court when needed. And I really didn't want to lie down in a field and sleep. That was just begging for trouble. What I really needed was for Bella to get her sparkly new fairy self back here, so I could get us to somewhere safe.

I walked past the door to the edge of the field and found a tree to lean against. I could see anything coming across the field, and with the tangled underbrush behind me, I could hear anything coming in that direction. I was hungry, and cranky. I half-hoped something would come out of the woods, so I could kill it messily and relieve some of the frustration.

Out of the corner of my eye I caught a flicker of movement. It was Bella, walking slowly toward me. She was picking a flower every so often, and I waited to speak to her until she was right in front of me. We spoke at the same time.

"Lom, I'm..."

"Sorry I didn't..."

I broke off, and she stopped and smiled at me. Her eyes were suspiciously damp, but if she had been crying it had stopped. She held out the flowers to me. "I am so sorry I hit you. That was uncalled-for, and I was being unreasonable. Forgive me?"

I snorted, and took the flowers. Talk about role reversal. "I'm sorry I didn't warn you. There's nothing to forgive, I earned that."

"I won't do it again." She said earnestly.

"Yes, you will, but in training, next time, and I will have my guard up. I still owe you lessons, Princess."

She laughed. "Deal. Now... where to?"

"Home. My home, and some food, and rest, and talk, not necessarily in that order."

She looked around the empty field and up at the unnaturally bright blue sky overhead. "How do we get there?"

"You're going to take us there. I can't use that much magic right now."

"But I don't... Oh, the library. Going to have to get used to that." Her eyes unfocused a little. "Got it. Ready?" She held out her hand, and I crooked my elbow so she could slip it under my arm.

She held up one hand and a slender crystalline wand appeared. I laughed. She didn't actually need one, but many fairies affected them while casting spells, or words, or even sparkly dust, and she had been using Alger's library. Her wand was prettier than his gnarled root, but it was the same school of thought. She smiled at me, flicked it, and a bubble of light formed around us both. When she collapsed the bubble, we were facing my front door.

"Neatly done. Now... can you Look while I check to see if anyone has tried to get in?"

Bella closed her eyes, and I bent to look at the keyhole. It wasn't keyed for a metal key like a human's door, but the spells in my warding would have indications if someone had tried to force their way in. It was dark and cool to the touch. She opened her eyes and blinked rapidly. She was getting better at that transition.

"I see... a lot. Not sure what all of it is, and the library is so full of information it's overwhelming. But I don't think I see anything harmful? Anyway, it's all very peaceful, nothing flaring, or moving very fast."

"That's about right. Not all baddies will have ugly color magical signals, nor will they flare, since you can will your magic to cloak. But the motion would indicate an ambush. I don't think we were expected here. Let's go in, and I'll tell you why."

I touched the door, and it swung open. "After you, Princess."

She stepped into my hallway and stopped. I closed the door behind her and let her take it in. I've had a long time to put my home in order, and I'm rather proud of it. It's not very big, but it doesn't need to be, and I'm not home very often, either. I looked around, seeing it through her eyes for a moment.

The walls are lined with bookshelves and windows. In one corner, a fireplace, cold and empty at the moment. Unobtrusive doors lead to the other two rooms on this floor, and a spiral staircase with wrought iron railings of leaves and vines twines around a central post into the upper level. There are six sides to the room, and windows on four of them, each one looking into a different season, something I had expended a great deal of magical effort on warping Underhill to create. The only windows that would open were the french doors on the summer side. Bella turned in place, trying to take it all in.

"Do you like it?" I asked softly. It was suddenly important to me that she did.

"It's amazing. This is your home? I'm embarrassed about my cabin, now."

"I had a lot of time to work on this while I was ill. Your home is every bit as much a home, maybe more, since I'm not here very often any longer."

"I didn't expect this."

I went to the kitchen door with her at my heels. I needed food, and to sit. "What did you expect, a bachelor pad?" I teased her as we walked into the warm room. There was another fireplace, this one lit and an armchair to one side that I folded into gratefully. She looked around, again caught up in the new place. My kitchen was half the size of my great room, but I intended it to be a dining area, sitting place, and the heart of the home. I enjoyed cooking, and guests at my house knew they would likely be sitting here, at the table, and usually helping if they had been more than once. I didn't entertain often, and it was only ever friends or family.

More to the point at the moment, my housekeeper Ellie loved to cook and entertain, and was always asking me to bring people home. She had gotten the message I'd sent while waiting for Bella to come back from her snit, and was ready for us. She was shy, and would likely not make an appearance while Bella was a stranger, though.

"Ellie?"

Bella looked at me oddly, no doubt wondering if I had finally slipped round the bend with pain and illness. I smiled reassuringly at her, an utter failure, I realized when she raised an eyebrow in disbelief and started toward me.

"I'm ok," I assured her. She bent over me anyway and laid the back of her hand on my forehead.

"You are burning up." She told me dryly. "You need bed, and rest."

I fended her off. "I have a naturally hot disposition." I raised my voice. "Ellie! Dammit woman this is no time..." I lost steam and my voice trailed off. Maybe Bella was right.

Ellie stepped out from behind my chair, virtually appearing by my elbow, and Bella jumped. To her credit, she didn't shriek. Ellie's face wasn't beautiful, she looked like something badly carved out of wood, but she had a sweet soul.

She looked at me and clucked. "Overdid the magic, eh?"

Her voice was as rough as her appearance.

"Ellie, this is Bella. Lavendar's granddaughter. She'll be staying with us until I present her at Court, and I'd appreciate it if news I'm home and she is here didn't get any further than these walls."

She sniffed. Gossip was bread and butter to her, and I took advantage of that on occasion. But she was reliable.

"Welcome, young lady. Can you help me get him to bed? Why he insists on stairs..." She grumbled as she grabbed one arm. Bella more gently took the other, and they both ignored my protests that I could do this myself, thank you.

Chapter 14

Pixie Monster Hunter

I awakened in my own bed, a bowl of soup gently steaming on a tray beside the table. My nose twitched. Ellie knew what I needed. I swung my legs over the edge, rubbed my eyes, and froze. I'd committed a grievous tactical error. I had left Bella and Ellie to talk alone, without telling Ellie what she wasn't to say. Two women talking about their man was always a dangerous thing. This was bad.

I stood up, swayed, and sat back down again. It would have to wait until I had eaten and put clothes on. I hoped Ellie had been the one to undress me, at least. She had been my nurse before. The soup beckoned me, literally, with a finger of steam. I sighed, and obeyed the hidden Ellie's dictate. When the bowl was finished, I set it down and it vanished with a tiny pop. In it's place was a plate of sandwiches and one of cookies. I felt the corner of my mouth crook up.

"You'll make me fat." I told the empty room. There was no response, and I ate them all, anyway. I needed the energy.

Belly filled, I contemplated clothes and the stairs. I could probably manage, but the damage was likely already done. I lay back on the bed and fell asleep again. I needed my strength to deal with an angry Bella again.

When I woke up the second time, I could feel that the toxins were gone. Well, as low as they were going to get. It was like an ache that never quite went away, but most of the time I could ignore it, at least until the levels rose. I didn't bounce out of bed, but I could move freely as I got freshened up and dressed. I wondered what time it was.

Time doesn't flow in fairy lands like it does in the human world. It passes, yes, but as with my windows on the different seasons, it can be manipulated. I've wondered if that accounts for the temporal slips. Something like earthquakes on fault lines, where a sudden release of built-up tension causes a rapid shift. Not every being could manipulate the fabric of Underhill. I'd had some help with my house. Necessary, since I couldn't use much magic myself. When we had made the house, I thought I'd spend the rest of my life holed up in it, too sick to leave. Otherwise I probably would have that little bachelor flat Bella had so obviously expected me to have.

And now I needed to gird up my loins and go face the music, with mixed metaphors and all. I left my bedroom and could see that there were lights on in the kitchen below me, the light streaming out into the dark great room like a golden invitation. Across the landing from me, the guest room door was closed and dark, which I took to mean that Bella was in the kitchen.

I could hear their voices when I reached the open door, Bella's soprano a counterpoint to Ellie's wooden baritone. I paused for a moment, wondering what they were talking about, but they felt silent, and then Bella called.

"You can come in. Ellie says you are out there, and that you need to eat."

I felt like a little boy caught eavesdropping.

"I was sure you would be furious with me." I told her as I walked into the big room.

She was sitting at the kitchen table with Ellie, steaming mugs of something in front of both of them, a plate of cookies, obviously much diminished, off to one side. Bella blinked in surprise. "I got over that. It's not your fault I'm a fairy, after all. I mean, yes, you didn't tell me I'd turn into..." She looked down at herself in dismay.

"A pretty, fluttery creature?"

She glared at me, and I raised both hands in a gesture of surrender. "I'm trying to make the point that you haven't changed in any way except the physical, and even that has perks you don't know about yet. And one you already used."

"What? Flying? It was pretty cool." She craned her head around to look at the tip of her wing.

I shook my head. "No, you have a lot more strength for your size than you realize." I fingered my still swollen lip gingerly.

"Oh!" She got up and came over to me, reaching up to take my face in both hands. She turned it a little to one side so she could see the damage she had done better. I stood still and tried to ignore that she was touching me with warm fingers and smelled so good up close... Mercifully, she let go and stepped back. I made tracks for the table and a safe sitting position.

"I did hurt you, I am sorry." She came and sat down, a rueful tone in her voice. "You're right, I don't know my own strength yet."

"You'll learn. We still have lessons to do."

I turned and spoke to Ellie. "Thank you for taking care of her."

The wood elf nodded. ""Twas no trouble." She looked at Bella approvingly. "She's a handy being to have around."

Bella just smiled. I wondered what that was about, but didn't dare ask. "How long was I asleep?"

"Couple 'o days." She informed me calmly. I was glad I was sitting down.

"Why did you let me sleep that long?" My voice went up in volume, and she frowned at me.

"Cos you needed it. Still need more, sounds like."

Bella cut in. "I told her about what you had done. She said you needed to sleep until you were ready to get up. Are you hungry?"

That sidetracked me. My stomach growled. "Very. How long since I ate?" The sandwiches and cookies seemed rather distant now.

Ellie got up and went for food. Bella answered. "Yesterday. Ellie told me you'd been awaken but not for long. How are you feeling?"

"Hungry, stiff, and sore, but the toxin level is minimal. I'll be back to myself in a day or so."

"And then court?" She sounded nervous, and I couldn't blame her. I wasn't looking forward to that, either. "You said they weren't looking for us here, at your house. What did you mean?"

"Not court, until you are ready. Because you are the target. They, whoever they are, didn't know it was me sent to escort you to Court."

"Why would you make a difference? No offense..."

"They sent a troll, a roc, and ogres. Singly. If they had known who was escorting you, there would have been a pitched battle."

Ellie slid a big plate of eggs, toast, and bacon under my nose. I started eating as fast as I could get it in.

Bella laughed, I wasn't sure if at my boast, or the way I was eating. "You aren't modest at all, are you?"

"I'm now wondering..." I started after a swallow, "why the Court sent me after you. What's special about you, Princess?"

She looked startled. "I'm not special at all. I didn't even know about..." she gestured, and I guessed she meant Underhill, and all of fairy land. "Until after my mother's death."

"I thought you grew up on stories of it?"

She shook her head. "Grandma Lavendar raised me. Mom was never quite there, and I was only eleven when they were killed."

"I'm sorry." I was sincere. My mother might make me furious at times, but I loved her and would miss her if she were gone. I didn't really remember my father.

"Why you?"

I sighed, I had been putting this off long enough. She wasn't going to let it go, this time.

"I'm a bounty hunter."

She blinked. "A what, now?"

"The Court sends me after rogue magic users. So if there is a being of the Folke, or even a human, running loose on the Human plane, they want me to collect them, bring them Underhill for punishment, or simply elimi-nate the problem. Rarely, I work Underhill, but for that, they usually use the Hunt. The Hunt is too... disruptive, to send into human realms. I'm a lot more discreet." Most of the time, anyway.

"And for that, they pay you. You're the only one?"

I nodded. "There are few who are willing to leave Underhill, these days, except the rogues. And I have a certain talent for it."

"I can see that, after what we have been through." She looked thought-ful. "So that is why I got the shakes after the troll, and you didn't."

"What about the ogre?" I asked her, curious. I had been out of it, and hadn't noticed.

"Oh, yes. You were asleep, but I had to stop for a while, I couldn't keep driving. That's when I got the T-shirt for you."

I nodded. I'd wondered about it, I had torn my shirt up when I used my wings, but had awakened in a new shirt. "And since then?"

She looked uncomfortable. "I haven't been sleeping a lot."

I raised an eyebrow at her. "Nightmares?"

She nodded. "I've hunted all my life, trapped, fished... but that troll, he was driving a car. And he spoke."

Now it was my turn to be startled. "He spoke?"

"Yeah. Didn't I tell you?"

"No. Trolls don't talk much, so I would have remembered. But it's been a long few days of running and hiding. Do you remember what he said?"

"He asked me where Lavendar was."

"What did you say?"

"Well, I couldn't talk." She mimed hands around her throat and made a face. "I don't think he would have liked to hear that she's dead."

I leaned back in my chair, my belly full of food at my mind working at top speed. Why would they think Lavendar was alive, and what did this have to do with Bella?

Bella interrupted my train of thought. "How do you hunt, er, monsters down when you can't use magic?"

"I can, just carefully. And I can cast spells that are pre-made for me. Mostly, though, I'm just a sneaky son of a bitch."

"Raven always told me, 'never hunt in a straight line if you can hunt crooked.'" she said with a small smile. She missed the old spirit.

"Wise Uncle. And how long have you known him?"

She looked surprised. "All my life. Dad told me he was the first one to hold me after I was born."

That explained rather a lot. Between Raven and Lavendar, this girl had a lot of patronage. She lived up to it, too, while remaining unspoiled. I didn't think Court would change that, and if it did, it was my job as her retainer to smack her back down to size. Speaking of which.

"Ready for your first lesson?"

"I thought that was what the library was for?"

I shook my head. "All the knowledge in the world - which, knowing Alger, is about what you have in your head - isn't enough without knowing what questions to ask. Come on, I want to show you something."

Chapter 15

Training in the Armory

She obediently got up and followed me out of the kitchen. Ellie had long since disappeared to her private quarters. They might be on my premises, but might not. I had never seen them, and I thought they were more likely in, or under, a tree.

I led her to the other door that was on the same wall. As I laid my hand on the knob and activated the unlocking spell, she looked interested. "I wondered what was in here. Ellie said not to touch the door, or an alarm would go off."

"She's mad she isn't allowed in to dust," I told her over my shoulder. "Anyway, not an alarm, but a rather interesting sticky trap that would keep anyone until I get there to deal with them."

I led the way down a stone staircase, feeling it get cooler as we neared the bottom. At the landing, I opened a second door that also had an interesting spell locking it. One that was suitably more lethal than the entrance. Upstairs, an accidental mix-up could lead to some being trying the door. Down here, there could only be mal intent.

Inside the basement, there were rows of racks, and she ventured from behind me to see what was on them. I could hear her chuckle. "Quite a toy box you have here, Lom."

"Well, all these years of killing monsters and confiscating weapons." I let my grin show and we shared a moment of amusement at my armory. "Yeah, it's a big toy box, but a lethal one."

She carefully didn't touch, but looked closely. "I recognize a few things, but some are just... odd." She pointed. "Like that one."

I came closer to see. "Ah, that's a troll-built crossbow. Ugly as it's owner, but very functional. I think he made it out of railroad track and a leaf spring. I saw it put a quarrel through a cinder block wall."

"I thought trolls were stupid?"

"This one was a freaking genius."

She kept walking down the row of shelves. "Wow, these are tiny, and so detailed." She was nose to nose with a shield and spear that were all of a few inches long.

"They aren't toys," I pointed out. "Those are Sprite weapons. There's a bow and arrows, too." I showed her the box I kept them in on a puff of wool. They were no longer than her thumb from tip to first joint.

"You fought a sprite?" She sounded surprised that I would pick on a being a fraction of my size.

"No one fights with Sprites if they can help it. Little buggers will swarm you until you're a pile of bones. No, I made a deal with them. They got a home, and work, and I didn't have to come back in a box."

She cocked her head at me, "you lost?"

I laughed. "I won, and they won, not all battles have to end with the victor's boot on his opponent's throat, Princess."

"I like that. Wish it could be true more often."

I sighed, "So do I."

She continued on down the aisle, and I stood still for a moment, remembering how I had acquired most of these weapons. I hadn't set out to bring back trophies, more memories, and interesting pieces that had caught my interest. Like that LeMat pistol, enspelled to fire incendiary buckshot by an angry fairy with a grudge against a lady who was no better than she should be, and probably much more pleasurable than most. He'd caught the Court's attention when his wild shots at her set the riverboat on fire, and it couldn't be put out easily. Fortunately for me, he had been a terrible shot, and I was able to take the gun away from him. He'd sagged like a candle near a hot stove, and I think he was relieved to be taken Underhill again.

Bella had gone on to the next aisle, and I let her wander, trusting her not to touch anything, while I opened up the workshop. In here, I modified weapons, built in spells, and generally employed the tricks that kept me alive at what I did. In one corner of the long workbench that lined the far wall was a Mosin Nagant I had picked up dirt cheap, and was prepping to fire wooden bullets that were jacketed in frangible metal. Dryads can't be killed unless you find and cut down their tree, and not always then, but they were vulnerable to wood from their own type of tree. They also can't be transplanted once they reach maturity. I had been preparing to find a grove that was luring unwary passersby in a California park. I wasn't in too much of a hurry, I figured that was a fate the eco-friendly would approve of, fertilizing trees.

I didn't think I was going to get to them anytime soon, either. Or the ogres infesting Mt. St. Helens. I had no illusions about having killed any of the pack that had ambushed Bella and I. Knocking them off a bridge into a river was only a delaying tactic. The ogre she had blown up was surely dead, but the one with the log in his chest was doubtless holed up somewhere with a she-ogre licking his wounds. Someday, I would have to go back there and take care of them. First, though...

I turned as Bella walked into the shop. Her eyes widened as she looked around.

"Oooh! Shiny!" she laughed. She looked at me with a raised eyebrow and I nodded permission to the unspoken question. Now she could touch, and she did, inspecting my reloading station. I guessed, given her upbringing, she was familiar with the process. She seemed to know what she was looking at.

"What!?" She stopped cold and held up a wooden stake. "Please tell me vampires aren't real."

Now it was my turn to laugh. "No, but other beings react badly to organics, where metals won't hurt them."

"Next you will tell me the silver bullets," she pointed to a small wooden box with neat rows of copper and silver cartridges lying in it, "aren't for werewolves."

"No, I won't tell you that," smiling, I went on with the lesson, "although a lot of the Folke are sensitive especially to silver, so I use that load more often than lead."

She cocked her head slightly to one side, considering. With the fairy wings at rest behind her, and her hair pulled up in a loose bun, this made her look utterly sweet and adorable. I bit my tongue and reminded myself this was a woman who was deadly with a weapon and not afraid to use it.

"Score the barrels of your guns much?"

I knew she mean with the harder silver than the soft lead loads. "Yeah, I go through them. Fortunately, this job pays well."

She nodded and looked around again, an encompassing sweep of gaze. "My cousins would be jealous of your shop, you know."

I blurted out before I could stop it, "well, there are times I have thought about putting together a team."

I had, too. Although the concept of bringing in half-fey Alaskan rednecks had never crossed my mind until that second. Now that I had said it, though, it was a way of being certain they were not double agents for Low Court. Or High Court, for that matter. I was struck by that, but it would have to wait. Bella brought me back to the present.

"What am I learning today, Lom?"

And this was why I couldn't lose focus. She needed me all in the game, because she didn't know what was being played, much less the rules.

"Not firearms. Fairly certain you are solid on those." We matched feral grins for a second. "No, I'm taking you to the spell room. We spent a lot of work making it into a safe place to try out magic."

"I had never thought about it before the library," she gestured vaguely at her head. I wondered if the full ramifications of what Alger had done had sunk in with her yet. I thought not, she would doubtless be... verbal... when they did. She went on, "where spells came from. Lavendar never really talked about it. I just realized days ago that it takes work to develop a spell that really works."

"Working is easy," I corrected her, "maintaining control is hard. Most fairies never bother to use anything new because it is much less risky."

"So how do I learn," she asked reasonably, "without killing myself or you?"

"Well, in here," I opened a third door with effort. It was solid steel, and the interior panel was scarred and marked with soot. "We can test spells with powered-down results. This room has a massive damping spell embedded in the floor that holds magic release to a minimum."

She eyed the big, empty room with a dubious expression. It was fairly dim and dark, lit only in a few places by weakly glimmering elf-torches. The magic for those globes of light common in Underhill homes was just not strong enough to endure for long in here.

"How safe is this?"

"Not completely. But it won't kill you." Now she did have a look of alarm on her face. I backpedalled quickly. "You know I have to deliver you safe and whole, still, Princess."

"That's not... terribly reassuring."

I snapped back, "good training isn't easy."

She sighed and braced her shoulders, which did interesting things to her... wings. "OK, where do we start?"

"Come on," I led her out into the middle of the room, closing the door behind me as I did so.

Once we stood shoulder to shoulder facing one wall, I instructed her, "close your eyes and think back to the troll on the bridge."

She closed her eyes and I could almost feel her flinch a little. She was upset at herself for not having cued in sooner to the threat, I surmised.

"You had no way," I reassured her, putting my hand on her shoulder, "of knowing that he was ambushing you. You weren't expecting that kind of danger, and you are trained to help. He was using that as your weakness to get to you."

She nodded with her eyes still closed. I felt her shoulder relax, and her chin came up. There was my hard-headed girl.

"If it happens again," I went on, "what are you going to do as soon as you realize he is a threat, now?"

She took a deep breath. I stepped to one side to give her room to work. "My strengths are air and fire. Yours is earth."

"Yes, go on." I had nodded, and then realized she couldn't see me, her eyes still closed.

"So I want to use fire," she told me, "He's too big for air to do much."

"Fire at will." I quipped.

"Um," she got that distracted look I was learning to recognize.

"Toward the wall. Don't worry about speed now, this is time to think, so later, you won't have to."

She held out her hand and I could tell she was summoning her wand. Then she flicked it at and released the spell, a glimmer that spun off the tip and slowly toward the wall. After a moment, a fireball splashed muddily against the sooty stones. I always got a kick out of the fire behaving like a liquid in the damper field, and from the look on her face, so did she.

"Good. Now, do it without the wand." she looked at me, and I explained. "It slows you down."

"How?" she asked.

"How to do it without, or how does it slow you down?"

She looked annoyed, "how to do it without. I see your point about slowing me down."I knew I shouldn't needle her, so I tried to tell her straight. "It's a display piece. Mortals fear the wand as a symbol of magic being done, but you don't need it to aim a spell."

She nodded and tucked an errant lock of hair behind one ear, with a serious expression.

"Ready?" I prompted. Without a word, she made a gesture, and again fire splashed against the wall.

"Excellent!" I really was pleased. She caught on very fast, and had a lot of power, this wasn't tiring her out at all.

She beamed. Literally lit up with happiness. This startled her.

"What just happened?" She was holding onto my arm, now, with both hands.

"Um, you're a fairy. You sparkle."

She backed away, her face a mask of horror. "Oh, no. No, no, no... I will not sparkle. Please don't tell me I leave a trail of pixie dust like Tinkerbelle when I fly."

I choked back the laugh. "Bella..."

I must not have succeeded in wiping the amusement out of my voice. She headed toward the door. "I can't do this right now, please let me out."

"You need to practice. I'm... " I caught up with her, started to catch her shoulder, and changed my mind. She was liable to rip off the arm that touched her right now and use it to club me to death with. I changed tacks. She had one hand on the door handle, and I knew better than to try and physically stop her. She might not be able to kill me, or really want to, but she might hurt me without realizing what she was doing.

"Bella." That tone stopped her. "You're acting like a child. This isn't about you not liking your appearance, what is wrong?"

Chapter 16

Delicate Flower

"I want to get out of this place." She spat it out, like I was going to argue with her. "I want to go home, spend long, quiet days with my spotting scope and a cloud of mosquitoes. I do not want to wear anything but denim and plaid. I most definitely do not want to become a delicate, sparkling, damned flower!"

The curse startled me. I knew she was under a lot of stress and hadn't been feeling well, I didn't realize how bad it had gotten.

"Let's go upstairs and talk?" I suggested, still not wanting to have my head ripped off. She growled, but nodded. I let us out of the training room and she headed into the room I thought of as my warehouse.

"Lom." She had stopped in front of a cannon that had teeth marks all around the muzzle, like something had grabbed on and used it as a chew toy. "How long have you been collecting trophies?"

"Well, I don't think of them as trophies." I reached out and trailed a finger through a deep gouge in the brass, and she did the same once I had touched it. I was really appreciating her restraint with the objects. Some of them were still bespelled, or in the case of the goblin weapons, fouled with filth and venoms that would act even through skin. "If they were trophies, they would be upstairs over the fireplace or what-not."

She patted the snout of the cannon and looked back up at me, her eyes still shiny with unshed tears. "Good point. But you are doing it again."

"What?" I pretended innocence and affected a shocked tone. Her smile told me I'd overdone it.

"How long?" she repeated simply.

I sighed and rolled my shoulders against the tension building up there. "Let's go upstairs, get some coffee, and I'll answer questions."

I put the coffee on, and indulged in something I rarely did unless I was alone. It gave me something to do with my hands and an excuse to stall. I started a pipe, finding more comfort in the motions of packing, lighting, and relighting than I had expected. My routines and home were upside-down, too. I'd never anticipated this little errand would become so complicated. It was supposed to be a straightforward pick-up and delivery. I'd show up, she'd sign papers, we'd fly to Seattle, rent a car, drive to a main gate Underhill (it was in a tiny used bookstore that mundanes loved, never guessing the real reason it was able to stay in business) and present her at court. Mission over.

Reality had been a fighting retreat from her home and state, a journey that had taken far longer than planned, an oath of fealty I was not going to back out of even if she didn't seem to understand its gravity, and no signature on the papers lying forgotten on my bedroom desk. I was also stalling on taking her to the shark pool that was Court. I'd gotten soft, I mused silently. Bella just sat still and watched me. She had kicked a troll in the 'nads, maintained a cool-as-a-cucumber demeanour through a midair furball with a roc, and blown an Ogre the hell up. I would confess I was a little afraid of her, especially with Alger's gift still unwrapping inside her head.

"You wanted to know how long I've been doing.. what I do."

"Monster hunting?" she supplied curiously.

I winced. "I don't call it that. Not all the beings, things, whatever, I go after are monsters. So I usually say bounty hunter, if pressed to it."

She nodded. I went on, "I started after I'd fully recovered from the elfshot that almost killed me, and left me, as a Pixie magician's apprentice..." The corners of her eyes crinkled, but she suppressed her smile. "Useless. I was in my young adulthood, what humans call late teenage years developmentally now. You know how boys that age are."

She gave me a rueful smile. I was willing to guess that with all her cousins, there were stories there. But we didn't have time, now. "I wanted to prove my value, and I didn't want to be Underhill very much. So we took on a small commission as a favor for the King."

She didn't question the we, and I found out later she'd assumed I meant Alger. "How did you work around not using magic?"

"I could risk triggering pre-made spells, and I learned to, as Raven put it so well, hunt crooked. There were some pretty close calls in the early days."

But we had been going after small prey, then, my partner and I, looking for the minor disruptive elements in human realms that were very close to our own. A brownie craving the old days. A changeling left in the wrong household, that could leave an angry mob hunting us to the very doors of Underhill. Back then, humans still had memories of where the major doors were.

I finally answered her question, speaking softly to try and lessen the impact. "Bella, that was two hundred human years ago."

She settled back in her chair. "Ah. I knew..." she gestured in frustration, a rare thing for her to not have the words. "You are different. You're not like any man I'd ever met, and I kept thinking, 'he's a Pixie, of course he's not like a human guy' but there was more than just that. You always keep your cool."

I laughed out loud without being able to stop myself. I was so uncool around her I might as well be the gawky youth who had taken on that first job all those years ago. She had me by the throat and didn't seem to know it at all. But I couldn't tell her that. I talked around it, instead. "Practice. Sometimes I'll see something I didn't expect," my mind flashed back to a pair of smoking ogre feet, "But mostly I expect very bad things to happen."

"I need to learn that," she mused.

"No, you don't. You never want to learn that." I retorted. "If all goes well, we show up at Court, endure a couple of uncomfortably formal weeks, and you can go home. You'll never have to come back Underhill or see me again."

That left me with a tight chest, but I knew it was for the best. She needed someone who could be human with her, not an old, sick, Pixie who couldn't live in the human realm all the time. It was the first time I'd thought about this rationally. I had been falling for her, from that first moment, and it simply would not do. Now I wanted to get up and leave the room, but she spoke and I sat still and listened.

"It isn't going to go well, is it? I don't know what's going to happen, but I have a bad feeling." She wrapped her arms around herself and looked small and miserable.

"I think it will get rough once you appear at court. I think it will be... both easier and more difficult when it is known I am your escort."

"How is that?" She looked up and I was glad to see she was keeping the tears at bay.

"Because I have a reputation. Which I think you understand better, now." She nodded agreement, and I went on. "But that means that when they do throw something at us, and they will, it will be bad. Hence..." I gestured downward, towards the room we'd just vacated. "Traning. You need to be able to use the library. I don't think Alger had any idea what he was doing, giving you that. I think he meant for you to be able to access the outer layer, the 'how-to' books so to speak. But you have the whole damn library in your head, and frankly, that's a little scary."

She looked surprised. She was used to being competent, yes, but the idea of being fearsome had never crossed her mind. "I didn't mean..." she started to protest.

I held up a hand to stop her, and leaned toward her. She sat forward in her chair again, intent on me. "It's our secret weapon. They think you are fresh from human realms, untrained, powerless, helpless. But Bella, you know more magic than they do, any of them. Alger is... very old. I'm not even sure how old the bas... er, old man is. And you have his entire wealth of knowledge," I reached out and pressed a fingertip to the soft skin of her temple. "Right in there, and no one knows that but us."

She leaned her face into my hand, and I had to catch my breath at the touch of it, such a sweet, intimate motion. I cupped her cheek. The temptation was there, but I had a hundred years of practice against that. After a moment, she sat up, and I dropped my hand.

"And I will miss you," she told me. "Maybe you could come visit."

I didn't even want to explore that invitation, there was a wealth of meaning hidden there, and I had a fairly good idea she didn't even intend all of it.

"Let's get through this, and I'll take you home." I promised. "But I'm stopping at your front door, because last time you threatened me with a shotgun."

She threw her head back and laughed out loud. "You have a point. Whatever happened to that paperwork, anyway? Even when you were unconscious, you kept hold of it."

"It's up in my office area. You don't have to sign it, you know."

She shrugged. "Is there any reason I shouldn't, at this point? I'm already committed to doing what they want."

I thought about what I had read of it. "I don't think it will be an issue, and it may be a good thing if you are under the protection of the Court, formally, while in attendance there."

"Go ahead and get it, then," she grimaced, wrinkling up her nose, "before I change my mind again."

When I came back down Ellie was sitting at the table with a steaming cup in front of her. I blinked. I knew it wasn't coffee, she turned her nose up at that, and she never sat at the table. Well, sometimes, in the lonely years, I had coaxed her into sitting and talking. But she was always fidgety and I never kept her long, unable to torture her. Yet here she was, relaxed and smiling her crooked smile at Bella, who was talking about baking. They seemed to be discussing the relative merits of yeasts and sourdoughs. For the second time since I had gotten home, I lingered in the doorway, fascinated by the sight of two women in my kitchen. it was very... homey. I sighed, and walked the rest of the way in to the table.

Ellie looked up but stayed where she was, and I smiled. Bella just smiled at me and said, "get on with it, then."

I pulled the stack of papers and vellum out and shoved it across to her with a fountain pen on top of it. She bent over it, leafing through until she found the page she wanted. "Aren't you going to read it?" I asked in curiosity. After her reaction the first time, this was different.

"No, I read it before. Most of it's genealogy, anyway." Her pen scratched across the paper, and she peered at it for a moment. "Little spell there. Must be making sure it's really me signing?"

I nodded, tickled she'd picked up on that. "Yes, and another to deliver them when you're done."

"Ok, but will that give us away?" She looked up at me in concern, the pen poised over another page.

I shook my head. "A little, but it's not going to give away that you are already Underhill. I'm guessing we will be the last ones to arrive at Court, as long as it has been." I would be checking on that with Devon later, too. He was doubtless wondering what had happened to me.

"Ok, then." Trustingly, she signed the last three times, and collated the papers back into a neat stack. There was a gentle glow, and then, with a quiet pop, they disappeared. She sighed, "now I'm glad I didn't do that at home. You'd be peeling me off the ceiling about now. So much has changed, so fast."

I agreed with her silently, but she went on without expecting a response from me. "So how long now until we go to Court? Will I need clothes?"

Ellie spoke up, and I detected a hint of humor. "How about dinner?"

"Yes, Ellie, please dinner." I told her fervently. Training, talking, and heaven help me, telling Bella about Court Dress, was going to mean I needed more energy.

"Go away now." She informed us cheerfully. "Back later, I call." She stood up and waved us out with both hands.

Chapter 17

Lom's Gift

Bella beat a giggling retreat. "I'm going to go wash the soot out of my hair," she informed me, headed for the staircase. I watched her go, reflecting on how nice it was to have company, particularly company that looked like that, walking up stairs. I tore myself away from the sight to go to my office desk and boot up the laptop.

Again, Devon must have been monitoring for me.

:Hello, Uncle.:

:Nephew, very formal this evening.:

:Not happy. So much gossip. My brain needs bleaching.:

I laughed out loud in my empty room. He had a point.

:So, report. We will arrive in Court within two days. You don't have to do more:

:Thank Goddess.:

After a few moments of the cursor blinking at me, the report came up.

:Of the original expected girls, there are five at court. Two more had "accidents" on the way, and one escort was lost as well. There is much curiosity about Bella at Court, only they don't seem to know her name, it's all Lavendar's progeny when they talk about her. The process doesn't get started until you two show up, Lom. There's no buzz about you at all. I think you are right, they don't know the King assigned you to her. All the other escorts were knights. I hear that Low Court is quiet, but I didn't put out feelers there, I was good.:

I nodded to myself when I read that. He was correct, I would not have risked having him stir up that ant's nest. It was going to rile up some with the selection of the Queen, and the process beforehand. No point in setting it off prematurely. The report went on.

:I was able to find out that the King seems unworried, although I know from you that he isn't, but Court takes their lead from him, so he must be playing to them. No-one at Court seems to show any alarm, they are taking all these "accidents" at face-value. You know, Lom, there are times I really lose hope for our society.:

:You and I both, Kid.: I typed back quickly. :You done good, thanks. Now drop back to a safe distance and I will take it from here. I was afraid of walking into an ambush.:

:There are no indications that anyone is aware of a conflict, or planning trouble.:

Which didn't mean that no-one was, just that they weren't being obvious about it. It was interesting that it was business as usual at Court. Presentation, at least, should go smoothly. It was all I could ask for.

:Good night, Devon. Got your homework done?:

:Ha! very funny. KThanksbai!:

He signed off, leaving me puzzling over the last word construct. Impertinent whippersnapper. Ellie's dinner bell rang, distracting me. Food would be good about now, I couldn't remember last time I'd eaten, off hand.

Over dinner, Bella wanted to talk clothes. I put down my fork for a moment and thought about it. I have two really good Court outfits, but I hadn't been to a formal affair for a few years, and as much as I hate to admit it, I know my limitations.

"Um, they need to be formal, and er, feminine."

She looked at me like I had lost my mind. I could agree with that assessment. Fortunately, I could call for backup.

"Ellie!" I bellowed, startling Bella. Ellie appeared at my elbow with a small pop and a slight smile. I gave her a dirty look. She was enjoying this whole thing entirely too much.

"Could you please fill Bella in on what she will be needing for Court Dress? I need to go make my own preparations, we are going in two days." I picked up my plate and beat a hasty retreat. I really did have work to do. Ellie's voice, raised abnormally high, rang in my ears as I went.

"Two days?!"

I spent the next day and a half in the armory. I'm not sure what they were doing, I had Ellie send me plates at mealtimes. One of them arrived with a scrap of fabric on the rim, so I was sure they were happily getting Bella ready. It was after lunch, with me planning on leaving after breakfast the next day, when I next found myself in the kitchen doorway.

"He's in the armory. No-one goes down there but him, so it's a good place for him to retreat."

That was Ellie's voice, I hadn't heard what she was responding to. I listened hard, curious what they had to say about me.

Bella spoke, "oh, he took me down there that first day he was up."

"He took you to the armory? He never takes anyone down there." Ellie's distinctive sniff, "not even I'm allowed to go in there. Must be dirty as anything."

Bella chuckled. "It was interesting, but not too dusty. He's really never let anyone else down there?"

I stepped into the room, clearing my throat to let them know I was coming. They looked up from the kitchen table. There were piles of fabric in what seemed like every color in the rainbow. Bella was casting small, marble sized spells with matching colors onto heaps of it. Ellie was rocking in a chair by the fire, a pipe in her hand.

"How is it going?"

Bella stuck her tongue out at me. "It's going, which you would know if you'd bothered to check."

"I'm checking now." I pointed out, a little stung. This was not my forte.

"I won't let you down," she promised, "You can be sure that everything I wear at court will be both formal and feminine."

Now I was sure I had stepped in it somewhere along the line. "I don't doubt you will be the loveliest Fairy there," I assured her. Ellie snorted loudly.

"Will presentation be in the morning when we arrive, or...?"

She was ignoring my sally. Ok, I was fine with just the facts, ma'am. "It will be in the evening, and then a formal banquet for the participants to all meet one another."

She looked up at that, suddenly wide eyed. A spell clung forgotten to her fingers like a ruby droplet. "Will I have to give a speech?"

The horror in her voice made me smile. "No, that's the King's job. I don't think you will be called on to do any public speaking."

"Good, because I suck at it."

She went back to her task. I spoke over her head. "I'll go pack, then. I suppose you will want your weapon when we go?"

"What weapon? I didn't bring a weapon with me." She was distracted into her task. The red fabric was... shimmering. I decided not to look too closely.

"The Ogre-Killer?" I teased her gently, "how quickly we forget that which saves our lives."

"Oh," she looked up again with a big smile. "Did you rescue that? I thought it had gotten lost when we came Underhill."

"When you have a moment, I'll show you what I did with it."

She stood up. "That's the last of it. Ellie, want me to clear it out of your way for dinner?"

The wood elf shook her head, her eyes half closed. Whatever she smoked she enjoyed, but it wasn't tobacco or anything I recognized. "I will pack for you."

"Oh. Thank you." Bella looked as surprised as I felt. Ellie never did anything for anyone but me, anymore. Even that had taken some negotiation at the beginning. I hadn't wanted her help, and she was determined to not let me lift a finger. We had compromised over the years, and it seemed Bella had made an impression.

Bella followed me out to the armory door. "Ellie was just telling me you don't let anyone come down here."

"There's a spell on this door, and now it's keyed to let you past." I unlocked it, and she followed me down the stairs. At the bottom where there had been a small landing and the single door, there was now a second door across the landing from it. I pointed to the old door. "I keyed the spell on that to not be triggered by you, but it's still locked. This one," I pointed now at the new door, which was still fresh enough to smell of the wide pine boards it was made of, "is yours."

"Mine?" She sounded stunned. I handed her a set of keys. "Yours, and here. You'll want to set a spell ward, I'll help if you want."

She looked at me, serious. "Lom, are you mad at me?"

I rocked back on my heels. "No, I'm not mad. Yes, this has gotten... complicated. But that happens." I shrugged. "Now go on and open it, I worked hard on this for you."

She opened the door and stepped in. I followed her silently, I wanted her to take it in. It wasn't as big as mine, but she had her own workbench on one side, and a single rack of shelves on the other. Ogre-Killer hung on one, and a few weapons I thought she could make use of were there as well. She walked around it, lightly touching a few things, and circled back to me, her face solemn.

"Do you really think I will be here long enough?"

"I don't know. But I was hoping it would help you with the feeling girly thing."

She grinned. "Oh, yeah! It's a great gift, Lom. Thank you!"

She reached out, and I remembered the last time she had thanked me for a gift. This time, to my half-disappointment, she just gave me a big hug. I found that I missed the comfortable pressing of her chest to my facel. Now that she was shorter than I, I had to settle for their pressure against my chest. I hugged her back, and then she was off to look more closely at what I'd given her. She came back with a small gun in her hand, and a oddly shaped holster. I laughed at the choice.

"Is that what you'll be carrying tomorrow?"

She nodded, "I want to be inconspicuous."

"Better to surprise them than going in with horns and trumpets. I approve. Now, I'm going to teach you how to attach a summoning spell to a weapon, so you don't have to carry it with you."

"Oh, goodie." She bounced a little, but it didn't distract her, even though she was definitely sparkling.

Chapter 18

Arrival at Court

The next morning she was demure in slacks and a button-down blouse. I did a double take, because I had never seen her like that before. Her face fell. "Is it not ok?"

"Well, you look like someone's idea of an executive, but you should be fine. We'll arrive quietly and you will have plenty of time to change. Remember protocol?"

She nodded. We had spent the previous evening going over how she would let me take point and be protective, and what she could expect from me, and floor plans, and it had been a very late bedtime. I, for one, needed coffee. Ellie materialized at my elbow with a steaming mug. I eyed her suspiciously. "Are you reading my mind? I don't advise it, it gets ugly in there."

I sipped appreciatively at the coffee.

"Who needs to read minds? I know what you want." She handed another mug to Bella. "Breakfast before you go, not leaving with empty bellies."

We obediently followed her into the kitchen. With this spread, we'd be lucky to arrive conscious. Ellie was worried, I translated it as. I followed her into the pantry, where she was fussing over jam pots.

"Ellie," I stopped her with a gentle touch on her coarse hands. "It's going to be fine. I can take care of us, and Bella's perfectly capable of taking care of herself. Me too, if it comes to it."

She looked away from me. "I like her. You like her."

"This isn't..." I rubbed my face. Memories I'd locked up for a long time were flooding back. "She's not part of our life forever. She hates it Underhill, and she will go home and forget about us. Which is as it should be."

The tiny wood-elf looked up at me with shrewd eyes. "You not happy about that."

"Does it matter?"

"You should be happy again. Nothing before your fault."

"My wants and wishes are not part of the equation. She deserves to be safe, and happy. I can't give her anything. Now, stop worrying over the marmalade and come sit with us."

She followed me to the table, and we both listened to Bella praise her cooking while we all ate. I didn't taste much. This had been a wonderful little interlude, and I was surprisingly comfortable with the girl who had invaded my life and surprised me in so many ways. Today was going to be the first step in letting her go again, and helping her get home safely. I was going to miss her.

Arrival at court couldn't have been simpler. Bella repeated her bubble spell that had gotten us to my house from the door to Underhill, and we walked into the suite of rooms the Majordomo directed us to. Bella looked around the little sitting room.

"Where am I sleeping?" she asked. I could see that she was nervous, and guessed that she wanted some alone time and time to get her mask on before the presentation.

"In here, would be my guess." I opened a door to show her a large bedroom, which I knew from experience would have an attached bath and closet. Court had lots of room, these days. The majordomo had been stone-faced, but I had detected a glimmer of relief when he had heard her name. So we had been ushered to a prepared set of rooms very promptly. I was certain that before he had even closed the doors on us, word was racing through the ancient halls that we had arrived. The game was begun.

"And you?" I thought I detected a touch of concern in her voice, and wondered if it was general nerves, or if she thought they had only given us one bedroom. I pointed across the room.

"I'll be right over there, Princess. Knock if you need me."

She tucked her hair behind her ear in a gesture I was learning meant she was unsettled, and I left her to unpack and settle in. I only had two formalwear outfits, and I was looking forward to appearing in one of them that evening. I recognized the old familiar rush of adrenaline, the thrill before battle. I didn't know that we would meet the enemy tonight, but it seemed likely, that whoever it was, would be there.

I climbed into my monkey suit and checked myself in the mirror. The James Bond style tux wasn't actually black, just a brown so dark it looked black. The sapphire blue silk shirt with the gold bow tie would look gaudy to her, I knew... right up until she saw the whole of Court. It was time to collect my princess and show her off.

She was standing in the middle of the sitting room when I opened my door, and I flashed back to the first time I had laid eyes on her. The dress she was wearing was about as far from the silk long johns as you could get, and yet, it reminded me of that. Revealing, without actually showing any skin. She was sexy enough to make my mouth water in the barkcloth blue gown, with sparkles... I narrowed my eyes and walked closer, focussing on the fabric. Yes, I was right, it was sparkling, lighting and dimming with magic. She chuckled.

"Neat trick, yes? Ellie suggested it. The night sky, she called it."

I raised an eyebrow at her. "Thought you didn't like sparkling?"

She shrugged, a motion that did interesting things to the curves she had highlighted. "If you can't fight it, might as well use it. If it distracts you, I know I'm onto something."

I had to agree she was right. She was distracting, dammit. I needed to get a grip. She turned, and revealed a lot of skin. Her hair was swept up simply into a thick coil at the back of her neck, and her back was bare all the way down to... "Any lower and I'd see your butt."

She looked over her shoulder, an expression of concern on her face. "Too much? I thought it was a nice contrast."

"We don't have time for you to change. Do you at least have a wrap?"

She laughed and picked up a sheet of gauze off the chair. "You're grumpy tonight."

I let her settle the drifts of black starry fabric over her shoulders and around her wings. I didn't dare offer to help, and have my hands so close to all that creamy skin on display. "I'm worried, and you are playing dress-up."

"True," she told me calmly, sweeping toward the door in a flurry of skirts. I had to hurry to get there before her, and she smiled at me as I gave her a dirty look. "But I have my mask on, and I am ready for anything."

The High Court, Underhill, has fallen from the glory years that were written and sung about in human history. Perhaps because we have retreated from a world above that has moved beyond us, or simply because we are so shrunken in numbers and power. Yet it still has the echoes of a past when nothing was unheard of, in these halls, and I saw it fresh through Bella's eyes that evening, as we paced silently side by side down halls carpeted in scarlet, and decorated in more gilt and rococo than any italianate palace.

"A bit overdone, I know," I told her out of the side of my mouth.

Her mouth quirked at the corners. "Just a bit, yes."

"The old halls are better." I was rather fond of the oldest part of the tor, myself. I went there when I was tasked to the Court for any length of time, to get away from the Folke and have some peace.

Right now, though, we had arrived. Two liveried footmen opened the doors for us, and I could read Bella's very straight face as mingled amusement at having fallen into a BBC production and horror at the idea of her being here. Inside the doors, the majordomo stood at attention. He rapped his staff of office on the hardwood flooring twice, and boomed out our names.

"The illustrious Princess Belladonna Maline ys Lavendar of Flora. Her escort, Learoyd Ortheris Mulvaney."

I winced. I hated when they did that, but no amount of bribery or cajoling would persuade them to forget my full name and simply use Lom. Beside me, Bella was struggling to contain her giggles and losing. As a result, when she met my mother she was smiling and sparkling vividly.

The dowager Mulvaney was a force to be reckoned with, in Court. Bella was, simply, an elemental force.

"Mother, this is Princess Bella." I turned to look at Bella, "And this is my mother, the Dowager Lucia Mulvaney."

"So pleased to meet you," Bella held out her hand, "Your son has taken very good care of me."

Mother sniffed, but I could tell from her face softening a little she was pleased. "He does his duty," she allowed, taking Bella's hand briefly. "You had a safe journey?"

"It had it's moments, but we are here finally." Bella looked around the room full of people. "I do feel a bit out of my depth."

My mother smiled, shocking me, but the artless confidence had been just the thing. She took Bella under her wing, metaphorically, and tucked her hand into her own elbow and then led her off, murmuring, "let me introduce you..."

Chapter 19

The Other Princesses

I trailed behind them, feeling much relieved. If mother was going to like her, then she would be cushioned from the usual Court snobbery. That made it possible for me to focus on watching for malice in the eyes of the glittering crowd. It was like a never-ending costume party. The denizens of Court saw no reason to limit themselves to just one era of dress. Some of them had been here, in this hall, while Elizabeth was crowned, and I don't mean the second one.

Most of them looked bored, in spite of the variety in their dress. Near immortality meant nothing changed quickly, and any excitement was savored slowly. Bella was something new, however, and many eyes followed her progress through the long ballroom. None of them, however, seemed to be unhappy with this interruption in their routine. Casually, seeming almost uninterested, they gravitated in our direction. I started looking for the other princesses.

It seemed logical to me that one of them was the instigator. Well, not the girl herself, although I had been cautious with Bella to begin with. No, this was an old mind, one that wanted power, which meant they were planning to be the voice in a princess's ear when she was crowned Queen. So I was looking at the people standing next to the princesses.

Five princesses besides mine, and each of them with a much larger entourage. We met the first one obliquely, my mother beckoning to another matron who was standing over a girl seated near the wall.

"Lady Herbale, please make the acquaintance of Belladonna ys Lavendar."

The matron, dressed in a mode I identified as late Victorian, touched fingertips with Bella, who was looking nervously amused.

"Chahmed, I am sure. Dill," she turned and gave the girl in the chair the hairy eyeball. "Come heah, deah."

The little thing couldn't have been more than fourteen or fifteen, a mere wisp of a girl in a very modern chartreuse dress that made me wince. "Hello, I am Dill ys Parsley." She essayed a curtsey, this time making Bella wince as she wobbled dangerously on the downdip.

"Princess Dill." The matron made sure her charge's status was known. "And you are the princess Belladonna?"

"I am. Very nice to meet you both."

The girl flicked an anxious glance at the older woman. "Pleased to meet you," she offered, along with a limp hand, which Bella took in both of hers.

"I have been curious," she told her, "About the other princesses. I've never met a princess, and I only found out I am one a little while ago."

Dill's eyes widened. "Really?" she squeaked, putting her other hand over Bella's, so they were holding hands like chums. "But you're very old."

Bella laughed. "I didn't grow up Underhill."

"Oh, I know. We talked about you."

"I am sure you did." Bella let go of her hands. "I am looking forward to talking soon, and I will try to answer your questions."

"Gee!" Dill at this point caught sight of the death glare her aunt was giving her, and subsided. "It was very nice to meet you," she mumbled, retreating to her chair.

Mother gave me a speaking glance, and propelled Bella onward. I watched the look on Lady Herbale's face as we left. Shock, and a touch of fear. She knew Dill had no chance to be chosen, and she was trying to calculate what Bella's motives were. I smiled to myself, knowing that Bella had just taken pity on the child. My mother continued on inexorably, but at this point I could see that her progress was not random, and I drifted behind them as mother smiled and nodded, and Bella just smiled.

The next group we intercepted was much larger, as it contained two of the other princesses. Both of them wore pastel, high-waisted gowns that were in a fashion a hundred and fifty years out of date in human lands. They were of an age, and similar in appearance, both being dumpy blondes of no great height. Bella found herself looking them in the eye, while I loomed over all four women. Their entourage had melted back a little as we approached. There was no dragon dowagers here, the oldest in the group I recognized, and gave him a slight nod in greeting. One of the knight escorts, Beaumont just looked slightly constipated. Then again, he always looked that way.

My mother gestured, her skin papery white over her thin bones. I reflected that she wasn't getting any younger, and I had been a very late child, after years of trying for an heir. My sister predated me by two decades.

"The princesses Apple ys Mulberry and Rowan ys Willow, may I present to you Belladonna ys Lavendar?"

The young women gave identical cool smiles, and shook hands lightly with Bella.

"Very nice to meet you," she offered.

"Likewise," smirked Apple. The expression on her aptly apple-shaped face was not pleasant, but I detected no deeper malice than jealousy there. Rowan just looked remote.

My mother returned the polite smiles and snipped at them, "I shall return you to your flirtations, girls, we must be on."

I hid my smile, doing my best to keep a professional aloofness as Apple tried to catch my eye. I knew her, and she had been hunting me for a long time. My mother evidently shared my feeling about the sour little thing, who'd I'd nick-named Crab as a girl just presented at Court.

We slowly progressed around the dance floor, mother greeting old friends and making introductions to people I had known most of my life. Bella was looking overwhelmed, but she was a trooper, smiling and making small talk when required. We were almost on the opposite side of the room from Dill, when we were stopped by a tall fairy hurrying towards us. The blonde with the very ruffly yellow dress was all smiles, her hands outstretched.

"You must be Belladonna," she cooed, leaning in for an air kiss.

"Oh, please, Bella." My princess looked like she wanted to bolt, because this princess was very much in her personal space.

My mother had glided closer to me, and now she whispered in my ear, "this one is the most likely."

I nodded to acknowledge I'd heard her, and paid more attention to the Folke in the vicinity.

"I am Princess Buttercup ys Peaseblossom, but you must call me Bea," she effused, her hand to her chest dramatically. "We shall be friends. Do come and tell me all about the human realm," she shuddered for effect. "How barbaric a place it must be to live!"

Bella gave me a wide-eyed, pleading look. For the umpteenth time that evening, I suppressed a laugh. I looked at my mother, who nodded with a very unladylike smirk, and came to her rescue.

"I'm afraid we really must meet everyone, dear. But I am sure that Bella will have time for you tomorrow, and you girls can all get together for a lovely gossip."

Bea ruffled her golden wings in an artful way and glimmered at my mother. "Oh, Lady Mulvaney, you are so right. I'm afraid I let my enthusiasm carry me away."

My mother smiled indulgently. "Quite all right. Now, if you will excuse us..."

As we were moving away, I caught the sulk of a spoiled child on Bea's face, and a very odd expression on the face of the elderly man whose arm she had retreated to. That would be a lead for following up, I thought. Her father, or uncle, someone who would have little access to the throne but through her. And she was a bubblehead.

We had circled back to the doors, and no sign of the fifth princess, which was not making Mother happy. My feet were starting to hurt, and Bella was likely wishing she were elsewhere. The majordomo approached on silent feet, and I raised an eyebrow at him, which he acknowledged with a slight hand gesture. Nothing urgent, then. I went back to my endless scanning of the crowd. He cleared his throat, catching my mother's attention.

With a bow, he offered a small white envelope, and then disappeared as quietly as he'd come. I'd spent some time practicing that silent walk of his, and it had come in handy at times. Mother slid the notecard embossed with a crown out and looked at it, then handed it to Bella, who made a surprised face.

"Is this customary?" She asked, and I wasn't sure if she was directing the question at me or Mother, who answered her before I could.

"Not at all, my dear, this is a signal honor."

I held out my hand and Bella gave me the note. When I read it, I understood her surprise. The King was requesting a formal presentation, tomorrow at ten o'clock am, to be followed by a private luncheon for her and her escort with him. This was something new. Normally if he wanted to see me, I made my way through secret passages to his private chamber and we talked like men, something I had come to understand over the years was a rare treat for a man who was surrounded by sycophants and intrigue.

"I think early to bed, then, so that we may have you fresh and bright for this." My mother decreed, then went on, "I would like you to meet my daughter before you go, however. And I do wonder where that girl has gone off to."

I understood she did not mean my sister, who was hardly a girl, but the missing princess. I caught the eye of one of the hovering footmen and gestured him over. The drinks from his tray for mother and Bella were appreciated, but the quiet word I dropped in his ear was my real reason. He nodded and headed toward the service doors, handing off the half-full tray to yet another man in livery. Then I caught up with my mother, who was headed single-mindedly across the room to my sister, who was fluttering her lashes at a man with his back to us.

"Margot," my mother caroled. "Meet Princess Belladonna."

My sister is a little bit of fluff, who lives to flirt and gossip, but she hasn't a mean bone in her body. Or, some days, a brain in her head.

"Oh, hello! It is so nice to meet you!" She stood and kissed Bella on the cheek. "You must meet Ivan, Count of Muscovy."

The dark man with curly mustachios rose and kissed her hand gallantly. "Enchanted," he informed her in a heavy accent. "You are one of the princesses, yes?"

"Um, yes, I am. And you are?"

"Oh, I am no-one. I am simply a fairy from Europe who visits the very charming Margot when I have business in Court."

Bella blinked at this. My sister laughed and patted the seat beside her. "Come, tell me all about your trip. Was it very exciting? When we found out family duty called an Escort, well, Lom had to be found who-knows where, and my poor son almost had to go and get you. He's far too young to leave Underhill, you know."

Bella sat next to her and let all this flow over her with a bewildered smile on her face. My mother sank into a spindly chair, leaving me to stand over all of them and look like the muscle, which I was. Bella finally sorted out what Margot had asked her, and answered, "I'm glad your son did not come, there were complications, and Lom's skills were invaluable."

Margot squeaked and clutched her hands. "I knew it! Such terrible rumors, but I have not been listening to a one of them."

I was having trouble keeping a straight face. Knowing her, she had made some of them up. Bella shot me a glance, and I shook my head just a little.

"Oh, what have you heard?" my clever girl asked, a look of calm curiosity on her face. Good, she wasn't going to give details to the greedy Margot.

"Well, did you know that eight princesses were called in, and only six arrived? They say you are the last one, but no one, simply no-one, knows what happened to the other two. And the Knight Forestall was sorely injured, and may not survive. Simply terrible, darling, and I was worried sick about you, because I do feel you are family. Such an old connection between our families, you know."

"No," murmured a now fascinated Bella, "I didn't know."

"Well, it goes back to great-great-grandfather, who was the groom of Queen Tansy. Pixies have always been in the service of the fairy court, but it doesn't mean we are servants, you mustn't think. Anyway, even your grandmother Lavendar had a Mulvaney in service, although he was our great-uncle or something." Margot waved a hand dismissively.

I broke in before my sister could continue. Bella was looking interested, but the footman had slipped a note into my hand, and I needed to pull her away.

"Bella, if I can pull you away... Margot, I promise you may see her soon, but we must retire early this evening."

Mother, reminded, backed me up. "Oh, certainly do take her, Leroy, her first evening, poor girl, she must be exhausted."

She took Bella's hand in hers and patted it gently. "Sleep well, m'dear, and do let us know when you are up to receiving, tomorrow."

Bella stood carefully, aware of her wings, I realized as she moved gracefully away, saying, "So very nice to meet you."

Chapter 20

Princess Maize

She walked at my side to the door, and once we were well out of the room and in the deserted hall, she heaved a deep sigh.

"Thank you," she murmured softly enough for no-one to hear.

"I figured you were beat and ready to retreat, but I'm afraid we have one more stop before our rooms."

"Oh?" She stopped and looked at me. I shook my head.

"Nothing to worry about. Just the last princess, who was indisposed, but asked to see you, anyway."

"Why are they so anxious to meet me?" she asked plaintively, again walking with me.

"Well, think of it this way. One, you finally arriving means the process begins. Two, now they know what the rival looks like."

"I'm not a rival!"

"They don't know that. Also, you're the dark horse. Underhill is like a small town in some ways. They all know one another, or at the very least, of one another."

She ran her fingers through her hair, knocking it loose. "Drat," she said, stopping to twist it back up hurriedly. I watched, enjoying the little show.

She gave me a dirty look. "You were having entirely too much fun tonight, mister."

I laughed. I couldn't help myself, it just came out. Bella screwed up her face... and then burst out laughing with me.

"I must have been a sight," she finally got out, between whoops. "The country girl in the ballroom."

"No, no..." this sobered me right up. "You were magnificent. You even won my mother over, and that is a very rare accolade."

She blinked at me. "But she was so nice."

"That's the point. She wouldn't have given you a second glance, but you... you're something special, and they all saw that tonight."

"Oh." She took a deep breath, and I could see her mind kick into high gear.

"It's not a bad thing, Bella." I pointed as we rounded a corner into a dustier corridor. We had left the main hall some time ago. "And here we are."

I knocked at the door, and after a moment it cracked open just enough for me to look down and see a suspicious eye glaring up at me. "Lom, and Princess Bella, here to see Princess Maize."

The door swung the rest of the way open, revealing a dimly lit room, and obscuring the body of the person opening the door. I stepped in and looked around it at her. She was hunched over the handle, still, her shoulders angled toward me, her long, curly white hair flowing over them and hiding her face entirely.

"Don't be afraid," I assured her. "Where is Princess Maize?"

"I'm here." The voice came from a bundled form on the couch. I turned to her, and Bella followed me into the sitting area. It was similar to ours, rugs over hardwood floors, and enough seating for a half dozen people to gather.

"I'm Bella," my girl said gently. "Are you all right, Maize? Why weren't you at the party?"

The girl on the couch burst into sobs. "B-because I l-look awful!" she wailed. Bella sat on the couch next to her.

"What happened?"

I decided to stay back, she seemed to have it well in hand.

"I g-got a note, and I went to see what was happening, and... and.. this happened!"

She threw back the blanket dramatically, revealing a swollen and blotchy face.

"Oh, dear," Bella sounded distressed, and I leaned closer to see. Maize's face was covered in small weeping blisters. Bella raised a hand and Maize flinched back.

"Oh, don't touch me... it hurts, and what if it's catching?"

I appreciated the sick girl's caution. "Have you seen a healer?" I asked her gently.

She nodded. "Granny Jenny had the king's personal healer come to see me. He said it was a spell, and we would have to wait until it wore off."

"A spell? Triggered when you got to where the note said to go?"

She nodded glumly. I went on, trying to keep my anger at her foolish behaviour from creeping into my voice. "And what did the note promise you?"

She curled up even more, but at least refrained from covering her face with the blanket again. "A love spell."

I blinked, uncertain I had just heard her correctly, and made eye contact with Bella. Yes, she had the look too, the "Oh, dear god, the next generation..." look.

"For the King, I'm guessing? Did you know the Queen is a political position, not a marriage, right?"

She sniffled. "I thought it would help."

I rubbed my face. Bella patted at the blankets covering Maize's shoulders. "Ok, can I please have the note?"

"I- I don't know..." she hicupped. "Granny Jenny?"

The woman with the wild elf-locks crept into view and held out a folded notepaper. I took it. "Thank you. Are you this child's caretaker?"

"Am not a child," Maize protested weakly. I ignored this.

Jenny nodded. She still wouldn't meet my eyes. "Keep her safely in her rooms. I will have the Majordomo send someone to stand guard."

"Oh, no..." Maize tried to sit up, whimpering a little. "How embarassing, I don't want..."

"Someone tried to harm you, this was not just a prank, my dear." Bella cut in. "There are bad things hunting the princesses, Maize, it's not just you."

The young fairy's eyes got very wide. "Oh, no. You think... someone wanted to hurt me badly?"

Bella nodded. Maize started to cry, silently. "We won't let anyone get to you. Lom and I are going to find out who is behind this, and make sure they can't hurt anyone else, I promise."

Maize nodded mutely, still crying. Bella stroked her hair. "You will be better soon. And you will be beautiful at the next party."

This did get a response. Maize whispered, "I like your dress."

"I'll come help you get all dolled up when you're ready to be out. Now, you think about that, and Lom will take care of the bad guys, that's what he does."

I hid a smile. I was a very unlikely hero, and it was making me feel weird to have the two women looking at me like that. I looked around for Granny Jenny, but she was out of sight again.

"We will check on you tomorrow." I assured the girl. Bella stood up.

"It was nice to meet you, Princess Maize."

The girl sniffed and tried a watery smile. "Thank you for coming."

Back out in the hall, I looked at Bella. "Teenagers. Such a wonderful word, with so much connotation. You know it's a recent invention, don't you?"

She laughed. "You're not saying reckless youth is a recent phenomenon, surely."

"No, I'm not." I replied ruefully, thinking of a few things I'd rather stayed forgotten. "Want to go check this out? I'm thinking that there might be traces of the spell still lingering, and with the library, you might be able to..."

"Hm..." she looked distracted for a minute. "Yes, I think I should be able to see something. I'm game to try, at least."

"First, let's set up that guard. And..." I looked back down at the note. "I think you will want to change into something more practical. This is liable to get dusty."

"Oh, thank you. First great idea I've heard all night."

"Sarcasm will get you everywhere, Princess."

I sent her to our rooms with a footman, and returned to Maize's rooms with a guard. There was no answer when I rapped at the door, but when I knocked a second time Granny Jenny opened it a crack.

"She's sleeping!" she hissed at me.

"You have someone watching over you, I wanted to let you know. If there is anything you need, just send a message to the majordomo. You have message spells?"

"Why would I need message spells?" She opened the door a little wider, and I could see her drawing herself up straighter. She did a very good job of looking down her nose at me despite being a head shorter than I.

"Because you're human?" I returned, amused.

"How do you know that?" she demanded.

"Long practice."

"Do not tell anyone..." she pleaded.

"It's nothing to be ashamed of. Now, do you have message spells?"

She nodded, and shut the door in my face. I sighed, and wondered how long she had been Underhill, and where she had come from. It wasn't relevant to tonight, though, but it made me curious. Humans Underhill were uncommon, and it had a difficult history of interaction with the world above. I made a mental note to come talk to the old woman again.

Less than twelve hours at Court, and I was already working on a suspect list, and clues. Making progress. Now to collect my sidekick and take a look at that clue. I made another mental note to never call Bella my sidekick out loud. I did value my hide in one piece.

Chapter 21

The Lower Halls

Bella was in her beat up jeans and a well-worn t-shirt when I got back, lounging crossways on a chair with her booted feet dangling and her eyes closed. From the rapid movement of her eyes behind the silken lids, I guessed that she was not asleep, but consulting the library. I let her be, and went to change out of the dressy clothes.

She opened her eyes when I came back out of my room. "I think I know what to do, now. It's like... magical DNA."

"Or fingerprints. Either way, I appreciate the help. I could do it, but..." I made a throwing-away gesture of frustration at my own inability to perform much magic. She nodded.

"I'm just happy to be able to help. It would really suck to have to sit in my room while you were out there having all the fun."

I raised an eyebrow - maybe both of them - at her. "You do know this gets dangerous. You remember the troll, and the roc, and..."

She laughed. "Yes, but sitting still won't help me feel better. And," she patted her hip, "it's not like I'm unarmed."

"Don't get me wrong. I'm not going to turn down help. Now, let's go.

I'm thinking we're going to be up late enough as it is, and I don't want to wait until morning."

"Yes, sir," she stuck her tongue out at me, standing and stretching. "I'm ready."

The note's directions took us into the long-abandoned gallery of portraits, in the oldest part of the halls. Court, the sprawling complex that rules Underhill is... underground, mostly. Especially the ancient parts of it, covered under a grassy hill called a tor. Some of the newer parts resemble a fairy tale castle, but that was the part in use, and we were headed further in, and deeper. Bella drew closer to my side as we got into the darkened halls that way.

"How long since these were used?" She asked, looking at tapestries that hung in shattered strips. I knew from experience that the old silk would fall to dust at a touch.

"I think when my mother and father were young... before I was born... this was the part of Court that was all the rage. See, every new generation seems to feel the need to expand, or improve."

"Fairies are like humans, then."

"Pretty much. I've spent more time than most in both worlds, and there are a lot of similarities. But differences, so don't assume the Folke will react the way a human would." I cautioned her.

She nodded. "It's awfully dark back here."

"The elf lights have all burned out and no one bothers to replace them." I explained, pulling a spell out of my pocket and activating it. The globe of light that popped into being bobbed up and floated over our heads. It would follow us for hours, until I put it away, or it burned out, which I didn't expect to happen on this short expedition. "Is that better?"

"Much, thank you."

"Not too much further. The halls go back quite a way, but I don't think Maize would have been willing to go in deep, there are rumors of nasty things taking up residence back there."

"Any truth to it?"

I shrugged. "I haven't been asked to take a look. I have a long list of bad guys to check out, and if you haven't noticed, there is only one of me."

"Yeah, about that..." she started to say something thoughtfully. I interrupted her.

"Take a look at that..." I'd seen it before, and now the hackles on the back of my neck lifted.

She looked where I was pointing. "What? I don't understand."

"Little tracks, in the dust by the wall."

"Too big to be mice."

"Right, and not the right shape."

She bent down to get a closer look. "Like tiny bare footprints. What made these?"

"There are a couple of possibilities. One of them is very unpleasant. Keep your eyes and ears open, and let's make this fast."

We had been strolling leisurely and chatting, unworried, but now I was on high alert. There was no real reason to suspect goblins here, almost in Court, but the way things had been going since the death of the Queen, I wasn't going to discount it entirely. I picked up the pace, and she kept up with me well. It was nice to have a partner.

"In here."

The double doors to the hall stood open, and we stepped silently into the vast, dusty emptiness. On the walls there were paler patches where paintings of ancestors had once hung, and every so often there was an abandoned portrait of some poor soul so obscure they had been forgotten here. I waved my hand, sending the light globe gently spinning out in a flat spiral. We could see where Maize's steps had disturbed the dust, and then a starburst pattern where they ended, and retreated in a crooked pattern toward the door.

"That's where the spell detonated," I observed. "Can you see anything?"

"It would be more of a 'feel,'" she pointed out. "And I think I need to be closer."

I tried to circle around the dusty footprints to preserve them, and we got to the edge of the starburst pattern. "Not too close, in case it still lingers."

She nodded and crouched down, closing her eyes. I turned and looked around the room, which was not fully in the light. The corners were full of moving shadows to match the still-circling globe. It was not a pleasant sensation to try and watch. Bella was mumbling to herself. I suppressed the urge to ask her to hurry it up.

She stood up and dusted off her hands, even though she hadn't touched anything. "I have a good feel for it. If I feel it again, I'll know it."

"Good. Ready to get back?"

She looked at me. "Why, Lom, I believe you are nervous."

"Yes." I didn't bother dignifying that with an explanation. She was looking over my shoulder. "What?"

"Come look at this, and bring the light." She set off toward the near wall. I stifled a curse, and followed her.

"Lom..." she stopped under the oil painting of a man, done at least four centuries ago from the style, and stared up at it. I stared, too.

"He looks like you."

He did, and I knew why. "My great-great grandfather, I believe." I looked for, and found, the plaque on the wall.

"Alonzo Mulvaney. Founder of my family," I read and commented.

"Why is he still hanging in the dark, then, and not at your home?"

"Well, my guess would be, my mother. She doesn't talk about it, but there was a scandal."

"Oh." She fell silent, still staring up at him. I had to admit the resemblance was pretty strong. I had other things on my mind tonight, though.

"Bella. We need to get back."

"Can we take..." she waved at the picture. Since it was a full-length portrait of the man standing with his hands on the rein of a horse, and enclosed in an ornate gilt frame...

"No. That thing weighs as much as you do. And why do you want it, anyway?"

"It's sad that he's all alone here." She brightened. "Oh, I know!"

I felt as much as heard the scurry in the shadows at the far wall. "Bella…"

She waved her hands in an intricate pattern, and the portrait vanished with a soft glow of light and a popping noise.

"What did you just do?" I demanded, distracted by the feeling that we were no longer alone.

"Sent it back to your house." She looked at my face for the first time, and her smile fell away slowly. "What is happening?'

"Move toward the door quickly, but calmly. Don't run, and get a spell ready."

She matched me stride for stride, a trick, since her legs were shorter than mine. She didn't look around, but I could see her eyes were alert. The shadows behind us roiled, like silt in a pond, disturbed by something moving under the water. I still hadn't gotten a clear look at it, but I was trusting my instincts, and every hair on my neck was standing up and shouting danger. We were three levels under the Court, and it was just the two of us. We needed to move fast.

Chapter 22

In Case of Fire

They came out of the shadows in the hall from the wrong direction: the one we had come from.

"Damn. Bella, stay with me!"

I didn't even slow down, just turned and headed down the dark hall, in the wrong direction. She ran at my elbow, or rather, flew, as I realized her feet were only hitting the floor every so often as she loped along next to me.

"What are they?" She shouted, as the war cries of the mob behind us rose to a shrill peak.

"Goblins. It had to be goblins..." I hated the little monsters. Born and bred in the dark, they served no masters, but occasionally did dirty jobs for the Low Court.

"Where are we going?"

Valid question. It had been a while since I had explored down here. Right now, I was looking for someplace we could get back upstairs, and the only thing I could remember was down another level and over about three hallways. We ran down the shallow stairs, and the goblins paused at the top of the steps. That made me look back to figure out why they had stopped. Bella shrieked. I snapped my head around, and saw why the goblins had stopped. They had herded us into the troll's lair.

I snapped the spell I'd been carrying in my hand toward the nearest troll, and pulled my weapon. Bella had her gun in the wrong hand, and was throwing spells with the other one. I started to correct her, and then realized that the troll facing us was falling. He threw his hands up as he fell through the massive hole that had suddenly appeared under his feet, and I saw a ridiculous look of dismay on his face as he went. The next spell dropped a lot of the ceiling on the other three standing trolls. The one I had hit with a fireball was rolling on the floor in agony.

"Great job! What the hell was that?"

"Um... an excavation spell?"

I laughed out loud, standing there in the dusty mess. We couldn't keep going, the trolls would get free of the debris in moments. There was a mess of goblins at the top of the stairs. But I wasn't worried. We might be surrounded, but that just meant better range of fire.

"Don't hold back! You don't want the goblins to take you alive."

She set her shoulders against mine, her wings folded tightly, but still a ridge next to my backbone. The trolls were still down, a slow thrashing all I could see of them. The old beams and plaster had more heft than I'd thought.

The goblins were dancing at the top of the stairs, jeering and gibbering. I couldn't catch most of what they were saying, and was grateful Bella didn't speak goblin.

"What now?" She asked me.

"Well, I don't think the structure is sound anymore in the direction of the trolls. So..."

"Got it." She spun round, her wings snapping open, and both hands flicked out, tossing an arc of spells up the stairs.

The spells she threw glowed redly, and when they hit, they splashed fire. Upwards, where it stuck to everything. Bella had created a napalm spell. She threw another handful, and this time, the goblins scattered as the orbs fell among them. The screams of those already burning replaced the chanting and jeering.

"Why did you do that?" I shouted, leveling a shot at the first troll to stagger to his feet.

"In case of stairs, use fire!" She caroled gleefully, flying higher and throwing more spells.

"How are we supposed to get out of here?" I demanded, trying to hit the troll's eye this time.

"Like this." She threw another spell, this time in the direction of the trolls, with her eyes closed.

"Holy mother Titania, woman, learn to aim!" My voice went up at least an octave as I tried to backpedal without getting into her sticky fire. The last of the goblins were in full retreat. The floor under me was starting to creak ominously between the holes and the burning stairs. My britches were getting warm.

The big blue spell bounced off the troll's head and hit the ceiling above him, where it detonated. I got a little confused at that point, because when the shockwave hit me, I hit the ground. Hard, and on the seat of my pants. I was afraid at first I'd fallen in the fire, and then realized I was just seeing stars from the force of the blow. Then the floor tilted and I grabbed for something, anything, to keep me from falling.

I got Bella's arm. She was saying something, but I couldn't hear her over the ringing in my ears. She bellowed and I got the message, "Hold onto me!"

I clung to her waist, and she took off like a rocket for the hole she'd blown in the ceiling. I went along for the ride, looking down at the destruction as we made our escape. I was about to unlimber my wings, when she had us up, and into a deserted hallway for a light landing. I sprawled on the floor and tried to catch my breath. Bella crouched over me.

"Lom! Are you OK?"

"Put it out! Put it out, put it out!" I gasped, trying to sit up.

"What?"

"The fire! Do you have a water spell or an extinguisher in your bag of tricks?"

I flailed frantically. Bella had no idea what she had done. The halls might be covered in earth, but they were largely wood, and tapestry, and... I was sending message spells spinning off my fingertips, and she had a look of dismay on her face as what she had done sunk in.

She might have saved us for a moment, but if the fire went out of control, the whole of Court could be lost. She took to the air again, and dove into the hole.

"No! That's not..." I threw myself flat on the floor as close as I could get to the hole and looked down. "What I meant, " I finished softly, knowing she couldn't hear me.

The heat and smoke in my face caused my eyes to tear up. I couldn't see where she had gone, so when I felt a hand on my shoulder I rolled over quickly, on alert, but didn't point my weapon. The Majordomo was on one knee next to me. I relaxed minutely.

"Lom? Are you injured?" he asked loudly enough I could hear him. The ringing in my ears was starting to subside.

I shook my head. "I don't think so. The fire..."

"We're on it."

"It's not just that, there are goblins and trolls down there." I pointed, and finished, "Bella is down there, too."

He looked alarmed. "She is fallen?"

"No, went to try and put the fire out. It got started while we were fighting them off. But warn your men, I don't know how many are left and they are likely crazy mad."

He nodded grimly and stood to call directions to the crew arriving with spells and tools to fight the fire.

I tried to stand, and sucked in my breath at the pain. Somewhere during the battle, I had been hurt. I gave it up, and lay back down. The Majordomo bent over me.

"I'm sending the healer to you. Stay put."

I waved him off. I wasn't likely to move anywhere right now, and I still didn't know where Bella was. "Go find Bella, Joe. Please... I can't right now."

His gnarled face softened. "Got it, Lom, don't worry, I'll see that she's safe."

I closed my eyes, and opened my Sight. Underhill, it was not usually as useful as it was above. There was just too much clutter, unlike the human realm where magic stood out like a flare. I knew what Bella's magic signature looked like, and if I couldn't go to her, I could at least help find her. She wasn't far from me, I figured out quickly.

From the position just slightly under me, and to one side, I guessed she was... standing on the ceiling of the hall below me? That was peculiar, as was the positioning of the crew Joe was holding back, below me, and in front of her, which I was guessing was well back of the top of the stairs where the goblins had been. I saw a few ragged green magic flares that were the verminous creatures trying to slip away past the crew. I saw one of them blink out, killed on the spot, I guessed. But why wasn't the crew fighting the fire, and what had happened to the trolls?

I gave it up, and with a grunt of effort, rolled over so I could see down into the floor below. It was still hard to make anything out through the smoke, and now, steam. The ragged hole that gaped in the floor below explained what had happened to the trolls. They had fallen at least one level, and were either disoriented or had decided to leave the crazy fairy alone. I didn't think we had killed any of them, my pistol shots were unlikely to have hit a sensitive place at that range in the chaos. Bella had been trying to slow them down or divert them with the spells she had used.

The goblins, on the other hand, had died in droves. I could see blackened bodies on the stairs, now that whatever Bella was doing to suppress the fire was working faster. There were no more flames showing, just lots of steam rising. Unfortunately, the hole I was looking through was acting as a chimney, and it meant I couldn't see again.

The wood elf healer came and touched my arm, helping me roll away from the hole. He spread a spell over me, and I could feel the warmth and a slight tingle as it sank through my body.

"You have cracked ribs, here," he spread his fingers over my chest. "Your tailbone is badly bruised, which I will help with, so you can walk."

"'Preciate that, Melcar." I told him. We had worked together many times, when I had come home busted up after a job. "What's going on below?"

"Ah, it is progressing very quickly. Princess Bella has the fire almost out, the crew is damping hotspots, and clearing... debris."

I knew from the distaste in the last word he meant goblin bodies. "Anyone else hurt?"

"I will look at Princess Bella as soon as she will let me. I think she has some burns, but she refuses to leave until the fire is declared out."

"Tell the crew to be careful with goblin weapons. They put nasty crap on the edges that can posion you."

He raised an eyebrow. "I will pass that along. This is, you know, the closest our ancient enemy has come in generations."

"Yeah." I tried sitting up. Still hurt, but not as badly. "It's not happy-making."

I didn't think any of them had had time enough to truly process how close the Court itself had come to being under attack. If Bella and I had not been out here, and tripped the offensive before they came to the inhabited halls, who knows what would have happened. Folke don't have armies, and Court doesn't even have trained fighting men in any great number. Melcar helped me get all the way to my feet, and although I swayed a little, I was standing.

I looked down at him, feeling every year of my age. "Better check on Bella. She's stubborn, and running on adrenaline."

He nodded, and rustled away, the leaves woven in his hair wilted from the heat of the fire. I followed more slowly. Getting down to the stairs wasn't too difficult, over a hall and down a set of servant's stairs I hadn't known were behind a blank panel. As I took the steep, narrow stairs cautiously, I wondered how many more of these there were, and if the goblins knew where they were.

At the foot of the stairs was a young sentry. His eyes widened when he saw me, and I realized I must look a sight. I gestured toward the hall behind him.

"All clear out there?"

He nodded, "They say the fire's out, sir."

I grunted and walked out into the chaos. Joe's crew was systematically cleaning, at this point, stacking bodies in one spot on a tarp of oilcloth for removal, and one guy with a pushbroom was shoving what appeared to be watery suds along the floor and down the stairs. There was soot everywhere. Another two were cutting down the wet, ruined tapestries from the walls extending some twenty feet back from where the fire had been stopped. I would have felt guilty, but I knew what condition they had been in to begin with.

I looked for Joe and Bella and didn't see them, so I started moving toward the stairs. They were surprisingly undamaged, with some fire-marked craters where I supposed the spells had initially hit and burned, but the old wood had not ignited wholesale. Bella's spell had been more restrained than my first impression of it was. I spotted her and Joe on the edge of the troll hole, looking down into it.

"Bella." I greeted her wearily. "Are you all right?"

She looked at me blankly for a second, her hair plastered to her cheeks and forehead, sooty streaks on her skin from shoving it out of her eyes. She looked exhausted.

Chapter 23

Aftermath & Punishment

"Lom. Oh, thank goodness." She held out her arms and I hugged her without thinking, feeling my ribs protest, but not caring. She was alive and whole. She let go after a moment and looked intently at me. "Are you hurt badly?"

I shook my head. "Are you?"

She showed me her left arm, which had a streaky burn from wrist to elbow. "It doesn't hurt too much. Yet. I wanted to make certain the fire was out. And we're wondering where the trolls have gone."

I looked at Joe, who was regarding us thoughtfully. "I think they will have retreated. Trolls don't like fire, or opposition, for that matter. We embarrassed them more than anything. I don't think you want to send a team after them..."

He nodded agreement emphatically. We both knew that was a good way to get people killed. I went on, "but there should be sentries at the stairs from now on. If there were some goblins, there will be more, and the trolls might come back."

"I'll take care of it. You two, go get some rest and clean-up, then the King will want to see you."

"I'd think he would want to see us now." I pointed out, not that I was arguing with some time to recover. I was swaying on my feet again.

Joe nodded. "He understands there are injuries to heal. Melcar..." Joe looked over at the little wood elf, who was coming with bandages in his hands. "Take care of Princess Bella, and then see they get to their rooms."

Bella submitted to the bandaging, then Melcar snapped his fingers and before I could protest, we were bubbled and in our rooms. I sank into the nearest chair.

"I need to examine you, Princess," he told her. "If you would prefer, in your room?"

She shook her head tiredly. "Here is fine. Do you need me to undress?"

"Perhaps the trousers off? They have metal in them."

She nodded and peeled her wet jeans off with difficulty. White bikini panties were revealed briefly before the T-shirt fell back down over them. I was in no state to appreciate the long legs revealed, instead seeing the bruising on her thigh already appearing. She'd banged something hard, there.

Melcar repeated the diagnosis spell he had used on me, letting it melt through her body. She sighed as it did. "That helps right away, doesn't it? A touch of analgesic?"

He looked pleased. "Yes, I put a little relaxer in there for the muscles. It's my own tweak to the spell of my grandfather."

"Well, thank you." She told him with a little smile.

"You are not injured, there is some bruising and the burn, of course. I put a salve on the burn, it ought to be better by morning."

"Magic works better than human medicine."

He shook his head, "I combine them, you know. Magic is not always efficacious against some diseases. Although fairy is not as likely to contract cancer, there is so much human intermingled now, it does happen."

He picked up the small bag he had carried the bandages and salve in, and made it disappear. "Now, Lom..."

He advanced on me, and I let him come. I was too achy to move already, and I knew I needed what he had. He set the spell on my forehead.

"You have ten minutes to get into bed." He cautioned. "Then you will sleep for at least six hours."

"I know." I tried to stand and groaned. Bella bent over me and offered a hand, which I accepted, and then leaned on her as we headed toward my room. Behind us, Melcar called out "Good night!" before popping off.

"Damn." I grabbed the door for support.

"What hurts?" She sounded concerned.

"What doesn't? No, this is about Melcar."

"He seemed nice, and very skillful."

"He is both. He's also an old gossip. He's going to cheerfully announce that we headed off to bed together." I sighed. It didn't seem like a terrible idea, but not when I hurt in every bruise, and was about to be knocked cold by a sleeping spell.

"Let him. Is Court that Victorian?"

I could see where she would get that idea, after some of the costumes earlier. "No. Court is... " I started to slur, and she got me sitting on the edge of the bed and undid my belt. I regarded the top of her head with affectionate amusement. She pulled my pants off. "Court is everything goesh. Like Shummer of free love..." She lowered me back into bed, one arm crooked behind my neck. I was rapidly going boneless. I tried one last thing. "Bella, thanks..."

I don't know if she responded to that. I'd like to think the warm lips I felt on mine were her response, but I think I was already dreaming by then. There were a lot of dreams, that night, some exciting and involving her, but those would blend into running from the monsters behind me, and the high note of the Huntsman's horn ringing in my brain.

Waking up hurt. Well, not the waking up part. The trying to move part led to me making undignified noises until I got vertical, and staggered for the bathroom. After that, I became aware that bathing was highest priority. It should help with the stiffness, too. I'm not sure how long it took until I was finally ready to face the world, but Bella was sitting at the table with a cup of coffee in front of her when I emerged from my room.

She gave me a lopsided smile. "I'll let Joe know you're up. Coffee?"

I think I did a reasonable zombie groan, because she chuckled and poured a cup before leaving me to walk over and open the door to the hall.

I didn't hear what she said, I was too busy inhaling the black ichor of the gods. She came back and sat down, picking up her own cup.

"I said to let you get through your second cup and then we would be down to the meeting. He said to tell you no rush. He's awfully young."

I nodded. One thing Underhill had few enough of were youngsters, so it made sense they would be assigned to safe places like our door. The older men would be in the basements holding guard against the darkness there. I finished the first cup, and prepared the second more slowly. Bella was in a chatty mood.

"You were serious, last night, Melcar would have said we were sleeping together?"

I winced. I had forgotten about saying that. "Yeah, probably. Don't worry about it, though."

"I will worry about it. It's none of their business who I sleep with, first, and second, I'm not having an affair with you."

"You wouldn't be the first princess to have a little fun with her escort. Sex is not regarded as a big deal, Underhill, because conception without magical intervention is so rare."

She raised an eyebrow. "Are you suggesting..."

The door opened, and we both turned to see who it was. Joe stood in the doorway in full regalia. I wondered if he'd had any sleep at all.

"We're ready." I put my cup down, reluctantly. I'd just swallowed the last of my coffee.

Bella murmured, "we will talk about this later," before sweeping past me to the door. I wondered what that meant, then shrugged and followed Joe to the King's small reception room.

This was not where I usually met him, which meant this would be a much more formal affair than our sessions usually were. Which, now that I thought about it, made sense, as this was a much more serious threat than we had faced in my memory. He was seated in a small throne, looking grayer than last we met, and we walked across the red carpet to stand in front of him. I gave him a small bow, my usual greeting to my sovereign, and Bella followed my lead, instead of the more customary feminine curtsey. He raised an eyebrow, but didn't say anything.

"Learoyd." His deep voice sounded tired, which matched his appearance. His use of my first name wasn't a good sign, as he usually just called me Lom.

"Majesty." I replied calmly. I knew he wasn't angry at us, just agitated about the threat.

He looked at Bella. "Princess Belladonna. I did not intend our first meeting to come about like this. I have fond memories of your grandmother Lavendar, and I would have liked to hear about her life in the human realm."

"I did not know you knew her. I know very little about her life Underhill."

He smiled a little, then. "We will have much to talk about when the chance comes. But for now, I'm afraid, treachery is afoot."

"The attacks on the princesses were just the tip of the lever." I filled in. "The lack of a Queen means our enemies feel Court is weak."

"Our Enemy." He corrected me heavily, "the only one there has been from the mists of time. The invasion into Court is merely minions sent to harry us."

"Nasty business." I agreed.

He regarded us silently for a moment. I'm sure he had been told all about Bella in the last few hours, her appearance and actions from the party through to the aftermath of the battle no one else had seen. He knew me, had known my capacity for violence for years. She was something else.

"Belladonna, I will not sugar-coat my words to you. When the initial reports came in, we were afraid and angry at the destruction you wrought."

She looked surprised. "What was I supposed to do? We were in danger of being killed."

He didn't protest her talking back to him, just nodded. "And on reflection, I saw that, too. I was also told, at length..." His gaze slipped beyond us, and I guessed he was looking at Joe, who would be standing at attention in front of the doors, in his Majordomo role. "That you minimized the damage at great personal risk to yourself, in the aftermath. Thank you for that. However, I am afraid that you are so powerful and adept, the rest of court may not accept your courage, only seeing that you are... different."

Boy, did he have that one right. Court was going to be a hotbed of rumor, lies, and fear at this point. And Bella would take the brunt of it, as she had revealed herself to be talented beyond most of their wildest dreams with magic.

"They are wondering, already, where you came from, and how you came to be able to do such magic, with such little effort." She opened her mouth to respond, but he held up a hand to stop her. "We will talk, at length, about this. But your recklessness is a grave concern to us all."

She blinked. She was being treated like a child, and I knew she didn't like it. I also knew he was wrong, that he was assuming she was well-trained, when in reality I had given her the barest of starts. Everything else was book-learning. To him, it looked like she had no judgement at all, and to her, she was only using what looked like it might work, in desperation. I started to speak. He went on, not even acknowledging me.

"Learoyd, you will assemble a team." His face showed his grief. "It's like the old, old days, eh, boy?"

I nodded. Not since I was a youth had Court been under this much strain, and it showed. "I can call enough, I think, of the old crew."

"But not her." he pointed at Bella. "Princess Belladonna, you are simply too valuable for me to risk allowing you to be in the dangerous situations Lom will have to face. Also, until I am certain your allegiance is to us, I cannot risk allowing you to be privy to our further plans. You are not a prisoner, my dear, simply confined to Court until further notice."

Bella gasped. "At least let me help. I can prove that I am not your enemy."

He shook his head. "You are so very powerful, and I don't think you realize the true extent of that. I don't think you are an enemy, but you will have to prove it to others."

"If you don't want me here, at least let me go home," she protested.

He raised a shaggy grey eyebrow again. "Up to the human realm? I'm afraid that is not an option at all for you any longer. Magic is too risky to expose humans to it, and potentially lead them Underhill, an invasion the Folke might not survive. We all fear that."

This was what had sent me on innumerable jobs into Human worlds, after all, the fear that we would be discovered and eradicated. Bella had no real way of knowing that, of course, unless Lavendar had mentioned it, and as she herself was a refugee from Court, I somehow doubted that. Bella might look calm to the King, but I could see she was about to break down.

"Then what is to become of me?" She asked, softly enough we almost didn't hear her.

"We will talk about that in time. For now..." He gestured, and Joe opened the doors. "This is your escort while Learoyd is unable to fulfill his duty. If you will follow him back to your rooms..."

She turned without speaking again and left quickly, forcing her young guard, who I recognized as Joe Jr., the Majordomo's son, to follow at a trot. He would take good care of her. I looked back at the King.

Chapter 24

The Team Gathers

"Sir..."

He stood up, with effort, and came down off the dias. "Come on, Lom, let's finish this like civilized men."

I followed him into the smaller room with overstuffed chairs. He folded into one, and I took the other. "Sir, you need to know that Bella..."

He held up a hand. "I don't want to talk about her. She almost burned down the Court, is the woman crazy? I don't know what we are going to do with her, she certainly can't be allowed out of our control."

I rubbed my face. I knew from experience there was no reasoning with him in this mood. King Corwin was a good ruler, fair, just, and usually, reasonable. I'd give him time, and he would come around. If he really did sit and talk with Bella, and she kept her temper, she would most likely win him over quickly. I shifted gears.

"I need Alger."

He winced. I knew how he felt about the old man, and usually, it was mutual. The problem was, Alger had forgotten more about the old halls of Court than anyone else living remembered. I'd done some exploring in my younger years, but all that made me sure of was that I didn't know enough. There could be anything back there.

"He'll insist on joining the Court."

"Yes, and you know I won't need him all the time, so he will be up here on occasion. I'll try to keep him busy, though."

Corwin huffed through his mustache. "All right, I'll lift the ban. He can come back to Court."

I nodded, not having expected to have to fight hard for anyone under these circumstances. "I'll give Joe a list of a few others, the rest can be your choice. I'll want no more than a dozen."

"Will that be enough?"

"If I need more, I retreat." I pointed out. "This is just an exploration, to see what we are up against. After Court is secure, I'll want even less for the next part of the mission."

He narrowed his eyes. "Are you certain, Lom?"

I shook my head. "Not at all. But I know where the root of this must be, and I can ask no one but myself..." and Bella, I silently added, if she ever forgives me for this day's words... "to venture into such dangerous territory."

"We underestimate, you, Lom."

I was surprised. The royal we, and the gentle tone were unlike him. "Sir?"

"Sending you on tasks, thinking you are simply a mercenary, and only bound to us by family needs."

"All true, my King." I grinned at him, and he smiled back.

"But you are truly loyal to us, are you not?"

I met his eyes squarely. "You're the best man for the position. You're screwing up right now, though."

"And why is that?" he demanded indignantly.

"Because you removed our best asset from the game."

"Ah." He sat back, and beamed. "Now, that I did not know. I see that you want her for more than a toy, and with her power she does have potential."

My turn to wince. There had been stories going around about Bella and I. "She is much more than a mere toy."

"I will talk to her. And I will be gentle, but she is far too dangerous to allow unchecked Underhill. She's a loose cannon."

I sighed. "Sir... she is not familiar with our customs. She did not want to come Underhill, hell, she threatened to shoot me if I came back a second time with the papers."

"Really?" He was amused, now, the corners of his eyes crinkling.

"Yes. She just wants to go home, and she's going to be very unhappy finding out she is a prisoner. She will blame it on me, and you know what? She's right." My mouth drew back in a rictus of a smile as the full import of it sank in, and the bitterness fully hit me. "I brought her here, and I taught her what little she knows about magic. So whatever she started to feel for me..." I remembered the kiss, and felt unaccustomed moisture spring to my eyes. "It's dead, sir, and I don't blame her. Now, if you will excuse me, I have work to do."

I got up, and out of the room, before he had a chance to say a word. I didn't care if I'd angered him. He needed me. All of Underhill needed me, which is why the one person I cared about in it, I couldn't go to when she needed me. Not that she was going to want to see me ever again.

I headed straight for the scene of last night's disaster, spinning message orbs off my fingertips as I went. I couldn't see Bella, but I could make certain she was not utterly alone and at the mercy of the cats of the court. For one thing, the last worry I needed was whether she was safe. I was going to have an interesting few days, as was my crew. I wasn't happy.

The clean-up was going well. The holes in the floor had been cut square, preparatory to replacing the floorboards and beams that supported them. The walls and floors had been washed roughly. I wasn't sure they would do more than that, this far back, appearances were unneeded. Some of the boards on the stairs that had suffered the most damage had been removed, so I stepped carefully as I made my way down them, to talk to the furthest sentries.

"What have you seen, boys?" I greeted them.

"Not much. Sometimes I think a shadow moves, but it's a trick of the light. We put up more globes…" he gestured above him, "and that helped a lot."

I nodded. "They are watching us. But they hate the light."

He looked nervous. I slapped him on the shoulder. "We'll chase them out soon. I'm putting together a crew now, let the guys know that I can take a few. We'll head out in the morning."

"Yes, sir… Lom. I'll do that."

I left him peering into the shadows intently. I wanted to see what the lower levels looked like, but I knew better than to go down alone. They would still be there in a few hours. Joe was waiting for me at the top of the stairs, still in full regalia.

"Will he forgive me?" I asked lightly.

Joe shook his head. "He's not angry with you, he never is for long. He's just worried, this time."

"I'm a touch concerned, myself."

I took a moment to study Joe as he watched the clean-up crew working. The old man didn't look old, and the only reason I called him old was that he had been Majordomo since I was a child. He was a pixie, like me, and our race seemed to gravitate towards positions of service. Not servants, always, but places where they took care of others. In Joe's case, that was the King, and Court. What my mother had been for the late Queen.

"Ever get tired, Joe?"

"What else would I do?" he asked without bothering to look at me. "This is my life, and it has its moments. Like this one."

Now he did look at me, and smile. "Are you tired?"

I rubbed my face. "Sore still, but no. Ready to fight. How fast do you think we can get supplies in place?"

He shook his head. "Ah, the impatience of youth. Discover a goblin horde in the basement, and you want to be off in search of little pricks..."

I laughed out loud. I'd forgotten how low his sense of humor could go. "Not all of us are made of wood, old man..."

He started to grin, and I finished up, "some of us are made of steel."

Now he laughed with me.

"Should be arriving any minute now, everything on the list you sent me."

"You move fast."

He shrugged, "no, I delegate. I just wish I could come with you."

I shook my head at him. "Best stay safe from all those little pricks. Besides, I need someone to have my back."

He grunted, and looked back up the hall. "Ah, there they are, now."

I'd asked for weapons, food, and bedding for a dozen men for a week. I figured if we couldn't reach the extent of the halls in that time, we were doing something wrong. Which was why we wouldn't leave until Alger got there, of course. While we were down there, we would be able to tag places with message spells so backup could be summoned and arrive within minutes. Without the tags in place, there was no way to have them come to a place they had never been and would have to find in the dark.

We would still be on the pointy end of the stick. Or, in this case, the myriad pointy ends. Why did it have to be goblins, in the dark?

"Lots of glow globes, right?"

"Enough to light the whole damn Court. We may run short up front, but you will have the ability to see."

"Joe..." I looked him in the eye. "If you need anything, magically, ask Bella. She doesn't have much experience, but she knows a lot, once she knows the question. Give her a minute to think about it, and she has the power to make it happen."

He blinked, and processed what I had said to him. "I will... take that under advisement."

"I made sure she has company, and I know your son's a good man. But once I leave tomorrow, I can't worry about her."

He nodded. "You won't have to."

"Alger's coming." I shifted topics to something less painful. "He should be here tonight, if I have to guess."

"I thought you would require his expertise. I have taken the liberty of preparing his rooms."

I shook my head. "You don't need me to tell you anything, do you?"

"Is there a mole in the court?"

I raised an eyebrow. "Yes, that I am sure of. But no, I don't know who it is, and with only a few itchy feelings, I can't point fingers."

"I will be watching."

"You're always watching."

Footsteps coming down the hall caught my attention.

The fairy walking towards us looked like something out of an old movie. Black leather jacket, white t-shirt, jeans, and biker boots. His black hair was gelled perfectly. I held out my hand, and he shook it gravely.

"Been a while."

"Not long enough," he responded, then nodded at Joe. "How're they hanging?"

Joe raised an eyebrow at him, and then shook his head. "Perfectly level, until I see you coming, and then they want to hide."

Dean guffawed. "I may steal that one."

"Be my guest. And now, I must return to the front."

Dean watched him stride up the hallway. "So, Lom..."

"Goblins, and trolls in the basement. That I know of. You in?"

He grunted. "How many of us?"

"'Bout a dozen."

"Just enough to trip one another up." He flexed his fingers and popped a tiny spell flame on the tip of one, then lit a cigar.

"It's my show."

"I'm in." He shrugged, looking down the hall into the shadows. "This is a new one on me. Could be fun."

"For your values of fun, yeah."

He clapped me on the shoulder and went to look at the equipment. I sighed softly. This had been fun when I was younger, now it was just work.

"Well, m'boy!" A voice boomed out of nowhere, and Alger appeared in its wake. "Together again!"

"I've had enough backslapping." I sidestepped him. "You're here to be a guide, and when it's over, we're going to have a word. Or several."

His face fell. "Lom, you take all the fun out of it."

"It's not supposed to be fun, it's just vermin clean-up."

He brightened again. "I have some new spells to try out!"

"As long as they don't involve fire."

He paused thoughtfully. "Maybe a little?"

"I'll take it under advisement. Take a look at the gear, and let me know if there's anything else you need."

"The Court is providing?" He rubbed his hands together and stalked off.

After another hour, there were five of us, silently getting packs of gear together, all of us old fools with a mission on our mind. Dean, Alger, and then the wood elf named Ash with his brother Olive. They were related to Ellie, I'd never been able to figure out quite how, but they were tough, uncomplaining, and moved like they could read one another's minds.

Melcar arrived with a rustle, and exchanged nods with Ash and Olive, who were probably also related to him. I think all wood elves are connected somehow. He held out his hand to me, and I shook.

"You're coming with us?" I was surprised the King would let his best healer go on a dangerous mission.

"I think I will be needed," he replied simply.

"No offense, but I hope you won't."

He looked around. "There are six of us? Then I will let Joe know to send a matching number. He has a list of volunteers we evaluated."

"I appreciate that. When they are ready, we will head out."

"It is late." Alger came up while we were talking and pointed out the obvious.

"There won't be a party tonight for you to attend. And down here, time is meaningless." I turned to face the group, which was swelling as Joe's men arrived. Now there were a full dozen, and the team was complete.

Chapter 25

Sealing the Halls

"A nyone tired?"

A chorus of negative replies. I looked back at Alger. "I don't want to go far, but I do want to shake down and get everyone in the proper mood."

It didn't take long to get everyone ready. We'd never worked together as a team, but I didn't have anything complicated in mind. If we had to clear out two halls at once, send six guys in each. Alger would set wards as we went, essentially creating tripwires that would alarm if enemies or unidentified passed through them (or rather, tried to), and we'd repeat until we had gotten to the heart of the tor.

If it went well, the goblins would retreat in front of us, back into their underground lairs that lay even deeper than the Court. We'd seal any entrances we found, and the King would set up routine patrols to make sure new ones weren't dug later. If it went badly... I'd blow that bridge up when we got to it.

I put Melcar and Alger in the middle of the group. Neither was a fighter in any trained sense, although Alger was a tough old bastard, I'd give him that. Dean took point. Dean always took point, and I wasn't going to argue with him.

We started out in the level below where Bella and I had made our stand against the initial invasion. There was still a mess down here, sooty footprints showing where at least one of the trolls had jogged down the hall deeper into the hill. With smudging and carpet, we couldn't be certain if there had been one, or more. I remembered three for certain from the fight, and when we found a nasty mess of congealed blood, we knew I'd injured one.

"What's behind us, sir?"

"William, right?"

He nodded. I went on "Joe and the clean-up crew checked the halls and set a ward there..." I pointed at the cross hallway. "So we are going to start here, but we'll check that stub before we go any further in."

I gestured. "Dean, Take William and..." The other man I indicated supplied his name.

"Henry, sir."

"Go with them. Let Dean take point. He's a bad-guy magnet, so he'll take fire and you guys can mop up after him."

That was the way it worked with Dean. He was a sucker for thrills, and a berserker in a fight. Not a team player, but still, useful in a fight.

Dean walked close to the wall to avoid the debris, and they disappeared around the corner. I turned to Alger.

"What can we expect from here?"

He picked up a splinter of broken beam and looked at it. "Holy Oberon, what did she use?"

"Excavating spell," I supplied laconically. I didn't want to get into an after action report.

"Clever girl," he said admiringly, then used the splinter to sketch in the sooty carpet. Where he raised the nap of the cloth it worked well to draw.

There were three parallel great halls for at least another short ways, then there were only two. Deepest into the tor, there was one.

"Once," he commented in a mournful voice as he drew it, "Lined with benches and tables, and rushes scattered on the stone floor. It was the hall of warriors, and horns of ale were drunk while songs of valor were sung."

"You're not that old." I pointed out.

He sighed, "no, but it was a simpler time."

"And a short, nasty, brutish life was all you could expect. All right, that is our destination, to clear to the..." I pointed at his sketch. "What is that?"

"Fireplace. Big enough to roast an ox in."

"No doubt stolen from some poor human farmer. No wonder our ancestors had such a bad reputation."

"Very true," he agreed.

"The tricky bit is going to be the three halls. I'm not sure I want to split us up into groups of four."

"We could always start off with the central one, ward off the side, and clear them one at a time down to here..." Melcar pointed at the angled joining of the third hall into the center one.

"Works. Alger, ward off the far hall, then. Let's wait for Dean and the boys, and tonight we'll head for there, then camp."

I straightened up from my crouch stiffly. I was still achy from last night, but moving would help that. I really didn't want to back goblins into a warded corner, so we would come back here and clear from top to bottom in each hall, driving them (hopefully) toward the exits.

We were a sloppy bunch. No attempt at military precision marching. None of us had the training for that. But there were enough hunters with us, used to moving slowly, quietly, and patiently, that I wasn't worried. We were a big enough group that walking into an ambush seemed unlikely. I sent a cluster of light globes spiralling into the hall, and we filed around the debris pile and deeper into the dark.

I had decreed that the rooms off all the halls were simply to be warded and sealed. We didn't have the time or manpower to clear each one of them. Even so, our progress was slowed by having to stop every so often and do this. Dean prowled ahead, restlessly. We had almost reached the junction when he came back and headed straight for me.

"Found something," he reported. I followed him back up the hall, Alger tagging along in curiosity.

Something turned out to be a familiar pattern in the dust. We bent over it, studying what the signs said.

"Someone brought in the trolls," I stated the obvious, looking at the starburst of a burst spell, and the three sets of dusty tracks coming out of it. Wherever they had come from, they had been wet, and their feet had thus made a little mud for the first few steps, which had dried into a crusty outline of footsteps. Tiny crumbles of this continued toward the front of Court for a few feet, and as we moved, some of those wavered and fell. The powdery dust didn't hold up well.

"Not that long ago," agreed Dean.

"Not a lot of people knew where Bella and I were going last night. This... clears up something."

I flicked a message spell into being and murmured a memo to Joe, then sent it spinning off in flight toward him. All three of us watched it go. The mole in the court was the only one who would have tried to ambush us last night.

"What about the goblins, then?" Dean asked, looking down the hall again, into the weird shadows.

"They are less controllable. I'm guessing that was a long-term plan, and the trolls were a hasty improvisation. We still have an infestation."

I took a few steps deeper into the hall, avoiding the evidence. Facing the shadows, I spoke in goblin.

"Go back to where you came from. Only fire and death await you here."

There was a scrabbling sound in the dark, but nothing else. I shrugged. It wasn't likely to work, but anything was worth a try. The rest of the group came up behind me.

"Keep moving. They are here, but not attacking yet. If you are hit, and it breaks the skin, see Melcar right away, even if it's just a scratch." I looked around, and made sure everyone understood me. Dean led off, at a slow amble. He wasn't as relaxed as he was making out, though, and I saw his hand slip into a pocket for a spell to fondle as he walked.

I was a rarity amongst my group, I pondered as we moved from door to door. I carried two guns, and had the ability to 'port more within seconds from my armory. The Folke relied on their magic, but I couldn't do that, with my disability. Today, I was carrying a shotgun slung under my arm, because a load of #4 shot would work just fine on goblins, and had a nice spread that might eliminate more than one.

We reached the junction. There was the angled hall off to our left, and on our right, a cross corridor to the other hall we would have to clear. Alger stalked from side to side at the end of the hall, muttering and waving his twig wand. I sighed. We still had two more to do, and this was getting tedious.

"Drink something, then let's get back to the left hall." I ordered, taking a pull at my water bag myself.

We didn't quite doubletime back to the top, but it was a much faster move now that we didn't have to worry about sealing doors. Alger set his wand to the seal between the cross corridor and the left hall, and I nodded. He brought it down, and as it came down, there was a shower of goblin arrows flying through it.

They had been waiting for us, knowing we would get around to that ward eventually. Dean skipped back about two steps, Alger just stood calmly, the arrows that hit him sparking and falling to the ground. The rest of us were out of range. Goblins didn't have the pull to effectively use the longbow, for which I was profoundly grateful.

They do favor a massed charge, and that was what we were facing now. Saliva dripped from jagged teeth as the leaders screamed and hurled themselves headlong at us. Dean flicked a spell that seemed to be an airburst of sticky liquid, while I calmly fired into the bodies of those nearest. Goblins are more translucent than anything, having evolved with their centuries underground, but their green ichor makes them look green. Especially as they explode.

Alger had calmly chucked a single spell into their midst, and as it arced to head-height on a goblin, about waist high to me, it detonated. There was, for a stunned split second, a spherical void, which then collapsed with a terrific 'boom.' I knew that noise. Alger was using the spell Bella had wrought such destruction with only last night. The difference was, he wasn't using it to drop the structure on our enemy (and incidentally, ourselves), he was using it to displace the bodies of the enemy.

The result was that we were all splattered with green goo as halves and bits of goblins rained back down on the floor of the hall. The ceiling was... indescribable. If there were any comments behind me, I couldn't hear them, partly deafened from the spell. I strode forward, the ground alternating between crunchy and slippery with every step. I was going to have to retire these boots after this mission. Dean's liquid had hardened instantaneously, with the result that at the leading edge, there were masses of clear resin with goblins trapped in them. It was a surreal scene.

I let Dean get clear out in front, and waved back Alger, irritably, gesturing for two of Joe's guys to get up with me and put him closer to center. I figured we were all a little deaf, and didn't even try to speak. A goblin came up out of a pile of corpse... bits, knife in hand, and face contorted in a snarl. I shot him, then reloaded. I only carried six shots, and that was with one ready to go.

Behind me, as I reached the far edge of the carnage, I could hear a muffled thump and curse as someone fell in the mess. I shouted over my shoulder, "See Melcar!" but didn't slow down, moving at a fast trot with weapon ready. There were doors ahead, one on each side of the hall, and some of the fleeing horde would have taken refuge in there.

I had a warding spell, and slapped it on the closed door. Dean, already on the other side of them, circled back and we took up stances on each side of the door that was hanging ajar slightly, the hinges rusted through so it was at an odd angle. It wasn't going to be easy to close or open; when they'd built Court they had liked to use solid materials, and this door was twice my height, and made of carved oak thick enough to stop bullets. I waved Alger forward.

"Can you seal it and somehow get the oxygen out of it?"

I spoke in a low voice, not a whisper. Whispers carry, and I wasn't worried about alarming the goblins. They knew we were there. I'd like for them not to make a suicidal charge, though, so I used words they were unlikely to understand.

Alger nodded. "A deflagration should work."

I eyed him suspiciously. He held out a spell, rosy pink and warm to the touch. I sighed. "This had better not burn the Court down around us."

He just grinned broadly, which worried me more than a fervent denial would have. He cupped his hand together and muttered into them, revealing a spell orb after a moment.

"Yours, then mine. Ready?"

I threw the spell in, triggering it at the apex of my toss. Alger slapped the spell he'd just made on the door lintel, and as the wall of flame hit the doorway, it stopped it cold.

"I thought you said no fire!" I yelled, jumping back a little in sheer surprise. The conflagration in the room was complete, a roaring inferno of heat and flame.

Chapter 26

But No Fire, Dammit!

"No, I said I wouldn't burn down Court." He pulled out a pipe. "This won't take too long, that's not a big room."

I watched in fascination as the flames slowly died out, starving themselves of oxygen. He'd done what I asked, I just had hoped for a less difficult to control solution. The walls and ceiling were blackened, and the floor littered with things I didn't care to contemplate, but there was no structural damage. Dean, who had leaned his leather-clad shoulders against the wall to smoke while the fire went out, stood and stretched.

"Ready to go, boss?"

"Yeah. We'll clear to the end of the hall, then set up camp and get dinner."

The next two doors held no surprises, and Alger sealed the end of the hall while i sent a pre-packaged message to Joe that we were ready for dinner. Joe showed up with it himself.

"Need a report?" I asked him wearily. I'd sat down on my bedroll and pulled my boots and socks off with a huge sigh of relief.

"And to give you one," he confirmed. Melcar came by and knelt to look at my feet.

"No blisters, doc, just sore and stinky. How's the boy that fell?"

"Leo will go back to the courts. He did get scratched on the hand, and it is already swollen and very painful."

"Do you need a replacement?" Joe offered.

I shook my head. "We really are just tripping over one another in the halls. Later, maybe. But there will be time for that. Today was tedium punctuated by a skirmish with goblins."

"A skirmish?"

I nodded. "There were only about fifty of them. Not that I had time to count, mind you."

"You expect more?" he looked concerned. I didn't blame him, we'd already had a casualty.

"Yeah, I expect the Great Hall to be crawling with them, and it won't just be a hunting party." I wondered if I looked as grim as I felt. I'd only had to go in after goblins once, and Kipling was on to something with his female deadlier than the male poem. I planned to call for back up then. I'm no hero. I also wasn't planning on relying only on magic.

"Tonight, I want food, sleep, and to check my messages, not necessarily in that order. Did the King have any instructions?"

"Only to carry on. He received your message earlier, and is implementing your suggestion."

"Ah, good. That will be your end of the action, I'm afraid, although I doubt it will be anything as direct as this is."

I got up and padded to the food and got a plate full. "Excuse me," I told Joe with no compunctions. I needed to eat, it had been a damn long day with too much effort and too little food. He just nodded understanding and went off to talk with others.

I'd chosen a spot outlying the group. Only Dean was further out, so as I sat and ate, I summoned my message spells. One at a time, set on my earlobe, I heard the voices of the senders. The first one yielded my mother's voice.

"I've heard all about this foolishness, and don't worry, I will deal with it. Bella is such a sweet girl, and will make a wonderful addition to the family. Margot and I are putting our heads together, and I am sure this will blow over before you return."

I closed my eyes in sheer disbelief. Mother had taken the bit between her teeth, decided she had seen something that wasn't there, and was likely to make Bella's life even more miserable. But at least it would distract her from being alone. I listened to the next message.

Scratch the alone. Ellie would already be with her, her terse message simply said, "yes." I went on to the next-to-last message. Devon's young voice, excited and voluble, chimed in on the matter.

"So, I went to see Bella, and I took Dorothy, because, you know, proprieties. Anyway, she is so beautiful, you didn't tell me that. And smart, and nice..."

I sighed. The boy was smitten, and in front of his girlfriend, too, who I liked. Dorothy's short brown hair, pointed ears, and steady good nature made her very endearing. He went on, and I listened with a smile.

"She talked to us about Alaska, and some of the adventures you two had - why didn't you tell me about those? We told her everything we could think of about Court, who to watch out for, and that sort of thing, to help her out. Dorothy and I agree that if she needs to be rescued, we want to help, Lom."

His voice was very serious at the end, and I felt the chuckle roll up before I knew it was coming. The last thing Bella would need was rescuing, like some fairy tale princess... more likely, the kids would step in it, and she would have to rescue them. I rolled the last spell around in my hand, wondering who it was from, and finally put it to my ear.

And immediately jerked it away again. The only thing coming out was an eerie, high-pitched wailing. The hair on the back of my neck rose, as I realized where I had heard that sound before. I'd thought she was dead, all these years, and to get a message, especially this message, from her now was a bad sign. I looked around the well lit area, with my men trying to sleep, and wondered who the banshee's wail was for. It wouldn't be me, or I wouldn't have gotten the message. And I'd rather it was me than one of them.

Nothing from Bella, but she was well-protected. I lay down, and closed my eyes. There would be no sleep tonight, but I would try to relax and let my body recoup at least. In the morning, I could make a liar out of the banshee. No one was dying on my watch, not this time.

I'd been a tough man for a long time, leading a life most of these sleeping here tonight couldn't imagine, sliding between two worlds with ease. I'd lost all concern for my own life, living from job to job, relying on bullets, not magic, to get those jobs done. If I didn't come back from one, no one would care for long. Oh, mother and Margot would wail, Devon would grieve, but there was no one loved me enough to lie awake wondering what had happened. When you deal with the devil, you become him, a little, and my job was monsters who had slipped their leashes. Is it any wonder I'd become one? Tomorrow I'd paint the wall with goblin gore, and then I would go release Bella from the prison I'd put her in. I rolled over and opened my eyes, giving up on sleep.

Morning in the underground halls was not heralded by a rising sun. We had left all the light globes illuminated, to help the watchers, and to keep the light-sensitive goblins at bay. Oh, they could attack in the light, but they were less likely to do so. No, what woke my crew was me banging on the wall and shouting, "rise and shine!"

There was grumbling, but I pampered them with a hot breakfast, and coffee. The coffee mostly shut them up, except for the tea drinkers. I gave them an hour, and then walked through, making sure each one was ready to go for the day. Alger stopped me with a touch on my shoulder. I followed him to the ward.

"What is on your mind, nephew?"

"Just the mission. Are you ready?"

He studied me intently for a moment. I held his gaze. "All right, then. Let's go," he touched his wand to the ward and it blinked out of existence. "Hunting time."

I waved Dean forward, and gestured Alger back. At least this time they weren't waiting for us right that second. Anticlimactic, but that was fine. I could live with boredom. Excitement could kill someone.

Having only two halls to worry about today was simpler. Knowing I had too many men to effectively move in one hall meant I could risk splitting the group. We checked the tops of both halls, and I sent Ash and Olive with four of Joe's men down the smaller side hall. They would check in with us at each cross hall. For once, I had appreciative thoughts for our ancestors and simple architecture.

Progress was a familiar reprise of the day before. Illuminate a stretch of hall, move to doors, seal them, repeat. We found a goblin campsite around noon, with a tiny fire ring in the center of the hall, and the dust disturbed all around in what I guessed was enough space for the mob that had attacked us yesterday. I read this as a good sign. They had been quite a ways from their home encampment.

I told Dean, "We'll smell it, you know, long before we trip across it."

He nodded, "And isn't that a wonderful thing to look forward to. Have you asked about missing folke?"

"No, and I'm not going to."

"I won't talk about it." He promised, his eyes going to a point far over my shoulder and about a century before. We'd both seen things no sane being should. Sometimes I wondered if either of us was still sane. Him, with his obsession with death and danger, and foray into the human world... me, with my monsters.

I grunted and went back to the group. "This is good. Means we're unlikely to have another ambush. Let's move."

I wanted to get this done, today. Prolonging it was only going to drag my untrained men down, and I hadn't slept the night before, and wouldn't until we were finished. Safety first, but speed next. We sealed doors and walked halls. The junior crew parallelling us was getting ahead of us, and I sent a messenger to tell them to hang back at the next cross hall.

Chapter 27

Nasty, Tricksy, Thieving

So there were only five men who saw the goblin's surprise. It was carefully placed on a teepee of sticks from somewhere, or maybe bits of broken furniture, right in the center of the hall, facing us. I raised my hand in the signal for stop, silent. We all stared at it, barely even breathing.

Bella's face in death was faintly greyish, her hair tangled and partly obscuring her features. But the bloody stub of her neck made it very clear she was freshly murdered. I felt a wave of rage well up, and pushed it back, locking all emotions aside. Behind me, there was a broken murmur, and then William stumbled past me. I caught him by the arm, and he almost pulled me off my feet.

"Hey!" I grabbed him in a bear hug, and he fought me. We wound up with Alger and Dean helping pull him back, while I looked past him at the very pale Henry. "What the hell?"

"M-my wife.. Lorinsa..." William sobbed, reaching out for the gruesome warning.

I looked back at it, at my princess...

Alger stepped past me and made a gesture so fast I almost missed it. In a hissing of dust falling, the object on the sticks was revealed as an ancient skull of some animal. Dean let go of William, who drew a deep breath ending in a hiccup. We all looked at each other, then the rag and bone totem.

"What did you see?" asked William.

I answered, "someone special," without going into further detail. They didn't need to know.

"Me, too... well, my mother." Henry supplied in a shaken tone.

Dean just lit a cigarette and took a deep drag. Alger shook his head. "This was not a goblin idea. We need to be prepared to face traps and mind-tricks, I think."

I ran a hand over my face, feeling the stubble I hadn't bothered to shave off. "I'll let the others know. Hope they didn't have one of these."

We walked around the goblin head game as close to the walls as we could get. None of us wanted to be near it, even knowing it was harmless now. I wondered what would come next. My team was shaken, even Alger and Dean, who had seen the elephant before. Beorn came strolling up from the cross hallway.

"Hey, what's that?" He asked curiously.

"Don't touch it," I told him. "Everything OK with them?"

I knew it was, he was too relaxed to be worried. I wanted to distract the young man from his curiousity.

"Yes, sir. There's nothing over there but empty rooms. They are waiting, at the next cross hall. Ash said he would ward it until we got there, just in case."

Good man, caution was a great idea in light of our new discovery.

"All right, let's get up there." I raised my voice a little. "Nobody touch anything. Don't believe your eyes, or ears... check with me, or Alger, if you have any weird things happen."

They all nodded, and Dean took his usual place. I shook my head, and followed. I was ready to get this over with. At the cross hall, Ash dropped the ward and we conferred. I'd made a decision and I needed his input.

He shook his head. "No sign at all, Olive and I have been looking for footprints or disturbances in the dust."

"Then I want to ward off the hall here, at the cross hall, and at the end of the cross, blocking the side hall altogether. We will concentrate on this hall. I want all of us together as we near the main encampment."

"You think there is one?" he asked, the leaves in his hair rustling as he looked up at me. Wood elves might be small, but they are strong, and tough.

"I know there is. This could get messy." I warned him.

He just nodded. I talked to the rest of the group while he and Alger set sealed wards. As soon as we could, I chivvied them into action. I'd been right on one thing. We could smell them first. It was like walking into a sewer wall. Dean stopped cold, one foot still raised. Then he lowered it, shook his head and snorted, then blocked his shoulders and went in like a bull charging in slow motion. I took a deep breath and followed him.

Behind me, I could hear gagging as my men experienced eau de goblin for the first time. Even Alger had turned a fine shade of green. None of them had thought through a whole settlement of little green guys living in the great hall, sewage not being something they had to think about in our land of magical disposal. They also didn't know what I did about the culinary preferences of goblin families. Not something you would talk about at the dinner table at Court.

Some smells fade with exposure, until you can't really notice them. This one had a life of its own, and that life was a violent one, assaulting our olfactory nerves relentlessly. Even my stomach was roiling, and I was concerned with the effect on our fighting ability. But it took a back seat to the concerns raised when we hit the edge of the trash midden.

I raised my hand, and brought everyone to a halt. Dean looked at me, having paused by himself before going into the tangled mess.

"I'm thinking prime location for booby traps." I told him, and he nodded.

Then he angled his body so we blocked the view of the men behind us, and made a subtle hand gesture. I followed his gaze.

"Dammit," I said, softly enough to not be heard by the others.

"Yeah. We've got enough green kids for this to be a problem."

We looked at one another. I didn't have time to linger over a decision, we were going to arouse curiosity, probably already had for Alger. The old man didn't miss much.

"Let's pull back. I need some time."

"I'd say a meal, but I'm not hungry." He followed me back to the group.

"We're so close, I want to pause and get ready." I told them. I didn't tell them, yet, about the bones in the midden.

I took them about halfway back to the last set of doors, and Alger set a ward between us and the goblin camp. Once they were as relaxed as they were going to get with the stink, I looked around at them.

"This is going to get bad. I don't know how many goblins are in there, but I'm willing to make a guess." I paused and looked around at the, "and that would be, a metric buttload. You know we already had a skirmish. That's all it was, a skirmish. No one was seriously hurt. Yes, Leo went back to the front, but Melcar" - I looked at the wood elf, and he rustled his hair with a nod of agreement - "says that he will recover, although he may lose sensation in some fingers. We rolled through them like a hot knife through butter. That is not going to happen in there." I pointed down the hall.

"I'm going to call for back-up. But just getting to camp is going to be hard, not physically, but mentally." Now they looked confused, except for Dean and Alger, who were half-listening, and mostly watching the wards. I went on, "I'm sure you've heard stories. I know I did, as a lad. Goblins are our boogeymen, and no tale is too gross to regale one another with late at night. The truth is... worse. Goblins eat anything. They have to, having adjusted to living underground so much that they no longer grow plants or keep animals like we can to live on.

"They do farm, though. Fungus, mostly, but in times of need, they eat one another, their own children... and whatever else they can catch." I took a deep breath, "that includes people. We know this camp had eaten at least one fairy, we found the evidence in the midden just now. The problem is, they also keep their captives to be eaten at leisure. So we don't know what we are facing, and we cannot just seal the Great Hall and obliterate them all."

Now they all looked more than slightly sick. Even Melcar was looking ill, and I knew he had to have a strong stomach. I wasn't going to tell them that even if we rescued people in this place, they would most likely have lost their minds. I had checked back with the three frail waifs we had taken out of Elc'hoor, and they had progressed to being able to feed themselves and and use a toilet. They were unlikely to ever emerge into reality again.

I also didn't tell them that despite my fears that this would be the case, I had still contemplated sealing and deflagrating the Great Hall anyway. It might be the most merciful thing for those poor souls. As the day had worn on, though, I knew that whatever kind of a monster I was, I was one who still had hope. This was going to get ugly, and the banshee's wail haunted me, but it had to be done.

"You're all volunteers, and you didn't sign up for this. If you need to go back to the front, no one is going to hold it against you." I made contact with William and Henry, who were both very young, and very shaken by the dirty trick earlier. "We know there is some malevolence at work here that is much more cunning than any goblin I have come across. So there may be traps in the trash midden, even before we reach the goblin encampment. Once we are in the camp itself, there will be trash everywhere. They are semi-nomadic, and when a camp gets too disgusting, they just move on.

"This camp may be close to uninhabitable, because they are being kept here for an attack on Court. Everything moving in camp will attack you. Women, children, and every weapon you must assume is poisoned.

They make up for their frail bodies by making sure they have every advantage over the enemy. You saw what happened to Leo, and that was just a scratch. Alger is going to help you with personal protection spells, but they will be powered off your magic, and they will draw down your energy."

I took a swallow of water and drew a breath. "Are there any questions?"

"How are we going at them?" Dean growled. I knew he was ready to go now, but I wanted to wait for backup and weapons.

"We're not just using magic. I'm having two crew-served machine guns brought in. I'll be on one, and Olive," the slight wood elf nodded at hearing his name, "on the other, because we have the experience. We'll each chose two men to be with us, and give you a quick orientation. I know some of you may protest that using them is not a fair fight, but -" I looked around, meeting eachI'd like to get a few sprites for her, since man's eyes - "we can't afford to fight fair."

Chapter 28

Rest & Reinforcements

Joe transported in then, at the back of my group, and I nodded at him in greeting. "We'll have a hot meal, and a few hours to plan and rest, then we go in."

I walked back to Joe, taking him a little further away. "It's bad, Joe."

"I heard some of that." He studied my face. "How are you holding up?"

"I'm ok. The younger ones are going to have problems. What's the news up front?

"The King told me to tell you that the Great Hall is stone, he doesn't anticipate an attack of nostalgia, and to cleanse it with fire."

That sounded like the old man. "I can't just do that, unfortunately." I explained to him briefly the reason we had to take the camp one step at a time.

He looked past me at the men, who were eating and lounging. There was no boisterous chatter as usual, though. "How many do you need?"

"How many do we have?" I countered with a sigh.

"Enough, I think. The Great Hall isn't that big."

"Only the size of a football field," I grumbled.

He gave me a funny look. I sometimes forgot that some things didn't translate well. I went on, "I would like to use a few sprites for reconnaissance, if we can find a few not afraid of their own shadow. I need to know where any captives are."

I handed him a written list, and he unfolded it and took a brief look before folding it back up and nodding a silent farewell. He walked back down the hall for a moment, then disappeared in a transportation spell. I stared after him, thinking. If Joe was rattled... I turned and looked at my men, lounging subdued with their food mostly uneaten.

I took a deep breath and headed back toward them, getting ready to stop by each one and try to give them a pep talk. We had a few hours, I wanted them to try and get some sleep, something I doubted any of them would be able to do. I put my hand on Henry's shoulder, and felt him jump out of his skin as he looked up at me.

"Oh! Lom..."

"Want to go back to the front?" I asked as gently as I could. Young men and their sense of amour propre.

He shook his head. "No, sir, I volunteered."

"Tomorrow, don't be a hero." I caught his eye. "I don't want to have to go talk to your parents."

He swallowed, but held fast. "I am ready. I don't want to die, but... Well, if we don't do this, then my parents, everyone at court, they're in danger."

I nodded. "You'll do fine. Follow orders, make sure you stay with your team."

"Yes, sir."

I walked away, and Alger came up next to me. "If that's your idea of a pep talk, you need to work on it a little."

"I know. I'm not used to working with..." I gestured at the hall full of my men.

"Anyone?" he supplied with a raised eyebrow.

"Pretty much."

"It's been a while since I did," he mused.

I looked at him. "When did you do it at all?"

"Before you were born. Anyway, carry on." He turned and walked away, leaving me grumpily contemplating his back. Alger being enigmatic meant there would be no answers.

I had made it through all the new men by the time the reinforcements started arriving. I supposed I was going to have to start calling them my old men, now. They had been through two days of goblin hunting in these dark halls, now. It's not a lot of time, but it can do things to a man fast under that kind of stress.

A very small transportation bubble popped by my head and revealed four sprites. They tumbled about in midair for a second, then one after another they formed into a diamond formation and snapped me a salute. I was amused, but tried not to show it.

"The McGregor brothers, reporting for dooty, sorr!" the one in front snapped. "We haird ye needed to rool t' skies!"

Now I did laugh. "You're insane, Ewan, you know that?"

"Aye," he grinned in a way that only reinforced my proclamation.

"They have poison arrows," I warned him.

"Aye. We ken that," he agreed happily.

I sighed. "Ok, here's what I need..."

I had just finished my briefing and was rubbing my temples to ease the McGregor headache when a more welcome face appeared.

I held out my hand as the shorter pixie walked up. We clasped forearms.

"Daffyd, glad you could come."

He shrugged, "What the hell? I have a new arrow to try out. And, goblins, man!"

"You're nuts, too." I laughed with him. Daffyd Ap Maple had a long-bow, and he was very good with it. It was just an English yew bow, but all his arrows were enchanted. He was also one of the very few in the hall that had spent any time above in the Human realms, and who I could call a true friend.

"I saw the McGregors flitting about. Now, they're bughouse nuts," he pointed out.

"Tell me about it." I pointed at the carts. "There's hot, good food, if you haven't eaten. I'll be briefing everyone in the morning, so take some time to meet people and take a rest if you can."

"Lom..." he sounded amused. I blinked at him. "It's morning in about, ah, now?"

"Oh, wonderful. Time to rally the troops, then."

He looked past me. "First, you have one more recruit, looks like."

I turned and groaned out loud. Daffyd chuckled behind me. "I'll line 'em up while you talk to him."

"Thanks." I growled. Actually, it was be good to have a lieutenant I could delegate to. I was going to need all my patience for the man I was about to tell to go home.

"Martin." I greeted him as civilly as I could. He was in his armor and he clanked as he walked toward me. "No horse?" I asked, unable to stop myself.

"Lom, frivolous as always, m' lad." He flipped up his visor, revealing a face lined with more years than I cared to think about. One eye drooped slightly. The grizzled cheeks hadn't been shaved in a while, but in the gauntlets I couldn't see the shake of his hands that no doubt was the cause of the stubbly face.

"Martin, are you mad? You can't fight in that get-up."

He scowled at me. "It'll keep the little buggers from biting my ankles."

I tried to put it as clearly as I could, "I can't let you fight, Martin."

"You can't stop me," he growled. "I've fought goblins for longer than any of you young pups, and when this old warhorse hears the call, he rides out!"

"And if you take others down in your ride to Valhalla?" I snapped back at him. "Everyone that goes out there..." I pointed through the ward to the shadowy hall beyond. "Is going to be relying on the ones nearest them for covering fire. Martin," I gentled my voice and put one hand on his breast-plate. "I understand. I don't want to die alone, myself."

"I am not here merely to avoid dying alone. I plan to die in bed with a winsome lass to cuddle me. But what's a soldier to do when there's a battle to be fought?"

I'd lost, that was more than I had time or energy to fight with him over. "Talk to Alger, then. He has his orders for the offensive, already. I must go... Martin." He had started to turn away, and now stiffly faced me again. I drew myself up, and snapped off a salute.

He nodded, very slightly, all his helm allowed him, and clanked off. I felt something bump my cheek and startled, catching it quickly. A message spell. I held it in my hand, remembering the banshee's wail in my ear. Or my mother's voice. I didn't know which was worse, honestly. I'd rather go out and face the goblins in my bare skin than her, if someone had told her what was happening this morning. I finally put it to my ear, and closed my eyes as I heard Bella's voice.

"I know what's happening. Joe, Jr. told me. I think he'd rather be down there with you fighting, than up here watching me be social. I have had more visitors... But I won't bore you with all that. I just wanted to make sure you know I'm not mad at you. The King seems to think... Well, I'm not mad at you. I know you didn't mean for me to wind up stuck Under-hill, and you wouldn't have pledged to me if you were planning to betray me." Her voice trembled a little on the last words, but she went on, "I've been looking up goblins in the library, Lom, and they are foul. I hope..." her voice choked up, and she cleared her throat. "Anyway, I need to talk to you, so please come back."

That was the last thing I'd been expecting. I had done my best to put her in a locked compartment of my mind while we did this, and I should have known she would kick down doors and take names if I did that to her. I formed a message spell carefully, feeling the nausea that magic use brought, and murmured into it as softly as I could. Then I let it go and watched it zip off, blurring out of sight in seconds.

Chapter 29

Goblin Battle

I t was time. I checked my own gear, then Dean's. Olive had selected Beorn to help him with the .50 cal. I had asked Ash to run the other as I had realized I needed to be, well, everywhere, in my commanding role. Dean would take lead when we were done with the guns. Everyone was geared up, all we were waiting on were the pixies.

Alger dropped the spell, and they flashed out silently into the dark hall. We waited as close to quiet as we could manage with now forty-plus men packed into the broad hall. I didn't want to put the ward back up, and possibly trap the sprites when they needed to retreat. It was a long couple of moments, with me flinching every time someone coughed, or shifted.

Then they were back, shrilly laughing as they circled my head, and Alger brought the ward up. I exploded, "What the hell?" at Ewan.

"Dinna fash yerself!" he came back at me, still chuckling. "Me 'n t'lads are full of t'joy o' battle, tis all."

"Report, now, then get yourself back to court." I growled at him, unamused that he might have given away the surprise attack.

The prisoners were being kept in the great fireplace at the end of the Hall, but they in turn were shielded from us by the throne dais, a vast block of granite. The columns of the Hall would also create shadow effects from the bullets, but we were free to have open fields of fire without harming friendlies. The sprites were vague on details, but insisted that the entire floor of the Great Hall was covered with the seething bodies of goblins, except, of course, where there were ramshackle huts or piles of trash. The trash midden that stood between us, and them, was a big obstacle, but I had a plan in place to deal with that.

I thanked them, then looked at my men. "Are we ready?"

A throaty growl of agreement came, and I nodded to Alger, who stood by the wards. He touched wand to the shimmering spell, and it dropped like a falling sheet. He and I waited for Dean to ghost out a few yards, then wave us forward. Alger and I, shoulder to shoulder, walked down the center of the hall. I knew we were vulnerable, but what he was about to do meant no-one could be in front of us, and that included Dean. When we reached the edge of the trash heaps, he fell back behind us, as planned. I took a breath, tried not to choke on the stench, and Alger raised his wand.

"Go." I said simply. He threw the spell. I braced against the impact of the backlash. The excavation spell that Bella had used was small, compared to this one. I shook my head to clear the ringing in my ears, and looked at Alger. He was still standing tall, wand at ready. Behind him, Dean had taken a knee, and even further back, I could see the machine gun crews ready for my gesture.

"Go." I said again, and imitated Dean, taking a knee against the force of the air pressure that blasted back toward us. This time, when the spell was done, Alger was leaning on my shoulder. "Time to get you back to Court," I told him, standing and taking his weight more fully. "Can you?"

He snorted softly, "The day I can't you might as well leave me in the midden. Lom..." He paused, and looked into my eyes, ignoring the clatter of the guns and men marching around us. "Be careful, boy."

"Always. I'll die as old and mean as you. Now git." I pushed him upright, and took a step back, so he could transport out. I was moving toward the machine gunners even before he'd blinked out of sight. We had known the two huge spells would leave him exhausted, and he had been up all night preparing the personal protection spells for the rest of the group. We had six hours, he guessed, before they would draw us down to nothing. I told everyone they had four hours from activation to turn it the hell off. I didn't think any of us were as tough as the old bastard.

The trash midden was scoured clear, but the floor was still slimy in spots, so we didn't move quickly forward, just steady. The goblins at the entrance to the great hall seemed to be stunned, not sentries, just unlucky SOB's that were too close. I unlimbered the shotgun and Daffyd took up the other side of the hall to give the machine guns covering fire close in. Then Ash and Olive opened fire.

I had known that in the stone hall, the sounds of the guns would be significant. I hadn't considered quite how loud they would be, and was glad I had issued earplugs and taken the time to explain how they worked. I could see the effect of the sound on the nearest goblins, who cowered, hands to their ears and mouths open in a silent scream. The guns mowed them down like grass. Ash and Olive created overlapping fields of fire, sweeping the hall with six to nine round bursts. They knew better than to get excited and go to continuous fire, risking overheating the barrel of the gun. When they had fired through one belt, I raised the shotgun over my head and bellowed "Charge!"

We'd planned for enough men to create a double line stretching from one side of the hall to the other, but I had also known that it wouldn't be precise. Unlike a trained fighting unit, we were not choreographed in our movements. But no one ran ahead of the line, either, as we were moving out onto the guts and gore of countless dead goblins. It would be too easy to fall on that floor. I stopped worrying about it too much as a goblin leapt out from behind the first column, wickedly curved sword swinging high. I shot him, and then the next one...

An outcry to my left caught my attention and I could see young William was in trouble. I veered a little towards him, knowing the man behind me held our line, and switched the shotgun to slung, while pulling my pistol. I shot the goblin that was latched onto his arm with a mouthful of needle-like teeth, blowing his body apart, and William shook off his head, gasping "thanks!" before charging forward again.

I returned to the gap in the line as best I could, leapfrogging forward of the man who'd taken my place. The goblins were thicker, now, coming out from behind columns and the dias and charging us with no compunctions about the state of the floor. As I watched the wave come on and braced for it, I could see one or two slip and go down, trampled under the feet of their brethren. I also saw a flaming arrow arc over the mob, then burst into impossibly white fire. Daffyd, with one of his special arrows, and if I had to guess quickly, white phosphorus.

Nasty weapon, that. I fired a round into the oncoming group, and then shouted one more time, "For the King! Charge!" and we hit them hard. Our line splintered, but didn't break, and goblins died in droves. I found myself suddenly at the foot of the dias, clutching a long blade in one hand, and the pistol in the other. I was covered in goblin ichor, and as I cut open the goblin backed against the stone, I wondered where the sword had come from, but at that instant, a deafening concussion blew me down.

I struggled back to my feet and looked in the direction of the blast. There was a lull in the onslaught, I guessed because every sentient being in the Hall was doing what I was doing. I couldn't tell what had happened, but a starburst pattern in dead goblins had cleared the left hand side of the dias, and the ones remaining were severely disoriented, one staggering to the edge and falling off as I watched. I headed for the steps on the right side to dispatch the remainder of them.

There were only a few, and they didn't put up much of a fight, so I was able to stop and scan the field with a better vantage point for a quick, comprehensive glance at the carnage. Dean joined me atop the dias. He pointed at the starburst.

"Young Henry," he informed me laconically.

"What the hell? Oh, shit, death curse?" The young fool could have wiped out a number of men on his own side had that been detonated while we were still in the line, instead of him having gotten himself cut off atop the dais.

"Aye." He reverted to the tongue of his childhood in stress, I'd noted. "Ye ready?" he pointed the blade he held in his right hand down at the fireplace, and our goal.

"Let's do this." I replied grimly, reloading my pistol with a fresh magazine. The .45 didn't kick as badly as the .50 I'd wanted, but it cut through goblins just fine. He led the way down, screaming. I followed more calmly, firing as I needed to keep his back safe. The others were sweeping in around the dais, and there were very few monsters left to oppose us as we came to a crashing halt in front of the fireplace.

Chapter 30

Prisoners or Food?

The room was suddenly, shockingly quiet. It wasn't soundless, there were the groans of the injured, and the occasional wet thunk of a coup de grace being delivered, but there seemed to be no goblins left standing. In front of us... I turned away for a second to catch my breath, and saw Beorn quietly vomiting by the dais. Everyone else looked sick, as well.

I stepped forward and, using the long blade I'd picked up during the fight, cut the man off the frame. He was very dead, half-butchered already, but still. There has to be some dignity, even after what had been done to him. The pen where the prisoners were was still shut tight. William started to walk toward the gate.

"Hold." my voice was hoarse, and I felt like my throat was raw. I rasped, "wait for Melcar. Someone call him up here. and tell him to bring back up. Dean, Daffyd, choose six men and start mopping up. Take more if you think you need it. Ash..."

I looked around, and belatedly realized my pistol was still in my hand. I holstered it, and beckoned Ash to me. The sword I just held in my left hand, I didn't have anyplace to put it, and it had served me well, I wasn't going to just drop it on the floor. "Ash... casualty check, please. Have Olive organize the pull-back of everyone who doesn't need to be right here, right now." I realized I hadn't seen Martin, the one man I'd like to have with me for the next part of this battle. I asked, "Martin?"

Ash shook his head, his leaves and hair too matted with ichor to even move. "I'm sorry, Lom."

I felt my throat constrict. "Damn," was all I could get out as I choked up. At least he had gone out like he would have wanted. "Go, then. I need to get this finished."

Melcar, two of his apprentices in tow, walked around the corner of the dais. I felt some of my tension release at his arrival.

"Ready?" I asked him, "I don't want them to wait any longer."

He nodded, his face pale. I didn't blame him, mine was probably pale under the green slime. I walked to the gate and undid the latch, then swung it wide. No-one was in sight.

"Shit..." I wriggled through the small opening, and found them, huddled into the furthest corner. Covered in dirt and rags, and utterly silent. They were too afraid to even scream. "You can come out. The goblins are dead. C'mon..." I beckoned to them, my heart sinking. They were too far gone to even understand me.

Then, one of the men who was trying to cover a child with his body sat up. He looked at me, silently, for a long moment, and I met his stare without moving. He slowly stood up, and I still didn't move, and I could see the moment when my non-threatening posture, and likely, gobs of green flesh and blood sticking to me, sank into his mind, and his face softened, just a little. He gibbered at me, and something about his appearance sank in. I backed through the gate, beckoning him onward, and called over my shoulder for Melcar. The man flinched at the raised voice, but kept coming. He paused again at the gate, and then slipped through it. He was skin and bones, so he fit easily.

Outside the fireplace pen, he looked around him at the carnage and my standing warriors with wide eyes. Then he fell to the floor at my feet, on his knees, embracing my waist and sobbing aloud. I tried to peel him off.

"Melcar! They're Asian, not sure which culture, but doesn't the Oriental Court speak mostly Mandarin? Do we have a translator? Can you get this guy off me?"

He was blubbering now, his face covered in tears and snot. No-one else had yet ventured out of the pen, although I could see movement in the shadows. Melcar put his head in and spoke in what sounded like Mandarin. One of his apprentices helped the man let go of me and led him off to the stairs, which were mostly clear of bodies and gore, and had him sit there. I noticed the body we had cut off the frame, and even the frame, were gone.

That had been quick thinking on someone's part. I wondered who I needed to thank, and then noticed Joe standing to one side of the fireplace. Of course. I hobbled over to him. Somewhere along the mad rush, I'd pulled a muscle. There were no doubt other things wrong with me, but that one was hurting like a bitch right now.

"Are we done?" I asked him, tired beyond expression. "I'd like a shower, and food, and sleep, not necessarily in that order, and only once my men are taken care of."

"We're already getting everyone up to Court, five at a time. I've got a clean-up crew coming here to evacuate the prisoners, and then we will deflagrate the Great Hall before sealing it off. I'd set up another crew to handle debriefing and clean-up for your men. The King wanted me to tell you 'well done' now, and that he will talk to you tomorrow once you are rested."

I nodded, my head feeling so heavy it might fall off. "I will be the last one out, then. I need to find Ash..." I didn't see him here behind the Dais.

"He's out in the main Hall. I'll come get you when it's your time."

I think I grunted a response before shambling off, but I'm not sure. Ash was standing still, looking at a tableau out of a bard's saga. I came and stood beside him, feeling a fresh wash of grief over my soul, knowing that I would be swamped with it, if that kept happening. Martin stood tall before us, his armor battered and smeared with blood and ichors, slowly puddling together into a muddy palette that illustrated the tale of the valiant knight's last stand. They had piled on him, literally, until in death he was unable to fall. Only his head sagged forward slightly, as though he were thinking about some unfathomable question.

"He was a grand old man." I rasped, my voice shot from the fighting and screaming, and from the unshed tears.

"Proud to have fought with him," was Ash's eulogy. He deliberately turned away from the scene, and I followed his example. "Henry was the only other death. Daffyd has a nasty gash on his calf, Melcar sent him up to Court already. I think almost everyone has cuts and bruises, even with the protection spells."

"And everyone has to have that looked at, no matter how minor."

"You, too, Lom." He scratched his jawline. "I need a bath."

"Thank goodness for magical water heaters." I started to hobble for the far side of the Hall, where another group was gathered around something. "Go see Joe and get that bath. Thanks, Ash."

He headed off toward the dais. I continued on, only stopping to pick up a stick to lean on as I walked. I still had the sword in the other hand, I had forgotten it entirely. I stopped and fixed a transport spell to it, and sent it to the workbench in my armory. With my stomach heaving, I tried not to look too much at the floor as I maneuvered my way toward Dean, an unknown man... and Alger. When had he showed up?

His clothes were clean, and his long hair slightly damp, leading me to guess that he had been good and not returned until after I'd given the all-clear to Joe. He was poking at something on the floor. I clumped up to them, too tired to be quiet, and not wanting to surprise them anyway.

"What did you find?" I leaned on my stick and looked at the mess on the floor. That was red blood. Who had been injured here? Alger flipped a layer of soaked cloth off a lump, and I realized I had been wrong. "That's a fairy. And not one of ours."

Now I bent closer, and could see that the head was still wearing odd goggles, probably enchanted to allow him to see in low-light conditions. He'd been struck in the torso with at least one .50 calibre bullet, and eviscerated.

"That explains a lot. They had a boss." I straightened back up, feeling that muscle and several others in my back grab all at once. I think I yelped, because Dean was suddenly at my side lending me an arm. I glared at him. "I suppose you're fit and chipper."

"They'll never kill me." He grinned, showing all his teeth in something that was not humorous.

"I don't suppose they will. Myself, I just feel old."

I straightened the rest of the way and he stepped back. Alger bustled past us. "Come on, boys, let's see what else is hidden in this mess."

I exchanged raised eyebrow glances with Dean, then shrugged and followed the old man at a snail's pace. Joe intercepted me after a short time, and I went with him with great relief. I didn't know how long it had been since we'd made that initial charge into the Great Hall, but it felt like days, even though I knew it could only have been hours at most. I needed to rest before I fell down.

Melcar's crew manhandled me through a decontamination process that left me wrapped in a robe and being handed a plate of protein-rich food. I wolfed that down, making myself stay on my feet and walk the length of the long room that had been commandeered for the purpose, checking on everyone. I knew that the after effects of todays work would stay with them for a long time. Even for me, it had not all been in a day's work. I might never see some of them again, but I still felt a responsibility for them.

I returned my plate, and found the guy in charge. "Do you need me for anything?"

He shook his head, "no, I think you are supposed to get some sleep, sir. Joe said to make sure you didn't push too much. Want a transportation spell? He said you might need one."

I hesitated, wondering how many of them knew just how limited I was, magically, then decided it didn't matter, tonight. "Yeah."

I stood still and felt the bubble form around me, then collapse. All I could see was my bed... I staggered for it, shedding my robe and falling... Into nothingness of sleep.

I don't know how long I slept. I rose and fell in and out of consciousness a couple of times, just enough to know I was alone, and safe, then back under again. The last time I did this, I could smell coffee. I swung my feet out of the bed and sat up carefully, my entire body screaming in pain. I felt like I had been beaten with sticks. Not little ones, either. Naked, I started to go into the other room, only belatedly realizing that I was not alone when Bella looked up from the couch and reacted to me.

"Oh, shit." I heard myself say as I turned as fast as I could and shut the door behind me. I leaned against the door groggy and wondering if I had really seen her there, smiling at me, or if that had been another fevered dream.

There was a light knock at the door, I could feel it send gentle vibrations through me. "Lom?" Her voice was concerned. "I can leave, if you'd like."

"No! I don't want you to go... just, let me find something to put on. I'm moving slowly."

"Are you ok?"

I grunted in pain as I tried to get the robe off the floor, and heard the door open behind me. "Bella..." I protested weakly, then she was there, picking the robe up and holding it for me. I let her help me into it, and then wrapped my arms around her and pulled her close. She stiffened, and I let go as fast as I could. By Oberon's Beard, I'm an idiot. Why did I think she would want a broken down old warhorse?

"I'm sorry..." I told her hurriedly, "just after battle, and I don't know what got into me. Juices are flowing, I suppose." I felt like I was babbling, and backed away as quickly as I could, into my dressing room, ignoring her plaintive, inarticulate protest.

Chapter 31

Jenny the Morris Dancer

I came out fully dressed, stalked into the sitting room and grabbed a cup of coffee. She was sitting at the table, and looked up at me, her wings drooping. She held out a hand, and I wasn't sure what she wanted.

"We will talk later," she promised, dropping her hand when I didn't acknowledge it, and I walked out the door clutching the steaming cup. I'd screwed it up. She was, so far as I knew, a virgin. Certainly by the standards of Court, she was extraordinarily loyal, and I guessed she was a one-man woman. She didn't need me, she needed a nice human man who could give her stability, a family, and a normal life. I needed to get some space, and stop tripping over my tongue every time I was around her. The last thing she needed was me... I stopped outside the door to the small throne room, taking a deep breath, clutching my empty coffee mug, and mentally folding her, with all the emotions tied to her, into a compartment in my mind and throwing away the key. Duty called, and that was my life.

I took a deep breath, and opened the door. They could banish me from Court. Alaska had possibilities I'd like to explore, with Raven and his kin. I wouldn't mind that, a forced retirement. I walked in to a room full of people seated at a conference table. They all looked at me, and I felt the aches of the day before as I stared back at them. I'd done my job, and lost two of my men. Now, I had to explain to the King what had happened to his friend Martin, and a young fairy with a future cut short. I took my seat at the opposite end of the table from the King.

"Good morning, Lom," he greeted me warmly, his face sternly belying his tone of deep affection. "Are you well?"

"Well enough. Majesty, I would like to apologize..." he cut me off.

"Lom, you did well. You took a team of men that had never worked as a unit, and wiped out a goblin infestation that outnumbered you more than ten to one. You fulfilled your duty faithfully, under daunting circumstances, and furthermore, rescued ten poor souls who had lost all hope without you. Now, let's discuss what I'm going to ask you to do next." He offered the table a humorless smile, baring his teeth. "Because we all know the reward for a job well done is another, more difficult task."

He went on, while I tried to catch my breath. "As some of you know, Lom had been looking into the mole in Court who was responsible not only for this infestation and the Trolls, but for the attacks on the princesses traveling to and in Court. He sent me some of his results before going goblin-hunting, and I asked Joe to delegate that to someone competent."

He looked at Joe, who nodded and looked at the man next to him. A fairy I was unfamiliar with, he stood and delivered his report in an even tone. "The two persons of interest were investigated to see if motivation could be found. In the case of the man, no motive could be found other than a vague jealousy, but he is also certain his daughter will be the next queen, so I discounted his ability to try and destroy the Court, for that is what this is.

"If the Low Court, or the dark court as I think of them, could gain ascendency by making it impossible for us to fulfill our charter by having both a reigning King and Queen, then they could gain the power to break our wards here at Court, something they came close to doing with the goblins. Before the room was cleansed with fire, it was found that the goblins had come in through cracks in the floor of the Great Hall, doubtless having happened after the abandonment of that area, and as we never considered it vulnerable, it was unwarded and unguarded. That is no longer the case for any outlying parts of Court."

He took a sip of water, and kept talking. "The other person of interest was difficult to assess, as so little was known about her. It took me two days to determine that she is, in fact, able to use magic, although I do not think it originates with her, as she is human."

A little murmur ran around the table. Humans were so uncommon Underhill we sometimes forgot that any lived with us, much less that they could do magic when taught. The feeling tended to be that they were sentient pets. I disagreed, but then, I wasn't here often.

"She was found to have in her possession spells of enough sophistication that they can only have originated with the Low Court. We have detained her for your Majesty's questioning just moments ago, in anticipation of this meeting."

When I walked through the doors, in other words. We all turned and looked at the doors as they opened, and two guards walked in, supporting her between them. She was as limp as a rag doll, but I felt no pity toward her. The poison of her ambitions was murderous and cowardly. They brought her to stand before the King, and let go of her arms. She slid to the floor and huddled there. He looked down at her is disgust.

"Stand up, woman!" he ordered, his voice a deep growl. She shook, but stayed with her head hidden in her arms. "I won't ask again."

She slowly stood up, but kept her face hidden behind her wild white elf-locks that had been the first thing I noticed about her. I wondered how long she had been using them as a shield against scrutiny. Our culture revered the elderly, those who had enough centuries to be wise. This human had played upon that, and her seeming service, to worm her way into the Court.

"Look at me. I want to know who you are." His voice was still cold and stern, almost remote.

She shook her head, and he nodded at a guard, who reached over and tipped her chin up so her face was revealed. He studied her for a long moment. "I know everyone in Court, and somehow I have not seen you, these many years. But I do know your face, or I did when it was young and comely. You were Jenny, the Morris Dancer who came with bells on her feet and hands to dance for us and make us all laugh and wonder at the skills of your troupe. You came many times, although the others changed. How does it come that you are here, and trying to overthrow Court?"

She twisted her chin out of the guard's hand and spoke for the first time. I was surprised at the volume, having only heard her barely more than whisper before.

"I was seduced by the decadence of the Court," she rasped. "Young, and beautiful, and then discarded like a broken toy. I could not go home again, I had been here too long, and was trapped. It took me decades to find one who would teach me how to use magic, but I was treated like dirt." She brushed her hair back and shook a finger at all of us. "You think you are so superior, being able to call on magic for every little thing. But I have caused your destruction, and then I will be where you sit, in a Court who does not require you to be a fairy to hold any power!"

She had been manipulated. Low Court saw humans as animals, fit only for the toy she felt like. But she had been an infected splinter we had never even noticed, festering for many years. She might have felt like her heaven had become hell, but it was by her choices.

"Are there others, who feel as you do?" the King asked, his face unreadable.

"In your rotted Court, I have acted alone." She raised her chin higher. "I was helped from outside when I needed resources, but it is I who have brought you low."

The King contemplated her for a long few moments, while she glared around the room at each of us. I wondered what he was going to do next. He looked straight down the table at me.

"I will grant Jenny's dearest wish," he spoke gravely. "in compensation for her mistreatment, and to keep her humanity intact. Lom, will you do me the honor of escorting Jenny home?"

It took me a moment to process what he was truly saying. Not where she had been living, but above...

"Yes, your majesty. May I have an assistant?"

"Of course. And if you please, be it done immediately, I would not prolong her distress any further."

I stood and bowed slightly, then gestured at the guards to bring Jenny, who was looking bewildered. She did not understand what she was being given. I followed them out the door, hearing the King say behind me before it closed, "now, the problem of the Oriental Court..."

I spun a message spell off my fingers and felt a wave of relief that he had not asked me to be in on the discussion of the other Court. I needed time to absorb what I had done, and what I was about to do. I might still feel numb, but that didn't mean I wasn't looking to the future.

We stood and waited until Bella arrived, dressed in jeans, flannel shirt, and boots, looking slightly confused. "Lom?" She slowed and looked at Jenny, defiantly erect in the guard's grasp.

"Come on, I'll explain on the way."

I murmured to her while we waited for the transportation spell to reach our destination. I'd ordered two so I would have a moment to tell her what was happening. It popped, and I looked at the elegant arch, with the shimmering door between the elaborately carved columns. "You don't have to do this."

"I do. I have something to prove, and Lom... You do too much alone."

I turned to the guards, who were holding a wide-eyed and struggling Jenny. "Time to go home, Jenny the Morris Dancer."

"No!" She shrieked, as I clamped onto her arm with both hands. Bella followed my lead on the other side, and we had to almost pick her up off her feet as we went through the door. The change was an old familiar bone tingle, and I let go of Jenny's arm. Bella sighed deeply and opened her eyes, almost absently releasing Jenny as well. I looked up at her and felt a ripple of amusement that died as I looked at Jenny.

She was stumbling forward into the dewy grass. The sun was up, but it was early morning here, on Earth. There were birds singing, somewhere. Jenny sank to her knees and put her hands to her face.

"What year is it?" she whispered.

"It's 2013, unless there has been a time slip since I came through." Bella responded quietly.

"Over two hundred years..." She slumped forward onto the grass, her body decaying as we watched, then crumbling into dust and partial bones.

Bella shuddered. "Even knowing that was..." she didn't finish.

"She asked to come home." I felt no emotion about it. She had been granted a merciful death, while my men had died in pain and terror.

I turned to Bella. "Did you bring what I told you too?"

She pulled the items out of her pocket. "Wallet, cellphone, and passport. But why?"

Chapter 32

Bella's Choice

Bella looked steadily at me, standing in the sunshine with the breeze in her hair and the bones of our enemy at her feet. I waved an arm at the grassy field.

"There's a road that way," I pointed, "And you can be in Alaska under Raven's protection before Court knows you are gone. Who are they going to send after you, me? Funny how that works, I just won't be able to find you. You're free, Bella, run."

She still looked at me without speaking, and I was too tired to try and interpret what she was thinking. I turned away from her and walked toward the door back into Underhill.

"Lom."

I kept going. I hated goodbyes. I hadn't gotten to say any to Martin, or Henry, but she at least had happiness and a future.

"Lom, look at me." She had a very firm note in her voice, and I reluctantly stopped.

She touched my shoulder and I looked at her. "I don't want to stay here. I can be useful to you." She tapped her head. "The library, remember? And I know I'm not... well, we work pretty well together. I was hoping to talk to you about a partnership."

"You want to come back Underhill?" I felt like I was thinking through molasses.

"Yes, and work with you, if you're interested. I..." She touched my arm again, softly. I could feel the warmth of her fingers as she looked down at me. "I thought we were friends. You swore fealty to me, but I want to release you from that. I don't..." She bit her lip and looked away. "I know this is bad timing, I'm sorry about that. I just feel like I'm needed, back there." She pointed at the door in front of us.

I sighed. "I can't stop you. You know how to pass through the door, and you are certainly powerful enough to not need me."

She frowned at me. "You never answer my questions."

"Bella, I can't. Not... not right now. I don't know, I'm tired and my brain is running about half speed."

"Then let's go home." She took my arm, tucking her hand into my elbow, and we walked forward together.

On the other side, she twisted her head around and let a huge, exaggerated sigh out. "Damn, I still have wings." She looked up at me. "Although I don't mind as much being shorter than you."

I looked down at her. There were times she was as opaque as any other female I had known. Right at this moment, I wasn't sure what to do with her.

"I'll take you back." I offered. She smiled sunnily.

"That would be nice. Have you eaten?"

"Um..." She popped a 'port spell around us and I tried to remember food.

"Right, then. Dinner it is." The spell popped and we were standing in our sitting room in the Court.

"Bella..." I couldn't think of the words to explain what I needed to do. "I have to go do something."

She snorted. "Not until you have eaten something. You are swaying on your feet. Sit."

She pointed at a chair and I sat, not knowing how to walk away from the inexorable momentum of a woman in full nurture mode. I hadn't experienced it in many years.

"Hang on a moment." She pulled open the door to the Hall, and spoke to Joe Jr. before returning to sit with me. "Ellie is here, you know?"

I nodded. I vaguely remembered sending her to Bella. Plates suddenly appeared on the table and Bella grinned at the look on my face. "She's been champing at the bit to feed you since she got here. She seems to labor under the impression you will waste away to nothing if she isn't feeding you."

I picked up a fork and realized I was starving.

"Thank you, Bella." I raised my voice, "and you, Ellie if you're listening."

I ploughed into the meal, watching Bella pick at hers. I set down my fork and then picked it up again. I thought I knew what was wrong. I'd added to her nightmares again. And she wanted to work with me, she had no idea what she was in for. I felt buried under a mountain of remorse. I should have said no to Martin's request to take the field of battle with us. I ought to have sent the youngest men back to Court when we swept the Great Hall. Hell, maybe I ought to have kept my mouth shut about the prisoners and just burned the Hall. I would never have known how many, or even for sure there were any survivors in there, and my men would be alive. I dropped my fork on the plate with a clatter.

"I have to go. I need..." I pulled the spell around me like a safety blanket and went home. There was a dusty cabinet, and in it were the bottles I had not touched in years, and in them, the numbness I needed to make the pain recede. I knew it wouldn't go away, nothing short of death could do that, but it would at least give me some objectivity, to step back and take a look at what had happened, and what I could have done better.

I was drunk, sitting in the dark, having pulled the blinds on all the windows, when she showed up. She watched me as I poured with one hand, then lifted the glass to my mouth with the other.

"I wasn't sure who to talk to when you ran off. I wondered if I should let you have some time, but you worried me with your... detachment. I considered your mother," Bella leaned back in the couch, almost vanishing into the shadows, only her calm voice letting me know she was there. "Who has known you the longest, and she certainly wants me in your life. She bustled into the room when you left to fight goblins, smiled at me, and announced, 'you two will be perfect together. Oh, I have wanted someone to make him happy again.'"

I took another drink, methodically pouring with my left hand and then using my right to lift the glass, squaring my corners as I did so.

"Margot came to mind, but although she has lived with you as her brother all your life, she does not understand you at all. Which left Ellie. You know, when I first came here, I thought she was your wife?"

This jolted me enough that I looked over. Her face was a pale oval in the darkness, her body melted into the couch, just her face turned toward me.

"Ellie has nursed you through many injuries, illnesses, and heartbreak, she tells me, but it was your first wife who you still mourn that she was in service to. She chose to stay with you of her own free will, although, she told me, you've tried often enough to fire her."

I grunted, and poured another drink in my methodical effort to get stinkin' drunk.

"She also told me not to let you mope. That if you have time to rebuild your walls, you might not come out again. That you've been easier with me than anyone else she has ever seen. Building me my own armory in your house... that was your way of making this my home, too."

Bella stood and walked toward me, and I realized she was wearing a red dress that must have been painted on. It sparkled, even in the dim room. Her hair was brushed out and loose. She was every man's vision.

I spoke for the first time. "If you can't pour out with your left hand," I demonstrated. "Then you're too drunk and it's time to go to bed." I picked up with my right, and belted it back.

"Lom," she bent over me and I could smell her, could feel the heat of her skin. "Pour me one?"

Chapter 33

Alger's Archivist

I have no idea whether I did. The next thing I remember was waking in my own bed, alone. I had a fleeting moment of disappointment that she wasn't next to me, and then I remembered that I had decided I would be bad for her. If she was going to stay here, Underhill, then our relationship would be frowned upon, should we become more than partners. Should she be selected Queen, it would be impossible. But she had looked so inviting last night...

I swung my feet out of bed and sat up slowly, fully dressed and feeling more than a little hungover. Ellie knocked on my bedroom door and walked in while I was still opening my mouth to respond, carrying a tray. I closed my mouth and glared at her.

She set the tray on the bedside table, clattering it and making me wince. "Mad at me?" I rasped through a dry throat.

She didn't answer, simply clearing her throat with a loud "hrmph" and pouring ingredients into a glass. I eyed it with trepidation. I remembered this concoction. It started to smoke slightly, and she handed it to me.

"Drink," she ordered, putting her hands on her hips and frowning.

I shuddered and held my nose, tilting my head slightly to accommodate the glass as I gulped it as quickly as possible. It burned all the way down, and then my head felt like it had exploded. I flopped back onto the bed.

"No, you don't." She reached over and took the empty glass from my grip. "Up, dressed, and you're due at Court in three hours."

"Why so early?" I sat up again, and the headache was already receding. My brain felt clearer, too.

"That's not early. It's past lunchtime now, and you will be there tonight."

I stood up. "I hear and obey. Now... can I take a bath?"

She collected the tray and left, again with a voluble sniff as she closed the door behind her. I tried to remember what was planned for tonight as I washed and dressed. A plate of food had appeared by the time I was out of the bath, and by that time I was ready to eat. A note lay next to the plate.

"Lom," Bella wrote, "sorry if I made you uncomfortable last night, but I'm not going to let you tell me what I want, or don't want. Partners doesn't imply that you get to be boss and I'm only doing what you tell me to. I will meet you at the banquet hall this evening, if you would do me the honor of being my escort."

When had we become partners? I let the paper flutter back to the table top, standing and looking out my window, not seeing the scenery, but a shadowy woman in red. It had been the fight with the Ogres, I thought. She had unflinchingly had my back. Then, in the hall while we were surrounded and outnumbered, she and I had stood back to back and she had made jokes while we fought. Sure, she needed experience, but she was smart, had the library on tap, and I thought I could stand looking at her once in awhile. I felt myself smiling broadly.

The rest of my afternoon I passed in working in the armory. The familiar rhythms of tasks that didn't make me think was a good way, I had found, to reset my mind when I was deeply upset. If I was going to have Bella's back tonight at Court, I needed to be able to focus. Her trial time at Court wasn't over, and the trouble with the goblins, and now, Low Court, were only going to prolong it. Also, I was increasingly afraid that if the King became aware of the true extent of Bella's power, he would choose her as Queen. That would make Bella pissed at me. At everyone Underhill.

I didn't remember that Alger was going to be at Court until I walked into the entry hall of the upper levels, where transportation bobble spells flickered and popped all around me. It was a very busy evening, so whatever was planned was a big function. Alger materialized nearby, looked around, and spotted me.

"Lom!" he greeted me enthusiastically, heading for me with open arms. He was dressed for the occasion in a suit that had probably been made more than a century before, with satin knee breeches and a tail coat. His hair was neatly restrained in a queue for once, and he almost managed to look distinguished. I ducked the hug.

"Alger, why are you here?" My own greeting was much less effusive.

"I would like to finally meet Bella." He sounded very pleased with himself for some reason. "I have been looking forward to determining if we have a new Family Archivist."

"She is not your librarian." I reminded him sourly, heading for the foot of the stairs. I'd been told to meet Bella here, but not a precise time, so I would loiter. Alger kept up with me. There were times I forgot he was as tall as I am. That reminded me of the portrait of Alonzo Mulvaney Bella had 'ported to my house just before the whole thing got complicated. I hadn't seen it when I was there, had entirely forgotten about it, and I wondered both where Bella had put it, and if he had been tall for a Pixie.

I realized Alger had not responded to me, and looked at him. Then I followed his line of sight, as he was staring, mouth slightly hanging open, up the stairs. Bella was making her entrance. I felt myself start to laugh, softly. I knew where the dress had come from, and it was an allusion that would miss most everyone Underhill. I'd also seen the dress before, I realized, the night before.

I met her at the foot of the stairs and offered her my arm. Alger still stood to the side, frozen. Bella smiled at me and slid her hand into my crooked elbow.

"Hello, Jessica..." I chuckled. "So, how do you keep that dress up, anyway?"

Bella grinned at me. "Magic, of course. Do you like it? I don't think you really saw it, last night."

"Oh, I saw it. So, what brought this on?"

"You said formal, and feminine." She nodded demurely at Joe, whose stone facade had cracked enough to allow a glimmer in his eye as we swept past him into the ballroom.

"So, this is a revenge dress for my not giving you better details?" I was trying hard not to laugh out loud, and this time, a belly laugh.

"No, my revenge will be making you dance with me."

"What if I tell you I can't dance?" I made the mistake of saying that just as Margot walked up to us.

"Lom, you dance beautifully! Bella, that dress is... amazing." She gushed, holding out her hands and Bella took her hand from my arm to take both of my sister's.

"Lom was most unhelpful when it came to designing a wardrobe for Court appearances. I'm afraid I'm very modern compared to the rest of you." Bella smiled at Margot and released her hands. "Perhaps we should talk about clothing sometime soon."

"Oh, yes! But my dear, I will be asking you questions, because you, Bella, are going to set the fashion. I am so bored," she emphasized the word heavily, "with what we have been wearing forever."

Bella blinked, turned slightly pink, and looked at me helplessly. "Don't look at me," I backed up a step. "You're the one in the knock-out dress."

"Oh, but I am interrupting," beamed Margot. "I do believe you were about to drag my brother out on the dance floor. Do have fun!"

She fluttered off, and Bella giggled. "She just has no filters, does she?"

"No, she doesn't."

"You don't have to dance with me tonight," she turned and looked up at me, flaring her wings so no one could see over her shoulder or hear her as she spoke softly. "I wanted to get you out of the house, but I know this had to be difficult."

I looked around the brilliantly lit room full of oblivious people. "There's a reason I'm not a social being."

"I know. I wouldn't be here if I didn't have to be. We could be curled up in your library room, reading by firelight and sipping coffee." She furled her wings, like a debutante tucking away her fan. "But tonight we have to pretend we fit in here."

"So, we dance." I held out my hand to her. She took it, and I led her onto the floor as they began a waltz. That dress was more suited to a tango, but I didn't think the Underhill musicians knew anything that lively.

"Why," I asked as we moved to the music, "is this a command performance for me?"

"Because we aren't done yet. Jenny may be gone, but the power behind her remains." She pointed out what I already knew. "And you pouring yourself into a bottle meant I was going to have to go after them myself."

I growled at her. "Not your job."

"Not yours, either. You haven't been assigned it by the king." she pointed out calmly, maintaining a little smile as we danced.

"Who else is going to take it on? Bella," She put a finger to my mouth as the music stopped.

"Hence, a command performance. I can't do it alone, I do know that." She walked away from me, as I stood still on the dance floor.

She meant that, I knew. She had every intention of coming with me to Low Court. The music began again and jolted me out of my reverie. I walked off the dance floor, and realized that Alger was leading Bella onto it.

"Alger!" he ignored me, of course, whirling her around in a swirl of red skirt and a low laugh from Bella.

I watched them from the edge of the dance floor, wondering why I was so uneasy about this meeting between her and my old mentor. She had the library in her head, and hadn't shown any signs that she couldn't access it at will. He didn't think that was possible... and I hadn't warned her not to tell him.

She was laughing up at him, her hair falling down her bare back in a cascade of blue-black waves. He was looking rather struck by her, and I wondered if she would distract him from his interest in her mind. But no... I could see that he was talking to her, not missing a beat in the dance, and her eyebrows were going up in a very amused reaction. I couldn't make out what they were saying to one another, the movements of the dance kept me from reading their lips, but I could guess.

Alger would ask her about how the library was working for her, she would tell him it was atrociously organized... I found my lips quirking up. She could handle him, and I could see from all the way across the room that he was looking disconcerted. She was not from Underhill, where the women were inconsequential by upbringing, and he had forgotten that. Underhill, it wasn't that women were oppressed, they easily equalled men in power by virtue of magic, and there was no reason for ours to have been a patriarchal society, unlike humans. It was simply that our society was stagnant, and so the little petty affairs were what had become important, not the work that Bella had been doing prior to her exile Underhill. She had been a scholar in her own way, and active physically in ways my sister, for example, could never understand.

I wondered how having the library of magic in her head was going to change Bella, was already changing her, as she circled the dance floor in a shimmering red dress held up by magic. And then, as she came to a halt in front of me, and came to me with a smile on Alger's arm, I wondered how she had changed me. Was it obvious? I looked at Alger, who was smiling besottedly at her. Well, he hadn't seen it, at least.

"Lom, M'boy!" he boomed at me, all smiles. "This is wonderful, wonderful!"

"What is, Alger? Bella, would you care to take refreshment?"

She took my arm as well and the three of us cut a path into the adjoining room where a buffet was laid out. Alger went on with his exhortation.

"I've never seen anything like it. She shouldn't be able to access more than a tenth of the library, but it seems..." he broke off to peer down at the woman smiling up at him. "How much can you access?"

"I'm not sure. I just... search for things, and find them. It never occurred to me to think I was being blocked from some of it, so I may be. How would I know?"

She sank into a chair at a small round table, and I brought glasses of non-alcoholic fizzy stuff for us. Alger was sitting with her, talking, and I stood and watched the others in the room while he tried to decide how much she knew. Or could know.

The Folke seemed unruffled by how close they had come to death, or worse. They still laughed and flirted and fluttered around the room, a dazzling display of color and glitter. I felt gloomy, watching them. Why had I bothered with the goblins? Was this really a society that was worth saving? Martin and Henry had been worth a dozen of these airheads. I spotted Joe, in all his Majordomo serenity, sailing through the crowd. I dropped a hand onto Bella's shoulder to get her attention and went to meet him. I knew without a word said that he wanted me, as he made eye contact and raised an eyebrow fractionally.

Chapter 34

Unwelcome News

Bella broke off mid-word and looked up, putting her hand over mine. "What's wrong?"

"We're being summoned, I believe. Alger, you will have to interrogate the Princess later."

He rose gallantly and took her hand, kissing the back of it and making her giggle. Then we strolled out of the room, following Joe out the side door. As soon as it closed behind us, I stopped, and Joe kept going for a couple steps before he caught on, then he turned and raised an eyebrow.

"What's going on?" I demanded. "You wouldn't have pulled us out of a busy reception for the princesses on anything less than the King's command, but I need to know what I am walking into with Bella. Last time the two of us sat down with him, he put her under house arrest."

He shook his head slightly at me, with no softening of his expression. I knew what that meant. If he could talk about it, he would. But he couldn't.

I debated turning and walking away. But Joe had never given me a reason not to trust him. I looked at Bella and she nodded. She trusted him, too. Well, alright then. I looked back at him. "Where are we going, at least?"

"The study," he replied simply.

Damn. That wasn't good. This meant that we were going to be prepped for a later, public announcement of import, and he expected a strong initial reaction, most likely from me. Had it only been me summoned, I would have known it was just a hush-hush assignment. Having Bella along changed everything.

I knew it was going to be an unusual meeting when he ushered us into the king's private quarters. The king wasn't there, and Joe left us alone. As he left the room he gave me a small wink. I wondered what had brought that on. He spent a lot of time cultivating the imperturbable look, and he wasn't given to dabbling in Court politics. He did his job and stayed quiet. Which is what he did now, silently shutting the door.

I might be alone with her, but it wasn't a place to talk about anything personal. I shrugged and deliberately put Joe's action to the back of my mind.

"Sit and make yourself comfortable," I suggested to her. "We might have a little wait."

She looked around the room, and I followed her lead, seeing it through fresh eyes. It was not an opulent chamber, but comfortable. I knew from experience the chairs were comfortable, and the wear was from centuries of use. They had earned the shabby. I had been here many times, meetings with the king when he needed a job done quickly and informally.

Bella finally took a seat in a faded blue chair, and looked a little tense. I sat opposite her on a small couch with plush cushions, remembering younger days lounging in this spot and trying to make the king laugh. I had succeeded from time to time, and over the decades had decided that it was better for him if I damaged his calm on occasion. This would not be one of them. My own calm was shaky.

Bella's wings were folded up tightly enough to be almost out of sight behind her as she sat with hands folded, but from the way the wingtips quivered from time to time betrayed her nervousness. She had chosen to stay Underhill, in a moment I considered foolish, and she had to be regretting that now, but there was no escape here. I was trying to think of a safe topic to divert her with, in this room where there were literally ears in the wall, when the king walked in.

He folded into his favorite chair, an overstuffed leather armchair that creaked under his weight. I wondered absently if someone kept repairing the old furniture to keep it going for him. He stretched his feet out in front of him with a sigh.

"Lom," he greeted me, and then, with a rare smile, "Bella."

Bella took my cue and responded as I did. "Your Majesty."

He might be acting informally, but I was erring on the side of caution and politeness. Also, I wasn't happy with him at the moment.

"I called you two to give you an informal notification, and job assignment, Lom."

I nodded. I had expected this. Bella just watched us. The king went on.

"Lom, I want you to escort our rescuees home. Melcar is afraid they will go witless dwelling on memories of their captivity, and has recommended that taking them back to their homes might be the best thing for them. We could, of course, simply transport them back, but I wanted a reliable emissary to carry a hand-written message from me, and assure the Eastern Court we will offer them all aid."

I thought I understood the subtext. He was appointing me to this so I could assess how corrupted Eastern was by the Low Court. Bell would lend this weight by her status...

The king interrupted my train of thought, "Bella, you will receive special training to ready you for coronation."

And the train of thought derailed with a noisy crashing of gears. What had he just said? I glanced at Bella, who was looking back and forth between us with confused eyes, and the wings were back to quivering.

He was positively jovial as he continued, "M'dear, you have the power, the presence, to be a magnificent Queen. I will be proud to share the ruling of Underhill with you, which our kingdom desperately needs to be in balance once more. But you need polish." He fixed her with an eagle-eyed glare. "You are a loose cannon and you must learn control."

I thought Bella really would explode right there. And he had no idea how much power and knowledge she really had. It was a good thing she was not the child he was treating her like, with the library in her head and no control. What she lacked was experience. I'd hoped to help her earn that alongside me, not immured in Court stagnating and becoming something she would loathe.

I spoke before she could. "Who are you going to appoint to teach her?"

Bella stood up, her wings flaring behind her. "I must decline to accept the position."

He stared at her for a moment. I sighed. I had half expected this reaction from her. She went on, her voice icy calm.

"I am in no way suited to a queenship. I have no real ties to Underhill, besides Lom, and he only because we work well together. I never wanted to come here, and did so only under duress. I feared for my personal safety and even more for that of my family. I understand that I would not be your wife, but that I would be in a place of authority, making important decisions for the benefit of this Court, and Underhill. I am not the right person for that. I don't know enough, and simply giving me protocol lessons is not going to remedy that. If you are so worried about my lack of experience and power, I have a solution to suggest. Let me work with Lom. If he can't deal with me, who else is going to?"

She stood there, wings trembling, but otherwise still and composed. He put his fingertips together and rested his bearded chin on them, looking at her through hooded eyes. I just leaned back and stayed out of it. That was my girl. She didn't need back-up, just moral support. She knew I was here for her.

"The reason I selected you, Belladonna, is the way you just spoke to me."

She blinked in surprise, and I tried not to let my lips crook up into the smile I was starting to feel. The king stood up slowly, and came to stand in front of her.

"I've behaved abominably toward you. I've done it deliberately, trying to provoke you. I needed to know how you would react to personal attacks." Now he grinned, the most boyish expression I had even seen on his face. "I have already had many reports of how well you handle yourself in actual combat."

Bella looked at me, and I shook my head. He'd had those stories from someone else. The king held out a hand.

"Forgive me? Would you be willing to work with me?"

She took his hand reluctantly. Bella's too nice to hurt someone looking at her with sad eyes. I had seen him manipulate people over the centuries, through sheer force of will, power, and discipline, but this was the first time I had seen this softer side of him. It was what she would need, though. She couldn't endure constantly at odds with him. I felt a little pang of loss. I had been looking forward to more time with her, and perhaps another kiss. This would end that little dream.

"I am not a creature of Underhill, sir," she protested.

"All the better. It will give you an objectivity we sorely need."

"And I miss my family." Bella admitted this after a long pause, and I knew it meant she did trust him a little, to say that. "They expect me home again, you know."

"There's no reason you cannot go home again, just not to live in Human Realms. In fact, I don't anticipate the coronation to be anytime soon. Once Lom returns from his little errand, he can escort you above."

She sighed, and I saw her wings droop. "I don't have a choice, really, do I, sir?"

"You do. You can choose to decline to become Queen. I will not force you into that. But know that if you do decide that, you can never return to your family and must remain watched even Underhill. You have too much power, and would be too tempting to Our enemies."

She protested, her face suddenly showing anger. "And being Queen protects me from that how? By making me choose between ruling and prison, you are forcing me."

The king shot back passionately, still showing more emotion than I had ever guessed lay in him. "Do you think I would choose this, if I could leave it all behind? I am alone, I can number those I trust fully on the fingers of one hand. But it is my duty, Belladonna. I was chosen for this, for some of the same reasons I am choosing you. You have honor, girl, and you know what duty is. It lies heavy on all of us, and shapes our destiny, will we or no. We are none of us fully free."

She looked into his eyes for a long moment, still holding his hand. I wondered what she was thinking. I knew something he didn't. She was fully capable of leaving this room, so carefully guarded, in a transportation bubble, fleeing Underhill, and precipitating a war with the Folke and Raven's kin. I wondered if she knew that. Better question, did the king know that she had such powerful mentors?

"I need time. I came expecting to while away the days until I went home. It was all an adventure. I never anticipated..." she let her voice trail off. The king gave her hand a squeeze and let go of it.

"You have time. I will appoint Alger, Lucia, and Lady Herbale to help you learn what you need to know. Lom will be away a few days, and then you should visit your family. I urge you to take counsel of your grandfather. I met him briefly many, many years ago, and he struck me as a wise man, even then, young as he was. Now I would imagine that has not changed." The king looked at me, and I nodded silent confirmation. Bob would ease her mind, even if he told her things she didn't want to hear. I made a mental note to ask at another time about how the king and Bob had met. There had to be a story there.

"For now, I need Lom to take the mission to the Eastern Court. You are welcome to remain in your rooms with freedom to roam through the Court. Will that do?"

She nodded. "Thank you."

I broke in. "Can she also go as far as my home?" I knew she could, of course, I had seen her there last night. But I knew she didn't realize she had been interdicted to the Court, and that ought to have been impossible. Bella had no idea of the full extent of her power.

"I don't see why not, if she needs to retreat. I know what a whirl it can be here, m'dear." They smiled at one another, and I could see the birth of an understanding between these two that relieved me. I had no desire to see Bella's power tested, and none at all to see Court in smoking ruins. I had a feeling she could do that, if she really were angry, and the loose cannon he had accused her of being.

"When does Lom leave?" she asked him quietly, her wings still and folded shut behind her. I recognized the signs of a calm Bella, but also guessed she was riding an adrenaline high under that exterior.

"Tomorrow morning?" The king looked at me and I shrugged. I could leave tonight, but it was up to him. The sooner I went, the sooner I was back, and I just wanted to get back and have a long talk with Bella, preferably outside the borders of Underhill.

"Then, if you will excuse us, sire, I would like to have another dance before bedtime." She smiled demurely at him. He looked startled for a second, surveying her in all her red-dress glory, then threw back his head in a bellow of laughter.

"Go on and enjoy yourself. Dam'me if I don't wish I could join you," he ended wistfully.

"And why not, sir? I am sure Lom would give up the floor to you - I practically had to drag him out the first time."

"You're good for him, girl."

I spoke up at this, "in the room, sir. And she's a menace to my peace of mind."

He laughed again, waving us out while his shoulders shook in helpless chortles. I fled before he decided to be even more unnerving and tease me. Bella took my elbow in the hall.

271

Chapter 35

Sealing the Deal

I realized she was steering me firmly away from the ballroom and felt surprised. "I thought you wanted another dance?"

"I want a raincheck on that. Right now, I need to talk to you. Somewhere safe?"

I realized she didn't know where was safe and where wasn't. She realized here at Court, listeners were everywhere. "My place."

The words were barely out of my mouth before the bubble snapped into place around us, and an interminable second later, we were in the still-darkened living room of my house, and I had my arms full of sobbing Bella. Startled at the sudden about-face from her cheer of a moment earlier, I rubbed her back and let her cling.

"So-sorry," she gasped out after a moment. "I- I didn't mean to do that. And I'm making you wet..."

I pulled her closer. "Cry if you need to and don't apologize. That was an unpleasant shock, I understand."

Through everything we had been through, I had never seen her cry. She might have late at night, I knew she had nightmares about the beings she had killed, because she had told me that. But she had never broken down, and I wasn't sure what to say to her now. I had just seen her life crushed, her dreams taken away, and she had laughed and flirted at the end of it. There was a steel to this woman, but also... She hiccupped to a stop finally and tried to pull away. I kept rubbing her back, feeling the ridges where her wings connected to bone, and gently working knots out of those muscles with my fingertips. She sighed, muffled, into the shoulder of my coat.

"That fe-feels good, thank you."

I wasn't sure if she meant the massage, or just being held, and it didn't really matter. She needed me.

"What am I going to do?" she whispered into my neck.

"I can't answer that for you."

"I know. I just..." She sniffed and lifted her head up to look at me. "I can't go home again."

"You did decide to stay Underhill just..." I had to think. So much had happened, had it only been a day? "Yesterday."

"But I had options, then."

"You have options now." I led her to the couch without letting go of her. I'm not sure if I thought she was going to fly away, or if it was an excuse to hold on to her one last time, but I didn't take time to analyse it. "You are stronger than you realize, Bella."

She cuddled into my shoulder as we sat together. "And if I ran away he would come after me. He sees me as a threat."

"You are a potential threat." I pointed out gently. "If he knew about the library he would have you under lock and key right now. You don't know the kind of power you can tap into with that. Alger has some inkling, but he's more interested in it as an academic."

"Can he take it out?"

I shook my head. "I'm sorry. I know I did this too you. Had I any idea..."

"I know you only wanted to give me the tools I needed to survive. And it's saved both of our lives, so... I'm glad I have it." She sighed and leaned her head back, closing her eyes. I looked down at her, seeing the teardrops still glistening on her lashes. She went on without opening her eyes. "Lom... what does the Queen do?"

"You have the library." I smiled down at her and then gave into temptation and kissed her forehead.

She tilted her head to one side and brought her hand up, pulling me down enough to reach my mouth and kissed me back. After a long moment, she spoke, lip to lip with me. "I'm not giving this up."

I leaned back far enough to look into her eyes. "Give what up?"

"Kissing you." She smiled and I let her do it again.

"Bella..." I wanted to let this progress, to go where we both so badly wanted it to take us. "It's not possible. This would not be good for you."

"Why not?"

"I'm a Pixie. I'm not... you can't..." I stopped, not sure how to tell her that, as Queen, she would have to choose her affairs carefully, and never with those seen as lower caste than the Fairy Court denizens. She would be expected to use pillow talk for diplomacy with foreign nobles, to seal deals with a kiss, and more. Human mores and Underhill ease with sexuality were two different beasts, and that, I was sure, she had no idea about. It wouldn't be in the library. Bella was a faithful woman, and if not a virgin, close enough to for it not to matter. She wasn't going to like this.

She surprised me with her little gurgle of laughter. "I'm an American. We don't respect the nobility."

And with that offhand comment I realized she was right. She would never see us as fairy and pixie, master and servant. She saw me as male, and herself as female. It would scandalize Court, but I had never cared about that before.

"What do you want, Bella?"

She started to open her mouth, and I hastily amended my question. "Tonight. From me... you wanted to talk?"

Damn the woman. I was perpetually losing my cool around her, and having an arm around those warm, bare shoulders and the taste of her on my lips was certainly not helping. She lifted an eyebrow, a small smile playing on her lips.

"You're offering to actually answer questions?"

"Within reason." I had to maintain my dignity somewhere.

Bella snorted and sat up a little, rearranging herself, and her wings, so she wasn't leaning entirely on me. I found I missed the contact, even knowing it would have put my arm to sleep.

"What was she like?"

I knew what Bella was asking. The Queen who had come before her. There were doubtless biographies in the library, but Bella knew I would have seen her in a way few others could. It wasn't a question she could ask anyone - well, perhaps Alger - and get an unbiased answer to.

"She was capricious." I stopped and thought a moment. I didn't want to give her a picture colored too much by my dislike, but I knew it would come through nonetheless. "I didn't like her, you understand. She cordially despised me, and my kind. We were... dust beneath her feet, simply pawns to move around the board and gain her what she wanted."

"Oh..." Bella's gasp as the import of what I was telling her sank in was followed by a kiss on my cheek. "I am sorry."

I shrugged, staring off into the dark room, remembering some of the bad moments. "There's a reason I spent most of my time hunting monsters. It was a way of doing something worthwhile, when I was power- less here."

She yawned, muffling it with her hand. "Sorry... It's been a long day, and a short night before it for me."

"Want to go back to Court?"

She shook her head. "Not yet, do you mind? I know you probably need to pack."

"No, my bug-out bag is here, in the armory. I can retrieve it as we leave."

She snuggled back into my shoulder, warm against me, and asked sleepily, "how does that work for you, anyway, since you can't do magic?"

I leaned my head back on the couch and answered, "I use pre-made spells that Ellie or Alger put together for me. And I can do some magic, but not a whole lot before it starts to poison me."

"You never did explain that."

I didn't that night, either, because I realized that she was asleep before I had gotten my thoughts together enough to answer her. I didn't want to disturb her, I'd wake her in an hour or so and take her back to our rooms... I drifted off, closing my eyes.

Chapter 36

Reluctant Departure

I was awakened by the smell of bacon, frying. Bella stirred and murmured slightly in her sleep, ending with a tiny squeak. She was curled up with me on the couch, and a blanket had been spread over both of us. I blinked at the soft knitted brown afghan for a second before I processed that the windows were uncovered and it was the first blush of dawn outside. I looked toward the kitchen. I couldn't see into it, but I knew it had to be Ellie, in there frying up.

It took a little work to extricate myself from Bella, who was between me and the couch edge. She snuggled into the warm spot I'd left with a sigh and kept on sleeping. I padded toward the kitchen, noting that my shoes had been slipped off, and stood neatly along with hers by the stairs. As I walked into the kitchen, shucking my wrinkled dress jacket, I got an unpleasant surprise for my morning.

"Alger," I growled.

He looked up with a sunny smile. "Glad you got up, m'boy, was just thinking I would need to grab a couple of pot and pan lids."

I snarled slightly at him, but my rejoinder was cut off by Ellie pushing a steaming cup of coffee into my hand. Black ichor of the gods... I cradled it and sipped appreciatively. It helped a little to ease the sight of Alger in my home. He had not visited in many years, knowing I would shut the door in his face if he turned up.

"Why," I got to the point, "are you here?"

"Bella." He replied quietly, "I came in with Ellie this morning, and your mother and Dill's dragon lady are coming later on."

I blinked at him for a moment, finally figuring out that by dragon lady, he meant the dowager we had met, guardian of the Princess Dill.

"Have them bring Dill along." I offered after sitting and thinking a moment. "Bella liked her, and you might be surprised how much having a little disingenuity will help."

I was also thinking it would make Bella laugh. I made a mental note to send messages to Devon and Dorothy, as well. Young company to offset the pompous droning she was about to be inundated in.

Ellie slid a plate of eggs and ham in front of me, and I ate dutifully. I wasn't really hungry, but the protein would help and arguing with her would just end in me losing.

"So what are you going to try and teach her?" I asked Alger.

"I don't know, I still want to figure out how she can access all of the library. I'm sure," he added thoughtfully, "that I can teach her how to find information more efficiently."

That made me snort, remembering Bella's acid comment about his organization of the library. "Maybe you should teach her how to put it in order the way she wants it in her head."

He looked struck by this concept. I stood up and stretched, feeling the stiffness from sleeping on the couch, and with another person. It had been... a very long time, since I had done that.

"Tell Bella I'll be back soon, and we'll finish our conversation." I was speaking to Ellie, but Alger smirked at this. I glared at him, and pulled up a bubble to go to the Court. As I stepped out of it, I reflected that I was running low on pre-made spells. When I got back, I'd teach Bella how to make them for me, and it should be interesting to see what she came up with. The woman seemed endlessly creative at spell casting.

They weren't ready yet, which I expected. I gathered a few things from our rooms, and made sure my bag was packed tightly for transit. I didn't know how long I would be gone, but planned for three days, and packed for a week. I was reading in the lobby, my kit next to me on the upholstered bench, when Melcar ushered in his charges. I tucked the book into my cargo pocket and stood to clasp forearms with him. Wood Elves are locked into a culture even older and more resistant to change than Fairy.

"Coming along?" I asked him, looking at the huddle of fairies he had shepherded into the lobby. A pair of his apprentices were with them, soothing and whispering as they shrank from the open space around them.

He shook his head, the fresh leaves woven into his hair whispering with his movements. "I am needed here. I have a copy of my report for the Eastern Court," He held out a small parchment envelope I knew contained a spell. I tucked it in another pocket. I had adopted the cargo pants when I encountered them in human realms. Pockets were wonderfully useful.

"My apprentices, Bertie and Alba, will accompany you," he offered.

"Let's get going, then. I think they need something to occupy their minds."

We repeated the arm clasp, and I walked toward the group of people. A large transportation bubble was trickier, and his apprentices would handle it.

"Ready?" I asked the man I recognized from the pen. His eyes were clear, but still haunted, and although the sparse stubble had been shaved, it just revealed him to be sunken cheeked. My question caused him to straighten a little. He squared his shoulders and a spark came into his eye.

He nodded, and gestured to the apprentices. I had guessed correctly, this was the leader. My handing over the reins to him, even symbolically, had given him something. I started to feel a little hope for these people. We might not share a language, but minds work alike.

The bubble sprang into existence, and we were on our way. Like most travel, the further you had to go, the longer it took. Even magic couldn't do away with that. We were standing on a flat floor, with an iridescent soap-bubble ceiling over us. The coordinates of the Eastern Court were our target, and I knew from experience we would land in a perfect garden, full of the scent of flowers and breath-taking plants as designed as sculptures. I was already going over my greeting. They knew we were coming, and would have someone who spoke English waiting along with a group of healers and relatives. It could be a noisy, emotional moment.

The bubble jolted, and I dropped into a crouch. Around me, people were screaming, some had fallen down, others had dropped to the floor as the bubble bounced like a plane in turbulence. This was decidedly not normal.

I had never felt anything like this, but my mind immediately went to the encounter between the Alaskan Bush plane and a Roc, not that long ago. Only here, I had no windows, and no way to shoot back. That part I could fix, at least. I triggered a call spell and felt the comforting weight of my shotgun fill my palm.

I barked an order to the passengers. "Get down, hug the floor!" I had no idea if they understood me, but most of them were already down anyway. Melcar's apprentices, a bonded pair, obeyed me without question, clutching one another and watching me with wide eyes. I rode out the jostling with loose knees, remembering rough seas and feeling that same queasy sense as I held the gun at ready, and scanned slowly in a full circle.

That we were being hijacked in some way I did not doubt, and I guessed by Low Court, but had no idea where they would land us, and what we would face once the bubble popped. There was a thud as we hit something, and the bubble stopped, tilted. I staggered, and recovered my footing just as the bubble went down. A chorus of jeers, screeches, and laughter greeted the sight of us. Me, with the questing barrel of the shot-gun, and the prostrate fairies.

It was Low Court, all right. I didn't recognize the setting, but the ragged bunch that surrounded us was unmistakable. For all the polish of my Court, here there was black, gray, and the red of eyes, teeth, and boils on the skin of a troll looming behind the rest. They held in a ring, taunting and hurling insults. I didn't think they were afraid of the small damage I could do with the gun - should they charge me, I might kill a few, but I faced dozens. My charges lay helpless at my feet.

Chapter 37

The Low King

The ring of onlookers broke, but not to allow a surge of violent beings toward us. Instead, they all fell silent as the Low King stalked through the gap. Inhumanly beautiful, where they were dressed in rags, he wore an elegantly tailored suit. He carried a cane with a silver top, swinging it lightly as he paced forward, eyes narrowed. I trained the muzzle of my gun on him.

"That's far enough." I told him when he was a pace inside the ring of his minions.

He stopped obligingly, an amused look on his face, and leaned on his cane, his hands crossed on the top. I took a step toward him, putting myself solidly between my charges and him.

"What do you think you are doing, little pixie?" he cooed at me.

I pumped a shell into the barrel. "Getting ready to blow apart your black heart. Bertie, get ready with another bubble." I spoke loudly enough for the prone wood elf to hear, and hoped he or Alba was rational enough to break through their fear and obey me.

The Low King shook his head slowly, mocking me. "Fool. You will not be able to leave until I allow it. I have this area interdicted against transport."

"That can be broken." It could, but it would require someone with more power than I had available. Being a cripple in magic sucked.

He sneered, revealing the first flaw in his appearance, with gray, jagged teeth. The idea of being bitten by them made me shiver, but I kept the gun steady on him.

He flicked a glance at the barrel. "We seem to have an impasse, then. You could shoot me, but then you, and all of..." he gestured limply at the Eastern Court people who had already been through so much at his instigation, "would die." He clucked his tongue against those teeth. "Such a waste. Pity, really..."

"What. Do. You. Want." I gritted out between clenched teeth. I really wanted to just shoot him, but he was right, damn him.

"Only you. The rest of the rabble can go on their merry way. But you must stay behind, surrender all your..." He looked at the gun again. "Spells, and be at our mercy."

"You know High Court will not stand for this."

He shrugged and yawned ostentatiously, pretending boredom. "They will never miss one little pixie. Errand boys are a dime a dozen."

"There is no way I am trusting you to let them go. If I surrender, you are just going to let your drooling anacephalic goons have them." I didn't look away from him, but I felt the beings glare at me, and heard the low growl at my taunt.

He raised one hand, revealing that he wore french cuffs with simple ebony cufflinks, and snapped his fingers. Out of the corner of my eye I saw the bubble appear, and then, as he dropped his hand, blink out of sight. The Low King smiled.

"Wasn't that easy? Now..."

I squeezed the trigger. His eyes barely had time to widen before the slug tore through his snowy white shirtfront. I fired again and felt a weight drop on my back and knock me down, blocking my view of the effect that shot had. I felt a searing pain as someone kicked me in the head, but my last thought before losing consciousness was a fierce exultation that at least I had made them pay for me.

I woke up slowly, in pain, and then vomit, as nausea racked my body. I rolled onto my side to keep from drowning on it - that would be a bad way to die - and curled into the fetal position. Everything hurt, but I didn't think anything was broken. Well, maybe a rib. That was a familiar pain, as I gasped for air when the spasms released me. It took an interminable time for my body to relax enough to let me become more aware of my surroundings. To start with, I was fairly sure I was blind.

I was lying in a rapidly chilling puddle of my own vomit and other liquid I didn't care to analyze too closely, and thankfully my nose seemed to be either broken, or bruised enough to not be able to inhale and smell it. One of my legs didn't want to support my weight, so I contented myself with belly-crawling to a drier patch of the rough stone floor. It hurt, a lot, so I rested once I got there.

I could tell, from the sounds I was making - mostly grunts and moans - that I was in a small room. I couldn't tell if there was a door or other opening, my hearing is not that good on the best of days, and this was not a good day. It hurt, even to breathe. And I had the growing conviction that being alive was not a good thing. Low Court has a reputation for a reason, and after killing their King, they ought not to have had the restraint to leave me alive. I pushed myself to a sitting position.

My head swam. I had nothing left in my stomach, which was good, as it would have come out then. I panted for a moment, listening to the reflections of sound. I couldn't see, but I could feel a breath of air on my slime-covered cheek, and there was no sound bouncing back from a portion of the wall. I took a break before heading in that direction, as the little effort of sitting up had taken all my energy. This was going to be difficult.

It took some time for another important bit of information to sink in. My clothes had gone. I don't know why I didn't figure out I was naked when I first woke up, but it wasn't until I started shivering uncontrollably that it dawned on me. With shaking fingers, I felt my forearms, and realized that all my pre-made spells had been stripped away. Someone out there knew far too much about me and my weaknesses.

So, I was naked, weaponless, and couldn't see. I didn't know where I was, and I was hurt, badly. I'd been kept alive for the further amusement of sadists, and I had no freaking idea where the Low King had sent the people I was responsible for before I had killed him. One could hope for the Eastern Court, sure, but just as likely the bottom of the ocean. My only regret was that I hadn't killed more of them.

I tried the leg again, and even though the muscle knotted and I had to bite my lips to keep the scream in, I made it to standing. Hands out in front of me, swaying, I shuffled toward the draft. I wasn't thinking about escape and evasion. There was no way out of this. But maybe I could take at least one more with me.

Footsteps sounded, and I stopped, one finger just grazing against a wall. The other hand flailed out into an opening before I pulled it back and tried to regain my precarious balance. The being was coming down uneven stairs, it sounded like. I wondered wildly if I could leap forward and overpower it...

A light flared up. Ah... I wasn't blind, then. I blinked fast in reflex, the light was painful after the profound darkness I had been in. My eyes teared up, and the captor, who I couldn't quite see, snickered in a high-pitched tone.

"Pitiful pixie. Poor, poor thing... alone in the dark. You like the light?"

My eyes started to clear and focus. The elf globe she had lighted was flying directly at my head, and when I reflexively ducked it, I fell. This time I couldn't suppress the scream. There was something wrong with the elbow of the arm I had tried to catch myself on. She laughed, a hair-raising cackle.

"It hurts, and screams, so delicious." She bent over me, close enough for me to smell her ghoul breath.

I gasped out, "you should..."

"What?" she giggled, trailing a finger over my cheek. "My, you are dirty."

"Meet my friend in Seattle." I panted for a second, then finished, "he could use a ghoul-friend."

She dug her nails into my cheek and scratched, shrieking. Someone didn't like puns, I thought fuzzily. Then, as she kicked me in the belly and as I returned to the fetal position, I had one more clear thought.

"That's going to get infected." I don't know how loud it was, but she evidently heard it.

I didn't quite pass out as she took out her rage on me, and maybe I should have. Without thinking about it, I threw up a magical shield. If I had either been out, or fully aware, I would have known what would happen. As she tried to get to me, I could feel the poison flooding me, setting my every nerve on fire. When she finally fled back up the stairs, calling for help, I shut the spell off, and then I did pass out again. There was too much pain, and my mind simply couldn't deal with it.

I didn't know how long I had been out when I woke up again. I knew that a significant amount of time had passed, because I could feel that the magic poisoning had ebbed. I also knew, before I even opened my eyes, that I had been cared for. I wasn't in enough pain, for a start, and secondly, I was lying on something soft. Cautiously, I opened my eyes. The ghoul girl's abandoned elf globe still hovered near the ceiling, so I could at least see. I listened for a long moment, until I was sure I was alone in the room, and then turned my head to look around.

I was lying on a pile of hay or straw. It was soft relative to the floor where I had started, and at least it kept me out of the sour mess I had smeared across the better part of the small cell. It was, I determined, a replica of a gothic dungeon cell, complete with stone walls, dripping moisture, and chains dangling from a rusty iron hoop embedded in one wall. The door was the only incongruity, as it stood fully open, stairs just visible beyond it. I took a deep breath, feeling my ribs scream in pain as I did so, and started the process of sitting up. At least this time I could see what I was doing.

I made it halfway up the stairs when I heard footsteps approaching. I froze, trying to decide if I should try and go back down - it had been slow, hard work to get this far - or try and rush for the top. I picked one trembling foot up and placed it on the next stair. My hind brain was gibbering at me to run, but I braced myself against the wall and waited for what would come.

The half-expected ghoul was not the being who hove into view above me. Instead, a brutish fairy who snarled at me, then, unexpectedly, turned and walked out of sight again. I tried to figure out what that was about while I took another step upward. My whole body was trembling now, and I was sweating despite not having eaten or drunk anything that I was aware of in.. days?

I was trying to reconcile my having the ability to even stand upright with that datum when a troll thudded into sight. The floor shook slightly with his every step. I grabbed the wall and hung on for dear life, having registered that falling down the stairs would be bad, and render my efforts to wreak vengeance futile. He snorted and shook his head, no doubt amused by the naked pixie trying not to collapse. I couldn't move as he came down the steps, forced to keep holding the wall or fall.

He slung me over his shoulder like a sack of potatoes, and I screamed through a raw throat as my ribs bent under this renewed assault. I twisted myself around his neck like a living stole, and reached for anything I could grab. One hand on his ear gave me enough leverage to get the other as far as his eye, and I hooked two fingers into it. He reflexively shook his head to shake me off, which was a mistake on his part. I decided the hell with it, augmented my grip with a little magic, and pulled. There was a pop, a scream, and we both fell down the stairs.

The troll grabbed me by the ankle as soon as he could, on his knees, his eye a bloody wreck hanging halfway down his cheek, and threw me against the wall. I hit the wall, and existence blinked out.

Chapter 38

The Death of Hope

I woke up to golden sunshine streaming across my face. I was lying on a soft bed, with cool covers pulled up to my chest. I stared at the white ceiling, watching the dust-motes dance in the light, and wondering where the hell I was. I heard a rustle to my left, and turned my head gingerly, realizing two things. One, I didn't hurt, and two, Bella was sitting at my bedside reading a book; the rustle had been a page turning.

"Bella?" I whispered, unbelieving.

She looked at me, her hair pulled back from her face and secured in a loose bun with what looked like a pair of chopsticks. With flowers on the ends. I tried to gather my scattered thoughts, but her lips curved up into a smile and she stood, bending over me. "Lom, you're awake."

Bella's cool lips on my forehead made me shake suddenly, as I realized how weak I was, how close I had come to death. "How did you..." I tried to ask.

She laid a finger across my lips. "Shhh... Here, let me get the sun out of your eyes."

Bella walked across the room with a sultry sway of her hips that riveted my gaze, and reached up to pull the drapes closed. My eyes watered in response to the change in light levels. Sure, that's what those drops were. She turned and walked toward the half-open door of the room, her footsteps silent on a heavy carpet.

"Don't leave..." I pleaded almost inaudibly. She paused at the doorway and smiled back at me, then slipped out, her white dress swirling at her ankles and lingering in my vision for an instant longer. I couldn't stop the trembling in my body, and tried to push the covers aside and get up, cursing my weakness. I might not be in any pain, but I had evidently been sick in bed long enough I could barely move. I almost made it.

She caught me as I was falling. I had rolled to the edge, but misjudged how close I needed to be in order to swing my legs over. I clung to her as she helped me to a sitting position, and pulled her into an embrace with all my strength, trying not to sob aloud, and staring over her shoulder in growing confusion. Something was wrong, and I couldn't quite think. What...

"Here, I brought you water," she held a glass in one hand, easing me back far enough that I would be able to drink. I opened my mouth... and it clicked.

"Bella, where are your wings?" I blurted out stupidly.

She paused, and the water slopped out and onto my bare arm. The pain was blinding. I screamed, and pushed - whatever it was, it wasn't Bella and why had I been fool enough to fall for that? - it away, flailing with the arm the acid had just spilled onto. Hope, the greatest torture of them all...

I felt a ripping sensation across my forehead, and the scene before my eyes rippled sickeningly. I reached up and blindly yanked at strands which squirmed against my touch, but yielded and tore when I drew on magic in my fear and revulsion to get them off, away, out of my mind. Warm blood gushed over my fingers and into one eye. I didn't care if it was mine, or.. the thing's.

With the penetration of my skin gone, I could see that I was still in the stone cell. The thing masquerading as Bella and raping my mind was a huddled lump whimpering in the corner. I still hurt, so badly... I leaned forward and vomited, a weak stream of mostly green bile adding to the steaming acid puddle on the stones. The non-mostly part was bright red blood. I idly noted that this was a very bad sign, before staggering to my feet and heading towards the foul lump of creature.

I'd insulted the first captor, injured the second, and I was going to tear this one to pieces with my bare hands and leave it to rot. I stumbled, and realized my vision was graying out on the edges. Dammit. This was no time to die, I had to kill it, first. I focused on taking one step at a time, and then I was there.

The blob of skin and tentacles withdrew into a tight, gelatinous ball, then, as I grabbed part of it, flew into action, pseudopods wrapping around my neck and arms. I ripped a few of them off, and it shrilled horribly. There.. the mouth of the skin gaped wide in pain. I knew what it was, in a flash of lucidity, and I knew how to kill it. A kind of succubus, the parasite would attach itself to a host, filling the host's mind full of endorphins and pretty fantasies, while the host slowly starved to death.

I seized the upper part of the orifice, then risked letting go of tentacles with the other hand, grabbed the other part of the mouth, pulling it as wide as I could. If I was going to die, so was this foul thing. I felt a pop, then another as something inside me gave way. As the creature thrashed, I vomited again, a gout of my life's blood pouring out onto the dying beast. I felt myself falling, almost a weightless sensation as my vision sparkled into gray fog and then, blackness. I never even felt the floor hit me in the face.

Chapter 39

Organizing Lom's Rescue

A long-forgotten alarm interrupted Alger's study session with Bella. He had slipped an unnoticeable tag onto Lom years before, that would only be triggered if his life was in mortal danger, if Lom was dying... and now it was flashing urgently, capturing Alger's full attention. Alger stopped mid-word, and Bella was staring at him in bewilderment.

"Alger? Is something wrong?"

"Everyone assumes that because Alger is old, I will suddenly become senile, or perhaps die," he replied. ""Yes, something is wrong. Lom is in trouble. Do be a good girl and scry him, will you? This is a perfect lesson opportunity."

Bella glared at Alger, her cheeks paling, then closed her eyes and took a deep, slow breath. Alger recalls wryly that he often has that effect on those close to him. With Bella, he knew it meant she was searching the library for 'how to scry.' Bella opened her eyes again, got up and walked toward the kitchen without another word to Alger, who trailed after her, curious to see how she had chosen to do this.

"Ellie, could I please have a shallow dish, and some water?"

Alger sat at the table and watched Bella prepare the water, pricking her finger and letting a droplet of blood fall into it, where it swirled and smoked, and then turned the liquid into a silvery colour. Fascinating, he noted, she was using a variation of the spell to find a loved one. Bella twisted her long hair up and secured it out of her way with a pair of hair sticks, then bent over the scrying bowl with an intent gaze.

"What do you see, girl?" Alger murmured encouragement to her, wanting a report. For once, he was hoping his spell had malfunctioned.

Ellie came and hissed into Alger's ear "What are you up to?"

He replied, trying to keep voice low and not disturb Bella, who was holding perfectly still with unfocused eyes trained on the bowl. "Something wrong with Lom, perhaps. I'd placed a spell on him back when he was a young pup in my care, to let me know if his life was in danger."

"And you never removed it?"

"Shh! Keep your voice down, the girl needs to concentrate." Alger remonstrated, as the wood elf's voice had risen considerably while she spoke.

"Exactly what would trigger this spell?" She had lowered her voice again, and Alger smiled at her avuncularly.

"Well, I didn't want to link it to his thoughts, you understand, a lad thinks of himself as immortal. So I linked it to his vitals directly, if his body is dying the spell is triggered."

She covered her face with both hands. Alger couldn't quite make out what she was muttering. Bella spoke, and they both looked at her.

"I just watched a troll bash him into a wall... he's so limp..." Her voice trembled. Then she straightened and started to give orders in a firm, clear tone.

"I need Alger to do a location casting. Ellie, do you know where Lom's cell phone is? I'll need that. And then, I'll break into the armory." She looked up from the bowl, her eyes bright with tears. "Hurry, please."

Alger shook his head. "If he is dying already, there is no way we will reach him in time... Plan for vengeance, girl."

She was eye to eye with Alger while he was sitting at the table and she was now close enough he could feel the warmth of her breath. "I will not give up hope. We will get him, and we will do it now! I don't trust you, I don't trust Court enough to call on them, but I am getting my family to help, and we are going to go get him. And we will bring Low Court to it's knees. I will. Not. Have this!"

She spun away from Alger, and stopped dead two paces away. Lucia and Lady Herbale stood in the doorway, their faces stern.

"We heard." Lucia told her. "And my dear girl..." she walked forward and took Bella's hands in her own, "we will do whatever we can to expedite. Ellie..."

The wood elf, who Alger had not seen leave, walked around the women from the outer room, and handed Bella the odd little device he had never been able to get Lom to let me investigate. Bella released the dowager's hands with a little squeeze, and cleared her throat. "I need to make some calls, and I understand I must be outside of Underhill to do so."

Ellie nodded. Lucia asked, "Do you need help to find the doorway and pass through?"

Bella looked surprised, "no, I don't, Lom showed me how the first time."

"Go, then... we will begin preparations here."

Bella ported out without further ado, and Lucia trained her steely eye on Alger, "why are you still sitting there? Shouldn't you be finding my son?"

Alger mused that the woman had the uncanny ability to conjure up shades of his long gone mother, who was not a nice woman at all. "I need something personal of his, something like hair, or..."

Ellie passed Alger a hairbrush. She seemed to have anticipated him and had brought it along with the phone. He thought quickly.

"I need a fire in the fireplace. And a spell..." He reached out, closed his eyes, and called what he needed. Holding the slightly warm ball of energy, Alger followed Ellie into the big room, where she kindled a fire. Lucia and

Lady Herbale hovered, not having anything else they could do. Alger looked at Lucia.

"I know Bella doesn't trust Court, but I think perhaps Joe and Melcar ought to be brought in on this. Call them here, let's keep this out of public view."

She nodded, her face pale and deeply lined. She was an old woman even by fairy standards, and for all her flaws, did love her son. The small fire sputtered and threw sparks when Alger tossed the spell into it, and a few strands of hair from Lom's brush. They stepped back, and he took a deep breath, knowing he had to prepare her for the worst.

"Lucia, I am so sorry. I know Bella thinks she can rescue him, but Lom is dying. With the time it will take to bring her family to Underhill from Alaska..." Alger trailed off, because she was not reacting the way he had expected. Alger would have thought tears, perhaps a case of the vapors... Instead, she was standing fully erect, her eyes flashing, and mouth crimped in a straight line.

"You will not give up on my son. Proceed with all speed. Bella is an extraordinary being, and I feel certain she will come through faster than you could conceive of. You abandoned him once, you *will not* do so again."

Alger wanted to protest 'I had not abandoned him, he had simply been too ill to finish his apprenticeship with me,' but he closed his mouth and went back to making the location spell work quickly. Lady Herbale 'ported out of the room, Alger assumed to take a personal message to the king, and to bring back Joe and Melcar. The flames got his attention, though, preventing him from asking questions, as a tiny image of Lom, formed from flames, appeared above the logs. He was lying on his side, curled up. To Alger's relief, the spell he had tagged him with was still active. He was alive.

"Can't you just... Bring him here?" Ellie asked from behind Alger. Alger kept his focus on the image, fluttering his fingers to weave the magic he needed for an illusory map of Underhill, with him...

"Ah, there." Alger muttered. A glowing dot, indicating Lom's location, appeared in a tangled web of energy lines that showed the various boundaries and fiefdoms of their world. Alger had spent centuries mapping, gathering information, and this was the first time he had ever called on it all at once. Lom was not at the Low Court, where they had expected to find him, but a remote outpost of that Court, a tower called Baelfire.

Alger answered Ellie as he used my hand gestures to bring up the tower, a blurry representation, Alger had never been there, of course, but informants had sketched in some details. Enough, he hoped, to reach Lom once we got to Baelfire.

"No... there is a very powerful interdiction spell reaching to a half-day's walk around the tower. Must be inconvenient for the inhabitants, and it gives us an advantage." Alger found Lom in the cellars of the tower and snapped his fingers, storing the whole thing for later recall. Alger looked at Ellie. "It means they can't call for back-up when we arrive."

Chapter 40

Backup Arrives

"Which will be shortly." Bella's voice startled them all, and she left the door open behind her as she walked in, not even pausing to greet them formally. "Alger, did you find him? Ellie, I need your help. Lucia, the boys will want coffee, if you don't mind..."

She didn't even look to see that they were following her orders, going straight to the door Alger had been curious about. Ellie had warned them not to touch it, and Alger had determined that it was guarded by a nasty little spell. Now, Bella simply opened it without preamble. She looked over her shoulder at him and demanded impatiently, "well?"

"Oh! Um, yes, I found him. Baelfire Tower." Alger heard himself blurt.

A male voice commented. "Sounds spooky, even."

A group of human men filed in the open doorway, each one carrying a pack, the last one cradling a huge rifle in his arms like an infant. He closed the door behind him carefully. The brown-haired one who had spoken met Alger with an outstretched hand.

"I'm Mark, Bella's cousin. Well, we're all kind of her cousins, 'cept for

Tex, there..." he indicated a tall, gloomy man with a jerk of his thumb, "and he's an honorary cousin."

They each greeted him with a handshake and a name. "Dan," The man with the big black beard and the hard eyes.

"Howdy," Tex shook and stepped back, allowing the last man to reach Alger.

"And I'm Mike." He had a mane of blonde-tipped brown hair that made me think of a grizzly bear.

They looked at the four men who made the big room feel much smaller with them in it. "How did you get here so fast?" Alger asked.

Mark shrugged. "Bella called us, told us we're going hunting, and it's something special. We met up at her place, and next thing we know, she's there, and we're in Oregon near the old homestead. She did that soap-bubble thing a couple times, and I have no idea where the hell we are now, but we're ready to go."

Mike chuckled. "Girl's had us all 'round her little finger since she's a baby. She doesn't ask much, so when she called, we came."

They all looked at Alger expectantly, and he realized they were expecting more explanation. "Well, this is Underhill," he began slowly.

Mark nodded. Dan and Mike looked thoughtful. Tex just looked confused. Alger sighed. "The world of fairies, sprites, and pixies. But don't go thinking that it's going to be easy. What Bella did to get you here... and don't tell anyone about that, you'll get her in you have no idea how much trouble, she shouldn't even have been able to do that, the girl has far too much power for me to explain. The beings you will encounter might not always look threatening, but every single one of them has enough magic to kill you. Or worse, not kill you. Just take your mind. Humans are..."

"Pets, Underhill?" Mark filled in for him. Alger winced, looking at these rough men. One could not imagine them as anything but what they were today. Hunters of monsters.

"Most humans who come Underhill are seeking oblivion, ease, rich-es... you are a rare group, here to help us. And we will need that. We can't call on our allies, we aren't sure who has been subverted by the Low Court - those are the enemy," Alger pointed out, and they nodded. Alger despaired of making it all clear to them in the time we needed, and sighed. "You're here to rescue Lom, I'm sure she told you that?"

They all nodded. Dan spoke. "Bob said he's a good man. And he gave me something for a king?" He pulled a small envelope out of his pocket and handed it to Alger, who felt a jolt of surprise. Who was Bob, and why was a human... he lifted the envelope to my nose and sniffed. Not a human.

Alger never finished that train of thought, as the simultaneous arrival of Bella from the basement Armory, Joe, Melcar, the Lady Herbale, and at least one of the healer apprentices arriving from Court, turned the room from quiet to chaos. Lucia, to his surprise, stepped in to brief both the Underhill people and the human arrivals, while Bella took everyone one at a time downstairs, and they each came back up with pleased smiles and weaponry. Alger sidled over to Ellie, who was standing by the door, a bow and quiver slung over her shoulder.

"Um, how did she..."

She grunted and raised an eyebrow. Alger backed off. While he hadn't been paying attention, Lucia had finished, and now everyone was looking at him.

"Um, hrmph..." Alger cleared his throat to buy time to remember what Lucia had been saying. Oh, yes, that he would guide them to Baelfire Tower.

"Can we leave now?" Alger asked Bella politely, as she came upstairs and leaned against the door, closing it and - he caught a flicker of light - resetting the spell.

She shook her head, fatigue showing. "I need to eat and rest. We all do. Joe..."

The majordomo, dressed in fighting gear rather than his usual sartorial splendor, came closer to her. "Yes, Bella?"

"I need your help to plan this. Can you coordinate with Mark and the boys? Ellie..." she and the tiny wood elf exchanged grim smiles. Alger sensed something there. "Is coming with us, but plan on her covering my back. Alger."

"Yes?" He was half afraid she would order him to hand over the map and stay behind. He could tell she was not happy about his pessimism over the boy's survival.

"Can you... If he is still alive?" Her voice quivered a little. Alger held out his hand and she took it.

"He's alive, I can feel that much through the spell. I'll be able to tell if... things change." Alger put both his hands around her small, cold one, and looked down at her. "I'm sorry if I sound bleak, m'dear. I have so many years behind me, I find hope difficult. I had no idea how fast you could move, or the kind of power you truly have."

She shook her head. "I just do what needs to be done. I'm not that strong."

Melcar took her elbow. "You need to eat. You have used an enormous amount of energy, and you are going to fall down if you don't sit."

She murmured an inarticulate protest, but didn't fight him as he led her into the kitchen. Lady Herbale came out with a tray bearing a coffee urn and teapot. Lucia followed with one of cups and accoutrements. Alger could feel the tension in his shoulders, cramping with anxiety to be going, but knowing that they should wait until dark, and travel on full bellies with rest.

"Waiting is something I have never learned to do, in all the years I have been forced to." Alger muttered to himself, Isitting with fingers steepled and thinking. They were all tense. Something had taken down the bubble Lom and the Easterners were traveling in. The poor wretches we had rescued from the goblins, along with Melcar's two apprentices, had turned up at Eastern Court only hours after the diversion of the Court bubble. Melcar had told all of us what he knew. Lom was facing an unknown number of beings, all vile, vicious, and wanting him dead.

Alger understood, probably better than Lom did, why they wanted him to die. The Low Court saw the human realm as easy picking for them, with magic and power to seize what they wanted. High Court wanted humans to remain blissfully unaware of Underhill as a reality, to let us fade into legends and tales. Lom was the tool who had kept the creeping incursion of Low Court's foray into human matters at bay. They saw him as a threat to their plans, and they were quite right. He would give everything to keep them from sparking a war that would certainly cause the death and destruction of everything we held dear. He had already paid a high price for it, beginning with being caught in the wrong place at the wrong time, innocently as Alger's young apprentice when they were trying to reach Alger.

Alger regretted that deeply, and Lom had blamed Alger for his distance while he recovered, but Alger had done it to keep him safe, to keep him out of the fight he eventually chose to enter into of his own accord as an adult. Alger was proud of him, of what Lom had become, and he would likely never be able to tell the boy. The spell was weakening, and that could only mean Lom was fading away.

It was time to rein Low Court in, and bring their power back into check. Alger had held back, under orders, but no more. He got up and walked into the kitchen. Bella had her head down on her crossed arms, apparently asleep. I touched her shoulder.

"We need to go. He is slipping away." Alger told her gently, hating the pain he was causing this young woman he was coming to be very fond of. She was a warrior.

She nodded, getting up and following me into the large room. "Let's go outside, everyone." Alger announced. "We need enough room to transport a group this size."

"Should we do more than one bubble?" Lucia asked. She was standing in the kitchen door, clutching a towel and looking oddly out of place. She had never been domestic in the slightest.

"No, that just invites defeat in detail when we are separated. We will go in as a group. Does anyone have any questions?" Alger looked around as the group assembled in Lom's garden, the overcast sky above a perfect mood setting for the somber crowd. Dan caught my attention.

"Yes?"

"What do you want us to do? Engage at will, or only when attacked? I get that they won't have weapons like we do, but they are still armed with..." he stumbled a little on the concept. "Magic, you say."

"Just before we get into the tower, Melcar and I will give you spells that will lessen the harm of any magical attack on you. They won't last long, you need magic to power them and only Mark," Alger nodded at the cousin who he needed to talk to, about his ancestry, "has any, among you humans. As for the rules... Kill them, before they can kill you, or any of us."

He nodded grimly. In one way Alger had made it easier, in another, harder. None of them showed any signs of sociopathy. They didn't want to kill anyone, they just wanted to bring Lom home and keep Bella safe and happy.

Alger bubbled the group without further discussion, grimly aware that while they might have some advantages, according to what little information they had, there were a lot more of the enemy.

Chapter 41

Tower Baelfire

B ella put a hand on Alger's shoulder, and he startled as he felt the surge in his magic. She was channeling power through him.

"Blessed Titania, I had no idea just how strong you were," he blurted.

"Get us through the interdiction if at all possible?" She murmured into his ear.

Alger took a deep breath, "I think I can, now."

"I broke the Court's interdiction without really knowing it until later," she offered him a partial explanation of how she knew to try this.

"Oh." Alger grounded the bubble gently in the Tower courtyard, but held the walls of it up. He spoke loudly enough to be heard. "Ready, now!"

When the walls went down it was rather anticlimactic. The denizens of the tower had assumed that because they could not go in or out, no one else could, either. Most of them were indoors. Mike took point, Dan the tail of the little relief column, and they marched in the front doors. Or rather, the hole that was left after Alger used his adaptation of Bella's excavation spell to take them down. It was a nice thing in that it removed all the matter from a sphere, and aimed correctly, left an open space to walk through. The debris was elsewhere. Matter in this case also included the door guards, if there had been any. There were a few stones that fell from above, that was all.

A small crowd spilled into the great hall they had just invaded, milling about in confusion. One, with better reflexes than the others, lobbed a spell. Alger blocked it, and the humans, seeing that they were under attack and their consciences were clear, opened fire. Mike's big weapon made the stones of the Hall ring, and the enemy all flinched back toward the doors they had come in.

Alger didn't stop moving. The enemy of any offensive, particularly a surprise one, is hesitation. Bella was a half step behind him, and to his right, so the two of them had the point as the humans-at-arms took flanking positions, firing until there was nothing moving in the hall, and whatever else was here, was hiding and had the sense not to come see what the ruckus was. Alger had the map up, floating in front of them and glowing brightly enough to illuminate the dim hall they took, the one that would bring them to the cellar stairs. They were not dungeons, Alger had been told by an informant years ago, in a putrid tavern, with a leer and a wink as she swilled the ale he'd bought her.

Bella stepped in front of Alger, suddenly, and held up a hand. They all stopped. Melcar and his apprentice were behind those two, and Ellie ghosted up on Alger's left, knife in hand. It was too close quarters for her bow.

Bella warned them, "close your eyes," then flicked her fingers and launched a spell, triggering a burst of light. As soon as the redness was gone, Alger opened his eyes again, blinking to be able to see. Even though eyelids that had been spectacular. Alger made a mental note that he would need to talk to her about weapons that harmed your own side.

There was a shriek that dopplered up high enough to be out of the range of normal hearing, and Ellie blurred into action. The ghoul that flew out of the side hall had to be blinded, but she was attacking anyway, her jaws unhinged and talons reaching out for Bella. Who side-stepped her neatly, and Ellie broadsided her. Alger almost didn't catch what she did, except it involved a mighty handful of stringy black hair, yanking the creature to a dead halt with a cracking of bones, then a swipe of that sharp little blade removed the scalp and hair. Ellie's other hand was on the ghoul's throat now, and she crammed the bloodied scalp into the unnaturally wide open mouth, neutralizing the venomous teeth. Then she stepped back as it thrashed against the wall, still scratching with talons for a target, and Bella shot it twice in the head.

The limp body thudded to the floor, and in the sudden silence, they heard Lom scream below, in the black hole that gaped and the stairs went into. Bella ran, one hand over her head, elf lights spinning off her fingertips, and the other holding the pistol she had just used to dispatch the ghoul. Ellie followed on her heels.

"Melcar, go. I'll stay here and cover her back." Alger ordered, pointing, and the wood elf healer went down into that foul pit without hesitation. With the new illumination Alger could now see the hellish scene below us, at the foot of the shallow stairs. Lom lay on the floor, naked bruised and bloody, under him, an amorphous mass. Alger deliberately turned his back. He could not rush down there to Lom's side, and he needed to keep his focus clear on threats from above. The small cellar was empty of life besides the wreck that had been a pixie warrior. The spell connection Alger had with him had severed with the eldritch scream, and he couldn't bear to think about that.

Ellie and the small apprentice ran up and past Alger, with her saying, "we need something for a cot or sling to carry him."

"Is he alive?" Alger blurted hoarsely. She didn't answer. Dan gestured for her to follow him, and they vanished around a corner. Behind and below him, Alger could hear Melcar saying something, but couldn't make out the words. Mark, Tex, and Mike were on guard at the entrance to the great hall, out of his sight, and he felt very old and alone for a fleeting second.

The little apprentice reappeared with Dan trailing him, carrying an armload of what looked like bedding. They went down the stairs. Alger could hear someone retching down there, and cursed his cowardice for not being able to look.

Melcar was the next one up the stairs, and he put a hand on Alger's shoulder. "He's alive, Alger. Barely, but there is still a magical essence protecting him. It's keeping his soul together with body, but also accelerating his death. He's incredibly weak, and I wish we didn't have to move him."

Alger shook his head, both to suppress the tears of joy, and to negate the implied suggestions. "We must leave here immediately. I have no idea how close reinforcements are."

"Moving him may kill him. I want to at least stabilize him first."

Magical transport is a curious thing. While less of an effort than any of the human methods Alger had studied, it still draws from the life force of those who use it. It's a tiny leaching of power, not even noticeable to a normal, healthy being of the Folke. For Lom, it had always been a tiring experience since the brush with the elfshot, and in his current condition, it might well be the last straw.

"At least we must move to a more defensible position. I will set the men-at-arms to clearing the Hall."

He nodded, and sent Dan up when he went back down. Melcar, Ellie, Bella, and the apprentice whose name Alger had never gotten, carried Lom up the stairs, each of them at a corner of the sheet he was on. Alger was guessing Melcar had told Bella not to use magical means to carry him. He was oddly pale, limp, and Alger could not see him breathe. He stood back against the wall to let them pass, then brought up the rear, using spells to ward and seal halls and rooms behind us. At the very least, they would be safe from that direction.

They placed him gently on a table, Ellie tucking a bit of rolled up cloth under his head for a pillow. He was swaddled in blankets, presumably for warmth. Alger knew well enough the harm shock could have, even in the absence of an obviously mortal wound. Melcar was rubbing his feet, and Bella and his apprentice each had a hand. Alger was so distracted with what they were doing, and just how dead Lom looked, that he missed the threat riding through the gaping hole in the outer wall.

Mark and Dan did not, both opening fire at the same time. The boom of their shotguns had everyone's full attention, and Alger ran forward toward them, shouting "cease fire!"

Half of the Wild Hunt was in the hall by the time Alger had reached the Huntsman, who had contemptuously stopped the slugs with a flick of his fingers. He stared down at him, and Alger refused to think about how he must look, a graybeard huffing and puffing at his armored knee.

"Why have you come?" Alger demanded, holding onto his stirrup with one hand, summoning a spell with the other. The Huntsman's riding beast, a giant and unnatural stag, stamped nervously, flicking his ears. The Huntsman was silent for an interminable moment, his visor concealing his thoughts. Around them, the hunt was equally silent, except for the slight jingle of harness as someone shifted.

"We came for our prey that was denied us." The Hunstman boomed. That deep, resonant voice shook Alger to his bones, as it always had.

"He is not yours." Alger shot back. "Moire LeFay gave her life for him, rest her soul." Whatever else the banshee had been, she had been devoted to Lom.

The Hunstman shook his head, and raised a hand to point at Lom's prostrate form. "He was afflicted by the elfshot that night, as well, and I claim him by the rights of the Old Ways. Old Man, stand aside. You know the Law."

Alger did know it. The Wild Hunt existed for those who were neither High nor Low court, for the lawless, to give them both freedom and an endless prison. Bound to the Huntsman, those who rode in the Hunt were no longer able to leave it. They existed only to hunt. None commanded the Hunt, in theory, although for the last centuries it had been aligned at least loosely with the Low Court.

The Huntsman spoke again, and Alger could detect a touch of emotion in that rumbling voice, now. "Yon Pictsie has done us a great favor, Old Man. We will not kill him. But he is Ours."

"A favor," Alger repeated incredulously. Lom hated and feared the Hunt, it was very unlikely he would have done anything for them.

"He killed the Low King. Who had gotten an unfortunate amount of power to control Us."

Ah... that was, interesting. Alger looked back at Lom. Melcar was standing by his feet, staring at them, and Bella was kneeling on the table, crouching over Lom and protecting him with her own body. The apprentice was under the table. Alger didn't blame him. The Hunt was the boogeyman. Children had been told tales of how the Hunt would get them if they were naughty. In a way, it was even true. There were no prisons Underhill, nor were they needed. Alger let go of the Huntsman's stirrup and stepped back.

Alger knew that in breaking the code they had kept for so long, he would break that protection given to all the innocents who feared, respected, and lived cleaner lives through that learned caution. It didn't matter if Lom was innocent, he was, through the Law and tradition, under the purview of the Hunt. And if the Hunt were not going to kill him, they might also be the best way to keep Lom alive.

Alger despaired, and his voice broke as he answered the Huntsman. "I concede."

The Huntsman nodded, ponderously, and with a gesture, released two of his men to dismount and start toward Lom. They hit the floor with a clash from their all-enveloping armor, and Alger tried not to think about Lom, forever hidden in black metal, speechless, all but mindless...

Bella stood up suddenly, and screamed defiance at the hunt, the Huntsman, and even Alger. Her fists knotted at her sides, her hair half falling down, and her wings vibrating like a plucked string, she shrieked, "he's Mine!"

She was standing on the table, straddling Lom's body, and we could

could see her moving her hands like she was pulling something upward, then hurling it toward the Hunt. She hit the two men moving toward them first, lashing them with rivers of sickly green energy that had them reeling backward, screaming. She used it like a whip, driving them backward, then moving on to the rest of the Hunt.

Alger was torn between wanting to watch her, as he saw that she was actually pulling the energy out of Lom's body, and knowing she was just as mad at Alger as she was the Huntsman, and from this angle he stood between her and the Hunt. Self-preservation got the better of Alger, and he dove for cover under the nearest bench just as she cracked that whip of energy at him. Safely out of the way, Alger was finally able to analyze just what she was doing. She was pulling the poison out of Lom's body and using it against them. Which was likely why it was so very effective; the elfshot turned on the Hunt had to sting bitterly.

The Hunt was in a full rout, now, the mounts running away with the riders even if they were not themselves spurring on the steed. Only the Huntsman, holding a disc of magic before him like a shield, was not moved. She sent tendrils after the fleeing men, and turned most of the energy on him. Lom screamed, a primal sound ripped from a throat that had been abused and torn from earlier screams. She looked down at him, and in her distraction, the Huntsman made his escape, slipping out of the smoking entryway in a clatter of hooves that slowly died away. The only sound in the hall was Tex's voice.

"What. The. Sam. Hill just happened?"

Chapter 42

Cogito Ergo Sum

I opened my eyes, disoriented and wondering if I were dead yet. No... I felt. I could feel the poison flowing out of me like water through a broken dam, pouring through a channel in my chest. The pain was easing with every second. My eyes came into focus and I could see Bella. Not the fake one who had tried to kill me, but mine, standing over me like some avenging war goddess, her hands full of eldritch fire, and her wings vibrating frenetically. I took a second to admire that tight, curvy ass so conveniently on display, and then realized what she was doing as she suddenly made a scooping gesture and pulled the last of the elfshot magic out of my body.

I couldn't help it; my back arched and pulled up off the hard surface I was lying on, leaving me on head and heels, and screaming. I couldn't stop it, it just came out and kept going... the pain was unbelievable, and then, like a switch, it was gone. I collapsed and tried to catch my breath.

When the stars that had filled my vision when my blood pressure spiked finally ebbed, Bella was kneeling beside me, holding my face in her hands and crying softly. I tried to talk to her, to tell her it was all right, but I couldn't make words, just noises. She disappeared from view, and

Melcar's face came near me. He laid a hand on my forehead, and with gentle fingers got me to open my eyes fully so he could see into them, then continued to examine the rest of my body.

After a few minutes I closed my eyes, but I could still hear voices. Sometimes they were close enough to make out what they were saying.

Melcar's voice, "he's much stronger. Pupillary reaction is back, pulse is stronger and faster - it was almost imperceptible before."

Someone else, "Can we move now?"

Bella, now, "I thought I had killed him..." she was definitely crying. I opened my eyes again, and tried to move my head so I could see her. She was standing right next to me, and I thought what a fool I had been to be taken in by the skin wife's illusion. She was dirty, her hair was flying all over, and her jeans had gotten a jagged rip in the leg. I didn't see blood, so hopefully she was uninjured. She turned to look at me and I saw the blood then, all down her front. I tried to reach for her, to find out if she was all right.

"Lom..." she bent over me, and I managed words.

"You... all right?"

She looked down at herself, where I had managed to put the back of my hand on her chest. "Oh. Yes, I'm fine, that's..." she choked up a little, "yours. We're going to take you home now."

"Good." I wanted to tell her she was beautiful, that this was better than the white dress and golden sunshine, but my eyelids were heavy and I needed to rest them.

I could still hear them talking, and now they were all close. I could feel hands, gentle touches, and then I felt the bubble pop up, and I gasped for breath, feeling my whole body twitch as the magic tingled through it.

"He can't take it!" that was Bella, a note of terror in her voice.

Alger broke in, "keep us going as long as you can. We don't know how many of them are coming, and we know they want us all dead."

I wanted to agree with him, but my shaking wouldn't stop, and the world filled with sparkles before blackness again.

I woke up in my own bed, weaker than a newborn kitten, but I would have known that stain in the corner anywhere. I stared at it for a long time before I dared try and turn my head. I ached. No sharp pains, but I knew I had a fever from the detached flying sensation, and I really didn't give a damn. Where was Bella?

Alger was asleep in the chair by my bed, lanky legs stretched out in front of him, and bearded chin down on his chest. I frowned. This was not the person I wanted to see right now.

"Bella?" I tried to ask, not certain if I could make a word happen. My mouth tasted like I had been kissing a ghoul.

He startled awake. "Ah..." He sat up. "So good to see you're back with us. Hang on, don't try to talk..."

He brought me a cup of water with a very prosaic and human flexi straw in it. I mused on the incongruity of that item, but it made drinking from a prone position much easier. He slid a careful arm under my shoulders while I sipped.

I tried to speak again when he set the cup down. "Where is Bella?"

That time he understood me, and the wrinkled old face broke into a smile. "Sleeping, m'boy. We made her go to her own bed, she's been in that chair more nights than was good for her."

"How long?" I asked him, suddenly aware that I was slowly healing, and shivered as I remembered the blood I had vomited on the skin wife...

"Six days since we got back here. We were only in the tower for a few hours, although it seemed like days."

I wanted to hear all about that, and how they had come to find me, much less rescue me. I had so many questions, there were so many loose ends... Bella walked into the room, and none of that mattered.

She came and perched on the side of my bed gently, then leaned over and came close enough I could feel her breath on me. "How are you?"

"I feel like an elephant ran over me, then backed up and had another go, but I'm alive. And you aren't wearing white."

"What?" Her brow wrinkled in confusion.

"I'll explain later. Right now, could you do two things for me?"

"Of course."

"Kiss me, and ask Joe to come see me."

She lit up with a smile that made my breath catch, and pressed her lips to mine. It wasn't the deepest kiss I'd had, but it was the sweetest one I'd ever been given. I closed my eyes, afraid the tear would slip out, and when I opened them, she had left the room again. Alger was still sitting in the armchair, grinning like a loon. I couldn't bring myself to growl at him, I was feeling pretty happy myself, right now.

"Alger, can you get mother? And I require you, Lord Alger Mulvaney, to summon a quorum of the Lords of the Kingdom."

He got very still for a moment, his whole face sagging oddly, and then raised an eyebrow. "That is not a title I care to lay claim to any longer," he told me stiffly. "Is that a command?"

I tried to shake my head, regretted it, and gritted out, "yes, it is, *Lord Alger*." I needed him to catch the clue, and not argue with me. I was too tired to argue.

He stood up and went to the door, opening it and looking back ame with an unholy combination of joy and fear that I had become unhinged. I feared that, too. I drifted in an unpleasant haze of pain. I didn't want to fall asleep. Ellie pushed past Alger, who stepped aside to make room for the tray she was carrying, then left the room.

"Are you up to some food?" She set the tray on the bedside table, and I could see a couple of bowls, one steaming a little. Even better, was that a cup of coffee?"

"I'd try." I wasn't sure, but the idea of it sounded wonderful.

She had me propped up on pillows and I discovered to my dismay that I couldn't yet feed myself without making a mess, when Joe came in. He stood, hands on hips, and eyed me for a long moment.

"You look dead," he pointed out, pulling a straightbacked chair away from the table and flipping it around before straddling it.

"You look good, too." I managed. Ellie held the coffee cup for me to take a last sip.

"Am I here to exchange insults with you? Not that I mind, it's better than what I thought last time I saw you."

I did manage a shaking of the head, now. "Josiah ap Colcannon ys Myrtle, I request and require a full audience with his Majesty Trytion ap Malise ys Wallflower. As I am invalid, it is incumbent that he succor me here in my desmesne the day after tomorrow at noon."

He blinked, but his face didn't show anything. "I shall inform him of your request…"

"Calling in all my chips, Joe. This one's important." I stopped. I wanted to tell him that he was a pillar of strength in an uncertain world, and one of the few people I really trusted, but I was too tired to say more. He stood up and came to the side of the bed. Ellie took the tray away, silently.

"I'll bring him, Lom. But you need some rest before you tackle… whatever this is."

I nodded slightly. He was right. I felt frustrated, but it was like opening a tap and having all the energy drain out of me to do anything at all. He put a gentle hand on my shoulder. "Get some rest," he repeated.

I obediently closed my eyes, and heard his footsteps as he went to the doorway. Odd how he was usually so silent, but I could hear him this time. I fell asleep, again.

For all I knew, my room was Grand Central station - yes, I've actually been there. They had an infestation of goblins in the lockers, and… but I digress - while I was sleeping. I was really out of it. I awakened sore, grumpy, and a dry as the desert.

I tried to sit up, and a slender hand pressed into my chest. "Here."

A straw at my lips got me to stop fighting and take a long sip. "M'Bella?" I managed when I could speak. My eyes were still not working right. I blinked, and the image resolved. She smiled.

"Ready for your public?"

319

"My public? I was to be wakened at ten, the audience isn't until noon." I felt a fleeting sense of fear, that I was losing my grip more than I'd thought at this point.

She shook her head. "They all showed up early, and from the level of gossip, you would think this was the event of the century. Intrigue and fear in equal measures. What have you done?"

I had decided to take my life in my hands, since it looked like there wasn't much of it left, anyway, and make something right with my last acts. My life was feeling like it had all been turned on its ear. "And the King?"

"Consuming Ellie's sand tarts at the moment."

"Tell her I'm sorry?" I realized I had invited people to the house without warning her. We never had company.

Bella chuckled. "She's in seventh heaven, in the kitchen with Margot and women I've never met, all of them gossiping like magpies. And the King is enjoying her food. What more could she ask for, she said."

"Bella..." I wasn't sure how to ask her what I wanted. She waited patiently with a smile, holding my hand. "I'm going to do something brash," I paused awkwardly.

She raised an eyebrow. "And this is different how?"

"I mean... this could result in my being banished from Underhill, or beheaded." I took a deep breath and winced. Sore ribs. "But best-case, it could mean I can finally ask you about something I've wanted for a long time."

"Do what you need to, Lom. I'm your partner, no matter what."

"Yeah. That's really good. I don't understand why, but it's good."

She chuckled. "Are you ready?"

"Please send Alger and Devon in. I will see you when it's time for the audience."

Alger walked in with that look on his face. He still wasn't sure if I had lost my mind in that dark cellar. "How do you plan to fit that Horde in here?" he growled, looking around.

"I don't. I need your help and Devon's to dress, get me downstairs, and then prop me up." I was thinking I'd be damned if I met my fate flat on my back. Maybe Martin had rubbed off on me.

He parroted back at me, "dressed? Downstairs, Standing? Are you insane, boy? Doing this might be survivable if you stay in bed, maybe out of the nightshirt into a proper shirt, but how the devil do you expect to get down the stairs and stay alive?"

"That's what transport spells are for." I snapped. "And not just a shirt. There are full formal court robes in a chest in the closet." I remembered who had made them, and then sealed them in there, after I let her know that dream of hers was not shared with me. For once, the memory was not wholly bitter. "As for holding me up, my East India Company Cane, and Devon's strong arm." I got a grateful glance from the boy, whose eyes were wide as he tried to figure out what his crazy uncle was up to. The cane would be a statement by itself, topped with a harpy's talons, clutching a bird's egg ruby. Gaudy, but effectively gruesome.

"Full robes..." Alger eyed me. "Alonzo Mulvaney lost the Family that privilege. Why... oh." I watched with a small amount of amusement as I saw the mental gears mesh. He knew what my late wife had been like. He remained standing, irresolute, for a moment longer, and then threw his shoulders back and marched off to the closet.

When he returned carrying the small chest I kept expecting him to set it down, rub his hands together, and cackle, from the way he was grinning. I did hear him mumble "bout damn' time," as he was unpacking.

He stopped and turned to me. "You sure about this, boy? The audience goes against you, they will strip you of everything and pitch you to the Wild Hunt."

"The Family is done paying through the nose for something none of us now living, not even you, were involved in. I have paid in my blood for this..." Unfortunately, this fervency brought on a coughing session. Devon caught me as I swayed, and I regretted having tried to stand up so soon. I thought I was going to hack up a lung, and I had given up smoking when

Kipling died. I wouldn't let him put me back in the bed, though. I did accept the coffee with plenty of cream that Alger offered.

When I could stand upright again, Alger popped the robe on me, and after I was fully garbed, flicked his fingers and it all stiffened.

"What the hell?" I couldn't move, except my head.

"Minor spell, m'boy. Relax, they will hold you up without you killing yourself standing.

"Oh..."

Ellie popped her head in the door. "They are in place..." her voice trailed off, and I knew she had registered what she was seeing.

Ellie swept an approving glance at me, from head to foot. "Right, I'll just get myself down in the kitchen and make sure everything goes smoothly." The proud look on her face, and set of her shoulders and she pulled the door closed behind her, told me that at least one member of my household was behind me all the way.

Alger transported us downstairs in a bubble, a breath-taking experience for me, again. I was trying not to think about the consequences of having lost my magic entirely. I wondered how long it would take me to die, like this... The first Lord entered the room, and I focused on the charade before me.

The startlement at my dress was something to behold. Win or lose, I was damn glad I had finally decided to do this. The King entered last.

He paced forward to stand in front of me when I did not come to meet him.

"You summon me, like a commoner?" his voice was low and grating. I could not read his face.

"I was unable to leave my home due to illness, suffered in line of service to you. I have right of redress."

"Ask ye." His voice was cool, his face aloof. I cleared my throat.

"King of Western Court, Lord of high from Tree to Sea, Trytion Malise ys Wallflower, I demand my rights as Duke High Tor, Marshal of the East. For too long my family has suffered for a deed none living committed. With the death of the Low King at the hand of the House Mulvaney, I declare the debt from the affair of the red cloak paid, and demand restitution of the lands and titles to the members of my house, and the return of suzerainty to the people of my lands." My voice broke, and I had to gulp for breath before I went on. My vision was tunneling down, onto the still face of my King. I was aware of a general rustle of movement in a room full of people. The world had narrowed down to the two of us. I didn't know where Bella was, and fought down the urge to look for her.

"I also demand the record of Alonzo Mulvaney be expunged, and my rightful place on Council as Duke Mulvaney be recognized. We have served in humble reckoning for long enough, and have proved that we are faithful to our King."

He stood like a storm cloud on the horizon. I hung trembling in the support of my robes. I couldn't say another word, it was all I could do not to pass out, and even that would come soon enough whether I wanted it or not. I had the Council as my witnesses, not that they loved me, or would care to see the name Mulvaney amongst them again, but this was properly done... and still the King was silent, his bushy grey eyebrows drawn slightly together as he stared at me in thought. I must look like death warmed over.

Bella materialized on the other side of me, gliding up on silent footsteps, and taking my hand. I turned my head slightly to see her solemn face, with her eyes fixed on him, and her hand in mine a significant gesture. I looked back at the King, and saw in his eyes that he had decided.

"Lord Mulvaney, Duke of Elleria Tor, Keeper of the Royal Horse, Learoyd Otheris, I hear you," he said. She squeezed my hand, and I imagined the look on her face as she accessed the Library to try and make sense of this. He stepped forward and took my hand. "We account you a faithful subject, harmless..." I tried not to let a giggle slip out, "and acclaimed here in the sight of noble witnesses, to be a House free of stricture. The debt has been paid."

He dropped my hand, and then stepped near. "Get well, Lom. We need you," he told me gruffly, then straightened and left the room abruptly, leaving an audience of gaping noblemen in his wake. it took a moment for the bubble of surprise to burst, and fill the room with a loud clamour. I closed my eyes. I had won. I could feel the dizziness pass through me, and knew I was going to faint.

"Out!" Alger's voice boomed over my head. "He's been close enough to death to spit in its eye, he's earned some peace and quiet!"

I opened my eyes to find myself back in bed. My mother was standing at my side, smiling down at me, with tear-dampened eyes. "Are they gone?" I asked.

"For now, son." she shifted her gaze, and I felt Bella move further onto the bed next to me. "Will you make him stay in bed long enough to heal?"

I started to laugh at that, and choked. My mother realized what she had said and blushed. Bella's giggle made me look at her, and she was holding one hand over her face, but I could tell she was blushing, too.

"Bella, will you marry me?" I blurted out. I had meant to do it with wine, and roses, and moonlight overhead... but here, flat on my back, with my mother on one side and Bella crosslegged on my sickbed, would have to do. It had been put off too long, while I couldn't ask her for her hand, while my family was disgraced in Fairy eyes and I would never have been accepted as a princess's suitor. I wanted her, her company, her mischievous laugh, and most of all, that brilliant, sparking mind of hers, throwing off ideas like electricity and lighting me up like a bonfire. Her body might have been the first thing I saw, but I'd fallen for her mind.

She dropped her hand, her mouth open in a little oh of surprise, and I realized that she had given up on me as anything but a friend and lover.

"Lom..." she started, then stopped again, looking at my mother. "Lucia. Can we?"

I snapped with more irritation than a man should have to use during a proposal, "we damn well can, and no one is going to stop me!"

My mother gurgled with laughter, suddenly girlish. "Bella, it would be a joy to call you daughter. And Lom's right. He could have done this before, but it would have been trouble. What he just did..." she choked up.

"Bella, please." I don't know what I was pleading for, her to answer me right, or just her to stop stalling and answer me at all.

She leaned over me, her long, loose hair falling like night around us, shutting out the world and making just the two of us in our own universe. Her eyes shone like stars.

"Yes."

The End...

In a small room far away, a raven poured a dragon a cup of coffee strong enough to float a mule shoe - with the mule still attached. The dragon shuddered, but sipped anyway.

"Should we call them for this?"

"We must. She is more powerful than either of us, and he keeps her in check."

The dragon sighed, and nodded agreement. He took another sip of the black substance his friend called coffee, and shuddered again.

For a Taste of Trickster Noir...

Miserable Wretch

There would be no happily-ever-after to this fairy tale. I was dying, to begin with. Not in the long-drawn out way that everyone is, dying by days. No, I was going quickly. Body damaged beyond imagining, magic gone, I was on the way out. And my biggest regret was that I had never slept with Bella. Not in the way you are thinking, although I'd dreamed about that often enough. No, simply in the warmth of her arms with the peace of the night wrapped around us. I wondered if I would be aware in the afterlife, to regret this eternally.

After the imprisonment at Tower Baelfire, the abuse I'd taken there, but most of all, the one thing I hadn't even been conscious for... Bella using my magic to fend off the Wild Hunt with a taste of their own medicine. The elfshot that had poisoned me for so many years, hurled back at them with the full power of the woman I loved behind it. Alger had told me the story, I was sorry I hadn't been awake to see it. In my last moments of lucidity, I'd thought at the time, I'd asked Bella to marry me. Purely selfish, I assure you, I thought at the time I was going to be dead before she would have to go through with it.

I also regretted the burden I was about to drop on Devon's slim shoulders. He was a good lad, but still a lad, and nowhere near ready to be Duke. Being my nephew and the last scion of the House Mulvaney was bad enough without my adding to it. Maybe I ought to have just died quietly in her arms, rather than letting my dreams out of the box at this late date. I didn't want the Dukedom, I wanted her. My fairy princess, who had brought me back to life in more way than one.

After the proposal, and my inevitable collapse, people came in and out of the room, but I don't remember who was there. Bella kept crying but not letting anyone see her. She thought I was out of it, and mostly I was, sometimes I was just too tired to look awake. It had been some time since I'd proposed, I wasn't sure how long. I wasn't staying awake long enough to know if it had been days, hours, or only minutes since I last opened my eyes.

My magic was gone. She'd stripped the elfshot, and with it had gone the magic. I tried for Sight, and got only the gray sparkles that happen if you squeeze your eyes shut for too long. So when Mark came and sat by my bed at some point, I was unable to confirm if he had magic, or I'd been mistaken back in Alaska. I did remember that I'd been told how he and some of Bella's family had helped come to my rescue, following her into unknown and definitely hostile territory.

"You didn't go home?" I asked, startling him. He had been nodding off and obviously not expecting the dead man to talk to him.

"Er," he rubbed his eyes and yawned. "Alger offered to teach me how to use magic. Seems I have some."

So my crazy great-uncle, the arch-magician, was at it again. Thanks to his meddling, I'd been targeted by the Wild Hunt as a boy. But he had balanced it with a gift to Bella, giving her the collected wisdom of the largest library ever, and she had access to all of it with her mind. Now, it seemed, Alger had collected Mark. Which didn't answer my internal question. I externalized it.

"So why are you sitting here?" I was genuinely curious. I'd barely met him, him sitting watch over me was hardly his debt to pay.

"Bella needed to sleep. Alger's sitting with her to make sure she does. Ellie's worn to the bone, and you mother was summoned to Court." His explanation was punctuated by a venture to the small table where a coffee urn stood. The smell wafting from his cup when he came back made my stomach growl, which startled both of us. I didn't remember the last time I'd eaten. I had vague memories involving a spoon, and something either warm or cool.

"Would you like some? Or can you have it?" He looked uncertainly down at me. Flat on my back, I couldn't drink it.

"Hell if I know." I admitted. I tried to sit up, the blankets an unendurable obstacle to that idea. He gently slipped an arm under my shoulders and I decided to let him. Once I was sitting, we found, I could stay up, wavering like a leaf in the wind. He grabbed cushions off the little couch and got me propped.

"Thanks."

"Don't mention it."

I was worried that I wouldn't be able to hold the cup, but that I could manage. I sipped slowly. It tasted wonderful with lots of cream and a little sugar.

"Ichor of the gods." I quipped with my old joke. He grinned suddenly, a flash of white teeth in dark brown beard.

"Longest I've seen you awake in a while." Mark was right, I realized. I didn't feel like I was going to fade out and fall over, either.

"I needed coffee." I reached up a hand to my own chin, letting the cup nestle in the coverlet folds to keep it secure. I was almost as bearded as he was. "By the Hunt! How long has it been?"

"Bella's the only one you will let near you, mostly. She was worried about trying to shave you with Alger's razor - I think cutthroat was the word she used - so it's been about six weeks. And man, it ain't becoming."

"I don't have face foliage like you do, no matter how long it's been," I shot back at him. My beard was straggly, so I was used to keeping my face smooth. I fingered the hair again. "You know where that razor went?"

331

A look crossed his face. "You kill yourself with that blade, Bella will kill me."

I snorted and leaned back against the pillow. "I have safety razors. Alger obviously didn't look in the cupboard."

I told him where he'd find them, and as he walked across the room, closed my eyes to rest the eyelids. They were heavy after so long not being awake, it turned out. I woke up again to daylight, and no Mark. But... I managed to touch my chin. I was lying flat again, but my arms were above the coverlet so I could move. I was smooth shaven. Good man.

"You're awake." And that was mother's voice, sounding rather pleased. I turned my head.

"How long?" I croaked. She fluttered a bit, finally coming up with a glass of water and a straw. I sipped gratefully.

"Since?" She was trying to deflect, not a good sign.

I sighed. "Since I talked to Mark?"

She relaxed. "That was yesterday. Or last night, rather."

"Bella?"

"She'll be up shortly, she's having lunch with Ellie in the kitchen. I took over for an hour, firm. Poor girl needs to rest, too." Mother sounded unusually grounded. She had spent most of my adult life cultivating all the mental depth of a sparrow, with an avid appetite for gossip and the social skills any honeybee would envy. Under it, I knew, was a keen mind for the byzantine politics of High Court. My reclaiming the dukedom had injected new energy into one member of my family, at least.

I knew I sounded bitter, "She does. And doesn't need to be tied to my wrecked old hulk."

She blinked in surprise. I suppose I also sounded morose. I growled a little under my breath. I just wanted to die in peace, was that too much to ask?

"Are you hungry?" she asked.

"Do I get to sit up if I am?"

She sighed. "Let me go get Mark."

She was almost out the door before I could respond, calling after her, "He's not my valet!" I finished in my head, having run out of breath, I don't have a valet, I don't need a valet, I'm not some old doddering fool or a Court dandy.

I lay there, panting slightly from that exertion. I could hear murmurs in the hall, but not what was being said. I wondered if Alger would give me grace. This was impossible. I would not be a burden for what remained of my worthless life. I rolled over, feeling like even that was a monumental accomplishment, and a wave of weakness washed over me. I wasn't going to be able to stand up, much less make it to the bathroom. I didn't want to think about those provisions for the weeks previous.

The coverlet was the next obstacle. I'd never realized before just how heavy the damn thing was. No-one was walking through the door just yet. In that moment of aloneness I realized just how oppressive it had been to never be alone, even if I had been unconscious. I wanted my armory, that ultimate man-cave, warded with spells that no-one dared tamper with to invade my space. The legs over the edge of the bed was a bad idea, in retrospect. They were heavy as lead, and about as easy to move.

Actually, once they had momentum, they worked just fine. As anchors. I slid out of the bed and landed on the floor with a jarring thud.

That worked. Time to start crawling, probably better than trying to walk just now. The nightshirt was tangled around my legs and not helping. I honestly wasn't sure if I was looking for a weapon to kill myself with, or just get to the bathroom. Footsteps sounded, coming through the door.

I looked up at Bella. She crouched down next to me. "Where are you going?" She had a funny look on her face.

"Bathroom," I gasped out. She nodded. Mark appeared on my other side, and together they got me to my feet. I refuse to admit that I whimpered when I took that first step.

"Bella!" My mother, sounding both scandalized and afraid.

"Lucia, he needs to move. If he stays in bed he's going to die. Or waste away to nothing. If he's out of bed, he's ready to walk."

Mother Titania, I loved this woman. Dying was worth having the right to call her mine. They got me in the bathroom, and I promised I would rap on the door when done. That business over with, I didn't want to go back to bed. Mark half-carried me to the little couch, while mother and Bella had a low-voiced but very tense discussion over my husk. I was beginning to feel like laughing at all the attention and angst in the air, when Ellie appeared with a tray of sandwiches, and my stomach made a rude noise again. She looked pleased to see me sitting up, at least. For once I didn't mind all the people in my room. As long as I was awake and alive to see them.

Food was both delicious, and exhausting. People were less and less welcome as I tired again. But I had been up for a whole hour, easily the most since... Well, I don't want to think about that.

"Bella..." I was now surrounded by what seemed like most of my family. I wasn't sure she could hear me over the talking, and I didn't have the strength to project. She stood up.

"Everyone out. Yes, he's better. But mostly he needs rest."

She'd read my mind. I leaned back, watching as she efficiently herded them out, gentle and inexorable.

"I'm not ready to get back in the bed." I told her after the last of them had the door closed behind them.

"Ok. When you fall asleep I'll go get Mark, though."

"I have questions," I started. She came to sit next to me, easy in her soft blue dress. I wondered about her jeans, and then realized that they wouldn't be available Underhill. Bringing my wandering mind back to my point, "No one is using magic around me. On purpose, or?"

She nodded. "When the smallest spell is activated in your room, you... twitch. It was decided," which most likely meant she had put her foot down, hard, "that we would not use it around you. I wanted to take you home, honestly, but they wouldn't allow it, and I wasn't sure what to tell a doctor was wrong with you."

Massive internal bleeding, broken bones, and complications from a mind rape. I felt my face flinch. She put a hand on my cheek. "I was sure I was going to lose you."

"You still might. Bella, I..." I swallowed hard. "I don't think I'm going to make it. I've been ill before, with the elfshot. This is, different. I can't even access the Sight. There's nothing."

She shook her head, smiling a little. "You had me worried up until last night. Wanting to shave was a sure sign that you were coming back from the edge."

"I lost my magic. I'm moody as hell, and have a serious case of the blues."

She shrugged. "There's a whole world of people without it up above. You're alive, and you have been doing very little with magic for a long time, I talked to Alger about it."

I sighed. I couldn't explain what I was thinking, that if I had to be helpless, dependent on others for everything, I didn't want to be alive.

"Will you sleep with me tonight?" Now I did succeed in startling her.

"I don't know..." she began dubiously, and I could tell she was trying to figure out how to say this.

"Just sleep."

"I've been sleeping here," she patted the couch cushions. "But yes, I would like that."

She put her head on my shoulder, not resting any weight on me, and I realized I was all skin and bones. No wonder I was having trouble moving, my muscles were shot. If I wasn't going to die, that was going to have to change.

I fell asleep like that, her warm against my side.

Read the rest of the series...

Trickster Noir

Dragon Noir

The East Witch

Also by Cedar Sanderson

Other Works by Cedar Sanderson

The Case of the Perambulating Hatrack

The Tanager Series:

Jade Star (a novella)

Tanager's Fledglings

WitchWard Series:

Snow In Her Eyes

Possum Creek Massacre

Children of Myth Duology:

Vulcan's Kittens

The God's Wolfling

Short Fiction:

Crow Moon: A Fantasy Collection

The Groundskeeper Tales

Raking Up the Dead

The Hoodoo that You Do

My Ghoul

Warp Resonance: A Science Fiction Collection

About the Author

Cedar Sanderson is an author, artist, and citizen scientist who makes her living as a technical writer. She is also the house designer for Raconteur Press, as well as running her own business, Sanderley Studios, which publishes her books. She has authored ten novels, countless shorter works, and edited several anthologies. She lives in a small town in Texas along with her long-suffering husband and a flame-point cat named Lightly Toasted Marshmallow.

www.ingramcontent.com/pod-product-compliance
Lightning Source LLC
Chambersburg PA
CBHW031133260626
47153CB00021B/239